Royal Vengeance

J.D. Ruffin

jdruffin.com

Copyright ©2022 by 3Aussies Press.

All rights reserved.

No portion of this book may be reproduced in any form without written permission from the publisher or author, except as permitted by U.S. copyright law.

Part I

Chapter One

Jess

Jess tumbled through the mirror and sprawled across the cold stone floor of the dimly lit catacombs. She tried to ease her fall but slipped and hit her head as she fell. Her heart pounded. She struggled to gather her senses and clear her vision.

Keelan hadn't followed.

She was alone.

As she finally caught her breath, she realized she was bracing her weight on the cold stone of her great-great-grandfather's sarcophagus. She yanked her hand away and clutched it to her chest while her eyes darted about the room trying desperately to orient herself.

The crypt should've felt familiar, somehow safe, but she'd never liked the place, with its creepy magical torches casting dancing shadows across the marble prisons of the dead. Her father had brought her down here when he'd wanted to impart some deep lesson about the weight of the Crown and their royal lineage. She knew she should revere the sacred ground, but it was hard to get past the idea of walking through rooms full of dead kings and queens who were likely more dust than flesh. To calm his disquieted daughter, Alfred would point out the place where he would rest, then where she would follow. It just made her skin crawl more. What child wanted to think about where they'd be interred?

She rose and took her first steps. The flickering flames made no sound, released no smoke. In the stillness of the chamber, her thoughts boomed like thunder in her head.

Keelan tried to kill me.

Why?

She remembered the crazed look in his eyes as he'd held her and knew it wasn't the noble Guardsman glaring down at her. Someone—*something*—had taken him over, commanded his actions, but knowing that truth didn't make seeing his face in her thoughts any easier or help douse the fear coursing through her veins. She tried replaying the last moments before she'd Traveled to the crypt, tried making sense of what had happened.

She'd been sleeping soundly. Then Keelan loomed over her with wild eyes and a knife. He'd been talking to himself—or wrestling with himself—she couldn't tell. In the end, Atikus had tried to pull the hulking man off of her but had been slammed into a wall for his effort. She hoped the kind old Mage was alright.

She'd barely squeezed out of Keelan's grip before he lunged across the room and pinned her against the shelving, his razor-sharp knifepoint quivering inches from her chest. She could still see the torchlight glinting off his silver blade. He'd struggled, fought against whatever, *whoever*, commanded him to act. She wondered at the strength it took for him to resist the powerful Compulsion, especially for a man with such a passive Gift.

She wasn't sure how she ended up flying through the mirror. She didn't remember breaking from his grasp, but somehow she'd gone from inescapable death to hurtling toward the safety of a room full of dead royalty. If it hadn't been so frightening, the irony would've made her laugh.

The crypt wasn't large, only a dozen chambers connected by a wide central walkway. Two bronze doors loomed at one end opening into a room she'd never visited. At the other end, plain gray stone mirrored their golden counterparts. The walls were polished and held only golden plates memorializing ancient monarchs. As she approached the towering doors at walkway's end, she looked to her right into the last grotto, the one that would soon allow her father his eternal rest. Her step faltered and she froze, staring blindly into the empty, unlit space. Its darkness mirrored her thoughts, as images of her father's face rose to the fore.

He smiled, and his hand brushed her cheek. He held her in a tight embrace, his warmth flooding into her.

With all she'd been through over the past few weeks, she'd yet to grieve or even focus on her father or brother—*or even her mother*—all of whom were lost to her now. Her younger brother Kendall was all the family she had left, and he was only eleven. In the silence of the stone chamber, surrounded by the kings and queens of old, Jess realized the weight of the Crown, *her Crown*, and that she now bore it alone.

Tears she didn't know were dammed broke free, and she slumped to the floor.

A half-hour later, Jess gathered herself, wiped streaks from her face, and stood. She reached for the wooden lever to open the doors, but a tiny voice in her head stilled her hand.

No one here knows I'm Queen now. That means they don't know about Father, or Justin, or Mother, or the invasion. Will they believe me when I tell them? What if they don't want me as their Queen? Am I ready for this? Where do I even start?

Tears threatened again, but she sniffed them back and stiffened her spine.

I am Queen *now. I can't act like a scared little rabbit. What would Father do?*

She thought back to the endless hours she'd sat in Council with her father listening to boring men droning on about taxes or land, farming or constables, fishing rights or disputed Ducal decrees, or a thousand other tedious topics thrust before the King. She'd tried paying attention, but most of it had felt so distant from anything she'd need as a teenager. And yet, here she was at seventeen—the Queen.

Father always said to surround yourself with wise men and listen to their guidance. I might have to amend that to include some wise women, *too. At least this gives me a place to start so I don't look completely lost. Start with the Council.*

She looked down at the rumpled riding clothes and shook her head, then she ran a hand through her tangled hair. She smelled the grime left on her fingers and winced. It had been weeks since she'd bathed and there was no way she'd look—or smell—like a queen until she had a bath and change of clothes. Her steely eyes and upturned chin would have to do. Her father always told her those were more powerful tools than the Crown, though she never fully understood the comment until now.

Without thinking further, she pulled the wooden lever and heard powerful mechanisms begin to creak. Sunlight began as a sliver, then grew into a flood as the doors opened.

"What—" she heard from someone outside.

Jess couldn't stop the chuckle as a startled cleric, bent with age, stumbled backward.

"Father, I have risen," she blurted out without thinking.

The man's eyes widened, and he tripped, landing on his backside.

She barked a laugh, finally realizing what the man must've thought, given her backdrop was a tomb. "I'm sorry. I didn't mean . . . Oh, never mind. Please escort me to the Palace."

As the priest's cart approached the Palace gate, a bored-looking guard in the shack nearby did a double take, then snapped to attention.

"Highness, welcome back. We didn't know you'd returned from your, um . . . journey," the man said, his eyes never leaving some distant point. She might've been a teenage princess, but the guards knew better than to make eye contact unless it was absolutely necessary.

"It's alright, William. Would you have the Chancellor's office assemble the Privy Council? I need to speak with them in an hour."

The guard's brow quirked.

She'd never used any of their names before. She never cared enough to learn most of them—and she was *never* kind or considerate to them. She'd heard the men often joked about how she'd been raised by the palace staff but refused to lower herself to learn their names. Her father tried to teach her the value of her people, if she'd only listened. She'd have to work on that if she was to become the Queen she'd envisioned as a girl.

"Um, Your Highness—"

"I know it's an unusual request. I'll explain everything to the Council."

She turned to the cleric before William could reply. "Thank you, Father. I don't think I could've done that long walk tonight."

The priest bowed respectfully and watched as Jess strode purposefully into the Palace grounds.

By the time she reached her chamber, the palace was abuzz with speculation regarding her unorthodox Council summons. Guards, servants, and even a few cooks scurrying to ready the kitchens for the return of their charge all whispered in corners about the Princess's sudden reappearance and mysterious demands.

One of her maids greeted her at her chamber door—the middle-aged woman. "I had a hot bath prepared as soon as I heard you'd returned, Highness. Will you want your ladies to help you bathe and dress?"

Jess placed a hand on her shoulder. "Thank you, Tena. I'll be fine on my own tonight. Would you please ask the kitchen to make refreshments for the Council in the throne room? We'll be meeting in an hour."

The woman couldn't hide her shock—or delight—at Jess's pleasant demeanor. She smiled, curtsied again, and scurried off.

Jess closed the door without looking back and slumped to the floor. Her head dropped into her hands and her chest began to heave.

An hour later, two green-and-gold-liveried servants opened the double doors to the audience chamber as Jess approached. She entered to the side of the thrones and walked directly toward the Council table where the Ministers were already assembled, at least those still living in the capital while the Kingdom pursued its war in the east. Only four of the eight Privy Counselors stood behind their high-back chairs awaiting her arrival, representing Trade, Foreign Affairs, Justice, and the Crown Treasury. Notably absent were High Chancellor Thorn, Minister of War Bril, High Sheriff Wilfred, and General Marks. At the far end of the table, a tall, thin man Jess didn't recognize stood; his long blue robes lined with one band of gold rustled as he bowed. The other men had their backs to the door and startled at her arrival, quickly turning and offering their own respects.

She approached the table and rested a quivering hand on the chair at its head.

"Thank you for coming. A lot has happened—is happening—in the east, and I don't know—I'm not sure, how much news made it through to you." She took a deep breath to calm herself and pulled the chair back to sit.

Foreign Minister Barcas cleared his throat and motioned with an open palm. "Highness, why don't you start with why you called us here. It is most unusual."

Treasurer Dask crossed his arms and frowned, clearly disgruntled by the presumption in the Princess's summons.

Jess nodded and took another deep breath. These men had never made her nervous before. Why was her hand shaking now?

"My father . . . the King . . . he's dead."

The room filled with sharp intakes of breaths and groans. Barcas ignored protocol and dropped into his chair while the others stared open-mouthed at the teenager standing before them.

No one spoke.

Jess looked from one face to the next and fought the urge to run from the room. Their eyes said it all. They didn't want *her* on the throne. In fact, she thought a thread of fear ran through their expressions. She decided to take Atikus's advice and play to their paternal instincts.

"No one feels this loss more than I do. It's been weeks since his passing, but it feels like yesterday."

"Weeks?" Dask exclaimed. "How are we just hearing of this? Why was no messenger sent to inform this Council?"

Jess sat in the High Chancellor's seat at the head of the table and stared into the glossy wood surface.

"After my mother killed my father—"

"Spirits, no!" Minister Carver said before covering his mouth with the ridiculous lace handkerchief he carried everywhere.

Jess looked up, and the tear she was holding back finally broke free and trailed down her cheek. Her eyes drifted to her hands and she sucked in a breath to steady herself, then looked up.

"Why don't you sit? There's a lot we need to discuss."

As the counselors took their seats, Jess glanced at the Mage. "Sir, please introduce yourself. I don't know you."

The man bowed deeply again. "Your Highne—forgive me—*Your Majesty*, I am Dane Ernest. Since the High Chancellor is in the east with our troops, Minister Barcas thought it would be helpful to have another Mage offer counsel."

This was the first time anyone had addressed her by the monarchical title, and a surge of nervous energy tickled its way up her spine. *This will take getting used to.*

Then the Mage's mention of the High Chancellor sank in, and she pursed her lips. Was this another snake like Thorn? She knew the other men at the table, but could she trust this one?

Before she could speak, Minister Barcas leaned toward her and whispered, "Majesty, he's a good man. Not one of Thorn's, if that's what you're thinking."

"How did you—?" Of course, he knew how she felt about Thorn. The other ministers had witnessed her reaction to Thorn's smooth talk at hundreds of Council meetings. Her dislike for the Spymaster was well known. She'd have to be more careful about how she let others see her true feelings moving forward.

She nodded once to the Mage, and the man took a seat near the table's far end.

A moment of silence hung in the air as everyone waited for their queen to address them. She eyed each man before finally beginning the speech she'd rehearsed a dozen times.

"My Lords, the King is dead. Prince Justin is dead. My mother, the *former* Queen, is thought to have killed them both in an attempt to take the crown for herself. Even now, she leads *our* troops in an unjust war against our Melucian neighbors—in the name of justice for my kidnapping. We have incontrovertible evidence that *she* was behind my kidnapping and attempted murder as well."

She paused as shock flooded into her advisors anew.

The massive chamber held its breath.

Each statement sounded more outlandish and devastating than the last, yet they all knew the truth when they heard it. Everything they thought they knew only moments earlier was radically outdated.

Their entire world had changed.

"The Children, the ancient cult based in the village of Irina's Pass, were responsible for the Gifted kidnappings that plagued *both* our nation and Melucia. They kidnapped me on my mother's orders and would've sacrificed my life on the altar of their evil plans if not for the bravery of our soldiers and two . . . others." Her voice broke with the next statement. "Prince Justin was lost during my rescue."

She steeled herself before her grief could take control. This was no time to show weakness.

"That's everything I knew before fleeing my mother's men. Your turn, gentlemen."

Still, no one spoke.

They stared blankly at her trying to absorb everything she'd told them.

In that moment, an odd sensation tickled the back of her neck, and a familiar voice whispered in her head, *"Jess, it's Atikus . . ."*

Chapter Two

Danai

Danai Thorn stared at the ornate crown in his hand, and his heart grieved for the one who'd worn it mere hours before.

He'd spent a lifetime—no, ten lifetimes—searching for clues that might lead to her return. The obsidian monolith left by her spell had offered more conjecture than instruction, but a thousand years after her death, he'd finally succeeded in restoring her to the world of the living.

And now she was gone.

Again.

Magical power tickled his fingers as it thrummed through the cold metal. The seven diamonds across the crown's golden base pulsed with an eerie crimson light. He shuddered, thinking how each orb was filled with the captured soul of a Gifted man or woman who was sacrificed for the greater cause of Irina's return, the bloodred hue of each diamond mirroring the sacred life force spilled to acquire its power.

He shuddered as his breath suddenly frosted before him. He swiveled, scanning the peak and nearby forest, but found nothing amiss. He rubbed warmth into his suddenly chilled arms and blinked several times to force moisture into thirsty eyes.

"Danai..."

Startled, Thorn nearly stumbled down the mountainside as a silky voice whispered in his mind.

"Danai, my dear, you found my crown."

He shuddered. *My dear?* She'd never called him anything other than his name.

"My Queen?"

"I'm here. My Vessel was weak and died when the Tower fell, but now my spirit is free."

Thorn's eyes darted around him, desperately seeking any evidence of Irina's presence. The only thing he found was the deepening chill in the air—and his bones.

"I don't understand. The circle—"

"—was destroyed when the Tower fell. Nothing contains me now, but my power is limited without a Vessel. I can influence, but never rule without a mortal form."

Realization drained the last color from his face. "You want to consume *me*? Take my body for your own?"

"No, my love, I want to share power as we always have."

My love?

He leaned against a tree, barely able to focus. He *had* loved her. From the day he'd met her, his heart had been hers. She'd been so broken by grief. He'd wrapped her in his embrace, supported her vision for a stronger, more prosperous Kingdom, and helped her gain her footing as she ascended to the throne. Even when her heart had turned to vengeance, he'd remained at her side, steadfast and loyal.

And yet, despite all their time together, he'd never had the chance—or bravery—to tell her how he felt.

What if he had? Would she have loved him in return? Would she have fallen into his arms and returned his embrace, as he saw in his dreams so many nights?

He regretted never trying, never learning what could be.

Yet he also feared she might have laughed and discarded his emotions as weakness. She'd mocked others for their frail minds and weak hearts. While he *knew* his love was a power in itself, he also understood that her heart had darkened by the time he would have opened up to her.

And now she called him *my love*.

His eyes, parched a moment before, brimmed. Yet he hesitated.

"Irina, I . . . I don't know. You *consumed* Isabel. I want to be with you, but . . . not like that."

Her presence was overwhelming in life. In death, it *compelled* allegiance. Unquestioning loyalty.

"Isabel was a weak, feckless fool. You are more worthy than any alive. We would wield power this world hasn't seen since the Sundering. Think of it, Danai!"

He felt a pressure against his chest, as though someone pushed against him, trying to burrow within him. He called his Light and pushed back.

"What *are* you—"

"Why do you resist me, my love?" Her voice held a new edge. *"I long to be one. Isn't that what you've always wanted?"*

The pressure intensified, and sweat beaded Thorn's brow despite the frigid mountain air.

"Irina, stop, please," he pleaded. "We can find another way, another Vessel."

Thorn held his breath as Irina's voice stilled. The tension against his chest eased as the moments passed in silence. His heart, long ago given to her keeping, shattered at the gulf now spanning between them.

"Irina?" he whispered. "Are you still there?"

What had been a palm pressed against his chest before was now an angry fist pounding against his heart, and Irina's spirit found purchase within. Her presence knifed his mental shield, desperately seeking a weakness.

"Never use my name again, Betrayer. Call me Vengeance, for that is all you will ever know from me. Your life is mine, your soul is mine, now your mind and body will be mine. Yield, and I may yet allow some sliver of Thorn to survive."

He could feel tendrils of power worming their way inside the crevices of his mind, searching for a way to seize control. White-hot bolts raced from his head down his spine and throughout his body. He dropped the crown, and his hands flew to his temples. He staggered but shook off the initial shock and thrust the might of his magical reserves at her invading essence. The tendrils recoiled, and Irina's angry screech echoed in his head.

"Resist me all you like. Your pitiful power is no match for my will. I will consume your mind and Spirit and force you to watch as the world burns."

A shaft of the rising sun glinted off the crown now cradled in the snow. Thorn snatched it up and slammed it onto his head. A wave of power swelled within his chest and drove him to his knees, but it bolstered his Light with immeasurable strength. He never knew the crown gave more than the seven Gifts, but now he understood it also magnified the innate power of its user.

His lips curled as he called out to his former pupil.

"No! You'll not have me like you did Isabel. I've not survived a thousand years only to lose myself to a *failed* sorceress." He clenched his eyes shut and began muttering a spell, each word stabbing painfully into the invading tendrils. He could see them writhing, feel them flailing and searching. When, he finally completed his incantation, the Spirit of Irina fled his body and materialized as a translucent vapor before him.

Hatred filled her eyes.

"This is not over, Betrayer. The circle was broken and I am free. When you are weakest, you will *become my Vessel, and this world will burn."*

"Irina!" he called out, but the Spirit turned and dissolved into the wind.

He tore the crown from his brow and hurled it to the frozen ground, its malicious intent and unyielding strength ebbing once cast aside. Tears formed as he watched the apparition of his lost love fade, leaving him again alone on the mountain peak staring blankly at the wintery sky.

Chapter Three

Keelan

Keelan's hulking form loomed over Atikus as the Mage closed his eyes and created a Telepathic link. Atikus agreed to speak his words aloud so Keelan could listen in on the one-way communication, but even with this assurance, the Guardsman wrung his dusty blue cap in his meaty hands as the words poured out.

"Jess, it's Atikus..." he spoke aloud and mentally at once.

Moments later, Atikus opened his eyes as his shoulders slumped from the effort. Telepathy wasn't usually exhausting, but he was communicating over an entire continent's distance, and that put a strain on his magical reserves. Keelan shifted from one foot to the other in front of him.

"Did she say anything? How did she sound?" he asked impatiently.

Atikus looked up with bleary eyes and chuckled. "You know it doesn't work that way, son. Telepathy only goes one way. She couldn't speak, and I couldn't hear anything on her end. I'm sorry, but you'll just have to ask her yourself when you get to the cave."

Keelan tossed his cap onto the chair beside Atikus and slumped into the cushion, mindless of how he crushed the cap.

Atikus raised a brow and grinned. "Weren't you calling Jess an immature brat before we came home? Why so nervous about how she's doing now?"

Keelan ran a hand over his rusty stubble. "Come on, Atikus. I tried to *kill* her. Why wouldn't I be worried? I mean . . . about seeing me . . . or me bringing her horse back . . . or . . . Spirits, you know what I mean."

The Mage's grin grew. "Uh huh, I think I know *exactly* what you mean. When *you* figure it out, come see me and I'll explain what to do about it."

Keelan's blank stare made Atikus laugh. "Just get ready for your trip. Time's passing while you sit here worrying."

Atikus wobbled as he stood and braced himself on Keelan's shoulder. "I'm going to check on preparations for the ceremony tonight and might stop by to see what cook's making for dinner. Why don't you come by my chamber later and walk with me to the Tower grounds?"

"I still don't understand why you don't want Declan there. He'd want to show his support to you and the Guild."

"Because he would outshine all of us, and tonight is for the Guild—and the one presiding insisted. We dare not ignore *her* advice," Atikus said.

"Alright. Not sure I understand any of that, but I'll go finish packing. See you in a couple hours."

The gray winter sky had dimmed to a moonless night by the time Keelan returned to the Mage's Quarters and rapped on the thick wooden door of Atikus's apartment. A long moment later, the door creaked open, and the Mage emerged in his long formal robe, two lines of gold glittering on the collar and cuffs. The gold *flowed* as if alive.

"Time to get this over with," Atikus said with a tight smile.

Keelan raised a brow. "I don't remember your stripes *moving* before."

Atikus looked down at his cuff and chuckled. "Theatrics and staging are powerful tools. That's a lesson you'd do well to learn, my boy."

"Well, it sure made me look twice. You still sure you want to do this? You're taking on the weight of the entire magical world."

"Look around. The Guild was devastated. Spirits, the whole capital is in ruins. Fewer than three hundred Mages survived—and that's in the entire country, not just here. The Mages aren't just men with Gifts; they are our teachers, our inventors, our historians. While most people will never know the role they play, every life in Melucia is improved by the work of the Guild and its members." Atikus sighed deeply. "It will take generations to rebuild our strength, and most who survived are young or highly specialized. I've never wanted the burden of leadership, but sometimes life calls us for a greater purpose. After everything our people have suffered, how can I refuse that call now?"

"I guess you're right. Besides, from what I've seen of those left, there really isn't anyone else strong enough to lead the Guild."

Atikus shrugged and walked out, closing the door behind him.

As they strode away, something in that simple act felt poetic to Keelan, the closing of one door heralding the opening of another. He'd always known his path—to serve in the Guard, to protect others. Now, after losing Tiana in his failed search across the border and their nearly tragic parting with Jess, he wondered if the course he'd set all those years ago was really meant for him. He loved the Guard, but was it truly *his calling*? He shook his head at the irony of *him* questioning his place in the world while his perpetually lost brother, Declan, blazed like a star for others to follow.

They exited the living quarters and turned toward the Tower grounds. In the weeks that followed the siege, hundreds of men and Mages had worked tirelessly clearing rubble and debris from the Tower's destruction. Now, a clear courtyard spread before them leading to the Tower's broken base. Every living Mage in the Melucian Empire stood assembled on either side of the path, forcing Atikus and Keelan to walk down the center. The path itself was littered with hand-sized cerulean petals of some foreign flower that flared brilliantly as their feet pressed them.

The Mages on either side bowed deeply and remained in that position until they were well past. Keelan was startled by the display of reverence, but Atikus marched forward, head held aloft, as though he expected the courtly reception. When they passed Mage Fergus—*Uncle Ferg* to Keelan and Declan—the portly old Mage sneaked a wink to Keelan before bowing as low as his belly would allow.

The Mages they passed straightened and followed in orderly ranks until Atikus and Keelan reached the Tower's base. Keelan made to step aside, but Atikus gripped his elbow and urged him to continue his escort up the stone steps, where three ancient Mages in billowing robes waited. When they reached the top step, it was Atikus's turn to bow deeply. The Elders echoed his respect.

The shuffling of feet behind them quieted, and Keelan glanced back to find every other Mage assembled in a semi-circle at perfectly spaced intervals behind them. Each Mage's right arm was stretched forward, palm held upward, with a ball of white light dancing above.

The withered Elder in the middle then spoke in a voice Keelan knew was magnified by magic.

"Brothers and Sisters of Magic, the Arch Mage has fallen. A new Guardian must be chosen to take his place. By the Light of the Phoenix, who here bears two or more lines of gold and offers to serve?"

No one stirred.

Keelan peered over his shoulder again to find every Mage frozen. The snapping of their robes and whistling of the brisk winter wind was the only sound in the courtyard. When he turned back, Atikus lifted his palm before him and bright azure flame flared to life.

The elderly mage bowed to Atikus and stepped back several strides. The other two joined him and began chanting in the Mage's tongue. Keelan could feel the tiny hairs on his arm rise as the magical energy swelled from their incantation. He nearly fell backwards when the Mage's words reached a peak, and the shimmering image of a woman appeared where the old Mage had stood a moment before. A broad smile parted her lips when her dark eyes landed on Atikus.

Then she noticed Keelan.

Her smooth brow quirked in confusion, then recognition, and her eyes opened wide. She stared for only a second before returning to Atikus and speaking in a clear, rich voice.

"I am the Keeper of Magic, and I bring warm greetings and heartfelt wishes from the Phoenix herself." Keelan barely heard the hushed murmurs of the Mages behind him as his mother's words rang in his ears. She continued, "For two-hundred-twenty-one years, Velius Quin led this Guild with strength, honor, and integrity. His was a life of service and duty. His loss will be felt for generations."

Keelan peered out of the side of one eye to see Atikus's eyes watering at the eulogy of his former leader.

"Now is the time for new beginnings." Her voice brightened. "Your beloved city rises from the ashes. Your people's spirit is renewed. So, too, must our Guild be. Tonight, we choose a new Arch Mage, and in doing so take our first step toward the future."

The Keeper of Magic made eye contact with each of the Mages closest to the steps, causing more than a few to retreat from her penetrating gaze.

"For over twelve hundred years, Arch Mages have been selected from among those bearing two or more bands of gold. To our knowledge, only three Mages alive today carry this distinction: Mage Atikus Dani of Melucia, High Chancellor Danai Thorn of the Kingdom of Spires, and Declan Rea, the Heir of Magic and son of the Isle of Rea Utu." The corner of her mouth quirked upward as she said the last words and noticed the befuddled look on Keelan's face. "High Chancellor Thorn fled the battlefield and has not been seen since. Declan Rea's path leads elsewhere. Mage Dani stands before you as the sole nominee."

The woman raised her palm, and a ball of flame burst into existence. "Each Mage must now bond his vote with magic itself. If you support Mage Dani's ascension, case your flame upward."

Atikus didn't turn to watch, but Keelan couldn't help himself. His jaw dropped as every Mage around them raised their flame above their head and released it into the night sky. No longer were there a hundred blazing stars but one massive beacon that writhed and sparked. When all were aloft, the Keeper raised her own flame, and it joined the others. At the moment her flame struck, the incoherent ball flared brightly and transformed into the outline of a Phoenix as tall as the Tower itself. Its head reared toward the sky, and it released a cacophonous roar. It belched a stream of magical flame, then dove and disappeared into the vein of raw power that coursed below the Tower's base.

Kelså called, "Arch Mage Atikus Dani, turn and face your Guild."

As Atikus turned, he saw the awestruck expression on Keelan's face and couldn't resist giving his adopted son a quick wink. Kelså raised her palm again, and flame blazed across Atikus's chest, leaving a golden Phoenix emblazoned across his robe as the fire winked out. The gold of the Phoenix flowed like the stripes on his collar and cuffs. Every Mage, including the three who now stood behind Atikus, kneeled and bowed their heads.

Atikus turned and whispered to Keelan, "Give it to the Mages, we know how to put on a good show."

He wiggled a bushy brow and was rewarded with a coughing laugh from the Guardsman.

Chapter Four

Danai

"Irina, how have we come to this?" Thorn muttered to himself as he wiped a tear from his eye, the first to fall in many years.

Their confrontation had left him shaken. She'd turned on him so quickly.

How could she think I'd turn against her? Me, Betrayer?

He'd spent years nursing her back to emotional health following the murder of her parents. He'd been her strength, her rock, and her shield. Thinking back, he could see the vulnerable girl in his mind, her ebony hair flowing beyond her shoulders. He saw the quirk of her mouth when she was amused and the way her eyes widened when she laughed.

He hadn't recognized the feelings that drove him. But a thousand years of reflecting helped him realize how much he'd fallen in love with her. Every night, for centuries, he'd dreamed of her return—her return *to him*.

He'd first thought it would be easy. The words created by her spell couldn't be that hard to interpret, but the answer to their riddle eluded him. So, he'd invented the Children to help him unravel the spell's mysteries.

How did that handful of magical geniuses devolve into a group of mask-wearing idiots?

And yet they'd proved their usefulness and succeeded in bringing their goddess back to the world of the living.

In his wildest dreams, he'd never imagined she would come back with only vengeance in her heart. Even when she led the Kingdom's armies east the first time, her goal was conquest, not death and destruction. He didn't recognize the Spirit that called herself Irina. She certainly wasn't *his* Irina.

Did she ever know how I felt?

He pressed his palms to his temples and screamed in frustration, and then everything tumbled into place in his mind.

Of course, she did. She's the most brilliant woman I've ever met. She fed me crumbs—a gentle touch, a warm embrace, a flirtatious glance—all to keep my hope ablaze. She knew I loved her and used it to turn me into her instrument.

And I did everything she wanted.

Simmering anger welled inside him, and he gave himself over to the power of rage.

Never again. I see you now, Irina. You *are the Betrayer.*

His internal battle finally quieted as Thorn bent to retrieve the crown. He absently brushed its band and realized no snow had stuck to the pulsing bloodred diamonds. As much as he'd learned of magic in his many centuries of life, he was still amazed at the mysteries it held. Unsure of what surprises the crown might still hold, he packed it securely in his rough spun sack, slung the pack over his shoulder, and began working his way down the steep slope of the mountain. His Gift of Travel could whisk him away with barely a thought, but he needed time to think through what to do next.

He'd never considered Irina's Spirit might roam free in the world; based on the malicious intent now consuming her being, the thought made him shudder. Even if she wanted him back in her service, she'd never fully trust him again. Now that he thought about it, how could he ever trust her? She was someone—*something*—he didn't recognize. She frightened him in a way no one had in many years.

No, following her wouldn't do.

So now what?

He could return to the Kingdom, but what welcome would await? He'd basically fled the field before the battle had even begun. While the common soldiers wouldn't know or care, he was sure Bril or Marks would clap him in irons at first sight and charge him with desertion. That's assuming they'd survived, which was a wild assumption based on the massacre he'd witnessed.

What about going home? he thought longingly.

He could simply Travel to Fontaine, directly to the palace if he wished. If Jess sat on the throne, she would likely dismiss him from her service in favor of some other Mage she thought more pliable. That wouldn't be so bad. He could pursue his own studies, or work with the few Mages remaining in the capital's Guild, but he hadn't seen or heard from Jess since she fled for her life with those two Melucians. She could be dead, or in hiding, or captive somewhere. It would've taken her weeks to return to the capital. She probably wasn't anywhere near the throne.

So, who would be in charge? The King and Queen were dead, Justin was dead, Jess was on the run, and Kendall was too young to rule. Bril and Marks were either dead or retreating with whatever was left of their army. The other ministers were too weak to step in.

What a disaster.

He stopped walking and slapped his head with his palm as a thought bloomed. In the absence of the monarch, the *High Chancellor* holds power. He was now the de facto ruler of the Kingdom of Spires until a new monarch could be installed. Given the disorderly state of the Kingdom's government, that could take months—or longer.

I could name myself Steward until a monarch is installed. That's actually the law, and no one would think twice.

But then he thought twice.

I've always been the hand of the monarch, advising and guiding, but never ruling. It isn't a Mage's place to rule. That would violate everything the Guild stands for—and has stood for since its founding. The Mages of the world would never accept one of us on a throne, even if the people did.

Besides, would I even know how to rule?

A voice deep within scolded him for his self-doubt. He'd counseled dozens of rulers throughout his long life. Who could have more experience, knowledge, or wisdom?

He savored the sweetness of that thought for a long moment before swallowing it whole.

Yes, I should *lead. They should beg me to rule.*

As images of *his* coronation flooded his mind, Thorn couldn't stop the vision of Irina striding through the palace to wrest the Crown from his grasp. He knew it was his mind playing tricks, making him doubt, but he couldn't stop the thrill of her touch. In that moment, he knew the first thing he had to do.

With a thought, he vanished from the mountainside and appeared before two golden-bronze doors.

Chapter Five

Jess

"Your Majesty, are you alright?"

Jess held up a hand to silence Dask as the counselors exchanged confused glances.

"Jess, it's Atikus." The Mage's warm, deep tone thrummed in her head. He paused to allow her to register the odd sensation and ready herself to receive more. *"Much has happened since we parted ways. Keelan is headed back to the cave with Dittler and can fill you in on the details. He should arrive in two weeks, possibly a day or two less.*

"The Kingdom army besieged Saltstone, eventually breaking through thanks to your mother's magic. She sent her armies to hunt the citizens of the capital who had fled east with orders to slaughter every man, woman, and child. The Phoenix returned, killed your mother, then struck down the Kingdom's army. Many died, but we estimate several thousand survived and are fleeing

back toward the border. Saltstone is in ruins, but the people survived and now work to rebuild.

"I can only maintain this link a moment longer, so two important things: First, don't blame your mother. Her consciousness was possessed by the Spirit of Empress Irina, and I don't believe she acted of her own free will. And second, please meet Keelan in the cave. Irina's voice is no longer a threat to him—or you. He carries vital information for both our countries and is most eager to see you again."

Jess's brows furrowed at the last statement, and she thought she could hear Atikus grinning through the Telepathic link as he spoke the words. She started to turn back to the Council, each of whom now shared concerned expressions, but Atikus spoke again.

"Jess, it was an honor to escort you for a time. You are a strong, brilliant young woman and will make a fine Queen. Believe in yourself and trust your heart. Both the Kingdom and Melucia count on you to be wise and true. When the time is right, we should meet to discuss how we might repair the damage done between our two nations. Until then, Spirits guide you, Your Majesty."

She looked up at the Mage sitting directly opposite her at the foot of the table. "Mage Atikus Dani sends his regards."

The table erupted in a flurry of gasps and questions.

"Gentlemen, please." She waved them to silence, then summarized what Atikus had told her, leaving out the part where she was supposed to leave the capital to meet Keelan. *Spirits, how did my tale become so strange?*

"Did he mention the fate of Marks, Bril, or Thorn?" Barcas asked.

She shook her head. "No. He said I'd learn more soon but sounded exhausted by the end of the message."

"It's remarkable he was able to send a Telepathic message that far for that long. Dani must hold a powerful Gift," Mage Earnest said.

"Did you say the Spirit of Empress Irina returned and inhabited *your mother*?" Minister Carver asked, incredulity punctuating his tone.

"That's what he said. It fits with the ceremony my mother performed in the Children's Temple. Queen Isabel was willing to kill her husband and both of her children. We didn't understand their goal at the time, but returning the Empress makes as much sense as anything."

Jess's words hung in silence for a long moment before Mage Earnest spoke again.

"Majesty, we must turn our attention to the needs of your people. No doubt we lost many fathers and sons in the campaign across the border."

The Mage's sincerity caught her by surprise, and she looked up, reassessing the man.

"Where do we even begin?" she muttered, more to herself than the assembled men.

Dask leaned forward and placed a hand on hers, violating every protocol prohibiting physical contact with the Queen. "Jess, your Council has far too many empty seats. Those sitting here cannot hope to repair the damage done without help. We need to rebuild this Council before we try to rebuild the Kingdom."

Jess looked around the table as Dask retrieved his hand, suddenly remembering propriety. The others were nodding their agreement.

"Fine. But I won't abandon General Marks or Minister Bril. They may yet live."

"Majesty, forgive me, but General Marks and Minister Bril took part in the invasion. Is it wise to return them to Council?" Foreign Minister Barcas asked.

Jess was about to snap at the man and defend Uncle Ethan, but Mage Earnest spoke first. "Minister, many followed the orders of their King and Queen. We may yet learn how they behaved honorably in the face of an impossible situation. Her Majesty is right to spare judgement until all the facts are known, especially for men who have served this Kingdom for decades."

Barcas looked as if he wanted to argue but kept his mouth closed.

Jess leaned forward. "Minister of War and General of Armed Forces can wait for now. Thorn *will not* be my High Chancellor, so that's a good place to start. What other roles need filling?"

And so, the discussion began. Names of nobles brought nods, jeers, and jabs as the Kingdom's inner circle began forming a new government. Jess forgot her fears and threw herself into the task at hand. Hours later, she noticed Minister Barcas staring openly at her, a broad grin spread across his usually placid face.

"Zumi, you look like you ate something odd. Out with it."

The man laughed, a rich sound. "I was just enjoying watching Her Majesty work. She has amazed this skeptical old man and might just renew his weary spirit."

Jess blushed at the compliment, then smiled and offered a nod of thanks.

Her mind was spinning as Jess made her way through the private passages within the palace, headed toward her chamber after hours of deliberation with her Council. The day had been challenging, frightening, and exhilarating. All her life, Jess had wanted to be taken seriously, to be seen as a competent, intelligent woman who would rule with wisdom. She couldn't admit it at the time, but the derision—even pity—she'd seen in the counselors' eyes months earlier had stabbed at her heart.

But not now.

They actually listened to her. She tried to remember the endless lessons of her father, allowing the ministers to talk themselves to exhaustion before weighing in. He told her many times that educated men needed to make their point long before they would ever hear hers. To act otherwise was fruitless.

She grinned inwardly every time the conversation would lull, and she would speak. All eyes would snap to the head of the table, as if she was the most important voice in the room.

And then it sank in.

She *was* the most important voice in the room. She was *Queen*.

Events had moved so quickly since she'd returned that she'd barely had time to absorb the weight of the crown she'd inherited. She felt it now. Alone in a dim hallway, the immense responsibility that rested solely on her seventeen-year-old shoulders bore down, and she feared she might crumble beneath its weight. Her skin turned clammy, and her heart raced. She clawed open her collar, gasping, but air wouldn't flow. Sweat beaded on her brow.

Desperate to gather herself, she slipped into the first room she saw. As she closed the heavy wooden door behind her, she turned and found herself staring at Justin's bed. Her mother had barred servants from cleaning her children's rooms in an effort to teach them responsibility, and several pairs of riding leathers still lay strewn across it, as if he was struggling to decide what to pack before leaving on the trip east with the army.

The trip to find *her* after she'd run away.

Her heart seized, and tears streamed down her cheeks. The scent of her younger brother flooded her senses. She could see his lopsided grin, his perfectly coiffed hair that screamed for her fingers to muss it.

She missed him so much.

"Little brother, what have I done? How am I going to get through all this without you?" she whispered. "So many people are counting on me now, and I'm all alone."

She hugged herself, clutching her sides as tears fell.

Long moments passed before she finally wandered aimlessly around the room. She raised a white linen shirt to her nose, breathing in Justin's scent, then clutched the garment to her heart. Her fingers trailed across his desk as she found random notes from his studies covered in scribbles and tidbits he aimed to remember. The simple script adorning those pages had somehow become precious in his absence.

She started to open an armoire, but a knock at the door interrupted.

"Jess? Are you in there, Jess?" the voice of her younger brother—her *only* brother—floated through the door.

She sniffed and wiped her face with Justin's shirt before realizing what she'd done. She clutched it to her chest once more.

"Yes," she sucked in a calming breath. "Come in."

Kendall pushed the door open slowly, then bolted across the room and wrapped his spindly arms around her. "I missed you, Jessie. I'm glad you're home."

"Me too," was all she could say as she fought another wave of emotion.

A moment later, Kendall looked up and asked, "When do you think Mom, Dad, and Justin will get back? They've been gone a really long time."

Her voice caught as she realized no one had told the boy anything.

She pulled away from his hug and took his hand, leading him to sit on the bed beside her.

"Kendall," she began, grasping for the words. "I . . . I need to tell you some things. They're going to be really hard, so I need you to be brave, OK?"

Kendall's wide eyes, now tinged with fear, bobbed along with the boy's head.

Jess struggled with how to tell an eleven-year-old such a grim tale but ultimately decided he deserved the truth. She started with running away with Danym and their harrowing escape through the Spires. To his credit, he listened attentively and maintained a firm grip on his emotions—until she reached the part about the deaths of their father and brother. It broke her barely mended heart as she watched her young brother's grief bloom across his face. She held him and tried to calm his quaking shoulders. His tears were infectious, and they held each other and wept until Jess's maid knocked.

"Hello? Majesty, are you in there?"

How do they always know where I am? she thought as she rose, smoothed her gown, and walked to the door.

Kendall refused to eat, claiming he wasn't hungry, and begged to be left alone in his room. Jess insisted her maid, Sarah, join her for dinner in the family's private dining room. The idea of a maid sitting with the monarch at the family's table nearly frightened the poor woman to death; they were halfway through the second course before Sarah stopped shaking and began to enjoy her meal. For her part, Jess simply couldn't face the empty chairs around the table alone.

Chapter Six

Jess

The days passed in a blur as Jess spent most of her waking hours attending Council or other meetings. With most of the men away in a foreign land, the work of keeping families fed and industry moving rested squarely on the women and elders. Jess found her chief responsibility, and her greatest challenge, was balancing the needs of the nation with the simple daily requirements of mothers and children. She could only push her people so far.

The ashes of her father and brother were expected to arrive in the capital within a week, and plans were made to honor them both. Jess overruled tradition and ordered Justin be laid to rest beside their father in the Crypt. He would be the first non-monarch interred in that sacred place, and different members of the clergy visited daily to try to dissuade her from violating sacred ritual. She listened patiently at first, but soon realized that small men with a modicum of power or influence found the need to challenge change at any cost. By the end of her first week in power, she politely refused to discuss the topic further.

Her coronation was another topic burning the tongues of her advisers. They argued her throne wouldn't be secure until the Crown was firmly seated on her brow. While she agreed with their sentiment and longed to give the people something positive to celebrate, she insisted the ceremony be delayed until she returned from a mission, the details of which she couldn't reveal even to her Council. She simply told them she'd received a messenger and had to personally attend some errand vital to Kingdom security. Fearful of who she could trust as her reign began, she dared not share the location—or even the existence of—the cave she and the Melucians had hidden in following their escape from her mother. The place had been a secret for over a thousand years, and she wasn't about to change that. It might soon be the only place in the world she could truly be alone.

Ten days following her return to the palace, she stood staring at the bronze doors of the throne room, a small leather satchel at her side. Mage Earnest, whom she was coming to appreciate for his candor and positive spirit, stood beside her chief guard, blocking her exit.

"This is a terrible idea, Your Majesty. You barely escaped multiple attempts on your life, are finally safe, and now you want to leave the safety of the palace again?"

"Majesty, I must agree. Surely there is someone else who could handle this errand for you. Any member of Council would go if you asked. I would go in your place. Please reconsider." Mage Earnest's tone was calm, in direct contrast to the captain's urgency.

Jess let out a deep sigh and peered up at the men. "Captain, Mage, I understand how this must look and sincerely appreciate your concern, but this is a journey *I* have to take. There is no one who can speak for the Crown on this matter. I'll be fine."

"At least let me send a couple of my men with you." The captain's voice turned stern but now held a note of desperation. She knew how hard he'd taken it when he'd learned of the recent deaths of three members of the royal family he'd sworn to protect, and he didn't want to lose another.

Jess put a hand on the burly guard, something she'd *never* done as Princess. "I'll be fine. Where I'm going, *no one* can follow. You're going to have to trust me, despite how I may have toyed with your trust in the past."

The captain gawked at her admission. He stared a moment, then relented and stepped aside, seeing no way to change his Queen's mind. Mage Earnest followed suit and bowed deeply as she strode through the gilded doors toward the palace's main entrance, where her carriage awaited her.

Jess peered out the window at the snow-covered city. They passed quickly, but she could see people stirring as the sun lit the horizon with a splash of brilliant orange and yellow. A few waved and smiled or offered respectful curtsies. She'd tried to keep her arrival quiet, to allow her father's ashes to return before news of her ascension became widely known, but she'd quickly learned a vital lesson: a secret known by more than two people would rarely remain a secret. The moment the Council had adjourned from their meetings on that first day, half the city was abuzz with the news of their new ruler. Wild rumors raced like wildfires, some making ridiculous claims about the King's death, others speculating on the insane things the petulant girl who now wore the crown would do next. Few held even a kernel of truth, but they stung all the same. Jess wanted to be a good Queen and to be loved.

The warmth she received as the carriage rolled through town was due to the work of Trade Minister Carver. She'd always thought he was a smarmy dandy in his frilly shirts and garish coats, but the man knew how to spread the word across the inns and shops of the capital. His little mice scurried and spread their own ridiculous rumors designed to boost the fledgling Queen's reputation. One claimed she'd fought crazed assassins in an attempt to save her father and brother while others talked of her valiant efforts to rescue the Kingdom from the iron grip of her now-maligned mother.

Jess protested the use of falsehood, and Carver tried to be gentle, but he ultimately explained that she wasn't well liked or respected as Princess, and some "stretching of the truth" would be required to win the people to her side as Queen. After that admission, she'd given him free rein to carry out his work, determined to focus on the myriad of other issues facing her people.

The carriage rolled to a stop at the steps of the Temple of the One, waking Jess from her thoughts. She reached for the handle, but the footman beat her to it, snapping sharply to attention as she emerged. The liveried man offered a crisp bow.

"How long will Her Majesty be at prayer?" he asked.

"You may return to the palace. I will be a few days," she said. "Thank you, Marcel," she added, placing a hand on his arm. The man's eyes widened as he looked down at his Queen's hand. He gave her a much deeper bow as she stepped back, and a smile bloomed on his face as he watched her enter the Temple.

The Temple's nave was empty. One lone priest knelt before the central altar near the far end of the cathedral. At the sound of her steps, the balding man's head turned to peek over his shoulder. She was only halfway down the long central aisle when he leapt to his feet and bolted toward her.

"Your Majesty! Forgive me. I had no idea *you* were coming this morning," he said through heavy breaths. "What brings you to the Temple so early? How may I serve?"

She waited for the priest to complete his bow and look up before speaking.

"I wish to spend some time in the Crypt. There have been very few moments alone since I returned, and I wish to mourn my family in private. Please see that no one disturbs me?" She raised a small book. "I wish to spend several hours alone."

"Of course, Majesty." He glanced from the book to the leather satchel in her other hand. He cocked a brow but turned and led her to the stairs descending into the Crypt.

At the top of the stairs, she placed a hand on his shoulder, causing him to turn. "Brother, please go about your prayers. I'll be fine from here."

The priest understood a dismissal when he heard it, bowed again, and resumed his position before the altar.

Jess continued down the stairs, pausing only briefly before the massive doors of the Crypt, then locked them firmly behind her from inside. The magical flames lighting the Crypt gave an eerie glow, but she didn't care. She marched to the far end of the marble hallway, peered briefly into the mirror resting against one wall, then walked purposefully through the glass and vanished, leaving the flames to ponder the dead without her.

The cave's magical flames mirrored those of the Crypt, casting a smokeless glow throughout the chamber. Jess took a few steps beyond the mirror and stopped, a chill running up her spine with the memories of her last visit. She knew Keelan hadn't meant to harm her—that the real Keelan would never hurt someone without cause—but she couldn't keep the trickle of fear completely at bay. Torchlight glinted off the silver pitcher resting on one of the round wooden tables, and a smile emerged. How had she forgotten about the mystical drink that waited so patiently for her return? She sat and poured a cup, the first fruity sip washing away her anxiety and fear, leaving a clear mind and hint of chocolate in her mouth.

Finally calm, her gaze traveled around the cavern. Cots, tables, shelves—just as she remembered it. Atikus had told her it would take Keelan a week or two to arrive, so she pulled out her book and leaned back for a good, relaxing read. She had been honest with the priest when she'd talked about how little time alone she'd enjoyed since returning. The quiet of the cave was a welcome respite from her long days shepherding the palace's efforts. Even a Queen needed a moment's peace.

Hours passed. When she tired of reading, she retrieved a small box filled with blank parchment, a quill, and tin of ink. For once, she had the peace and quiet to think, so she turned her mind to the most pressing issues facing her kingdom, starting with key roles she had yet to fill.

A messenger had arrived from the army a day before, and she was relieved to learn that General Marks had survived and was leading what remained of her forces home. She scribbled

"Minister of War," then wrote *Marks?* beside it. She thought a moment and put another note to the side of the name: *Chancellor?* The idea had come to her as she lay awake a few nights earlier, unable to sleep with matters of state spinning in her head. Uncle Ethan had been her family's closest friend and confidant. He might not make a great spymaster, but he could lead her ministers effectively, and she trusted him. He might be the only person in the Kingdom she could truly say that about. The sad *aloneness* in that thought made her pause.

She made notes of several other roles and possible candidates, then decided to think through other items. The Kingdom faced a dwindling Gift. Thorn might've been a snake in the grass, but he wasn't wrong about the desperate situation with their magical bloodline. She wrote "Gift—exchange with Melucia? Island tribes? Eastern states?" She had far more questions than answers when her quill stopped moving. After a moment's pause, a thought struck and she wrote, "Atikus/Melucia's Guild." The old Mage seemed to want to talk about the future, and she intended to do just that.

For the next several hours, she grappled with rebuilding the Kingdom's military, dealing with the poor educational system in towns outside the capital, the plight of farmers whose crops had been confiscated for the war effort, the endless stream of orphans and widows created by the war, and dozens of other problems she had no idea how to solve. When she finally set her quill down and leaned back, her mind felt numb.

That's when she heard a horse whinny and the clomping of hooves striking the rocky shore outside the cave. She shot out of her chair and froze, her unwavering glare fixed on the cave's far wall that she knew was actually a hidden entrance. In the space of a breath, the most beautiful creature she had ever seen poked his head through the magical stone.

"Dittler!" A giddy young girl's squeal flew from her lips as she raced forward. Dittler met her halfway and buried his head into her shoulder. She wrapped him in the biggest hug she could manage. The clatter of his hooves made her giggle as he danced with the thrill of their reunion.

"I missed you so much, my baby boy," she said. Dittler whinnied again and licked her face with his slobbery tongue.

"Your Majesty looks good in drool," a deep, amused voice said from the entrance.

Jess's head snapped up, and Keelan's eyes met hers for the first time in weeks. She saw only kindness and warmth, no trace of the malevolent evil that had stalked her before. Keelan's face broke into laughter as drool fell from her forehead into her eye, forcing her to swat it away with the back of her hand.

"You realize it's a crime to laugh at the monarch? I could have your head... or something... I'm sure it would be *very bad* for you," she stammered, trying to walk the line between stern and witty.

Keelan snorted. "A nation of laws. I like it here."

She tossed an empty silver cup in his direction and grinned when he ducked.

He looked up, sarcasm dripping from his tongue. "Regal as ever, Your Majesty."

She grinned and offered a mock curtsey. "I'm so glad you approve, Lieutenant."

The ice now thoroughly shattered by Dittler's slobber, Keelan stepped forward and gripped the horse's reins. His confident face suddenly betrayed a nervousness Jess hadn't seen a moment before. He looked down and absently stroked Dittler's side. "It's good to see you again, Your Majesty... I mean Jess. I... I don't even know how to apologize for... well..."

She almost let him continue to struggle with his apology, simply for the amusement of watching the huge man struggle, but she finally saved him. Her voice was firm, yet gentle. "Keelan, stop. It wasn't *you* who attacked me, but it *was* you who saved me in the end. I know that. It may take me some time to get used to everything, but I don't blame you for what happened. Besides, you forced me to face my future, and I'm grateful for that."

He cocked his head like a confused pup.

Jess grinned. "Come, sit. I remember how much you loved this wine, and my cook insists I take cheese, bread, and meat with me everywhere. We can catch up with a snack."

Keelan ran a hand over his stubble and smiled. "That sounds good. I *am* hungry, and that wine might actually calm my nerves a bit."

"I make you nervous?" she asked playfully.

"Uh, well, maybe. I don't know," he stammered inelegantly.

She laughed again. "I'm teasing you. Just sit and tell me, how is Atikus? I miss that funny old man."

The cave made it easy to lose track of time, and they talked long past the afternoon and into the night. Keelan left out few details of his trip back to Saltstone and the weeks he witnessed following the failed siege. He hadn't been there when her mother fell but described the events as Declan and Atikus had explained them to him. When he told her about Isabel's order to hunt down the mass of fleeing civilians, tears began to trickle down Jess's cheeks.

"She was horrible," was all she could say.

"Jess, it was Irina, not your mother."

Her voice steeled. "My mother *chose* to bring Irina back. She *chose* to sacrifice her husband, son, and daughter on the altar of Irina's ambitions. In the end, it might have backfired when Irina consumed her soul, but it was *my mother's* choices that led to all of this. As much as I may want to forgive her, to love and mourn her as a daughter, as Queen I cannot forget or forgive the treachery and death that woman thrust upon our two nations."

She peppered him with questions, and he patiently answered each one. By the time he'd concluded his tale, Keelan's stomach was telling a completely different story.

Jess chuckled. "I take it you're hungry again?"

"I'm a big boy. I like to eat." He grinned back. "And I happen to have purchased some salted fish and vegetables from the ferry that brought me across the bay. Would you like some?"

She wrinkled her nose, but said, "Sure. I'll try your salted fish, but don't hate me if I go back to my bread and cheese after the first bite. It sounds suspicious, especially coming from a ferry's stores."

While Keelan retrieved the fish from his saddlebags, Jess walked to the shelving and found plates and cutlery. When she turned, he was standing by the table staring at her back. She looked down quickly to see what was out of place.

"I'm sorry," he said as his face colored. "It's just that . . . well . . . the last time I saw you, we were in filthy, dusty riding clothes with tangled hair and dirty faces. I don't think we bathed the whole time we were on the run. And now . . . well, you're . . . beautiful." He looked down as he muttered the last word.

Jess blushed at the compliment, then grinned at his discomfort. She took a long look at the Guardsman in his crisp navy uniform. He'd removed his coat and laid it neatly on one of the cots when they first sat to talk, and she hadn't given it much thought. But now her mind was spinning. When had he changed into a clean uniform following his journey here? Surely his clothes would stink of the road and the bay, but they didn't. Why would he change his uniform before entering the cave?

She was puzzling through those questions when Keelan found his courage and took the plates from her hand. She startled and took a step back.

"Sorry," he said with a sheepish grin and began setting the plates on the table.

As if seeing him for the first time, her eyes traced the outline of his strong jaw and watched the muscles in his back shift in his tight white shirt. She chided herself for staring and turned back to the shelves, pretending to retrieve something else for their meal before joining him around the table again.

Chapter Seven

Danai

Danai's eyes roamed along the golden doors, taking in the detailed etching of the Phoenix that dominated their mirror-like surface. He knew no one tended this chamber, yet the doors remained as shiny and perfect as the day they were laid on their hinges. He traced a finger along one of the Phoenix's talons. He'd never touched the etching before, and despite his centuries of work with magic, it brought a boyish grin to his ageless face.

Finally tired of his rumination, he reached up to the plain metal plate on the wall and spoke the words, "E vesh Irina," *Take my life, Irina*. As the doors swung open, he made a mental note to find a way to change the words required to enter this chamber. Irina was dead to him now; at least, that's what he kept telling himself.

He slipped inside, impatient for the door to fully open, and was shocked to find a cloaked figure knelt in prayer at the altar. As he stepped closer, he could see the outline of a mask, feathers protruding where ears would normally be on an animal. One of the Children.

"Child, turn and face me. What are you doing here?" Danai demanded.

The figure didn't move, and Danai could hear the incessant muttering of the man's prayer as he approached within a few paces. The prayer ended, and the cloaked man rose to face Danai. His mask was of a snarling bear with what appeared to be an eagle's wings for ears. These people were creative, however twisted.

Lifeless eyes widened with recognition, and the man bowed at the waist.

"Forgive me, High Lord. I didn't know you would arrive today."

Danai's impatience grew. "I asked you a question, Child. Who are you and why have you disturbed this place? None of your order should even know of its existence."

"Do you not know me, High Lord? I am the Elder of the Children." The man's head cocked to one side in confusion. "I felt our Mother's passing and returned to her stone to mourn. It is a grievous end to our cause."

Is that sadness in his voice? Can Children feel sadness? Or anything, for that matter? Danai wondered.

"Irina failed us all." Danai said with indifference, causing the Elder's eyes to widen at his sacrilege. "I have come to release us from her grip."

Danai stepped around the Elder and beyond the altar to stand before the onyx monolith that loomed over the chamber. Its lettering glittered in the magical light of braziers posted throughout the room. He reached into the pack he'd carried following the siege and removed a coil of thin rope, wrapping one end around the stone and tying it securely. He walked back around the altar, releasing more rope with each step, until he stood inside the edge of the pool, again facing the monolith. He reached into his pack and removed the crown.

The Elder sucked in a breath and fell to his knees. "High Lord! How? Why do you have her crown?"

"*My* crown," he corrected sharply, then placed the ancient relic on his head.

Power coursed through him, and the Gift of Enhanced Strength contained in one of the diamonds answered his call. He gripped the rope, braced his feet against the inner lip of the pool, and pulled with all his magic-enhanced might. By the fourth draw, sweat was beading on his brow, and the pulsing crimson of the diamonds flooded the room with an eerie, bloody glow. On the tenth pull, the monument teetered slowly, then quickly, until it fell with a crash against the altar. Both shrines to Irina's legacy cracked and shattered, and the golden script burst into flame. When the last of the fires died, once majestic words in gold were replaced by charred remnants.

Danai dropped the rope and wiped his brow, smiling at his handiwork. He'd actually done it! There would be no second return of the Empress Irina.

"High Lord, what have you done?" the Elder sobbed. "Our Holy Lady is lost to us now."

Danai pitied the fool. Even in his hollowed-out state, he felt the loss of his mistress, the loss of his purpose. And then an idea struck.

"Elder, what do you know of the prophecies of the One?" he asked.

The man looked up cautiously. "Irina was the One foretold, and now she is lost. By *your* hand."

Danai cocked his head. "No. You *believe* Irina was the One, but she clearly was not, or she would be standing at the center of the continent, triumphant. She was a false fork in the prophecy, however compelling we both may have thought her to be."

Danai threw the last part in to make the man think he shared his loss, to create a sense of common purpose. He was proud of that bit.

"What if the One has returned, but *he* wasn't Irina?" Danai asked.

The Elder staggered back, propping himself against the shattered altar. "High Lord, what you say . . . I . . . we would follow the One into the abyss, should she, *or he*, return."

"Good. I will need your support, especially in the months to come, if we are to unify this land and fulfill the prophecy."

The Elder's eyes practically bugged out of his mask. "You can't mean—"

"I mean exactly what you're thinking. I declare to you, Elder of the Ancient Order of the Children, Keeper of the Flame, I am Danai Thorn, *the One Returned*, the One prophesied to unite lands and people. Bow before me and pledge your allegiance so we might begin our work."

Danai called his Light, and the diamonds on the crown flared brilliantly. He hadn't known that would work, but figured the dramatic flair was worth a try. The stunned look in the Elder's eyes told him everything he needed to know as the masked man threw himself to the floor and pressed his forehead to the stone.

"High Lord," the man whispered reverently.

"Enough of that. Address me properly," Danai commanded, having no idea what title he should use, but understanding the need to conform to the people's beloved prophecy.

"Emperor Thorn," the Elder muttered into the stone. "Your Most Serene Excellency."

Hmm. Not what I would've chosen, but it does have a nice ring to it.

"Rise and remove your mask. The time for hiding is over. The Children will continue to wear the holy robes, but your masks must be cast aside if the people are to accept you as their Priests."

The Elder rose slowly and removed his mask. His hands moved so slowly that Danai thought it might've been painful for him, but what surprised him most was the smooth, unmarred face that looked up at him once the mask fell away. The Elder appeared to have seen only thirty winters, his skin smooth and pale from years hidden beneath the bear's snarl.

The two locked eyes and Danai nodded once in approval. "Elder, I name you leader of the Temples across the land. I charge you with preparing the way for my return. Spread word of the prophecy's fulfillment, and ensure the people know the One will restore order and might to the Kingdom."

The High Priest bowed low. "It shall be done, Excellency."

Danai started to leave, but looked back and scanned the room again, intending it to be his farewell to Irina's resting place. A glint of silver poking out of the monolith's rubble caught his eye. He climbed and discovered a slender silver staff embedded in the heart of the black stone. *Irina's staff!* He gaped as he reached out to touch the ancient weapon his protégée had crafted a thousand years ago. How many times had he seen her wield that staff? How many times had he wondered at its power? She never told him its purpose, or what Gift might've been Enchanted into its length, but now he planned to find out. A grim smile curled his lips as he grasped the metal and it slid from its hiding place.

Without thinking, he turned and pointed the staff at the Elder. Calling his Light, he channeled and felt the thrill of life course through the silver stave. Unable to contain the raw energy, the staff bellowed white flame that hungrily engulfed the man. Living fire crawled up and down his body, yet he did not burn. His lips parted as if to scream, but the magic rushed in and filled his chest. When his lips closed, no trace of the magical flames remained. He looked up at Thorn and quirked a brow, as if something utterly perplexing was taking place.

Danai took a step forward. "What are you feeling? Speak to me!"

The man opened his mouth to speak but found no sound would emerge. And then it started.

Thorn stared down.

Slowly, understanding replaced terror, understanding of the *true* Gift that lay before him. The Gift that would place him on the throne at last.

Part II

Chapter Eight

Declan

D eclan stared out at the island landscape, his feet dangling over the edge of the cliff. He'd been there for hours, thinking through the events of the past few months. The last time he'd sat on this ledge, Órla had been by his side, chiding him for his lack of progress in mastering the many facets of his magical Gift. He smiled at the memory of her barbs, missing that perky voice more than he ever thought possible.

"The sunrise is incredible, isn't it?" His mother's voice startled him out of his musing.

He turned his head. "This may be the most beautiful place in the world. It's certainly the most peaceful."

"Come back during storm season and say that." She leaned down and kissed the top of his head, earning a warm smile.

As he found his feet, Kelså said, "I've made some breakfast if you're hungry. It's early, but I had a feeling you would want to start your journey soon."

He gaped at her. "How did you know I wanted to leave today? I was going to talk to you this morning about it but hadn't really decided yet."

"You'll learn that a mother *always* knows, especially when it involves her baby leaving the nest again."

He snorted and looked down into her twinkling eyes. "Baby?"

"You'll always be my baby boy, and don't you forget it Declan Rea!" She winked and turned toward the cave's entrance but hesitated. Her expression darkened. "I still want to hear more about what happened with Saltstone and Irina. I didn't press when you first got here, but it's important I know everything before you leave."

Declan nodded soberly. "Not the best breakfast conversation, but it'll have to do. After you."

They wound their way through the ancient tunnels. The smell of freshly cooked bacon greeted them before they could see the entrance to the kitchen. Declan's stomach growled loudly.

He was pleased to find piles of food waiting for them on the round wooden table. Eggs, bacon, steaming scones, and a small bowl of assorted fruit. "Did you make enough for the village? Spirits."

She beamed. "I can't have *my baby* going off hungry, can I?"

He grinned and thumped her arm playfully.

He filled his plate while Kelså poured piping hot tea into mugs and set the kettle back on the stove. Long moments passed in silence as they enjoyed their morning meal, but Kelså's curiosity and concern couldn't resist for long.

"Why don't you start from the beginning? You said Grove's Pass was destroyed by the time you returned, but I could tell you saw more than you were willing to discuss."

He took a sip of tea, set his fork against the edge of his plate, then stared into the grain of the table's wood for a long moment before speaking. When he did, his voice was barely a whisper.

"I grew up in the Guild in Saltstone, but Grove's Pass had become my home. There were over a thousand rangers who lived, worked, or passed through the town. They were my brothers and sisters, my family. And the people of Grove's Pass . . ." He had to take a few deep breaths to keep his rising emotions in check. Kelså set her own fork down and cradled her mug in both hands as she listened.

"The innkeeper was like another uncle. When I first joined the Rangers, I was young and stupid, getting into every kind of trouble you could imagine. I probably spent more time at his bar than I did in the mountains or HQ. He helped a lost boy find some measure of peace and focus. I probably wouldn't be alive if he hadn't taken me under his wing.

"And I could say the same about a dozen of the Rangers." His voice broke and he paused. "They were all dead when I got there. And the people . . . Who kills innocent children in their mothers' arms? Who does that?"

Kelså reached across the table and placed her hand on his. "Show me," she said solemnly.

His eyes widened with horror at the thought of bringing such memories to life, but he nodded and called his Light. Images flickered, then Grove's Pass solidified above the table.

He picked his way through the town's snow-covered streets. His vision displayed bodies, burned-out buildings, the remains of the Rangers' home. Declan's skill with Illusion had grown since his first time on the island, and they could almost smell the death in his images.

Then he moved to Saltstone, showing her the city's growing fortifications before the Kingdom's troops arrived. People, horses, and carts bustled through the crowded streets in preparation. Soldiers were everywhere.

He flew over the ranks of Kingdom trebuchets and soldiers, an ocean of destructive force aimed at Melucia's heart. Tens of thousands of men, many on horseback, watched as stone after stone was hurled against the invisible barrier of Declan's magical shield. The view through Órla's eyes was disorienting, but the inevitable outcome of the scene unfolding below was obvious. The city could never stand against such an assault.

Declan could only recall snippets of the battle between Irina and Arch Mage Quin, as he'd been tumbling down the Tower stairs when most of it occurred, but he was in position to remember the blinding light of Irina's fires as she blasted the city's dwellings again and again, killing and burning indiscriminately, exacting a millennium's worth of pent-up rage. They felt the grinding of stone against stone as the Tower cracked and began to break apart. Kelså stared in horror as Arch Mage Quin fell, then Isabel's body crumpled.

When the Phoenix streaked down and wrenched Irina's crown from her head, Kelså clapped a hand over her mouth and emitted a gasp. She watched as the evil Empress's Spirit evaporated into the sky, and the Phoenix sailed out over the Silver Mountains, trailing plumes of magical smoke from her massive chest.

A few seconds passed before Declan's images shifted, and they watched as the Phoenix, many leagues away, hurtled from the sky into the Kingdom's army. Brilliant light flared across the land as magic's guardian sacrificed herself a second time so innocents might live.

The images vanished, and Kelså found herself gripping Declan's hand, her knuckles now white. She released him and sat back, eyes downcast.

"Sweet Spirits."

After another eternal moment, Declan said, "We survived, as did most of the civilian population of Saltstone. Our army, such that it was, lost most of its men, but the Guard remained intact. We've had to recall the Rangers from the eastern border to begin rebuilding our border force, and our leaders have invested in a new navy, since most of our fleet consisted of unarmed merchant ships. I don't think the Kingdom fared much better, but we'll be prepared if they try anything again."

"What about Irina? What about her crown?"

"Irina? Didn't she die when Isabel was killed when the Tower fell?" he asked. "No one's seen the crown since the Phoenix took it. Couldn't you ask *her* somehow?"

She nodded. "Yes, I could ask about the crown, but Irina's Spirit worries me. The currents never fully calmed after the battle. I can still sense great turmoil, and in the images, I saw Irina's spirit flee Isabel's body. If she'd died and been taken beyond the veil, I shouldn't have seen her Spirit unless we'd summoned her. She's still out there, though I have no idea what she could do in ephemeral form."

Declan thought a moment. "When you taught me about Spirit Communication before, you said Spirits could cause great harm if not contained by a circle. You were insistent I learn to draw the circle perfectly with no breaks. When the tower fell, wouldn't that have broken any circle containing Irina?"

She nodded.

"Could she inhabit another person, like she did with Isabel?"

"I'm not sure. Probably. She wouldn't want to inhabit just anyone. She'd want someone with a strong Gift but a weak mind so she could control them. That's a hard combination to find. Most with strong Gifts have a mind to match, making their ability to repel Compulsion much greater. Plus, based on what you've told me and what you learned from Keelan, she gained most of her power from the crown, which is missing."

"But if she found the right host, and then found the crown . . ."

Kelså stood on the porch of the Keeper's cottage, staring into her son's eyes.

"Seeing you again was more than my heart hoped for, but a few days isn't nearly enough. Please come back when you can."

Declan stepped onto the first step, bringing their eyes to the same level, and wrapped her in a tight embrace. "If I had my choice, I'd never leave this place again. I love you, Mother."

Kelså's self-control cracked, and she swallowed hard to hold back her tears. She pulled away from Declan's hug and slapped his chest teasingly.

"Don't you dare make me cry, Declan Rea." She wiped a tear with her other hand.

He smirked and gave her a peck on the cheek.

"Oh, I should've mentioned this before," he said.

"Uh oh."

"So . . . I kind of told Keelan."

Her arms crossed and her arching brow rose further.

"Yeah. So, I told him about . . . um . . . well . . ." He looked down, trying to avoid her gaze that was now stern. "I told him about *everything*, but I used magic to bind him to silence and mask the knowledge in his mind. He can't speak about it, even if Compelled."

Her face softened. Her mouth set and she gripped his arms. "What is done cannot be undone. But son, no one else. *Ever*. Do you hear me?"

He nodded.

"I'm serious. Órla gave you—gave both of us—a great gift in letting you keep your memory. More than that, she gave you the ultimate trust. The security and fate of magic itself rests with the secrets you carry. If Irina—or anyone with ill intent—learned of the location of the Well, it could mean disaster beyond imagining."

He nodded solemnly. "I know, but Keelan is the most trustworthy person I know. His whole life, even his Gift, revolves around the truth. Add my binding, and I'm confident he will never betray that trust. Wouldn't you . . . someday . . .?"

Her eyes flew wide. "Oh, Declan, *of course* I want to see him, to know my son as an adult, to see the man he's become. There's nothing my heart craves more, but my heart can never take precedence over the welfare of magic and this world—and neither can yours. That's the burden we both bear."

She stared into his eyes for a long moment, then drew a deep breath and cupped his cheek.

"Enough of that. I *refuse* to say goodbye. I love you. Travel safely and come back to me soon, alright?"

Declan wrapped her in another hug and turned to make his way down the mountain path.

Chapter Nine

Atikus

Weeks had passed since Atikus watched Keelan ride into the distance, headed toward the cave. He longed to hear some word of his journey, hoping beyond hope that Jess would receive him well and the rift between the two nations could begin to heal. He knew it would take time, but the months immediately following the Siege of Saltstone were critical in ensuring the people's faith that peace was possible. Without visible, positive action, fear and animosity would quickly cement into irreparable hatred.

His new Arch Mage's robe, emblazoned with a living, swirling image of the Phoenix on his chest, rustled as he walked toward the audience chamber. He paused to examine busts of prior members of the Triad and artwork depicting Melucia's vast countryside, reminding himself of the history he would now take part in writing. Since his ascension to Arch Mage, he'd barely paused to ponder the weight of his new responsibilities or how his name and actions would be scrawled permanently in history's tomes for all time. Walking the length of this hallowed hall, the immensity of his new role settled into his mind. The last statue before the grand oak doors to the audience chamber was of the first Arch Mage. Her gaze looked high and far, her slender neck leading to a sharp chin and square jaw. There was a majesty in her pose. Moreover, the artist somehow captured a depth of feeling and wisdom in her eyes. Surely, this was some work of magic. It took his breath.

"Is it getting to you, too?" a deep voice rumbled from behind, snapping Atikus from his lost gaze. He turned to find the Guard's Captain-Commander Dev Albius a few feet away, quietly observing the Mage.

"And so it begins." Atikus smiled wanly, then turned and strode into the audience chamber, where the new Merchants' Guildmaster and the Eye awaited their presence. Albius grunted and followed.

The Triad adjourned their first session as Melucia's governing body. They'd barely begun to outline the impossible task of rebuilding the capital and repairing the damage to their nation. While Grove's Pass and Saltstone endured the brunt of the Kingdom's attacks, many port cities faced naval blockades while a few lost ports to bombardment. Much of the merchant fleet had also been destroyed, crippling a significant portion of the mercantile nation's ability to move goods. The Melucian military, such that it was, had been devastated, and the Rangers now numbered less than a tenth of their original force. The Captain-Commander replacing the Armsmen's Guildmaster among the Triad was testament to the state of the armed forces, something which would take years to correct.

And then there were matters closer to home—the people of Melucia who had suffered the incalculable loss of fathers, sons, mothers, and daughters. An entire generation of men had been wiped out by Irina's fires and her armies. The returning women, children, and elderly faced lonely gaps that could never be filled, but it felt good to start, even if it was a humble beginning.

Atikus grasped forearms with Albius, and the two men smiled warmly at their newly shared sense of purpose. Beatrice stepped into the center of the two men, gripping each man's forearm and pulling them apart. Her next move shocked them further, as she pulled them both forward and embraced them awkwardly.

"We've got a lot of work to do, but I'm glad to be doing it with you two. I'll do my best to keep the petty politics of the Merchants at bay so we can move things forward."

Atikus noticed Albius's wide eyes and winked at the Commander. "Dev, I believe she may match you on backbone. You might want to watch yourself." The old Mage chuckled and looked down at Beatrice with affection.

She slapped him on the chest. "Don't you get all comfortable, Mage Dani. It's *my* people who make the food, and I've seen how you like to eat. You'd better behave if you know what's good for you."

A rough bark of a laugh slipped from Albius as Atikus feigned offense. "My dear lady, I'm shocked you would threaten an old man's hunger."

The embrace broke apart with all three rulers feeling a sense of relief at their camaraderie. Atikus had turned back to his seat to gather his notes when a wave of dizziness caused him to stagger wildly, then collapse on the cold stone before his chair. The other two raced to his side.

"Atikus, are you alright? What happened?" Beatrice said with alarm.

Atikus didn't hear her. His head swam, and his eyes turned glassy.

In his mind, a shrill voice echoed. *"You may have won the day, but you will not defeat me. I claim you, Mage Atikus Dani. You will be my Vessel now."*

Atikus's eyes widened, and he struggled to breathe. His hands flew to his head, as if pressure would stop the presence from devouring his self-control. He reached within himself and seized his Light, a brilliant flame that exploded through him as he unleashed its raw power. Irina's spirit screamed an otherworldly howl, and he could feel her writhing within his skull. The pressure began to ease, and he laid his head back to gather himself, but Irina's spirit redoubled her effort as searing pain lashed his weary mind.

Tendrils of malice slammed against his brain searching for a weakness. Atikus's mental shield held, but barely. Sweat poured down his face.

"Atikus, can you hear me? Please, open your eyes," Beatrice called.

But the battle raged within, and Atikus dared not spare a moment lest his attacker take advantage. Wave after wave of mental intrusion hammered his protections. He'd been caught by surprise and was unable to turn the fight and take the offensive. It was only a matter of time before Irina wormed her way inside. He felt his will fading, his magic dwindling, while hers only grew.

How is she capable of such power without a connection to the world of life?

Irina's laugh raked at his consciousness. *"You always were a dense old fool. You are my connection now. I have access to your reserves and your link to the currents, but without your petty human exhaustion. I will never tire, so you may as well relent. Be my Vessel willingly, and I will allow a sliver of your consciousness to survive."*

"NO!" he screamed aloud.

"I was hoping you'd say that."

Irina narrowed her focus into a single, needle-sharp point, then rammed her will into his shield with all her strength. The concentration of magical force was too great for Atikus, and he felt her presence flood through, consuming his individuality and sense of self. The mighty Mage whose mind could never forget anything cowered in the face of Irina's ravenous desires. She dove into the recesses of his memories, searching, clawing—until she found something that shocked her into stillness.

In that moment of respite, Atikus drew into himself and gathered the last remnants of his power. Knowing his end was near, he held nothing back, clumsily hurling all that remained of his waning strength at the Spirit. For no discernable reason, she didn't react and didn't raise her own defenses. Atikus's magic bore into her as a wave crashing against rocks. Her magical balance lost, Irina's spirit tumbled out of control and was flung from the Mage's mind. He braced himself and walled off his mind from further intrusion, but it was for naught. Irina's Spirit had fled.

Weakened from the conflict, Atikus fell limply on the chamber's floor. He reached toward the Eye, but his vision clouded, and darkness enveloped him.

Chapter Ten

Irina

Irina's Spirit hovered above the Eye as she watched the Triad fret over the sagging form of their resident Mage. Atikus had defeated her efforts to excise his soul just as Thorn had before. She wasn't used to others having more power or strength. In her first life, she was one of only eleven humans alive with a connection to magic. It wasn't until the others had turned against her that she'd finally accepted her birthright as a Mage and turned her eye toward conquest and control.

She wasn't used to failing or having her magic rebuffed, certainly not by creatures like Atikus Dani and his pathetic two-power Gift. What was happening to her, to the world, that she would struggle with such a simple task?

The battle for Atikus's Spirit hadn't exhausted her. She was certain her ethereal form couldn't be tired or feel pain; yet something felt different, wrong. It felt as if the shimmering form of her likeness struggled to hold together. Maybe the fight *had* weakened her. She thought back to her battle with Thorn and realized that failure, too, had affected her Spirit's strength, possibly diminished her just enough for Atikus to have the upper hand in their struggle. There was so much about life beyond living that she didn't understand. She'd never cared about what happened in death—until she actually died.

She knew a Spirit could be contained. The Spell of Return that allowed her to be restored had initially contained her in that awful black monolith. When she was alive, Thorn had taught her about the power to interact with Spirits and the need to draw a summoning circle lest they be set free to wreak havoc. And here she was, the perfect example of that havoc-wreaking Spirit, set free by the breaking of the circle in Mages' Tower.

Even if weakened, she was *free*.

Then she wondered, could a free Spirit expire? Or could one be weakened beyond the point of its ability to interact with the living world? A spike of terror shot through her. What would she become if that happened? Would she be consigned to wander a land and watch a people she could never touch? Would she become some ghostly voyeur who could never again cross the threshold of life? That scared her more than anything.

She realized in that moment she needed a host more than she'd originally thought. Within the body of Isabel, she'd been able to rejuvenate her strength, become brighter and sharper, more in focus.

There is so much to learn about this new life of mine.

It was the idea of learning that made her realize something. When she had inhabited Atikus, even for the brief moments before he'd expelled her, she had touched every part of him, including his memories. Surely, there was something in that vast mental library to help her understand herself better.

She focused on the point within her Spirit that had brushed against the Mage's mind and was rewarded with a replicate version of his every understanding. At first, she saw only a smattering of recollections; but the more she delved, she realized that all the Mage's memories had transferred to her. She hadn't inhabited his mind, but she had stolen a valuable part of it.

An excited energy thrummed through her as she hungrily devoured the ancient man's knowledge. Every gift imaginable, some she'd never imagined, was cataloged neatly, enumerated and defined, allowing her already immense understand of magic to deepen and grow. Gifts of Healing and Warfare, Farming and Horticulture, Travel and . . . every other Gift known to exist. It was overwhelming and exhilarating. So much knowledge.

And then she saw it.

If she could draw breath, she would've sucked in a deep one.

There, lodged in the memories of the man, was an image of the most beautiful place she'd ever seen. At first, his mental vision was of a small village on an island, an idyllic setting that appeared to be little more than the fond memory of one stop in his travels, but something felt more important about this place.

She dove deeper.

She felt herself climbing a mountain, the path at her feet flaring with an odd magical glow with each step. As she ascended, she could feel the island air cool with the ever-present breeze.

She passed a simple shack, somehow knowing it was unimportant and would not impede her journey, yet also understanding it served a vital purpose linked to the overwhelming power she sensed. She continued unimpeded until the mouth of a cavern gaped before her. The dim light cast by torches bearing ever-present magical flame greeted her as she stepped forward. Rough-hewn rock turned smooth and translucent, vibrant with color and light.

After a moment's descent, the tunnel opened into a massive cavern, and she froze, awestruck. If her eyes had been dazzled by the colors and light of the walkway, her senses were now over-

whelmed by the tapestry of shimmering power before her. She looked down and saw a flow—no, a current—in perpetual motion beneath a glassy surface. As she strode forward, mist swelled up from that river and reached toward her feet with each step, as if yearning for her embrace. The crystals thoroughly encasing the walls and ceiling glowed and twinkled with a dizzying kaleidoscope of hues.

As stunning as the cavern was to her eyes, it was the intense sensation of power she felt emanating from across the room that captured her attention.

She ascended the steps and again stilled as she took in the opening before her. The mist was gentle, even playful before. Now it raged out of the opening and engulfed her. The hair on her arms and neck straightened and tingled, and she arched her head backward and laughed at the ecstasy of magic's touch.

Thirsty for more, stretched out a tentative hand. The mist swirled eagerly between her fingers and parted as she neared its source below. Her skin breached the surface of the river and swells of magic tore into her. It felt like trying to hold a wild beast, so frightened it fought and scratched as she held it tighter. Only when she relaxed and allowed the power to flow through her freely did its anger and fear abate.

In that moment, she knew true power. It was nothing like the pathetic imitation of mortal power she'd sought a millennium before or even in her latest quest for vengeance. It was the power to destroy and the power to create. It held the will of the gods and could make one a god—or goddess.

She grinned at that.

Then another memory slammed into her from the Mage's mind.

A woman with rich, dark skin and deep brown eyes stared up through Scrying water. Her vision was as clear as if she stood before him. Her smile was warm, her eyes sincere. Behind her crystalline walls shimmered, though only a small portion of the cavern's majesty was visible.

". . . must help me. Atikus, you and Velius are the only ones alive with knowledge of the Well's location—and of the Spell of Sundering now guiding its flow. For the safety of magic itself, no other can know of this place. The people of Rea Utu have stood vigil for thousands of years and remain to guard our secret, yet even they do not fully understand what it is the Keeper keeps. Only you and Velius."

Irina knew this was where she'd lost her power. Where they'd *stolen* it. This was where her supposed brothers and sisters had ripped true magic from her grip and given Gifts to the mundane people across the land.

And this was where she could seize her power once again.

Chapter Eleven

Declan

Declan stood a few dozen paces below the Keeper's cottage and let his eyes roam the landscape.

The day was bright and cloudless, and the tangy ocean breeze tickled his nose. Lush palms dotted the sandy shoals, and squatty plants with broad leaves spread lazily across the ground. Gulls called in the distance. The ocean could be seen from most places on the island, but from halfway up one of its mountains, the undulating carpet of blues and greens and brushstrokes of glittering white stole his breath. He could feel his spirit soar as he breathed in the beauty and couldn't imagine a more tranquil place in all the world.

And then he heard the scream.

Piercing, anguished, and clearly his mother.

Declan dropped the pack he'd slung over his shoulder and sprinted back toward the cave.

"Mother!" he yelled as he raced through the Phoenix-hewn halls.

He found her a few dozen paces inside where they'd parted, sitting on the cold ground, her back leaning against the cavern wall. Tears marred her ageless face, and she stared into the opposite wall, into nothing.

He squatted, gripped her by the shoulders, and shook her gently. "Mother. Mother! Are you alright? What happened?"

She looked up at him with a hollowness in her gaze and said, "It's Atikus. His Spirit is weak, so faint I can barely sense him."

"Is he alive? How weak is he?" Then Declan realized what she'd just said. "Wait, you can sense Atikus's Spirit?"

What other powers had she never mentioned?

Kelså patted his arm and nodded absently. "Something's happened. He was attacked. I don't understand how or by whom, but this wasn't a physical assault. It was magical. He's still alive, but his connection to the currents . . . I don't even know how it's possible, but it's *gone*. Atikus has been severed from magic."

Declan ran a hand through his hair and sat back. "But he's the Arch Mage. How could someone—"

"I don't know, but I don't think he was the first attack. I sensed *something*. I don't even know how to describe it—a stabbing? That doesn't sound right, but it's how it felt, like someone stabbing into the currents."

"When?"

"A day or two ago. I thought little of it at the time because it happened so quickly and then was gone. I didn't sense any damage."

She began to stand, bracing herself with one hand against the wall, but Declan shot to his feet and gripped her by the elbow to help her rise.

She looked up at him, her brow knitted with concern. "I know you want to get back to the mainland, but I'd appreciate you staying a few more days. Atikus may need help we can only give him at the Well. It'll also give us time to figure out what's going on."

"Of course," he nodded. "There's nothing urgent pulling back. I'll stay as long as you need me."

They made their way to the cliff's ledge, where the stone circles and magical wine awaited. The latter soothed their frayed nerves and energized their minds while the former focused their conversation. They talked for hours, examining what they knew of the two attacks in an attempt to uncover some piece of information they'd missed. At Declan's urging, Kelså tried to touch Atikus's consciousness a few times but failed. How could one so knowledgeable, so long-lived, simply have his tether to the currents cut like some flimsy ribbon? She'd never heard of such a thing, and the implications frightened her.

When the sun finally faded over the horizon, they returned to the kitchen for dinner. Unlike breakfast, which had been playful, if a bit wistful due to Declan's departure, dinner was somber. He quietly helped his mother prepare a meal of cold cuts, cheese, and bread. Neither had uttered since coming inside, and few words were spoken throughout the meal. Kelså was nearly finished with her last bite when she suddenly stopped chewing and gripped Declan's arm.

He looked up, startled. "What? What's wrong now?"

She gulped down the cheese and swallowed a sip of wine. "I don't know why I didn't think of this earlier. We need to go back to the Well and speak with an old friend. She may be able to help us puzzle some of this out. Come on."

Kelså puffed through labored breaths as they entered the chamber of the Well of Magic.

Declan had been in this cavern many times since returning to his mother, but the place still filled him with awe. The floor appeared little more than a sheet of clear ice with an ever-moving river beneath. With each step, the mist curled up to meet the pressure of his presence. Despite the urgency of their task, the little boy inside Declan couldn't resist bending down to trace a finger and watch as the mist raced to catch up.

As he rose to his feet, Kelså watched, arms crossed with a slight grin quirked across her lips. "Done playing yet?"

His cheeks flushed as he rose. "I'll never get used to this place."

As they strode across the chamber to the Well, Declan sneaked a glance at the light playing off the crystalline walls and ceiling. A thousand reflections danced throughout the cave, something that had been disorienting the first few times he'd see it.

Kelså stood at the edge of the Well and breathed deeply as tendrils of wispy power curled to greet her. Fingers of magic tickled her feet, then crawled up her legs until her entire form was bathed in pearlescent mist. The effect was otherworldly—and strikingly beautiful. She turned at Declan's gasp, and smiled broadly at his mouth, which now stood agape.

"It tingles. Come, feel," she said. "You'll need to approach the Well for this to work. I need your connection."

He closed the distance to stand beside her, and the magic responded, instantly crawling up his lanky body. He shivered involuntarily, but a giddy grin spread across his face. He looked down at the magic coursing above his hands and played at interrupting its flow with his fingers.

"Connection to what?" he asked distractedly.

"*To whom*, not what," she said.

That got his attention. He looked up, perplexed.

Kelså's eyes closed, and she muttered ancient words, barely audible though he stood only a hand away. As she intoned, the mist glowed brighter and sped in its flow across both their bodies. Another gust of mist rushed from the Well to gather and hover in an undulating mass above the opening. It pulsed like a heartbeat, then began to resolve and take form.

Kelså continued to chant. Declan had only seen the Phoenix herself once, high above the city of Saltstone, but there was no mistake; his mother had called the majestic beast. Her shimmering form grew until it towered above them and spread across the ceiling. Finally formed, the beast's head snapped downward, and she locked eyes with Declan.

A familiar voice brushed against his mind as magic's principal guardian observed him intently. *It is good to see you, Bond-Mate*.

He staggered back a step, and the mist scattered before reforming across his body.

"Órla?" The name croaked out of his dry throat.

"Hello, Bond-mate," her voice boomed through the chamber.

He gaped at the ethereal Phoenix's form.

"Órla, I've missed you so much," he said in a hoarse whisper.

"And I you. But I cannot maintain this form more than a few moments, and I bear dire news." Her gaze shifted to Kelså. "Keeper, the currents remain disturbed, and Irina still haunts the world of the living, though only as a Spirit. While her power is diminished, she may inhabit and subsume others who possess

Gifts. She may also sever them from the flow of magic, as the Arch Mage has learned. Atikus is lost to our arts . . . for now."

"How can we help him? Get his connection back?" Declan asked.

"His Gifts will return in time as his body and mind heal. There is nothing you can do beyond wait." She paused, and her intent gaze became a distant stare. "Atikus will heal, but I fear the threat is greater still. I sense Irina's presence, her rage, and know she will stop at nothing in service to her vengeance. No one remains safe, especially those with a Gift, while her Spirit roams the land."

Kelså sat on one of the crystal pillars surrounding the Well. "Where will she go? What will she seek to destroy now?"

"*Since her return, her purpose has been single-minded—vengeance. Her defeat at Saltstone will have enraged her further. Her mind is veiled from my Sight, but I sense a roiling sea within her. When she comes, she will billow and rage as the storm. Her Spirit must be banished, or all will be lost.*"

The mist began to dim and blur at the edges. Orla's voice sounded far away when she spoke again.

"*Irina's tomb has been destroyed, and she cannot return once banished. Declan, you are the only one capable of banishing her for good. This world will never be safe as long as her Spirit wanders freely.*"

Before he could speak, the Phoenix shattered into flashes of Light. Thousands of pinpricks glowed like embers but were icy cold against his skin before fading into nothing.

In the sudden stillness of the cavern, Declan stared into the Well, wishing for one more moment with his lost friend. The river of ancient power beneath their feet flowed but didn't speak.

Sometime later, Declan and Kelså again sat around the wooden table in her kitchen, each cradling a steaming mug. The sweetly bitter scents of honeyed black tea offered some comfort to their frayed nerves following Órla's message.

"Can Irina really destroy the world of magic? She doesn't even have a body."

Kelså shrugged. "I don't know. She can obviously do damage to individuals, albeit temporarily. If she learned how to permanently separate someone from magic, that could be disastrous."

"What would stop her from devastating the Gift across the mainland? The Kingdom's bloodline is already thin, and Melucia is weakened following the siege." He looked up and saw fear in his mother's eyes for the first time, but he also saw something that frightened him more: doubt. She had no idea what to do or how to respond. She was the Keeper of Magic. If *she* didn't know how to protect the people and their magic from Irina's wrath, who would?

Chapter Twelve

Atikus

Atikus stood on the shore of a massive river. He could feel immense power wafting up as mist tingled against his skin. Currents crashed against unseen rocks buried beneath the torrent.

Where there should've been the briny scent of life, there was none but crisp, cool air. The river was mute as its frothy indignation passed without voice.

Curious, Atikus knelt. He stared, realizing the river flowed not with water, but the essence of magic. Tendrils of translucent mist reached up and entwined his fingers as he held them above the flow. His eyes widened as it crept up his hand, yet he felt no pain, only the tingle, almost a tickle, of magic's gentle touch.

Emboldened, he extended toward the river's flow and allowed the tip of one finger to breach its surface.

The world flared with brilliant light.

The Mage's head swiveled as he now stood on a mountain's peak. The horizon burned with hues of red, orange, and gold atop an endless bed of forest greens. The fresh scent of pine filled his nostrils, and crisp autumn wind pimpled his skin. The vision's transition left him disoriented, yet he smiled at the simple pleasure of witnessing the awe-inspiring sunset.

A moment passed as he watched the sun's rays surrender to the horizon with evening's first touch. Something dark disturbed the view a hundred leagues to the west. He squinted. Rank upon rank of heavily armored men rode astride equally armed horses. At the head of the columns, he saw a man—no, a woman—wearing a brilliant crown. She clutched a silver stave in her right hand and pointed forward with her left.

Irina? Where am I? When . . . ?

The world flashed with brilliance again and Atikus struggled to gain his bearings.

He stood in the center of a large city. Men and women raced in all directions as screams of terror fled their lips. He called out, but no one heard his cries. He was an invisible witness to history. His head swam.

Charred rubble from nearby buildings littered the cobbled stones of the thoroughfare. He scanned the area to find few structures untouched by fire and destruction. A few bodies lay unmoving amidst the stones, but he found no evidence of the true carnage of war.

Bells began to toll, slowly at first, then urgently.

His gaze rose above the din, and he recognized the gleaming turrets of the Palace of Spires, the heart of the Kingdom in its capital city of Fontaine. Smoke rose from watchtowers—not the warm, curling smoke of their hearth, but the angry plumes of unwelcome intruders.

Atikus stumbled a few steps before finding his footing, then ran toward the palace. He rounded the corner of a stately manor, and the palace burst into view. He skidded to a stop as his mind again struggled to process what his eyes witnessed.

Soldiers in green-and-gold livery lay scattered and broken before the ornate iron gates. In their place, men in brown robes wearing odd masks, each holding a heavy cudgel, stood vigil. They scanned the street before them, ready to strike, but none appeared to notice the Mage striding toward them. He was invisible still.

He reached the first of the palace guard and peered down. The smell of waste and bile assaulted his senses, and he stumbled back a step. The man's throat bore three vicious lines, as if rent by massive claws. His arm lay a few paces away; he'd been ripped apart.

He moved to the next guard and found similar wounds. Some wild beast had devastated the ranks of the royal elite.

How is this even possible?

He looked up and realized he now stood face to face with one of the masked figures. Human eyes glared out where once a bear cast its gaze. To his surprise, they held no anger or enmity, only emptiness. Fear raced through his chest, yet the hollow eyes could not see him.

He took a step toward the gate.

The world flashed again.

When his vision cleared, he found himself in the royal audience chamber, paces from the Throne of Spires. Jess stared out, the sunset auburn of her hair trailing across the shoulder of her pristine, white gown. A trail of blood trickled from her nose, and her eyes bore the glassy stare of one departed. The bulky form of a man in blue lay on the bottom step of the dais before her.

"NO!" he screamed. He fell to his knees before Keelan's unmoving form.

It was impossible to tell how long he hovered over his adopted son's body before the scuffling of feet on marble turned his head. Again, what he saw threatened to overwhelm his mind.

Five animals stood in a line before the towering bronze doors of the chamber: a horse, a wolf, a bird of prey, a bear, and a mastiff. Each beast dripped blood from fang and claw. Each stared directly at Atikus, and he knew they saw him.

The world flared again.

Atikus stood on the Eye in the Chamber of the Triad. Tendrils of terror laced into his chest with white-hot rage. He tried to raise a shield, but it was too late—insidious barbs were already buried deep within his Spirit. He could feel their hunger, their hatred. He screamed in pain and felt something precious rip from his soul.

And then he heard a voice, barely a whisper. "Atikus, it's Órla. Follow my voice."

Kelså took Declan's hand in her own.

"Declan, tell me what you're thinking."

He squeezed her hand and stood, running his fingers through his unruly mop of sandy curls. "I . . . I don't even know what to think. If I go back through the Gate, I can be in Saltstone in two weeks, maybe a little less if I can find fresh horses along the route. Is there any food we can pack for the trip?"

"Declan, wait. There may be another way. But—"

"Will it get me there faster? What is it?" he asked, hope entering his voice for the first time.

"You could ride the currents."

Declan's mouth dropped. "*The* currents?"

She nodded.

"I didn't know you *could* ride the currents. They seem so . . . I don't know . . . not good to touch."

"Eloquent, as always." She smiled wanly. "And no, they aren't welcoming of human touch, but you aren't fully human, Declan. You are the Heir. You are *of* magic. I believe the currents may answer if you call."

He looked at her dubiously. "May? You aren't inspiring confidence here."

"I don't think anyone has actually ridden the currents before. I'm grasping at ancient knowledge here, trying to gain Atikus valuable time."

"But, what if—"

"I don't know what might happen. The mist welcomes you just as it does me. I felt Órla's warmth just as you did. I *think* the currents may also welcome you." She tried to project confidence, but her eyes showed only doubt and fear. "Son, magic always demands a price."

"Yeah, I got that. Órla said something like that at the end, before she . . ." He took Kelså's hand again and offered a weak smile. "This isn't just anyone hurt; it's *Atikus* in danger. We have to try everything we can."

Kelså stared up at her son for a long moment, then whispered, "I know you're right, but you're asking a mother to let her son leap into the unknown, into the most powerful force in the world. How am I supposed to be okay with that?"

But she knew Atikus was more than just a distant friend, more than an adopted father to her sons. He was the Arch Mage and last surviving great magician of his time. More importantly, with his Gift of memory, he was the keeper of hundreds of years of history. She couldn't tell from Órla's message whether it was his Gift or his life at risk. Órla had said his Gift would return in time, but something in the currents now told her otherwise.

Losing him—and his mental vault—would mean losing the past, losing vital perspective. They had to do everything possible to save him.

"Mom," Declan whispered and pressed his forehead to hers. "I have to do this. Atikus is a father to Keelan and me, and he means the world to the people of Melucia. They've lost so much already. They can't lose him, too."

She searched Declan's eyes and found strength and determination. Here *he* was the one placing himself in danger, and she was hesitating. Dueling emotions bloomed in her chest. Pride as she observed her son and his unwavering commitment to those he loved. And shame. Shame at her hesitation, at her questioning, at her selfishness in wanting to keep Declan safe when the whole world needed him most. She was the Keeper. She should put magic and the welfare of others ahead of every concern, especially her own desires. Yet she still hesitated.

She let out a breath she hadn't realized she'd been holding and nodded once, then looked away so he couldn't see her wipe the tear now trailing down her cheek.

"You're right, but I don't have to like it. Neither of us knows what this will do, what price will be demanded, if you can even *survive* the currents. Forgive a mother's fear, even if the Keeper knows this is your path."

He cupped her cheek and turned her face back to him. "I love you, Mom. Everything will be ok."

She tried to smile, but it wouldn't reach her eyes. He leaned down and kissed her cheek. Then, without warning, he turned, took two strides, and jumped feet first into the Well.

"DECLAN!" Kelså screamed, but he vanished into the swirling mist that now raged against the crystalline floor of the cavern.

Chapter Thirteen

Declan

He didn't think, didn't wait for his mother to protest or for logic to talk him out of anything. He just jumped directly into the most powerful force ever to exist. The last thought that repeated in Declan's mind as he leapt was, "Stupid idea! Stupid idea! Stupid idea!"

He looked down and watched his boots hurtle toward the open space in the crystalline floor. Then the world transformed into a kaleidoscope. A few feet away, his beautiful mother, robed in elegant white and gold, became little more than a reflection, a smear of white against the backdrop of hues reflecting against glass. His own golden tunic flared. He had to squeeze his eyes shut to stop the blazing spots that appeared.

Heat turned into knives of flame against his skin. The further he sank into the magical river, the stronger the sensation of being burned alive grew. And yet, oddly, he felt a chill.

He struggled to keep his head wedged in the pocket of air between the river's surface and the cavern's floor as his arms flailed and feet kicked uselessly against the endless pull. The current quickly drew him away from the opening, and he watched through the glassy floor as his mother's image faded from view.

His head was fully submerged now, and he felt the pressure of the watery flow carrying him away, yet he didn't struggle to breathe. If anything, sucking in the blueish mist filled his lungs with warmth and exhilaration. It felt as if magic wanted him to draw it into himself, to let it live within more than just his Spirit.

So he did.

He stopped struggling and lay back, allowing his body to float and be buoyed along. Magic sensed his surrender, and the surrounding glow grew. Aches that plagued him from years of hard service in the Rangers vanished, and his body was renewed. He'd experienced magic's healing in the bottomless pitchers of wine found in the Traveling caves—but while the wine's healing repaired injury to body and mind, the current's power restored the soul. In a single moment, Declan felt reborn, his flesh replaced with perfect, never-worn skin. He could feel his muscles tingling, knitting together where scars caused pain, becoming whole and unmarred.

Without thinking, he opened his mouth and laughed at the myriad sensations hammering his body and mind. Mist and syrupy thick liquid-that-wasn't-liquid rushed to enter. He panicked, but quickly realized it wouldn't harm him—it couldn't—it was *part* of him, and he was part of it. This torrent of power was his home. No, it was more than that. It was an extension of his Spirit and soul. He belonged here.

And that's when she spoke. Her voice wasn't muted or muffled; it echoed in his mind, clear and sonorous.

After carrying me for so long, it is now my time to carry you, Bond-Mate.

"Órla?" He wheeled his head around but saw nothing but mist. "Where are you? I can't see you anywhere."

She laughed in his head, and he thought it was the most joyous, pure sound he'd ever heard. *Have you learned nothing? I am everywhere—in the mist, the currents, the air above, the stone below. Thanks to your heavy breathing, I even flow within you. That's weird, by the way.*

Declan coughed involuntarily, and Órla laughed again.

I have never truly been a tiny owl, as you knew me, but an eternal, limitless Spirit of magic. One day you will learn that we are not so different, you and I.

Her laughter turned into a serious tone.

Declan, I would embrace you every day, but this is not your time. This world needs you. Atikus is in more danger than I thought. He can't wait for his connection to heal naturally. You must restore him. If Atikus falls, I fear this world will be powerless to resist her power.

"But I—how do I restore him? I don't know what to do."

Trust that small boy deep within you, the one who fears and aches. He knows the way. Trust the boy.

"The boy?" Declan's head spun in confusion.

The currents move quickly and will deliver you to Saltstone soon. Time for Atikus draws short, and I fear he may already lie beyond our aid. Do not tarry.

"Órla, what do I do? I still don't understand!" he shouted, but she didn't answer. The river's light pulsed brightly, and a wave of force swelled beneath him, lifting him above the surface. Without warning, the river drove upward and spat Declan onto cold, dry stone.

Declan leaned up on his elbows and stared back at the mystical river flowing a few paces away. The moment he'd been expelled from its currents, the surface had calmed, returning to its steady flow. He looked down, expecting to see liquid dripping from his clothes, but was stunned to find himself completely dry.

"Of course you're dry, you idiot; it's a *magical* river, not a watery one."

In contrast to the crystalline beauty of the Well's chamber, the cavern where he lay was rough, little more than a hole gouged out of the mountain. The only light came from the river's flow and the mist that reached up to tickle his skin.

The trek along the winding path back to the Mage's complex was covered in pristine snow. Declan took a deep breath of the crisp air and smiled. The thought of seeing his brother and adopted family of Mages once again put a spring in his step, and he found himself standing at the base of the ruined Mages' Tower ten minutes after leaving the cave. He gaped up at the once majestic symbol of magic, now barely a half-tower surrounded by the rubble of massive broken stones. He was here when the Tower fell and had seen it many times since, but returning home to its decrepit state was sobering.

"I come out here to think sometimes."

Declan nearly fell over at the voice that spoke from around the tower's base. A head covered in a blond mess of hair poked around, and a devilish grin parted the boy's face.

"Sorry, didn't mean to startle you." The boy stepped around and took a long look, his eyes growing wider by the second. "You're . . . you're . . . Declan!"

Now it was Declan's turn to chuckle as he righted himself. "Glad to see I made an impression last time I was here. And who are you, Mage-Apprentice?"

The boy locked eyes with Declan, then his eyes widened further, and he staggered back several steps. Fear bloomed in his eyes, and he ran away.

"Wait! Wha . . ."

Declan watched the boy's oversized blue robe flutter away.

"Not exactly the triumphant return I expected."

As he approached the Mages' Quarters, other apprentices approached, excited to greet the man bearing the golden Phoenix on his chest. In turn, they met his eyes, and their expressions morphed from curiosity into fright. In the moments since his return, Declan had managed to clear the yard, leaving him standing at the entrance to the Mages' Quarters alone and befuddled.

The door opened, and Mage Fergus bowled into him, nearly knocking him off the steps.

"Watch yourself, young man!" Fergus bellowed without looking up to see who he'd nearly knocked down.

"I would if you'd stop trying to knock me off my feet." Declan grinned as Fergus recognized his voice and finally looked up.

"My boy!" the Mage exclaimed, gripping Declan's arms with both hands, pulling him into a bear hug. "Welcome home, son."When Fergus looked up, his smile fell, and his eyes widened. "Declan, what happened to your eyes?"

"My eyes? What do you mean? Nothing that I know of."

Fergus scrunched up his nose as he leaned forward and examined Declan's pupils. "Son, I think we need to go inside and let you see for yourself."

The old Mage waddled back into the doorway and led Declan to a sitting room with a large mirror leaning against the wall. A happy fire snapped greeting and warmth in the hearth. Declan turned to the mirror and froze.

"I—Ferg—what...?"

The whites of his eyes now blazed with the intensity of the noon sun, and swirled with light the same intense blue of the Well's mist. As he leaned toward the mirror, he thought he saw the mist curling out of the corner of each eye. He blinked a few times, but the swirling, blazing brilliance remained.

Fergus sat in a large chair by the hearth and poured himself a glass of brown liquor, downing it in one gulp, then refilling the glass.

"How does it feel? I mean *they*, how do they feel? *Your eyes*? How do your eyes feel?" he stammered.

Declan reached up with a tentative finger and rubbed one eye, then shrugged. "They don't *feel* any different. I didn't even know they were glowing, or whatever they're doing."

"Well, I'm pretty sure everyone else will notice. It's rather, um, alarming, especially when you don't know the swirly, glowing magic man is going to glare at you."

Declan turned. "Did you just make fun of me? In my time of need?"

"I would never do such a thing!" Fergus said with mock indignation before breaking out into a grin. "But seriously, we'll need to figure out what's going on, if there are side effects or something. Before we do, though, you came back just in time to see Atikus. I fear we may not have him much longer."

Both men sobered. "He's that bad?"

"I don't think he's in physical pain, but for one steeped in magic to suddenly have that connection ripped away, well, it would make anyone question their will to live. Seeing you might help—but Declan, he's not the man you knew when you left. You need to brace yourself."

Declan nodded slowly. "My eyes can wait. Let's go see him now."

A moment later, Fergus was lightly rapping on the heavy door of Atikus's chamber. A muffled voice bellowed, "Go away!"

"Atikus, it's Fergus. Declan just arrived and we're coming in."

Without waiting for a reply, Fergus pushed the door open and strode into the room. Two strides in, Declan stopped and stared in disbelief. The stones of the floor were completely hidden beneath a layer of scattered clothing and books. Tomes of magic appeared to have been tossed thoughtlessly about. As he absorbed the scene, he found a curled lump in a heavily wrinkled blue robe on the bed. Atikus's silver hair had thinned, and Declan could see dark spots of age spreading across the man's pasty scalp.

"Atikus." Declan said in barely a whisper.

"I said go away."

"Atikus, it's me, Declan."

"I don't care if you're the Phoenix herself. Get out."

Atikus's voice didn't sound angry. It was hollow, devoid of meaning or life—or more likely the *will* to live.

Fergus patted Declan's shoulder and stepped out of the room, closing the door behind him. Declan stepped forward and sat on the edge of the bed.

"Atikus, please. I came to help."

The lump didn't move. "You're wasting your time. No one can help me. I'm useless now."

"Atikus—"

"Just leave me alone. You're better off without me."

Declan stared into the man's back. Seeing his adopted father in this state shocked him more than any of the wonders he'd seen and experienced over the past year. The once jovial, perpetually positive Mage had been reduced to an immobile, helpless man filled with self-loathing and self-pity. Declan's gut turned at the thought.

And yet, amid sadness, he found righteous anger. This man had raised him, gave him hope, taught him to laugh and love. He'd taught him to read and write, to think for himself, and to challenge the thoughts of others. He'd taught him everything that was good and right. What right did he have to shun that love now? *How dare he give up* when the world needed him? When *Declan* needed him?

In response to his rising rage, Declan's tunic flared to life, lighting every corner of the chamber with the brilliance of a hundred candles. Declan stood and stepped back from the bed, then spoke in a measured, commanding voice. "Arch Mage Atikus Dani, get out of that bed before I lift you out."

Atikus's head slowly turned, and he squinted through the tunic's glow. "Fine. I'll get up. Just turn that thing down, will you?"

Declan couldn't suppress a small grin and willed the tunic to dim, but only slightly.

Atikus finally sat up, his spindly legs dangling off the side of the bed, then rubbed his eyes with both palms. "I'm up. You happy?"

"Look at me," Declan commanded.

"You sure got bossy since somebody taught you magic," Atikus said before looking up. When he saw Declan's eyes, he froze, mouth agape. "Sweet Spirits. What in the—"

"We don't know, and it's not important right now. I came to restore your magic. Do you want my help or not?" Declan wasn't sure if this tougher approach would work, but he sensed the comforting he'd planned was doomed to fail against the rocky shoals of the Mage's languishing misery.

"You're wasting your time. I've been severed. There's nothing to restore."

Declan reached forward and gripped his arm, shocked at how wraithlike the formerly hale man had become. He focused his intent into the center of Atikus's chest and allowed his magic to flow into the man's Spirit.

There was nothing.

His Light flowed through every memory and thought, through every emotion, through every part of the Mage he could search, and still he found no remnant of magic. He searched for more than an hour.

"See? Nothing there," Atikus grumbled, ready to be done with this farce and return to his wallowing.

"Shh. I'll be done when I'm done."

Frustrated, Declan allowed his Light to dim, as if resting between exercises. His attention had nearly turned to other thoughts when something caught his mental eye. It was a tiny, almost imperceptible dot, something so small and dim that he never would've seen it while his own brilliant Light shone. He focused his inner sight and approached the dot, surprised that it didn't grow larger as he came closer. But something changed when he neared. *It pulsed*—faintly.

Excitement thrummed in Declan. He reached out with his magical sense to grasp the dot, hoping beyond hope, but was repulsed by an impenetrable wall that sent a shock wave through his soul. It wasn't a wave of pain, rather a sickness or *wrongness* that oozed through his mind.

He shivered at its touch but was determined to save his mentor. He redoubled his effort, drawing ever more power from his internal well and the tunic. He hammered into the barrier with all his might only to receive an equally powerful retort. Bile rose in his throat. His mind swam. He staggered and lost his connection to Atikus before tripping backward to land on the floor.

Atikus was down in a flash.

"Are you alright? Declan, can you hear me?" Concern marred the haggard man's face. "I knew this was useless. Please, stop. I can't have you hurt on my account."

"I'm fine." Declan shook his head to clear his mind, then looked up at Atikus. "But I think you're wrong about being severed. I saw a Light, but it's heavily blocked by . . . something. When I tried to break through, it tossed me back as if I was made of paper."

"That's impossible!" Atikus said, shocked. "Our Mages searched for my Light. None of them could see anything. Are you sure?"

Decan nodded and gave a lopsided grin. "You didn't let the most powerful Mage alive take a look. You know, the one with the mystical, blazing eyes and brilliantly floppy hair?" Declan flicked his hair back dramatically.

Despite himself, Atikus laughed. It was small at first, but quickly grew into a deep rumble that consumed his entire frame. Declan watched as something within Atikus broke free of the malaise that had gripped his soul.

"You always were *impossible*, never minding a word I said. Why did I think you would just leave me alone when I told you to?"

"No idea. You are a foolish old Mage, you know?"

Atikus wiped his own tears and gripped Declan by the arm. "Declan, I'm sorry—"

Declan cut him off, wrapping the Mage in a tight embrace and burying his face in his shoulder.

Long moments later, Declan pulled back with a start. "Not to ruin the mood, but I have an idea. We need to get back to the currents."

Atikus looked up utterly perplexed. "What currents? You mean *the* currents?"

"Sorry, you call it the *vein*. You know, the vein of magic that runs under the old Mages' Tower? That's how I got here so quickly."

Atikus stared in wonder. "You traveled *the currents?*"

Declan nodded. "I'll tell you about all that later. Right now, we need to get back there and try again. I can draw power from the mist. It might give me enough strength to break through whatever that barrier is blocking your Light."

They helped each other up and started for the door, then Declan stopped and turned back toward Atikus. "Um, we need to hurry and all, but, well, you stink of wine and who knows what else. I'm guessing you haven't bathed or changed clothes in days."

"I think it's been weeks." Atikus looked sheepish.

"Right. At least splash water on your face and change into a fresh robe. We can't let the Mages see you like this. You *are* still the Arch Mage."

"I'm pretty sure no one will notice my robes when they see your eyes. Let's get on with this."

Declan shook his head and turned to lead them out of the Quarters and toward the vein.

Part III

Chapter Fourteen

Jess

Jess stifled a yawn, covering her mouth with the back of her hand. Keelan grinned at her effort to mask her sleepiness but chose to save her embarrassment and yawned widely, stretching his arms to emphasize the point.

"I didn't realize how long we've been sitting here. It must be well past midnight," he said, feigning exhaustion he didn't feel. "We should probably get some sleep soon. How do you think we should handle the morrow?"

She finally released the imprisoned yawn. "We should return to Fontaine tomorrow."

"We?" he asked. "Is that the *royal we*, or actually you and me both?"

She snorted. "I think you and I are past royal formalities such as referring to me as *we*. That phrase still makes no sense to me. There's only one of me, even if I'm Queen. Why am I a *we*?"

He grinned. "I believe, Your Most Royal Majesty, the *we* refers to the monarch representing all the people and the land . . . and whatever else she claims as her own."

"Look at you playing amateur royal. I'm not sure you're right in your definition, but I'm too tired to argue." She stood. "I meant that you should return to the palace with me. The Council will want to hear your account of the siege firsthand. We have received a few messengers with updates from before the siege, but only one with news from the time after. You will be able to fill in the gaps."

He eyed her thoughtfully. "You've changed."

"Changed? What do you mean?"

"You were so afraid, so alone. Atikus and I did everything we could to make you feel safe and to get you to talk, but you were locked up tight. And there were times you'd bite at anyone nearby. I suppose all that's to be expected after what you survived, but the woman before me is so different from the girl I knew only a few months ago."

Now it was her turn to eye him thoughtfully, and a long moment of silence passed. He started to fear he'd gone too far when she finally spoke in quiet voice. "My father always said the Crown changes anyone who wears it. I watched how it changed him over the years. He seemed to always be debating something in his mind." She walked to her cot and sat facing him. "When I was a little girl, he was so carefree, often carrying me on his shoulders into the gardens, tossing me into the air before plopping me down on the back of a horse. He loved to ride with me sitting in front of him, his arms wrapped around my sides. I would snuggle into his chest and watch as the world passed by from the saddle. As I got older, he became more serious, lost that playfulness."

"Maybe *you* lost a bit of that as you got older, too? We all do."

She nodded thoughtfully. "Maybe. But I was in many of his Council meetings and stood by the throne as he heard petitions and negotiated trade or whatever pressed that day. He loved being King, but the weight of the Crown took its toll over time. I guess . . . I'm scared it will do that to me, too."

He stepped to his cot, sat, and leaned forward, taking her hands in his. He met her eyes. "Jess Vester, you are the strongest woman I know. You've lived through things . . . things that would've destroyed other people, but *you* never gave up. Of course, the Crown will change you. How could it not? But you have the power to choose how that change occurs, whether it's positive, whether or not you hold to all the special things that make you, well, you."

The sincerity pouring through his words—and in his eyes—caught her completely off guard. Her eyes fell to her tightly clutched fingers.

"You think I'm special?" she asked quietly.

"Very." He smiled and squeezed her hands, then pulled back. "But you were right about us needing rest. If we're going to return to face the palace tomorrow, we both need to be at our best."

A moment later, Keelan was wrapped in his blanket, eyes closed. He heard a small girl whisper into the night, "Thank you, Keelan."

"Good night, Your Majesty," he replied with a grin in his voice.

By some amazing feat of magic, the torches lit and grew brighter with the rising sun the next morning. Keelan had forgotten that trick of the cave from their last visit and stared in wonder as the flames danced gradually higher.

"I never knew magic could do so many amazing things." Jess said from her cot. "I mean, Gifts are everywhere, but to make something like this cave, or those torches, or *that wine*, it's wonderful."

"It's definitely something," he grunted in agreement as he rose and began rummaging through his pack. "May I fix Her Majesty's breakfast? We have dried meat and cheese or cheese and dried meat."

She smiled and sat up, her head tilted dramatically upward. "My royal pleasure commands cheese and meat, kind sir."

He lifted two wrapped bundles, turned, and offered an exaggerated bow. "As you wish, Your Most Bedheaded Majesty."

"Bedheaded?" Both her hands flew to her hair. "Is that even a word? And don't look at my hair! I need that mirror to just be a mirror before you see me again."

He laughed, a deep rumble that made warmth crawl across her chest. "No need to fret, Majesty. Your humble servant will busy himself with preparations for our journey while you, well, do *whatever it is you do* in that mirror."

She tossed her pillow into his back and strode to the mirror. "How dare you mock me! The Queen!"

When he muttered, "Not *my* queen" under his breath, another pillow slammed into his back, spilling a bit of the magical wine he nearly had to his lips.

"Hey!"

She giggled as she hurriedly brushed the tangles out of her hair. Dittler, who'd remained near the cave's entrance all night, clomped over to the table and nudged Keelan's shoulder.

"I know you're hungry, boy. We'll get you some breakfast when we're at the palace, ok?"

"You two seem to be getting along much better now," Jess said, packing her brush away and smoothing out her dress. "I swear he just sent me an image of you feeding him some kind of fruit. I'm pretty sure that image is his way of communicating affection."

"You mean *hunger*. We've reached a sort of agreement, but I wouldn't call it affection." He said, patting the massive stallion one last time before turning to face Jess. He froze and his eyes widened.

"What? I did the best I could on short notice."

He shook his head but struggled to speak. Nothing had changed since they'd spent the last day and evening talking, but it felt like the first time he'd really looked at her. She wore an elegant emerald gown with white lace around the neck and ends of her sleeves. The green of the fabric shimmered in the torchlight and brought out the auburn tint in her rich brown hair. He'd never noticed the red tint before. In fact, he'd never really noticed *her* before. She'd been a girl he rescued, not unlike many other victims of crimes he'd helped back home. But for some work of magic he couldn't explain, he saw a very different person standing before him now.

"No, no. You did fine. I mean . . . you look good." He stammered, then ran his hand over his stubbly chin. "I'm an idiot. Just ignore me."

Her smile brightened the magically lit cavern more than any sunrise he'd ever seen. She offered a mischievous wink and said, "We need to work on your complimenting skills, but that will do for a start." She sat and began spreading cheese across what was left of their crusty loaf. Dittler made a sound Keelan thought bordered on a laugh.

"Thanks a lot, *friend*," he said to the horse, patting him playfully one last time before turning to sit.

An hour later, their packs were fastened, skins were filled with wine, and the trio stood before the mirror.

"What's it like? Going through that thing?"

Jess shrugged. "It's like going through a door. One minute you're in this room, the next you're in another. I didn't feel anything unusual, maybe a little disorientation at returning in the Crypt. That part might be a little creepy."

She turned and reached up to pat Dittler. "Maybe I should lead him through. He'll probably have the hardest time walking through a portal."

"Okay, but he led Atikus and me into the cave, and he didn't have any trouble walking through faux solid stone," Keelan said. "For the record, *that* was really creepy."

She grinned, then turned to Dittler and gripped his reins. "OK, baby boy, you need to follow me." She sent a touch of her Gift into him, a light command to follow her, then stepped through the mirror, horse in tow.

Keelan watched them vanish, sucked in a nervous breath, and followed.

Keelan emerged through the mirror and bumped into Dittler's flanks with his first step.

"Oof! We're going to have to practice that some. I'll be picking horsehair out of my mouth all day now."

Dittler and Jess shared a chuckle at his expense.

"Woah, this place is . . ." He trailed off as his head swiveled, eyes taking in the Crypt's majestic creepiness. That's what he called it in his head, but he didn't dare insult Jess's royal line by voicing that opinion.

"What's in here?" he asked, running his hand across the Phoenix etched in the golden doors that towered to the right of the mirror. He yanked his hand back as magic's glow followed his touch.

Jess shrugged. "No idea. My dad didn't know how to get in there either. We guessed it's some ancient king or mage, but nobody knows for sure."

Keelan's investigator-brain kicked into overdrive as he examined the door and the metal plate on the wall beside it. "Well, someone knows what's inside."

Jess's head snapped around. "Why do you say that?"

He pointed to the plate, his face only a few hands from its gleaming surface. "Look here. There isn't any dust on this plate. That would've helped us see if it had been disturbed recently, but you can still see parts of a very faint handprint. Look here." He pointed and stepped back for Jess to look. "The oils on a person's hand almost always leave a trace on metal, especially when it's cold like down here."

Instinctively, Jess reached up and pressed her palm to the plate. The Phoenix flared and magical light swirled in its grooves, but the door didn't stir.

"Well, it was worth a try. I thought the monarch's touch might open it, but there's likely something else required, like a password or magical phrase that's been lost to time." She turned back to Keelan. "You ready to be scrutinized by the entire royal court? The moment we return, tongues will wag about who you are and what you've done to me."

"Done to you? What do you mean?"

"I left alone but returned with a Melucian. That'll be curious enough to start all sort of rumors, but when I actually listen to your advice and ask you to join in Council meetings, some will grow jealous or suspicious—or both."

"You want me to join in Council meetings?"

She nodded. "Some meetings, yes. They need to hear from you firsthand what you saw when you returned to Saltstone and what your people experienced. They'll want to question you, some quite aggressively."

The concern creasing her face touched something in him in a way he didn't understand. He studied her face a moment before responding. "I've spent the past few years being questioned and scrutinized by the toughest old man in Melucia, the Captain-Commander of the Guard. On occasion, I've stood before the Triad on the Eye. There's nothing quite like that experience. I'll be alright, especially with you there." He said the last words with a tiny curl of his lips that she didn't return, and her tone turned serious.

"Keelan, listen to me. I won't be able to help you. When we walk out of here, I will be the Queen. You'll have to address me as such, and I will need to treat you as a visiting . . . hmm . . . dignitary? Emissary? What are you?"

"Guest is fine. I don't need a fancy title."

"I see you've never been in the palace. *Titles* are everything. Without one, you'll be invisible, barely worth their notice." She thought a moment before her eyes lit up. "*Ambassador*. You're Melucia's new Ambassador to the Kingdom. That'll work nicely."

He barked a laugh and shook his head. "I'm pretty sure the Triad has to make that appointment on behalf of our country."

"It'll be fine. This can be temporary until they appoint a permanent one. I'm sure Atikus will smooth things out on his side of the mountains." She nodded proudly to herself, satisfied with her cleverness. "That's settled. Let's go home, Ambassador."

Without another word, she gripped Dittler's reins, strode to the end of the Crypt, and opened the doors leading up to the Temple.

Chapter Fifteen

Keelan

By the time Jess and Keelan entered the palace, the whole of Fontaine was abuzz with news of the Queen's return, though more rumors revolved around the handsome Melucian in the blue uniform who had escorted her through the city's streets.

"Your Majesty, it's good to see you returned to us safely." Mage Earnest bowed deeply as Jess entered the throne room with Keelan in tow. The Mage straightened and appraised her escort without a hint of expression. "And Lieutenant Rea, it's a pleasure to finally meet you. You're quite the famous investigator."

Keelan was surprised anyone this far from home knew who he was and couldn't think of anything to say in reply, so he simply offered a curt nod. He knew the man greeting them was a Mage by his robes, but his Gift remained quiet, indicating no deception or falseness in the man's welcome.

Jess looked between them, then remembered Keelan was a stranger in the palace. "Forgive me. Keelan, may I introduce Court Mage Dane Earnest. With High Chancellor Thorn missing, Mage Earnest is sitting in to provide the Council a magical perspective."

Before either of the men could speak, Jess began walking quickly through the chamber toward the door to the royal residence. "Come along, Keelan. I'll show you to your chamber. Mage, please assemble the Council in two hours. We have matters to discuss."

Without looking back, she barreled through the door and disappeared. Keelan shrugged at the bemused, bowing Mage and followed in the Queen's wake. When the door closed behind him, Jess was waiting.

"If you let these men start talking, you'll never get away. My father taught me that when I was eight. It might've been the most valuable lesson I ever learned." She smiled up at Keelan. "Now, let's put you down the hall. I can't have you near the family chambers, but I'd rather have you in our wing and out of arm's reach of nosy nobles."

A maid happened by at that moment and curtsied.

"Lydia, please show our guest to the Emerald Chamber. He will need a bath drawn. As you can see and likely smell, he's had quite a journey. He'll also need a few outfits appropriate for court, and his Guard uniform properly cleaned. See if the clothier can figure his size; it's somewhere between large and enormous." She chuckled at the maid's stricken expression.

Lydia colored but curtsied again. "Right away, Majesty."

"Please tell cook we'd like a quick lunch in thirty minutes. Something easy before Council." She turned conspiratorially toward Keelan. "Never meet with Council on a full stomach.

You won't be able to stay awake through the whole thing if you do."

Jess nodded, turned, and disappeared down the grand hallway, leaving Keelan staring speechless at her vanishing form.

The maid cleared her throat. "Sir, if you'll follow me, please."

When he turned, the middle-aged woman's eyes were roaming up and down the length of his body, her eyes alight with interest.

"Oh, right. Yes. Um ... thank you." he sputtered and blushed.

Keelan's head had just emerged from the steaming water when a tentative knock sounded at the door to his chamber.

"Sir, may I come in? I have your clothes." Lydia's muffled voice called through the thick wood.

"One moment, please." Keelan rose quickly from the bath, toweled off, then tied the towel around his waist. With his height and the size of the towel, he was barely covered halfway from his knees to his nether, but it would have to do.

"Come in."

The door popped open, and Lydia strode in, arms loaded with several sets of clothing. Her eyes took in Keelan's bare, muscled chest, then fell to the rest of his nearly naked form. She blushed and bustled quickly to the armoire to hang the outfits.

"There are three sets of coats, shirts, and leggings, each different colors and styles. Let me know if they don't fit right, and I'll have the tailor visit. I'll be back in a moment with shoes and small clothes," she said without turning from the armoire.

If his own blush hadn't reached his ears, he would've grinned at the woman's embarrassment. Instead, he simply said, "Thank you. Your name is Lydia, right?"

She turned, careful to keep her eyes locked on his. A surprised expression filled her eyes at his remembering her name. Keelan guessed that most barely noticed the staff, much less knew them by name. "Yes, sir. That's right."

"I'm Keelan. I don't know what they'll make up for people to call me, but please just call me Keelan." Without thinking, he stretched his hand out as if to shake hers. His towel unfurled and it was only his quick reflexes that prevented an awkward situation from becoming far more so.

Lydia's blush matched his as she curtsied quickly and scurried out of the room without a glance back. She was so flustered leaving that she forgot to close the door.

"I'll be back with your shoes!" she shouted from several steps down the hallway, a nervous giggle in her voice. Keelan rolled his eyes and shuffled to close the door, struggling to hold his towel in place lest the palace see all he had to offer. Before he made it halfway across the room, he heard Lydia gasp and giggle even louder.

Jess beat him to the open entrance, and her eyes widened nearly as broadly as her grin. However, unlike Lydia, her gaze was unflinching, taking in every inch of Keelan she could see.

"Should I worry about leaving my staff alone with you, Guardsman?" Her tone was playfully serious.

Keelan fumbled with his towel, trying desperately to tie it securely around his waist.

"I, um, just need a minute," he said, color fully flooded back to his ears again.

Amused at his discomfort, Jess took a step into the doorway. The panic on his face was her greatest reward. With both brows raised, she grinned wolfishly and said, "If I'd known Melucians were so well put together, I might've told Lydia to forgo the outfits and simply give you towels to wear."

She glanced below his waistline at the soaked, sagging towel, winked, then turned.

"Why don't you get dressed? Lydia will check back in a few minutes and show you the way to the family dining room." Jess paused a moment, then smirked. "I'll see about getting you some longer towels."

He couldn't help the grin that parted his lips as he leaned against the wooden frame. This visit to the palace was turning out very differently from anything he and Atikus had planned.

He could hear Jess laughing as she vanished down the hallway.

Jess was staring pensively at a painting of what Keelan assumed was a great-grandfather, perhaps several greats back, when he entered. Her head turned as a page announced his entrance, yet another tradition he'd have to get used to on this visit. The formality of the palace was almost as imposing as the idea of dining in the Queen's private hall. Keelan fidgeted with the stiff golden collar of the charcoal-gray doublet Lydia had provided. He looked up and caught Jess staring.

"What?" He looked down at his clothes and then back to her with a curious gaze. "Gray coat, black trousers. It's about as neutral between Melucian blue and Kingdom green as we could get. The stiff cut will take a little getting used to. Is it alright?"

"That's the style these days—the more uncomfortable, the more fashionable." She waved a hand and smiled absently, her voice turning subdued. "The clothes suit you well. Please, come and sit. We only have a short time before the Council assembles, and I want to prepare you."

Over the next half hour, Jess walked him through the key advisors who would be in attendance, the office each held, and what she'd tasked each with prior to leaving to meet him in the cave. Keelan appreciated her efficient, direct style as she walked him through her court. The conversation reminded him of his many briefings in Captain-Commander Albius's office. That man wouldn't know how to flower a word if his life depended on it.

"Keelan, you saved my life—*twice*. I will always be Jess to you in private, but once we stand before my subjects, you must remember to address me as Your Majesty. Anything more familiar will raise suspicion and fuel unwanted rumors, neither of which we can afford right now." She took a sip of her tea, then set the delicate cup on its gold-rimmed saucer. "This is an unscheduled meeting, so there will be no formal agenda. The Council will want to hear your account of the siege and aftermath and will probably question you on the condition of the Kingdom forces following their retreat. They will also want to know the attitude of Melucia's new leadership toward the Kingdom and our overtures of peace. To a man, those you will meet were opposed to the invasion, especially the Ministers of Trade and Foreign Affairs, but they are fiercely loyal to the Crown and will be cautious of you. I doubt they will report anything openly while you're in the room, so don't be disappointed if you learn nothing new.

"Oh, one more thing, under no circumstance should you reveal the nature of your Gift, the cave, or the mirror-portal. Even if I trusted the Ministers completely, I would hold those secrets between us."

Keelan leaned back, surprised by her caution with her own Council, many of whom she'd known for years. "I understand the need to protect the cave and the mirror, but my Gift? Anyone who's read the papers in Melucia knows what my magic can do. Why hide it here?"

"Another lesson my father drilled into me was to be wary of who you trust—and question those people carefully. I wish no one knew of your Gift. I would keep you at court just to advise me on deception and lies, which are more common in court than frills and lace. Such insight would be invaluable to a monarch."

"You almost sound afraid of your own people," he said, wishing immediately he'd kept his mouth shut.

She didn't flinch, just looked up with sadness in her eyes. "I'm seventeen, Keelan. If I rule for fifty years, a day will not pass when I do not question someone's honesty. I know it's part of the job—my father knew it, too—but I hate that part, the scheming and wheedling for position and power. Everyone thinks the monarch is the big fish, but sometimes it feels like being a minnow in a pond of sharks hungry to devour you and everything you care for."

Her hand shook slightly as she reached for her tea once more.

Keelan regarded her in silence. When they'd met, she'd been battered and bruised, frightened, and mourning more loss than anyone should experience in a lifetime. She'd drawn into herself, only opening up when she wanted to lash out at someone. He'd seen her as a petty, immature teenager whose life was spiraling out of control. He didn't like that girl very much, but he'd sworn to protect her.

Now, sitting at the royal table, dressed in elegant silks with her head held aloft and speaking with the dignity and grace of a queen, he saw a woman reborn. She spoke deliberately and with purpose, measuring each word as though the whole world depended on what she said. Perhaps it did—and he still struggled to think of her as the ruler of the largest nation in the world, but here she was.

This time she looked up and caught him staring.

"What?"

He smiled. "Her Majesty is *remarkable*."

The unexpected flush of heat that rushed into her chest caught her off guard, and she would've struggled to compose herself had the page not interrupted.

"Your Majesty, Council is assembled in the throne room." The page bowed and backed out.

Jess straightened in her chair and nodded to the page. In a blink, her confident, regal mask fell into place.

"Guardsman, follow me."

The first two hours of the Council meeting went exactly as Jess had predicted. Keelan was given the floor and was asked to walk them through everything he'd seen following the siege. The Ministers listened quietly for the first hour but peppered him with questions as the afternoon wore on. By the time he'd finished, the mood at the table was more collaborative than interrogative.

Jess sat back, relieved. The sharks hadn't eaten Keelan alive.

"Your Majesty." Mage Earnest rose as the conversation lulled. "The ceremony for the late King and Prince will take place in three days, and your coronation five days later. We have planned each event in great detail but need your approval to proceed."

Her face fell at the mention of her father and Justin. She'd barely had a proper moment to grieve for them, unless you count the time she'd spent with Keelan and Atikus running for their lives. The idea of laying them to rest weighed on her heart.

"Mage, you are new to me, but the others of this Council have been known to my family for many years. I trust each of you to honor my father and brother as you know I would wish it. I will leave the details to you." A moment of silence stretched before she spoke again. "Let's discuss the coronation tomorrow. One day will not spoil any plans you've made, and I believe we could all use an adjournment. I could certainly use some fresh air."

She rose and led Keelan back through the door to the royal chambers. When she reached the point where they normally went in opposite directions, she turned. "Come on. I want to show you something."

They followed a series of hallways, then paused before a plain, unmarked door that could've easily been a storage closet for the maids. Jess pushed the door open, and chill winter air rushed to greet them. Keelan wrinkled his nose at the sweet scent of some flower or herb he couldn't name. A few paces farther, they were surrounded by the beauty of the famed Royal Gardens.

Jess smiled at the wonder on his face. "This is one of my favorite places. I used to hide here when I didn't want to do my lessons or whatever chore my mother insisted was important. There's nowhere in the world I feel more at home."

He watched as she trailed her fingers across a prickly bush with pink flowers. As he looked around, he realized he didn't recognize most of the colorful and lush plants surrounding them. Then he remembered something.

"Jess, it's *winter*. How is this garden blooming?" The dumbfounded look on his face made her laugh.

"Do you not have gardeners with special Gifts back in Melucia?" Recognition dawned, and he felt silly for not thinking of magic. Of course, someone with the right Gift could make things grow, even in winter. He still couldn't account for the incredible variety of flowering plants. The maze of colors and smells was bewildering and breathtaking.

Jess had stopped to watch him as he took in her garden when he turned suddenly and nearly knocked her over. He gripped her shoulders with strong hand and caught her from falling.

"I'm sorry. I wasn't paying attention."

She looked up, their bodies only fingers apart, a thrill of tension racing between them. She tried to speak, but only whispered, "It's ok. I . . ."

Then he realized he was still holding her and stepped back quickly.

They stood frozen a moment longer, staring into each other's eyes until a call from the palace rang out, shattering the garden's peace.

"Jess! Are you out here? JESS!" a young boy's voice called.

Jess let out an annoyed sigh, then grinned at Keelan and led them back toward the palace.

"Time for you to meet the royal chatterbox," she said with a smirk.

Before they'd made it ten paces, Prince Kendall Vester wheeled around the corner and slammed into Jess, wrapping her in a tight hug.

"Hey, little man. What's this all about?" she mussed his hair, then pulled him away by his shoulders.

"Kenna wants me to study the inside of frogs. She said we have to kill one and cut it open. I can't kill a frog, Jess! You remember Felix? How could I cut up Felix? Or one of his cousins. Any frog could be his family. Jess, this is terrible!" The tow-headed boy was so upset he hadn't even seen Keelan looming a few paces away. When his eyes landed on the giant man, they widened, and his face lit with recognition.

"You're *the Melucian*! The famous Guardsman who's solved a hundred crimes and stopped a thousand more! I heard you can read minds! Is that true? Read my mind now. What am I thinking? Can you tell me stories about your investigations? What's the craziest thing you've seen? Are all criminals deranged? Are you ever scared? I bet you're never scared. Have you ever killed anyone? Who's the most famous person you've captured? Is it true you can't be stabbed or shot with an arrow?"

Keelan opened his mouth, then closed it.

The boy prattled on about the supernatural powers he believed the famous constable possessed, barely taking a breath between wild claims and even wilder questions. He was so enthralled with his new idol-made-flesh that his fear of the frog dissection vanished, and he completely forgot his sister, *the Queen*, standing behind him.

When Keelan finally looked up, desperate for help, he found Jess's face covered in tears of laughter. It must've been quite the sight, the hulking investigator paralyzed by the prepubescent Prince.

Jess finally decided to save her guest. "Kendall . . . Kendall! Take a breath." He startled and turned to his sister. "Why don't you go inside and find something you'd like to show Keelan. Just *one* thing, okay? We'll be there in a minute."

Excited, Kendall darted away without a word.

"Well, I think it's safe to say he likes you." She looked up laughed.

Keelan couldn't wipe the befuddled expression off his face, making Jess laugh even more. "How could you tell? I don't think he came up for air the whole time."

"And that's pretty much how family dinners go." She meant the comment to be light-hearted, but it suddenly reminded her of how different family dinners would be now.

"I'm sorry," he said, recognizing the change in her bearing. "Everyone expects you to keep moving forward as if nothing happened, but so much of your world has changed. I don't understand how you do it, how you hold it all together."

She examined his eyes and found deep empathy and . . . something.

"I honestly don't know, Keelan." She turned and gently cupped a fist-sized pink bloom. "Some days I think the seams will tear and I'll just fall apart. I'm just taking it one day at a time."

A moment passed, then she turned, looked up at him, and placed a hand on his arm. "But I know one thing."

"What's that?" he asked.

"I'm glad you're here."

Chapter Sixteen

Danai

Thorn sat in the high-backed throne on the dais of the ceremonial chamber of the Children's Temple. Braziers blazed throughout the chamber, their magical flame snapping soundlessly in the cavernous hall. The marble statue of Irina had returned from its perch above the Temple's retracted roof and now rested in its original position, where it towered over the most sacred room in the building.

A dozen men in silky brown robes and masks knelt before him, heads bowed.

Prophecies had fallen out of favor centuries ago when most religions of the day were discarded in favor of loyalty to the earthly Crown, yet there was always a pocket of people who yearned for communion within the unknowable, people who craved mystery and mysticism, though neither answered their longing or questions. Where men of learning saw veins in a leaf bearing water and nutrients, these believers witnessed the flow of their god's lifeforce, driving them with purpose and meaning. In these men and women, in their open minds yearning to receive unfathomable truths, Thorn knew his seed would bear fruit.

The Priests now crouched before his throne had spent the past month poring over ancient texts Danai had supposedly found deep in the mountains on the eastern border—at least that's what he'd told the blind, robed fools. At first, they had doubted the faded words on the yellowed parchment represented more than the writings—ravings, more likely—of a deranged mountain hermit, but Danai urged them to dig deeper, to discern every meaning, to find whether these documents held valuable truths or would be kindling for his hearth. He openly mocked them. He tested and pressed when one or more would assert divine meaning. He forced them to defend their positions, and in doing so, to *commit* to their arguments, transforming their views into tenants of a new faith.

The transformation in their work—and in their eyes as they watched him—was remarkable. Their belief was palpable.

Danai could barely contain himself.

Buried within that holy script—just deeply enough to require some effort to uncover it—a prophecy foretold of the return of the One. The Priest who discovered the foretelling thought it odd. The text predicted the return of a false prophet would precede the true One. How was it possible for prophecy to be so clear, so direct?

Everything fit perfectly with the timeline of events occurring over the past year. It was almost as though Danai had written them himself—which of course, he had. It had taken him weeks to mix ink in just the right proportions to saturate the page as was the custom centuries before. He'd struggled to perfect the spell that would age the parchment well enough to fool even the sharpest scholars, but he'd done it. Now all he needed were followers willing to buy what he was selling.

He looked no further than Irina's Children, a group he'd helped establish nearly ten centuries ago after his mistress's first demise. Their sole purpose had been to unravel the mysteries of the golden text on her monolith and carry out their instructions to bring about her return.

After Irina's failure, the Children were lost, adrift. They'd labored a thousand years to return Irina, and she'd failed them. It was a simple thing to turn that blind adoration for her toward a new scion of faith. He couldn't proclaim himself; rather, he needed them to discover his nature and, through their faith, call him to serve as their master. It had to be *their* discovery and *their* divine providence.

In the end, the morsels he'd buried in his holy texts worked better than he'd ever imagined. He had been prepared to send them on quests, force them into trials, induce them with intoxicants that would produce visions and prophecies of their own—all magically controlled, of course—but none of that had been necessary. These men and women were devoid of purpose and clung to the first life raft to pass by.

He couldn't have been more pleased.

"Rise, my Children," Danai said. "It is time the people learned the tenants of our faith. You, my most trusted disciples, will carry word of my return to every city, town, and village throughout the Kingdom. You will feed and clothe those in need, teach those who cannot read, and minister to the sick and dying as if they were your own kin.

"But remember this, the return of the One is a foretelling. None may know I am already here. You must build anticipation and hope in the hearts of our people. Only then will the path be laid for my return."

"By your command, Excellency," the robed figures intoned in unison.

The figure on the end dropped back to a knee and spoke. "Excellency, what if the people resist your words? What if they refuse the call?"

Danai smiled down at the sheep wearing a mask of an actual sheep. Such an odd custom.

"My Child, you will help them follow our path through benevolence and compassion. From this day forth, you are no longer Children, but *Priests* of the One. You are my voices on the wind, whispering my return to our people."

"And what if the people resist?"

"Do not trouble yourself with those who fail to believe. Others among our Order will follow to help those reluctant souls see our Light."

"And what of the new Queen, Excellency? How should we speak of her to the people?"

"Hear my words," he said in a formal tone, as if issuing an edict. "Today, there is the State, and the Faith. Soon, the State and Faith will be one. We welcome the Queen into her new role as the leader of mortal men and invite her to hear our words and subjugate herself to our spiritual guidance. Should she refuse to bow before our righteous call, the Order will do what is necessary."

"Yes, Excellency," Sheep looked up, and an evil, understanding grin twisted the eyes glaring up through the holes of his mask.

"Now go. Our brother, the Voice, attends to the new Queen in the capital. Hold to the faith, and know you bring peace and prosperity to our people."

The ten robed figures bowed deeply.

"By your command, Excellency."

When the last of the disciples vanished through the doors, a tall man strode out from behind one of the massive marble columns clutching a mask in his right hand, an odd mix of a bear with feathers in place of ears. Danai was striding down the steps of the dais when Bear approached and bowed.

"Excellency, I have chosen five. They await your command."

"Five more will do nicely." Danai steepled his fingers and grinned at the man. "You've done well, *Priest*. Bring them to me."

Chapter Seventeen

Jess

Weeks passed in rapid succession following their return to the palace. Jess was consumed with the work of rebuilding the military and reassuring her people of the Kingdom's commitment to peace with their neighbor. Rumors still ran throughout the country carrying wild tales of Melucian demons summoned to strike down their righteous king and prince, and no manner of royal decree would stop them. Thorn's carefully crafted stories of Melucian malevolence hadn't simply taken root through his town criers, it had grown and flowered through taverns and inns and born bountiful fruit in temples and shops throughout the land. Hatred of their eastern neighbor didn't wane with the conclusion of hostilities as Jess had hoped—it had actually grown with each tale of soldierly valor or Melucian deceit. She marveled at the willingness of the masses to believe such lies and innuendo.

Amid this atmosphere of misplaced loathing, Jess's popularity soared. Sympathy for the princess who'd lost everything, combined with nationalistic fervor fueled by beleaguered and wounded troops returning from their bitter defeat, made her the single point of hope across the land. Miraculously, the people had forgotten the petulant teenager who tried to abandon her duty and outrun her birthright only months earlier. All they saw now was a beautiful, fierce queen giving her all to knit together a war-torn Kingdom.

Conjecture surrounding Keelan's relationship with the new Queen buzzed among nobles and servants alike. Keelan was well liked, but the idea of the Queen consorting with a commoner, and a *Melucian*, left a bitter taste on some tongues, though they rarely stopped wagging long enough to savor it. He didn't accompany her as she rode among her people, even in the safety of the capital, but the new Queen was rarely without his company as she strode through the gardens or palace proper. The Council had even become accustomed to the towering Guardsman attending their sessions with his perpetually stern features and humorless advice. They'd come to appreciate his thoughtful, direct insights despite their gruff delivery.

Jess tried to ignore the idle chatter. She'd known her father had spun many plates as King, but she'd never truly appreciated the ever-present burden that rested on his shoulders. Being a sovereign wasn't like a commoner's vocation, where the workday ended, and family time began. She was *always* the Queen, *always* on stage, *always* on call. Even when she managed a moment of blessed quiet to herself, a maid or messenger often sought her out to deliver news or request her attention. It was overwhelming—and she loved every minute of it.

She'd delayed her coronation twice, insisting her Council focus on the needs of families who'd lost fathers or sons, and those of returning soldiers who'd witnessed calamity that would change them forever. She had argued her people were more important than a ceremony to assuage her ego. By the sixth week, sentiment among the Council had turned against further delay, arguing the need to cement her rule, and, more importantly, the need to give her people something to celebrate.

She was settling into the rhythm of the palace well but still felt lost in the art of understanding her people and their needs. Gazing into the eyes of a widow and her daughter, she could wrap them in her arms and provide for their needs, but it was impossible to look *her people* in their collective eyes and understand their needs, much less provide for them. There was no magic salve to soothe public fears or the irrational wave of emotions that wafted through crowds unseen and barely contained. Those unwieldy phantoms mystified her, though she knew she'd need to master them if she was to rule well.

There's so much to learn. Sometimes, I feel so small and lost. How did Father do it for so many years? she mused as she stared up at the golden blooms of starflowers in the garden. Their petals spanned twice the length of her palm and shimmered in the sunlight. Against the emerald of their thick, leafy vines and the white of the freshly fallen snow, the tear-shaped golden fronds were ever more brilliant. The subtle sound of footfalls turned her head. Keelan, sporting his sharply cut Guard uniform for the first time since their return, strode toward her.

"Want to run away before they can put that golden cuff on your head?" he teased.

"Golden cuff? You make it sound like a criminal sentence. Besides, cuffs go on your wrists. This is a holy relic they'll place gently on my head." She snorted. "You realize the Crown has been passed down from sovereign to sovereign for more than two thousand years? It even graced Irina's brow when she claimed to be Empress—before she decided to *acquire* a new crown this year."

He smiled and nodded. "Criminal sentence? That's probably a better description, although I might amend it to fit with the legal code and call it a *life sentence*."

She stood and shook her head. "Thanks for giving me confidence before I go to the executioner's block."

"Woah . . . I was just *imprisoning* you. Nobody said anything about *execution*—yet."

She slapped his meaty chest with her palm then laughed. "You're impossible. I think putting you back in that Guard uniform addled your brain." Her eyes roamed his striking figure.

He grinned and studied her for the first time since entering the garden, from her glittering pearlescent shoes, up the golden lace that trimmed her exquisite jade gown, to the three rows of dangling pearls across her bosom that disturbed the velvet field. By some magic, the sash that crossed her chest glittered at its edges and swirled as if a river of gold flowed within its cloth.

And then he looked up.

Her hair crowned her head in a majestic chignon, much like the one often worn by her mother. Its effect was breathtaking. Her long graceful neck met her curved jaw, and Keelan was transfixed. She looked every inch a queen.

He stepped back a half step and avoided her gaze.

"What?" She looked down and self-consciously adjusted her pearls.

"Jess, you look like a queen . . . I mean . . . regal . . ." he breathed more than spoke, then met her eyes. "I mean, you've always been beautiful, but now . . . um . . ." He ran a hand over his freshly trimmed hair.

She blushed but raised her chin and smirked. "Your way with words is . . . *um* . . . impressive."

"Just let me get this out, alright?" He looked down, then back into her eyes. "You are so much more than beautiful, so much more than just a queen. I mean . . . not *just* a queen . . . you are a queen, you know. Spirits!" He huffed in frustration at his mouth that wouldn't work. "You see people, really see them, and not just who they are, but who they can become. You see their goodness and their possibility. And when you set your mind to a problem, *nothing* will stand in your way until you've solved it. I've never met someone so strong and sharp and determined. I guess what I'm trying to say is . . . I admire the woman standing before me and respect the Queen she's becoming."

She'd had a sharp retort waiting on the edge of her tongue, but his words made her breath catch, and a wave of head flooded through her. She found herself struggling to focus, so she did the only thing she could think of in the moment. She winked and began walking up the path toward the palace. "Come along, good sir. The golden cuff awaits."

Keelan shook himself free of her spell and followed like a lost puppy.

As they marched from the hallway that spanned the royal family's private residences into the public passages of the palace, Keelan was struck by green-and-gold-liveried servants. No matter their task, each attendant they passed stepped aside and bowed or curtsied deeply. Every twenty paces, a pike-wielding soldier stood rigidly against the wall. As they passed, the soldiers smacked the butt of their spear against the marble floor in salute to their monarch.

Jess chuckled as they passed the first pair of guards and Keelan jumped at their salute. "Is the big, bad Guardsman scared?"

"I didn't expect . . . whatever that was. Um, Your Majesty."

She spit out a laugh as he *finally* remembered to address her properly in front of the servants and guards. None dared look directly at them, but she thought on maid's brow raised along with an amused corner of her mouth.

"Fear not, my brave Melucian friend. It is I, not you, who face the gallows on this day."

He knew her words for a jest but heard the clear undertone and felt the weight of the Crown pressing on her heart. *After all this poor woman's been through to save herself, she is expected to save a nation.* He shook his head at the irony but said nothing.

They entered the throne room through the side door closest to the dais, and Jess was surprised to see her Council assembled, each dressed in traditional black robes with golden chains of their office. The ceremonial black hats trimmed in glittering gold made her grin. As a young girl attending her first state function, she'd asked a little too loudly why the council wore fancy cooking pots on their heads. Her father, ever present in his role as monarch, lost all composure as her tiny voice filled the audience chamber and stricken looks spread throughout the assembled nobles. She'd never heard the King laugh so hard in the throne room.

And now they wore the cooking pots for her.

She stifled a laugh and strode forward. Each Minister bowed deeply, far more reverently than she'd experienced from the nation's leaders before. Each in turn grasped her outstretched hand and kissed it. She was so distracted by their display of respect that she'd missed the man standing by the massive chamber doors. With a start, she ignored the remaining counselors, lifted her billowing gown, and raced into the stunned man's arms.

"Uncle Ethan!" she squealed in a most un-queenly manner.

General Ethan Marks had finally returned to the capital after the Kingdom's crushing defeat in Melucia. The wintery journey covering hundreds of leagues and two mountain ranges had taken nearly eight weeks. She had given up on him making it back for her coronation, yet here he stood, shoulders draped with the ridiculous hunter's fur he'd insisted on wearing since his youth. But she didn't care about any of that now. With her father, mother, and brother gone, Ethan represented one of the last vestiges of family she had left.

"I would've moved the Spires to be here for you today." He held her shoulders at arm's length and smiled. "I'm so proud of you, and I know your father is proud of you, too."

At the invocation of her father, her smile drifted from jubilant to wistful, yet it did not fall. "When the ceremony is complete, let's talk. There is something I need to ask you."

He released her shoulders and bowed deeply. "My life is yours, Majesty."

A moment later, she turned to face the Council, each of whom had watched her exchange with Marks. "I suppose I can't run away again, can I?"

The stricken looks on the Ministers' faces caught her by surprise. She'd meant her question as lighthearted tease, but it appeared to strike too close to some unseen mark.

Ethan whispered from behind, "They fear exactly that, Majesty, after your most recent—adventure."

She straightened her back and made eye contact with each Minister. "You are my Privy Council, the heart of my government and my most cherished advisors. Each of you has pledged your life to my Kingdom and my reign. Today, I pledge mine in return. Hear the oath I speak from the dais, and know I willingly offer myself in service to this Kingdom until I draw my last breath."

The Ministers, moved by her passion, dropped to one knee and bowed their heads. Ethan quickly followed their lead. Jess was startled, but then noticed Keelan still standing quietly in the corner by the door they'd entered. He nodded once, and she thought his lips curled slightly upward. Dozens of butterflies fluttered within her chest as she turned and, alone, passed through the chamber's entrance toward her waiting carriage.

With festive, cheering crowds lining the thoroughfares leading across town to the Temple of the One, it took over an hour of the carriage's stately pace to reach her destination. Jess's gilded box-on-wheels was sandwiched between a hundred men on horseback. The streets had been cleared of the prior day's dusting of snow to ensure easy passage and clear viewing for the anticipated throng.

The park that sat across from the ancient Temple was overflowing with well-wishing commoners while nobles in their finery stood quietly behind rows of sharply uniformed palace guards, who lined the walk that led into the marbled building.

As Jess emerged from the carriage and took her first few steps, men and women on either side bowed and curtsied in a continuous wave that preceded her. She had to remind herself not to look but to hold her head erect and proceed in a slow, dignified manner befitting the incoming monarch. It had all been scripted and rehearsed, but nothing could have prepared her for her racing heart and moistened palms. *Thank the Spirits*

Mage Earnest insisted I carry a kerchief secreted into the sleeve of this gown!

She approached the gilded doors of the Temple and was greeted by the High Priest, a kindly old man with only unruly wisps of winter remaining of his once raven hair. He wore simple white robes trimmed in faded gold that spoke more of a humble servant than the exalted leader of the country's dominant faith. She had always liked him.

The High Priest bowed deeply, adjusted his ceremonial cap, and said in a familiar, fatherly tone, "Welcome, child. Forgive me while I set my cook pot to rights."

Upon later reflection, resisting a laugh at his unwitting use of her private childhood joke might've been the most challenging thing she did that day. Only a small snort escaped before they were moving again.

Two towering guards in the royal green and gold snapped to attention, smacked their pikes into the ground, then opened the Temple's doors in a painfully slow motion. The old vicar rose, took her proffered hand, and led her inside. She breathed in the light, sweet scent of incense as the tightly knit harmonies of the choir rose and fell in melodic beauty.

The Temple's interior consisted of a massive aisle lined on either side by five ascending rows of padded benches that faced each other. Jess always thought it looked like two opposing armies waiting for the bugle call. Her father insisted it was simply a house of worship, though her innocent analogy held more truth regarding schisms in the faith than any child could ever understand. Nobles stood before the benches in ascending rank, with those highest in the order of succession standing nearest the dais. Most of the men wore powdered wigs, another tradition Jess had never understood nor appreciated. The women in attendance each wore gowns, outlandish hats, and jewelry designed to over-match the other women in attendance. Weapons were never allowed in the presence of the monarch, but the women of the noble class needed no steel. The daggers of their eyes were deadly enough. More than one eye flared jealously at Jess's unmatched beauty, though as Queen, they *almost* forgave her for outshining them all.

The rows of soldiers who had lined the walkway outside filed behind Jess and the High Priest and formed ranks along the aisle. As the procession reached the far end where the throne had been installed for this day, Jess noticed foreign representatives standing before pews to her right. Tribal leaders from the islands of Vint wore brightly colored blouses with even brighter plumed wicker hats while clan leaders from Baz were covered in dark fur from head to toe. The continent's easternmost nations of Amnel, Pantrel, Orn, and Drea had each sent small delegations. The ancient isle of Rea Utu had sent only one representative, a bent old crone who leaned on a gnarled staff and smiled at Jess through gapped teeth. She couldn't turn to view the woman better with the procession moving forward but thought there was keen intelligence in her ancient gaze.

And then, last among the foreigners, stood the lone Melucian. At least three hands taller than any of the other representatives, Keelan was a beacon in the night compared to his counterparts. The palace staff had worked miracles with his worn navy uniform, and the golden Lieutenant's chevron on his shoulder glittered nearly as brightly as her own trim. He was careful not to turn his head, conscious of the hundreds of eyes anticipating his reaction to the young queen, but Jess thought she caught a slight widening of his eyes as she passed. Her own lips rebelled and curled a bit.

Standing before the final seat on the final row, the seat reserved for the Crown Prince or Princess, was a terrified-looking Kendall. Jess shattered the protocol of the tightly scripted ceremony and stopped to face her brother. His wide eyes rose to meet hers, and the loneliness she saw in his gaze pierced her heart. She cupped his cheek in her palm and whispered, "I love you, baby brother. I'm *so* proud of you."

Kendall gripped her hand with his own, kissed it, and eyed the impatient High Priest who was trying to get her attention. She squeezed his hand one last time then turned to resume the ceremony.

At last, she stopped before the first step of the dais, staring eye-level at the Throne of Spires: a gaudy, gilded monstrosity that had bruised the bums of kings and queens for generations. It was an impressive piece of furniture, but no monarch who graced its seat had ever admired its comfort. Her father certainly hadn't, insisting plush cushions be added while he sat for unending hours listening to petitioners and Council. Unfortunately, tradition dictated only the throne be present on this day, sans cushions. Jess groaned inwardly.

The back is padded, why not the seat? she thought aimlessly. The randomness of her thoughts kept the nerves at bay but nearly caused her to laugh aloud as the chamber reached a moment of utter stillness.

The moment passed with the rap of the High Priest's stave, a whip-crack that brought her back to the solemn present. She bent to rest her knees on the pleasantly *cushioned* faldstool a page placed before her, and she allowed another slight grin as she sank into the plush, feathered pillow. *So many silly rules.*

Minister of Justice Willa Parto, the first woman to serve on the Privy Council, appeared from behind the throne. Unlike the High Priest's simple garb, Minister Parto's ceremonial robes billowed with splendor. Seven hues of green representing the seven forested regions of the Kingdom ebbed and flowed throughout her gold-trimmed gown. Three ancient chains of office dangled from her neck, with a saucer-sized silver pendent depicting the scales of justice beneath a crown consuming the center of her chest. She wore a powdered wig with curled temples favored by the legal class beneath a tall black stove-pot hat of her own. Jess saw only the hat and grinned again before schooling herself back into the gravity of the moment.

Minister Parto looked down at Jess and offered her own comforting smile.

"Your Majesty," she bellowed for all to hear. "Your Royal Highness, Lords and Ladies, Honored Dignitaries, and guests, the King is dead. Now comes your Queen. Rise and face her."

As one, the assembled nobles and dignitaries turned from facing the opposite benches to the throne at the end of the aisle. Jess rose and, with a guiding hand from the High Priest, ascended the four steps, turned to face the crowd, and sat. In that moment, looking out at the nobles, *her* nobles, the entire world settled on her shoulders, and she felt its weight pressing against her chest. She placed a calming hand to her stomach and sat up straight as her mother had taught, breathing slowly and deeply. No one in the gallery seemed to notice, but the High Priest whispered as he bowed before her, "Breathe, Majesty. You're doing well."

Before she could think, the old man rose, walked around the throne, and raised the Crown from its velvet pillow with two hands, facing east. He bowed with the Crown raised above his head and cried out, "I present to you Queen Jessia, your undoubted Queen. All you who come this day to do your homage and service, are you willing to do the same?"

Those now facing the vicar cried aloud with one voice, "Aye, we will serve. HAIL, QUEEN JESSIA!"

The High Priest turned toward the south and repeated his call, then the west, and finally the north, each time receiving an even louder reply, as if each set of nobles sought to outdo the others in their public pledge to their new sovereign.

The High Priest bowed to Minister Parto and stepped back to allow her the fore. The Minister faced the Queen from the side, bowed, then spoke.

"Madam, is Your Majesty willing to take the Oath?" she asked.

"I am willing."

"Will you solemnly promise and swear to govern the Peoples of the Spires according to our laws and ancient customs?"

"I will."

"By the Spirits, and before these witnesses, I beg Your Majesty, rise and make your pledge."

Jess stood and drew one final breath of freedom, then spoke in a clear, unwavering voice.

"I, Jessia of House Vester, do pledge to lead, serve, and defend the Crown and its people from all threats within and without, without fear or favor, affection or ill will. I pledge to do right to all manner of people after the laws and usages of the Kingdom. To the people and the Spires, be it long or short, my whole life is yours. By the Spirits, this is my pledge."

Minister Parto bowed low again and stepped back into her spot behind the throne. The High Priest stepped forward, raised the Crown, and bowed again.

"The Crown of the Spires! Come all and look upon its majestic favor. Spirits, we beg your blessings on this Crown and the brow beneath it. Sanctify this symbol and our servant, Jessia, upon whose head we place this sacred relic, that she may be filled with royal majesty, abundant grace, and princely virtue."

He moved to stand facing Jess, bowed once more, then carefully placed the Crown on her head. As soon as his hands lifted, brilliant Light swelled from both the crown and the Seal of Office, the ring Jess now wore as sovereign. The High Priest stepped back to the lowest step and fell to one knee as the magic swirled around Jess, bathing her in an otherworldly glow. The crowd's collective intake of breath echoed through the chamber just before the magic flared one final time and exploded outward in a sea of sparkling shards above the heads of the awestruck nobility.

The High Priest dared not rise from his prostration, but bellowed, "HAIL, QUEEN JESSIA."

The crowd rushed to mirror the priest's pose, falling to their knees with heads bowed, and echoed again and again, "HAIL, QUEEN JESSIA!"

Jess had known the magical light show was coming but was still stunned by its intensity. For the first time since entering the Temple, she allowed her eyes to roam about the vaunted chamber. Kendall beamed up at her, calling out in his squeaky pre-teen voice. She gazed across the visiting dignitaries and nobles, and her heart both raced and swelled with pride. Her father had raised her for this moment, for the day she would succeed him. She'd always known he would miss her coronation, as it was rare to succeed a living king, but she still smarted at his absence in her moment of glory. The vacant seats beside Kendall underscored other absences she felt deeply.

She found Keelan again, kneeling along with the other dignitaries. Even on his knees, he towered over those around him, and she caught him stealing a glance. He winked before returning his head to the correct position.

He winked at me! Right after I received the Crown!

She tried to ignore the beginning of a mental debate over whether to be amused or annoyed with the Guardsman. What remained of her Privy Council was to her right behind the Royal Pew. A sea of nobles spread beyond. All were bowed low, only plumed bonnets and backs visible from her vantage on the dais.

And then her eye was captured by a lone figure standing in the back of the Temple nave, his brown robes catching the light just enough to make her notice.

Why isn't he kneeling like everyone else? And those robes . . .

Something familiar drew her to the man. She knew but couldn't place it. Was it his posture, the set of his jaw, his shoulder-length hair? Something was *so* familiar.

And then she *knew*—and her breath caught.

Chapter Eighteen

Jess

Jess blinked a few times and looked back at the end of the Temple as the assembled mass rose. The back wall now stood empty, though she was sure a man had been there only a moment earlier. She allowed herself to breathe again.

It wasn't him. You're just overwhelmed by the day. Relax.

An hour later, her gilded carriage pulled up to the front entrance of the palace. Dozens of guards lined the circular driveway. On either side of the grand entrance, rows of neatly dressed servants stood to greet their new sovereign. They all knew Jess. Many had helped raise her, but today she emerged a new woman, a Queen. They beamed with pride and dared to look her in the eye as she passed. Some wept with joy at seeing the once petulant youth grown into a stunning, strong young woman. When she came to the first row, she stunned them all by slowly greeting each person by name and thanking them for their service to the Crown. This alone took another thirty minutes but endeared her to her staff in ways she didn't immediately realize. She couldn't explain why she'd done it; it just *felt* right in the moment.

She made her way into the throne room. Miraculously, her staff had moved her throne from the Temple to its usual resting place while she returned. She smiled to herself and thought to reward those responsible for a job well done. Before she sat, she turned to a young page who stood nervously behind the throne and asked for a cushion. When he gaped but didn't move, she smirked and whispered conspiratorially, "If I have to sit here and listen to Lords drone on for the next two hours on this hard chair, my bum will fall asleep. Your Queen *needs* your help. Get me that cushion."

The page, now more shocked by her familiarity than her request, couldn't contain his smile and bowed. "At once, Majesty."

Once seated, Jess nodded to the Royal Master, who then nodded to the guards standing by each of the gilded doors. As the doors opened, Jess's eyes widened at the endless line of Dukes and Barons and every other flavor of nobility queued and waiting. Each came to offer the Oath of Fealty to their new Queen.

The Warden of the East, the portly Duke Kinsley Parna who'd become a tad too familiar with Jess's shrimp fork in a previous encounter, waddled before the throne. "Majesty," he bowed as low as his stomach would allow and whispered, as though they had some private, personal relationship she was unaware of. "This one is pleased to see you safe and enthroned."

She raised a brow but said nothing.

For once, Parna took the hint and lowered himself awkwardly to one knee, removing his sword from its scabbard and raising it in both hands above his head toward her. "I promise to be faithful to the Queen of the Spires, never to cause her harm, and will observe my homage to her completely, against all persons, in good faith and without deceit. Long live the Queen."

She waited a bit longer than ceremony dictated, enjoying seeing Lord Piggy submit, then answered in a clear tone. "The Crown accepts, and pledges our justice and protection, now and for all time."

The next few hours passed exactly as Jess had expected. Lords, Ladies, and visiting dignitaries flowed in to pledge, in many cases bearing gifts of gold, silver, perfumes, or silks. One of the islanders presented her with an odd bird with colorful feathers in a gilded cage. She nearly lost her stately composure when the creature looked her in the eye and said, "Hail, Queen Jessia!" Nobles in line burst into delighted applause while the islander simply smiled and bowed.

By late afternoon, the Royal Presence was fading quickly. Jess's neck and back were sore from sitting straight under the weight of the Imperial Crown, and the rush of being coronated had worn off, leaving her physically and mentally exhausted. When the end of the line finally appeared, she made another mental note to award her young page a kingdom of his own for bringing her a cushion, though her bum had *still* fallen asleep.

Keelan approached the throne, last of the dignitaries, the traditional position of highest honor afforded to the Kingdom's largest neighbor and trading partner. Jess hadn't noticed Keelan until he stood before her, and her features brightened immediately. She had to school herself to stop a broad smile from escaping. Keelan wore the annoying smirk of a man who knew what she was thinking. Again, she schooled herself, this time to stop from throwing the royal cushion at her honored guest.

Keelan bowed and offered his respects on behalf of the Melucian people. He gave the scripted speech Atikus had prepared, proclaiming the Melucian Empire's deepest desire to again walk hand in hand with their Kingdom neighbors. The turn of phrase made one of Jess's brows rise and a smirk of her own form. She wiped it away quickly and offered the Crown's sincerest hopes for the same.

"Guardsman, Rea," she said once the formalities had been completed. "Please remain a moment while the throne room is cleared. There are matters of relations between our peoples I'd like to discuss."

Keelan wasn't officially the Melucian ambassador and thought it an odd request, but he nodded and stepped aside to wait for the guards to clear lingering nobles from the hall. When the doors finally slammed shut, Jess reached up, removed the Crown, and placed it on the smaller throne beside her. She let out a deep sigh and stretched her neck.

"That thing is *so* heavy."

Keelan stepped forward and chuckled. "I'm sure you'll get used to it, Majesty."

"Oh, don't you start bending and scraping, at least not while we're in private. I need somebody other than my little brother I can talk to."

"Whatever you command, Majesty. I'm at your service." He smirked again.

This time she threw the pillow and nailed him in the chest.

"Royal abuse! The Crown is assaulting its guests! Help!" he cried to one of the guards standing rigidly against the wall.

She snorted and stepped down, yanked the pillow out of his hands, and tossed it haphazardly back onto her throne.

"Enough, Guardsman. Please escort me back to my chamber. I need to change and freshen up before the banquet."

"I'd be happy to." He smiled and offered his arm, which she took a little more quickly than he expected. The way she squeezed his bicep was also a bit of a surprise, but one he relished.

They'd made it nearly to Jess's room when a horrified maid scurried from somewhere down the hall and blocked their path.

"Majesty, please come with me. We've moved your items into the royal chamber."

Keelan started to tease her about moving up in the world but noticed a somber shift in her demeanor. It was subtle, and the maid probably hadn't seen it, but he was a keen observer—and he'd spent a fair amount of time studying her expressions lately.

"What is it?" He leaned toward her and whispered.

"The royal chamber is . . . it's *my parents'* chamber," was all she could say before her voice broke.

Now it was his turn to offer her arm a gentle squeeze.

The maid stopped at the door and turned. Keelan caught the hint and stepped back, untangling himself from her grip.

"Thank you for your time, Your Majesty. I'll see you at tonight's banquet," he said with a deep bow before disappearing down the hallway.

Jess spared a glance over her shoulder before allowing the maid to shuffle her into the suite, where an army of dressing ladies assaulted her the moment she entered. She never had a moment to catch her breath or take in the regal bedroom she now inhabited. Oddly, she was thankful for the distraction of her clucking hens.

Keelan tugged at the tight, scratchy collar of his coat as the page announced his entry into the banquet hall. Most of the guests were already seated and the chatter of hundreds echoed throughout the chamber. Oddly, the chatter turned to hushed tones at many tables as Keelan passed on his way to his seat. His collar might have itched, but scrutiny of so many nobles made his skin crawl.

Keelan was seated with several nobles and ambassadors from the smaller countries. Jess had been quite thoughtful in seating him with those whose interests most aligned with his home country. The table's conversation began with pleasantries surrounding the coronation and banquet, but quickly turned to the Siege of Saltstone. Each of Melucia's neighbors had heard varying accounts of the battle and the months that followed, and their representatives were eager to glean any new information they could from one of the capital's top lawmen. After Jess left the hall, the men and women huddled closer around Keelan, and the conversation turned to hushed whispers as they asked more direct, inflammatory questions regarding their hosts in the Kingdom.

At one point, the ambassadors from Pantrel and Amnel finally decided the wine had gone to their heads. As they rose to retire for the evening, a man in elegant brown robes wandered to stand behind the empty chairs at the table. All heads turned and eyed him curiously.

"Mind if I join you?"

Keelan thought he sensed the others tense as the young man pulled a chair back and sat without waiting for their reply.

"You're dressed like a holy man. We don't see many of your lot around these days. What are you doing here on the Queen's Day of Celebration?" the ambassador from Orn asked with a bit of a sneer.

The man's pleasant smile never faltered. "I am a Priest of the One, come to inform Her Majesty of my appointment as representative of the Order to the Crown."

"The Order? I thought you said you were a Priest of the Temple," a man to Keelan's left asked.

"Forgive me. The Order is what we call the movement behind the Temple's teachings. Think of it as the new name given to the Children."

Keelan sensed no falsehood in the man, though his non-magical intuition rang with something uneasy he couldn't identify. The robes were consistent with what he remembered of the Children, though the man wore no mask and did nothing else to hide his identity or intentions.

"Please forgive our rudeness, especially at a royal banquet, but the Children's recent history gives many of us pause when we see brown robes." He paused a moment to let others at the table realize who really sat among them. "Where is your mask?"

The Priest cocked his head at Keelan's question. "Ah, you know of our Order. The day comes when the One will walk among us, spreading his word and good deeds to the people. We have shed our masks so everyone may know us for our good intent. Our recent . . . history . . . no longer defines us."

When he was greeted by questioning glares, the Priest continued. "We seek to care for the sick and poor, teach children their letters, feed the hungry. Through these humble acts, we hope to build bridges of Light in the hearts of the people we touch. Ours is a message mercy and compassion with the goal of a brighter future for the Kingdom and our people."

The Ambassador from Amnel snorted. "That sounds like wine and a song, very different from the Children's aims only a few months ago. For centuries, your cult fed on the people's ignorance and laid groundwork to return *evil* to this land. Why should you now be greeted as benevolent holy men instead of the murderers you are? The Queen's justice couldn't be too harsh for your lot, from what I've seen."

"Gentlemen, you must let forgiveness enter your heart."

"Forgiveness?" Keelan spat a laugh at the obvious whitewashing of the man's cult.

When the Priest continued to stare at Keelan, he decided to take a different approach. "Perhaps introductions would be in order."

The Priest stood and bowed to the table, again unfazed by Keelan's inference. "I am a humble servant of the Temple of the One and will serve as the One's Voice and ambassador here in the capital."

Keelan offered the ambassador a shallow nod and watched as the others at the table made their introductions to the Priest. None appeared to have warmed to the man or his tale of his Order's new direction.

"Holiness? Father? Ambassador? I'm not sure how to address you. I am Guardsman Lieutenant Keelan Rea of Melucia."

"Lieutenant, please, there is no need for titles or honorifics. Please call me Danym."

Chapter Nineteen

Keelan

Keelan could hardly believe what he was hearing. He was a seasoned investigator, used to strange situations and even stranger characters, but the Priest smiling across the table had stunned him into silence.

"Lieutenant, are you alright?" the Ornish ambassador asked, gripping Keelan's forearm.

"Fine . . . I'm fine." Keelan stammered. He nodded in thanks and returned his gaze to the Priest. It had been months since Jess had cowered in their fleeing boat and described her secret boyfriend's betrayal. He strained, trying to remember if she'd described what he had looked like. The Priest before him was tall, which matched his recollection, but streaks of silver peered through the sandy blond of his hair, which was now tied tightly behind his neck with a black ribbon. Fine wrinkles webbed the tender skin around his eyes. Surely, the gray marked him a man in his thirties, more than a decade older than the High Sheriff's son. The bemused smile on the man's face might've triggered Keelan's alarms if the Priest hadn't worn that annoying smile the entire time he'd sat at their table.

Keelan dismissed the idea this was the same Danym and pressed forward.

"What brings a Priest of the One to the capital? I don't recall seeing you in the receiving line earlier today when the nobles pledged their loyalty to the Crown."

"My loyalty is to the Faith," Danym said simply.

"Surely, the Faith serves Her Majesty?" the Ornish ambassador asked.

Danym inclined his head to the man. "We recognize the Queen's place as a leader in *worldly matters*, but the Faith answers to a master far above any ruler. If you would come to know the One . . ."

"I thank you for the invitation but will pass. We Ornish have our own ideas of divinity, and they do not include murderous cults."

The balding representative stood, bowed to the others, and strode from the table, shaking his head and muttering to himself. On cue, the other ambassadors excused themselves and scurried after their Ornish counterpart. As Keelan scrutinized the Priest, he realized the massive chamber was now quiet, the royal guests having finally departed. Servants, still in their finest royal livery, cleared plates and platters while others scrubbed tables and floors, returning the hall to its usual pristine state.

Keelan rose slowly. "I believe it's time I also took my leave. Good evening, Priest Danym."

One of the Queen's maids bumped into Keelan as he made his way back to his chamber. He was so lost in thought that he barely noticed her walking toward him—until she was pressed against his chest.

Did she do that on purpose? he thought absently as he watched her disappear down the hall, giggling.

He shook his head and continued down the passage, only to encounter another maid. He decided Jess might want to know about the new Priest before talk spread throughout the palace.

"Excuse me," he said, causing the maid to freeze, bow, and stare at her shoes. "I need to speak the Queen. Would you let her know, please?"

The maid bobbed a curtsy but didn't make eye contact. "I'm sorry, Ambassador, Her Majesty has retired for the evening."

Keelan nodded and smiled. "Fine. It can wait until morning. I'm sure you're right and she needs her sleep."

The maid vanished down the hallway, and Keelan found his way to his own chamber, disrobed, and threw himself onto the bed. He hadn't realized how tired he was from the day's celebrations. Comforting darkness closed in, and thoughts of the odd Priest fled his mind.

Part IV

Chapter Twenty

Laurie

The sun was just peeking over the horizon when Laurie groaned, stretched her arms as far as they would reach, and struggled from under her thick woolen blankets. She shivered at the cold and frowned at the darkened coals in her bedchamber's hearth. She blew out a sigh, stretched one last time as she threw on her robe, and set about her morning routine.

First, she had to do something with the bushy tangle of sandy hair. It had somehow found ways to tie itself into knots that would make a sailor proud. The first few pulls of her brush tugged painfully at her scalp, and then—no, the successive pulls hurt, too. Her hair was a mess. Had she wrestled a bear in her sleep?

Once satisfied she was presentable for her father's guests, she rinsed her face in the frigid water of her washbasin and donned her uniform, a dove gray dress covered by a pale pink smock embroidered with a sparkly silver crown. She looked down as the smock settled and traced a finger across the stylized symbol of the Kingdom's royal household.

Years earlier, King Alfred and Queen Isabel had visited the town and stayed at their inn. The weeklong stay had transformed Oliver's sleepy but reputable inn into a palace away from home for the couple. At least that's what Laurie's father told anyone who would listen. To hear him tell it, he'd laid marble in every room, polished cherry wood (though the walls were oak) to a mirror-sheen, and sold his soul for a chef straight from the Isle of Vint.

In truth, they'd dusted and cleaned as best a family of common innkeepers could, but the boarding house was the same as before the royals had arrived, if a tad less dusty. The King's household even provided the chef and foodstuffs for their visit. All Hershel, Laurie's father, had to do was help haul it into his storeroom and kitchen. The royal seneschal had explained that only royal servants could attend their Majesties, which included serving food or wine, cleaning their chambers, or anything else that involved direct interaction with the vaunted rulers. Hershel and his household would be introduced to the royals upon their arrival, but there would be no further interaction once the King and Queen were settled into their chambers.

The day after the King and Queen had departed, Laurie had woken to a series of loud bangs outside the door of the inn—*on* the door of the inn, actually. Hershel had commissioned another artisan to create a new masthead for the business, one bearing the name *The Crown's Glory* in sparkling silver, complete with a stylized replica of the royal household's symbol. He'd changed it enough to comply with laws forbidding use of official royal symbols but kept enough to make it clear to all that the royal couple had blessed his establishment with their presence. *The Glory*, as the townsfolk called it, was immediately the center of culture and entertainment. Traveling minstrels and players were present most nights, and the ale was never watered as it was in the lesser establishments down by the docks.

Most respectable nineteen-year-old women in Oliver, the quaint town halfway down the continent's coast from Fontaine, were still snuggled warmly in their beds, likely enjoying the warmth of the husband snoring next to them. It was unseemly for them to work, even more so at an hour when the most common of commoners were expected to rise.

But not Laurie.

She was not a common commoner.

She loved to work. She loved interacting with the minstrels and players, the cooks and washerwomen, the farriers and stable hands. They gave the inn life, and she loved them all, but mostly she loved their guests. Whether they were weary workmen, curriers traveling to some faraway destination, or wealthy nobles spending their time and fortune on leisure, she loved living through their tales, learning what made them laugh, and living vicariously through their journeys she longed to enjoy for herself.

Oddly, the other women of the town held no grudge for her passion, certainly not the way they flung petty jealousies toward each other. Maybe they didn't see her as a threat to their vaunted position. Maybe they accepted the royal blessing on her household. More likely, they were infected by her self-deprecating wit and ever-present smile.

When Laurie entered a room, even when laden with a tray of food and drink for a raucous table, heads turned. Her bright brown eyes sparkled when she smiled, making most men—and even a few women—mirror her warmth. Her laugh sounded like the rumbled gurgling of some ancient creature who'd risen from the depths of the sea to find what lay near the surface.

It was infectious. It was heartfelt. It was Laurie in sonorous beauty.

She splashed her face one last time with the wintry water and wiped her eyes. *Some mornings just come too early,* she thought. Then she padded downstairs to begin chopping vegetables and cracking eggs for the guests' morning meal.

The common room was dark and chilly, though a small fire still danced in the hearth thanks to the night clerk. As she wove her way through the tables toward the kitchen door, Laurie felt a tingle, that unsettling feeling that often meant she was being watched. She froze and scanned the room. The stage was clear. The bar, with its hefty marble top, stood silent. The tables near the hearth were empty.

Maybe her mind was playing tricks and she still wasn't awake. She shrugged off the feeling and resumed her trek but was arrested by a single cough from the darkened corner of the room directly behind her. The one corner, she now realized, she hadn't checked.

"Hello? Is someone there? Breakfast isn't for another two hours."

A second later, a man stepped out of the darkness. Raven hair fell to his shoulders with slight curls at the tips; shadowed eyes bore into her. The chiseled features of his face marked him handsome, and the tautness of the fabric across his chest hinted at muscled strength beneath his shimmering robe. She wanted to smile, to offer welcome and respite, but something in the man's bearing made her take an involuntary step backward.

"Child, don't be afraid. I am a Priest of the One, here to offer help and comfort to those most in need. I arrived late in the evening, and there were no rooms. Your clerk allowed me the warmth of your common room. I'll take my leave now, but only if you'll accept my thanks for your kindness." As startled as she had been by his appearance, she couldn't help feeling drawn to the man. He had an easy smile and a confidence that made her *want* to sit and chat—and stare. Now that he stood in the dim light of the room, she could see his deep brown eyes matched hers and weren't the pits of swirling black her overactive imagination had conjured when he'd first appeared.

The Priest bowed as if he were a commoner attending his mistress or a royal.

He rose and grinned at her unease, winked once, then turned to exit. As he gripped the door's handle, he turned and smiled. "You really are beautiful. Your husband is a most fortunate man."

Before she could protest that she wasn't married, the strange, strikingly handsome man disappeared, leaving a dumbstruck Laurie and her furrowed brow staring from the center of the empty room.

Hours had passed since her encounter with the strange Priest. Laurie had cracked and whipped hundreds of eggs, diced dozens of potatoes, and sliced more tomatoes than she could count. Her smock remained spotless somehow, though she still absently brushed and picked at is as if crumbs clung to its surface.

Why did I want to tell him I wasn't married? What a stupid thought. He's a Priest of some weird new religion—and a creepy one at that. What difference does it make if he's handsome, or if he has eyes that made my legs wobble, or a smile—

"Hon, you alright? What's got into you today?" her mother asked as she tossed a fresh towel in her daughter's direction. "Help me wipe down the kitchen and get some rest. We've a full house for dinner tonight. Your da thinks the Duke might show up, though I can't see why. It's the normal troupe on stage playin' the same old tunes.'

Laurie woke from her daydream and tossed a devilish grin back at her mother. "You love those players, and I seem to recall you staring at a certain lead man last time they were here. You know, the blond with the tight pants that show off his—"

"Laurie!" Ma swatted her with the towel still clutched in her meaty palm. "I'm a respectable, *married* woman of society. I would never—"

Laurie barked a laugh. "Never? Oh Ma, you *did*, and expect you'll do so again—tonight!"

Ma swatted again, but Laurie leapt out of the way, leaving nothing but air and another round of highly amused giggles in her wake. The older woman couldn't suppress her own chuckle and began whistling as they cleaned.

"See. You only whistle—"

"Not another word if you want to see another name day!"

Laurie's laughter rose again.

The rest of the day passed with the practiced routine of the simple life of commoners running a business in a small village. Cook for the guests, clean, cook again, shop, clean the stalls, cook, clean the rooms, cook, do the laundry, cook again. It seemed someone was always appearing in the common room asking for a bite to eat, despite the clearly posted times for meals, but Ma wouldn't hear of a guest being turned away. *The King wouldn't have it*, she always said, as if she and the royal family remained in touch after their decades old visit. Most guests humored her, thankful she accommodated their stomach's every desire.

As they prepared dinner, Laurie could hear the swell of conversation and laughter in the common room as guests, both guests of the inn and families from town, streamed in to claim their tables. It seemed the usual players were even more beloved than she'd thought. *Maybe Ma wasn't the only one to notice Blondie with the Bootie.*

She chuckled as she chopped.

She'd lost herself in both her thoughts when a strange feeling crept across her arms. It took her a moment to realize the raucous banter from a hundred voices had stilled and only one voice rang out, loud and clear. She recognized that voice.

The Priest? she realized. *That has to be him. Why is he here?*

For reasons she didn't understand, her heart raced. She hadn't even noticed the sound of chopping had ceased as she strained to hear the man's words.

". . . from the war. We believe every life is sacred and come to serve those in need with love and peace in our hearts. Each of us in this room is blessed by the Spirits with wealth and comfort, else we would not *be* in this room. I ask for your help, for the people of this beautiful town, for the—"

Whatever he said next was drowned out by the sound of Ma's cleaver slamming through the evening's meat.

"Gonna stare at that door all night or help me get these meals out?" Drill Sergeant Ma barked with a tinge of playfulness—but only a tinge.

"Sorry. It's just—"

"Chop now. Talk later."

"Yes, ma'am," Laurie resumed her work, but reserved part of her effort for more straining, though the stranger's clear tone had vanished in favor of the guests' raucous chorus once more.

The last guest finally retired to their room, allowing Laurie to remove tankards and wipe down their table. The evening had been a success, with the players and Mr. Pretty Bum stealing the stage—and more than a few hearts. Ma chattered away, but Laurie heard none of it. She couldn't stop thinking about the Priest. She could see his eyes, he rounded lips, the curve of his chest beneath that clinging, silky robe.

Stop that. she chided, wiping her now sweaty brow with her shirtsleeve. *He's a Priest, for Spirit's sake, and probably lives by some code of celibacy or reclusiveness or self-loathing. Who knows? Just stop thinking about him.*

She looked down and realized she'd been cleaning the same spot for several minutes, then laughed at her own silliness.

"Do you always laugh when you clean?"

She nearly jumped out of her smock.

"Forgive me," the amused Priest said from the doorway. "I didn't mean to startle you."

"Well, you did!" she said sharply, immediately regretting her tone. "Can I help you?"

He smiled and gave her another deep bow.

What is it with him and his bowing?

"I didn't see you earlier. Were you able to hear my words?"

She eyed him with a mix of suspicion and curiosity, unable to resist his eyes. "I heard a little from the kitchen. It's noisy back there, so I didn't get all of it."

"The players were kind enough to allow me their stage before the show. I used it to introduce myself to the town, and to ask for their support in caring for those affected by the war. Their needs are great, and the Crown can only do so much."

Laurie stiffened. "I'm sure the Queen is doing all she can. She's a good woman and only took the throne a short time ago."

"Yes, I'm sure you're right."

"I assume you didn't come here to talk about the royal family. Is there something I can do for you, Father? What do I even call you?"

"Seth, please just call me Seth. I may wear the frock, but I'm just a man trying to do his best in a dark world."

She couldn't decide if her suspicion rose or fell at that.

"Alright, Seth, what can I do for you? We're trying to wrap up for the night."

He smiled and bowed his head—*again*. "I came to see you."

A flush of heat ran through her arms and into her chest.

"Me?"

He smiled innocently. She shivered.

"Yes, you. I understand you're *not* married, as I had thought. It seems that no one in this town has managed to win your hand."

Another flush. She dabbed her cheeks with her towel, then tossed it on the table when she realized she'd done that in front of this man.

"I . . . well, no, I'm not married. What's that to a Priest?" she said with as much strength as her weak knees allowed.

He took a step forward, and her heart raced faster.

"It has nothing to do with the Priest, but much to do with the nervous man standing humbly before you."

She coughed a laugh. "Nervous? You? That's not a word I've thought to describe you all day."

"You thought about me all day?"

Her eyes widened at the net she now saw wrapped neatly about her.

"Well, no. I mean yes, I may have. Oh, bother, what do you want with me?"

"I would very much like to have a glass of wine with you and to learn more about the most enchanting woman I've seen in all my travels. Would that be alright?"

"Well, uh, I have to finish—"

"Two wines, coming right up." Ma's voice cut through the tension in the room. "She needs a drink 'bout now, I can tell."

Seth failed to suppress a grin as Ma chortled from behind the bar. Neither of them had heard the portly woman enter, nor did they realize she'd heard the whole conversation.

"Ma!"

"Hush. I'll finish up. We wouldn't want a man of the cloth—whatever cloth that is—to stand around waitin', would we?"

Laurie rolled her eyes. "I suppose I could have *one* glass."

The thunk of a newly opened bottle slamming onto the wooden table sounded before she finished speaking. Two glasses appeared a second later.

"Take yer time. She's off t'morrow, whether or not she tells ya that."

And with a flourish, Ma vanished back into the kitchen, leaving Laurie staring at the bottle and Seth shifting nervously from one foot to the other.

Later that night, as she lay in bed staring out the tiny window in her room above the kitchen, Laurie thought the stars shone a bit brighter than they had all winter. She leaned forward and squinted, then shook her head at the girl who'd apparently had a little too much wine.

Still, thinking back to the hour with Seth, she couldn't help but smile. He wasn't anything like she'd expected. When they'd first met, he was cloaked in darkness and shadow, giving her the impression his life would likewise be veiled in secrets, but that hadn't been the case. A few sips of courage had him recounting a childhood in the countryside with his brother and two younger sisters. He laughed freely as he recounted antics that must've driven his mother mad.

As they'd talked, she realized his life—at least his life before donning his robe—had been strikingly similar to hers. He talked of tending his family's land and herds, and she was reminded of her daily chores in the inn. She didn't have brothers and sisters to terrorize, nor did she tend livestock or till soil, but she did have routine and duty to her family and their business. She understood his upbringing and quickly admired his openness and quiet strength.

Her mind wandered to his square jaw.

Enough of that, silly, she told the girl inside. *He's still a Priest, and you barely know him.*

But the flush flared through her again as she saw his eyes in her mind. She pulled the covers over her head and giggled before rolling over and drifting off to sleep.

The next morning began as the previous one had, with annoyingly chipper sunlight streaming through the window. She lay awake, staring out the window, not really seeing anything.

When it was clear sleep would not return, she released an annoyed huff, wiped her eyes, and rose.

She was supposed to work today. In a family-run inn, there was no such thing as a day off. Her mother had made that up last night when she saw a glimmer of hope that Laurie might finally have an attraction. She'd been nagging her for years to "find a good man," though Laurie couldn't understand the rush. She was happy working with her parents in the inn, happy seeing guests every day and making them laugh, happy being part of something special. After all, The Glory had been her home since, well, forever. She'd lived there her whole life. Why would she ever want to leave for some man?

But the night before, when Seth's persistent smile had made her heart flutter, all thoughts of the inn were replaced by deep pools of brown and locks of ebony (with little curls at their ends). She giggled when she realized she was twisting her own locks with her fingers as she daydreamed.

Despite her mother's unfathomable grace, Laurie knew her day off would include a trip to the market to purchase essentials for the evening meal. There could be no respite from their guests' grumbling stomachs. She donned her dress, fumbling awkwardly as she put one arm in the wrong sleeve. Blearily, she wrestled until things were righted and she could drape a fresh smock over her head. After a quick visit to the kitchen to grab a steaming biscuit and affectionate kiss from her mother, she ambled out of the inn. It was too early for the stalls to be open, but she had nowhere else to be and enjoyed the thought of an aimless stroll on a chilly day.

She'd made it halfway to the docks when the cheerful squeal of children woke her from her daze. Someone had worked a pack of little monsters into a frenzy, and they were screaming and laughing with reckless abandon. The merry sound made her smile, and she turned to follow it, curious to see what had the little rascals so energized this morning.

She rounded the corner of the apothecary and stopped mid-stride, her grin widening at the scene before her. A tall man in a brown robe faced away from her. A toddler clung to each of his legs while another had her arms and legs firmly wrapped around his waist. She could see the girl's tiny hands clasped across the man's back. Two others ran in circles around the man, poking him playfully with their "swords," which were little more the willow branches that bent with the wind as they waved them. A slender woman, her silver mane blowing wildly in the winter breeze, sat some distance away, covering her laughter with one hand. Laurie could see the glimmer of a smile in her eyes from across the road.

The man let out a grumbling roar and raised his hands, fingers crooked like claws, as he lifted one leg in a dramatic stomp. The attached toddler squealed with delight and screamed, "Get him! He's trying to flee!" The two swordsmen renewed their assault.

Laurie couldn't help but laugh with the children. The sillier the man acted, the grander his gestures, the louder their giggles and screams became. At the sound of a newcomer's amusement, the man turned, and their eyes met. The monster's mock snarl was immediately replaced with a warm, broad smile as Seth straightened then bowed deeply, a gesture made even more comical by his dangling darlings.

"M'lady, save me! I am but an innocent beast wrongly attacked by these ruffians. Please, have mercy, fair maiden!" Seth's plea caused the thin woman to double over with laughter and sent the children into a frenzy. High-pitched cries of, "No! He's mine. He's a monster," rang through the yard.

Laurie held up both hands, palms out in surrender. "Dear monster, you're on your own in this fight."

She walked around the fray and sat beside the older woman, and they laughed until tears streamed down their cheeks. When the swordsmen finally found their opening, the raging monster stumbled awkwardly to his knees, the barnacles still clinging to his legs. He let out cries and moans of pain, then dramatically uttered, "Oh, if I only had more time to live." That made the women's sides hurt and the children cheer in victory. When he finally lay unmoving on the paving stones, the children danced around him, swords held high, and proclaimed their heroic victory.

Seth peeked up from the stones with one eye and caught Laurie's attention. He winked once, then closed his eye again. The smug grin on his lips nearly made her piddle with laughter right there in the yard. She turned to her new companion and tried desperately to avoid looking at the man lest she find herself incapable of, well, anything!

Before she realized it, Seth was before her on bended knee, one child now firmly attached to his back with her head poking over his shoulder, tongue extended toward Laurie. "M'lady, might a humble monster accompany you on your errands this fine day?"

The older woman giggled at the handsome Priest. Clearly, she'd fallen under his spell. Laurie, a stronger woman (she told herself), straightened her back and looked imperiously down her nose at the man's proffered hand.

"Monsters aren't welcome in the market," she said. "But perhaps they may allow a Priest to visit—if accompanied by a lady of respect and renown, of course."

Seth lowered his head and shook it in mock disappointment. "Alas, I have found no such woman this day. I must go hungry then."

Laurie slapped him playfully, then rose. "Come on then. I would love the company." She looked back to see the older woman grinning from ear to ear. It took a few moments to fully extricate Seth from his tiny pursuers, but the three adults finally pried them away, allowing the Priest and innkeeper to make their escape.

"There's a story for the bards: the Priest and the Innkeeper's Daughter Fleeing the Pack of Ravenous Children." Laurie laughed and shook her head again at Seth's open warmth that contrasted so deeply with her initial impression of the man. He caught her looking at him and raised a brow.

"What? Is there something still clinging to my neck?"

"No. You're free of knee-high knights." She grinned. "I guess, I don't know, I never imagined seeing you—or any man of the cloth for that matter—carousing with a pack of wild children."

"You envision every religious man hunkered in his stone temple, on his knees, forever praying to his gods or the Spirits, right?"

She gave him a sheepish look and nodded.

"That's okay. It's what most people think, but the Order is different. We're actually here to help those in need, to be part of the community, rather than simply take from it. Everything we receive, we return. It's a vital tenant of our faith."

Laurie wasn't sure she enjoyed the religious turn of their conversation, but admired what Seth had to say, and even more the commitment with which he said it. She could see in his eyes, feel in his words, that he *meant* it—all of it. She'd encountered priests and monks of other orders, and most of them struck her as hollow, self-serving men who cloaked themselves in beliefs that never transformed into deeds. The Priest walking beside her seemed so different. Seeing him with the children, hearing their laughter and witnessing his obvious pleasure in their play, made her wonder if there wasn't truth in his words.

"You're doing it again."

She looked up. "Doing what?"

"Losing yourself in your thoughts. Care to share?"

His gaze was so intense, so beautiful. She looked away suddenly. "I was just walking through what we needed at the market in my head. That's all."

She thought she saw a grin out the corner of her eye before his head turned back to look ahead. "Taming that pack of wild dogs was my only appointment today, so consider me at your service, m'lady."

Days turned into weeks, each mirroring the last, with Laurie going about her routine, and Seth finding excuses to accompany her. Ma had taken to saving him a table each dinner and beamed each time he darkened their doorway, racing forward to grip him by the arm and usher him to his seat. She chittered about how happy Laurie seemed these days, and how she credited the Priest for her buoyant mood.

For her sake, Laurie thought her mood always cheerful and harrumphed at the thought some man made her more so—until Seth appeared each day and her smile widened ever so slightly. The flutter of her heart and flush of warmth throughout her limbs stirred with his gaze, more so now than before. After their third week of market strolling, she'd allowed him to take her hand. She'd never understand the magic he'd used in that simple touch. Sparks prickled her arms, and her chest swelled. He squeezed her hand affectionately, and the world stilled.

In their fifth week, Seth invited her to hear him address the people in the town square. Neatly scripted flyers had been strewn about town, calling all to hear the *man of the Order* speak. By this time, everyone knew him. Talk of the handsome Priest was on the tongue of nearly every hopeful, whispering maid. He would have no trouble drawing a crowd. Laurie dreaded facing the tittering biddies who already spoke of her with jealous barbs, but she wouldn't miss supporting Seth as he spread his warmth and works among her neighbors.

". . . the weak, those who cannot do so well for themselves." Laurie stifled a yawn. She'd heard this speech from Seth so many times she could recite it from memory.

She looked around her. Practically the whole town was there. Spring was poking its shy head above the surface, and heavy cloaks were no longer needed. Farmers in coveralls and fishermen in rough leggings stood beside women and girls in their finest gowns and dresses. Laurie couldn't stop her eyes from rolling at the obvious contrast and the townswomen's desire to out-impress at the largest public gathering so far this year. *Some things wouldn't be changed by the appearance of one good-natured Priest*, she thought.

Seth's voice drew her attention once more.

". . . the Queen." Murmurs trickled through the crowd at whatever he'd just said. She couldn't tell if the crowd agreed with whatever it was, but the Priest's words had clearly drawn a reaction.

Seth held his arms out, asking the crowd to calm. "We respect the Crown and its role in keeping order among our people.

They uphold laws and keep us safe, maintain our roads, and encourage trade with our neighbors."

The murmurs turned to nods and grunts of assent.

"And yet, who declared war on our neighbor?" Seth paused and looked from face to face. "Who spread the false tale of then-Princess Jessia's kidnapping at the hands of our Melucian brothers? They were innocent of this charge, yet this vile accusation was the bedrock on which our righteous anger was built. Who laid that foundation?"

He paused again and felt the mood of the crowd shift. The bitterness was palpable. He'd struck a nerve. A man's voice several rows back from Seth called out, "One who wore the Crown, that's who!"

Seth held up a hand again to quell the rising tide.

"That's right. It was the Crown itself who led our husbands and brothers to defeat and death. The Crown discarded a thousand years of peace in exchange for personal power. The King himself, Spirits rest his soul, was fooled into ordering our boys east. Is there a family present who hasn't lost a son or brother or husband? How many widows and orphans must the Crown create before we challenge their right to absolute power?"

Laurie glanced nervously around. Even society's finest had forgotten their silk and lace in favor of anger and resentment. Every family knew loss from the war. Every mother knew the ultimate grief and pain, the agony no parent should ever know. He was striking the flint, lighting the flame, drawing it skillfully into his palm.

Why, Seth? What are you doing?

The Priest allowed the flame to catch before begging for calm once more.

"Good people of Oliver, you know me now. Your children know me most of all." This brought a few nervous nods and tentative smiles from knowing parents. "I came here to serve, to minister to each of you in your own time and need. I did not come to fan the flames of rebellion."

Brows knit in confusion. Wasn't this man just talking about the ills of the Crown?

"Of course, the one who wears the Crown is human, like each of us. He or she is bound to err, some more disastrously than others, as we've recently learned. And yet, our faith doesn't teach revolution. Our mortal masters fulfill an ancient and worthy purpose when they serve and lead, rather than conquer. We praise the efforts of our new Queen. Tragedy tested her will and strength beyond what most could fathom, yet she endured to rise and don the vestments of power."

More nods spread among the crowd. Queen Jessia had indeed become a popular figure, a beacon of hope following the disastrous war of her mother and father.

"What we believe is that faith and order must coexist, must rule the mind and body and Spirit *together*. The Crown and the Order should stand side by side in service to the people of this land. The will of mortal men must always be balanced by the temperance of spiritual guidance. Only through faith and good works can we hope to reclaim the mantle of righteousness our Kingdom once possessed."

An impatient woman on the front row raised her hand and shouted, "I don't get it. You hate the Crown, then you respect it. You don't want rebellion, now you preach the faith should rule with the Queen. What are you saying?"

Seth smiled and nodded toward the woman in acknowledgement.

"Thank you, madam. We Priests do love the sound of our own voices a tad too much."

This drew chuckles and more than a few nods.

"We all know the ancient prophecy that foretells the return of the One. There isn't a child among us who cannot recite tales of Irina and her return by heart, but we now know Irina was a false prophet, a false goddess. She was never the One spoken of with reverence in ancient texts. She was a usurper who used magic and power to further her own evil designs and drive our nation into the ground!"

The ever-shifting mood swung instantly to anger once more at the mention of Irina.

"I come before you today, not with a message of anger and despair, but of hope. I come to proclaim the return of the true heir of prophecy, the true bearer of faith. The One returns—"

Gasps spread through the crowd. The woman who'd spoken earlier crossed her arms and shouted, "What does he *want*? We've got nothing left to give. The old Queen took my sons and husband!"

"My friends, The One comes to us with arms spread wide, inviting us into a warm embrace of love, kindness, and beauty. He comes to *heal* and usher in a new age of peace and prosperity for our people. He seeks neither land nor riches, nor does he care for conquest." Seth paused, tapped a finger to his lips thoughtfully, then corrected himself, drawing the crowd further to his words. "No, that's not right. He *does* seek conquest. He would conquer *every heart* and bring every loyal subject the *joy* and *peace* only found in righteous works and passionate, sincere faith.

"Tonight is a beginning. I am but a humble servant sent ahead of his master to prepare for his return. You are *my* family now, and I ask only for your open mind and heart. Go in peace, and think on my words."

No one moved for a long moment. They weren't sure they should. Then Seth stepped down from the makeshift stage and made his way through the parting crowd to where Laurie stood. She gaped up as he stood before her.

"Was I *that* bad?"

She looked at her hands as her fingers fidgeted. "You spoke well, but..."

Her face held a stricken look, and she struggled to raise her eyes from her feet.

"It's a lot to take in. I get it," he said. "May a humble Priest walk a lovely lady home?"

She looked around and saw the crowd dispersing, some casting glances their way, their faces unreadable. She nodded and allowed him hook her arm in his and begin their stroll toward the inn.

Chapter Twenty-One

Laurie

Laurie returned to the inn to find her parents alone in the common room, whispering angrily and trying not to raise their voices and disturb their guests, though her father's voice rose with every word.

"You can't tell me what that man was saying isn't treason!" Hershel slapped the table, then rubbed out his smarting palm.

"Dad, he never said the Crown should go or anything like that. He just said it should coexist with his faith." Laurie strode into the common room and plopped down in front of her father.

He fixed her with a sharp gaze, one meaty finger pointing in her direction. "He *said* King Alfred led us to disaster and needed a leash. He *said* his prophet should be a check on the

Crown. Imagine that: a *check* on the Spirits-anointed sovereign! He *said—*"

Laurie leaned forward and gently pushed his hand down, holding it once she felt the table. "Dad, I was there. He would never mean the Queen or the monarchy any harm. He just believes in the prophecy and wants this One, whoever that is, to be respected and listened to. That's all." She leaned back, releasing him. "Have you *seen* all the good he's doing around town? There isn't a widow or child who hasn't felt his positive influence, mostly in the form of food or clothes."

"Exactly!" he spat. "He shows up here in his shiny robe bearing pretty gifts. He's pure and innocent, *I'm sure.*"

"Hershel . . ." Ma said in a warning tone.

"Don't *Hershel* me. I know what I heard, and there's *no place* for folk who talk against our Queen, especially this new One who hasn't even done anything yet! If I hear that nonsense again, you won't be seein' that boy anymore. You hear me, young lady?"

Laurie folded her arms and glared at her father. "I'm a grown woman. I'll see who I want."

Hershel held her gaze for a long moment, fire blazing between them, until his face softened. He sucked in a deep breath and looked down at his weathered hands. "Laurie. . . I'm sorry. I don't mean to talk down to you. Of course, you're a grown woman. I'm just worried you're getting mixed up with a bad sort, that's all. Can't a father worry for his daughter?"

Her fire flickered out.

"I know, Pa, and I love you for it, but Seth is different. He's a good man. I know it."

Hershel grunted but didn't say anything.

"Laurie, go on upstairs and get some sleep. It's been a long night." Ma shooed her away from the table with a look that said,

I need to talk to your father alone. Laurie didn't miss her meaning, hugged Hershel tightly around his neck, then bounded up the stairs to her room.

Ma sat across from Hershel in the seat still warm from her daughter. "Listen, you old coot. That girl hasn't been happy like this in a long time. Why are you tryin' to ruin it?"

He shook his head firmly. "I want her happy as bad as you, but something about these Priests isn't right. All this talk about the Crown—there's treason in that man's words. We've been loyal to the throne our whole lives. I won't put up with such talk, not in my own town, and certainly not in my own inn. There are others in town who feel the same. We talked after that farce of a meeting, and plenty aren't happy."

"Hershel, you be careful now. You get the men all worked up and bad things can happen."

"Bad things are going to happen if we let those robed devils spread lies about our Queen. I won't stand for it, and neither should you. Spirits! First Irina comes back, now this. What's the world coming to?"

Ma stood and placed a hand on her husband's shoulder. "Just be careful, Hersh. Please."

He looked up and held her eyes for a long moment. She'd stood by him for nearly twenty-five years, and he loved her more than life. He couldn't ignore the plea in her voice, no matter how mad he might be about the Priests and their words. So, he nodded once, kissed her hand, and watched his wife vanish up the stairs to their bedroom.

Over the next two weeks, Seth stood in the town square each night to ever-growing crowds and spoke of the prophecy and return of the One. Most of his hour-long message centered on spreading good works, helping the poor, and turning one's beliefs into actions. These ideas were met with universal approval, filling donation bins to overflowing with each session.

And yet, woven within his message of good faith and better works, he sowed seeds of loyalty to the Spirits and one's faith over worldly concerns. He'd learned from his first sermon and never again used the Queen by name or title, but his meaning was clear. The faith should be the first place people looked to for leadership and guidance, not the Crown.

Hershel and several men and women of the town met each night at a large round table in the back of his inn following the gatherings. Hushed tones contrasted with loud music from the stage and the cheering that accompanied it. As the players' tunes swelled, anger festered and grew in the back of the room. Ma begged him to focus on the inn and mind his own business, but he wouldn't be pacified. The King himself had graced their inn, beginning a long span of prosperity for the town and their family. He wouldn't repay that kindness with betrayal. No, the King—and his daughter—deserved better.

What began as disgruntled griping evolved into plots and plans. Some favored speaking in opposition to the Priest, offering a counterpoint for the people to consider. Hershel argued Seth's carefully planted seeds had taken root far more quickly than anyone could've imagined, and, while talk might pluck a few leaves, it would do nothing to the roots as they twined ever deeper.

It was too late for talk.

It was time for action.

The evening was unseasonably warm, nearing pleasant springtime temperatures. Clouds dotted the sky, occasionally blotting out the sliver of moon and her chorus of stars. Seth's evening presentation was unusually well attended, drawing folk from surrounding communities throughout the countryside. Warm smiles mirrored the warmth in the air as the people stood and listened to the Priest and his good words.

He paused once, a wide smile parting his lips, as he was distracted by a pack of children racing through the crowd. A mother began scolding her son, but Seth called out, "Please, let them play so the sounds of their laughter may lift our spirits. Would that each of us had the light heart of a child once again." The mother seemed unsure, but chuckles rang through the crowd as they watched the boy dart after his friends.

Seth never mentioned the Crown, nor did he speak of mortal leaders and their failings. He spoke of green sprouts he saw everywhere he looked, tiny glimmers of hope rising above the field of winter white. He extolled the virtues he'd seen demonstrated by townspeople, from simple dockhands to wealthy landowners, and described how blessed he felt to be a part of their family.

Laurie stood transfixed in the front row. How had this man crept into town and stolen her heart? She looked around and realized he'd stolen more than just hers. Smiles, once rare in the post-war Kingdom town, now spread on the light spring breeze. She couldn't remember ever seeing the poor stand shoulder to shoulder with their betters, yet here they were, listening and nodding, raising their own voices each time Seth lowered his. She'd struggled to understand what she'd felt as she'd strolled through the market, but now she knew for certain. It was pride. Not the haughty assertion of one's dominance over another, but the humble satisfaction of a job well done. It was the elation one felt as she watched those she'd helped recover and rise anew.

When Seth's last words echoed through the yard, and the final rambunctious youth was rounded up, Laurie twined her arm in his and reveled in the warmth of his gaze. They strolled from the square, headed nowhere in particular, returning cheerful nods and "good evenings" to others headed home. Laurie didn't think she could be any happier than in that moment.

Hershel and two other men stood at the edge of the square and watched the crowd disperse. They painted on smiles and nodded as expected, but they brooded beneath.

"We can't wait much longer," Hershel whispered. "If he keeps this up, the whole town'd defend him if tried to stab the Queen in front of them."

"They'd say he was spreading his good works," an embittered butcher grunted in agreement.

"Tomorrow night. We finish this tomorrow night," Hershel said. The other men's eyes locked on his, then each man nodded once. The butcher and wainwright turned and vanished into the night, leaving Hershel glaring where Seth once stood. His stare could've burned the place down, if only he'd had the Gift of Fire.

The Order and its band of slicksters wanted the same thing most men standing in the square wanted, attention and power. If he was any judge, Hershel guessed the latter was far more important to the Priests and their prophet.

Their prophet. The One. What did *he* want? Seth was laying the groundwork for his grand entrance to the Kingdom's stage, but to what end?

He walked through everything that had happened over the past year as he wandered home, oblivious to the falling temperatures and deepening darkness. When he finally looked up to see thickening clouds obscuring the moon and stars, thoughts of winter's last gasp pushed to the fore, and he knew the coming days would cast a blanket of snow over the town's spring-filled dreams.

Nothing to do about it but dig out, he thought as he kicked a rock further down the path, thankful for the momentary distraction from the town's troubles.

He loved this place. He'd met Ma here, raised his daughter here, and planned to see his last sunset spread across the ocean's shores here. There was no way some outsider would show up and tell him these people, *his* people, weren't decent and good. He just couldn't let that happen.

A chill gusted by and pimpled the skin on his arms. He laughed at himself when he realized, in his aimless wandering, he'd walked nearly a half league out of town.

Time to go home, Hersh. Ma's waitin'.

He kicked another rock and turned back to head home. A couple strides later, he heard a rumbling roar from behind. As he turned, he had to blink to comprehend what he saw. A massive bear, fur dark as the night, towered over him. It roared and bared its teeth as a head-sized paw flew out of the darkness, and dagger-sharp claws tore into his chest.

Hershel staggered backwards, eyes wide from shock and pain. He tried to breathe, but fire bloomed in his chest. The bear lumbered forward, eyes never leaving its prey.

As another swipe descended, the one that would sever the arteries in Hershel's throat and snuff out his dreams of another sunset, a flicker passed through the bear's eyes. A recognition. An almost *human* understanding.

Chapter Twenty-Two

Jess

"Your Majesty." General Ethan Marks bowed deeply. "The last of our troops has returned. Of the eighty thousand we assembled, ten thousand bogged down in the mountains and never made it into the theater. Their units were primarily composed of newer recruits and archers. I've posted them at Huntcliff to guard the border and continue their training."

Jess strummed her fingers against the arm of her throne, waiting for the bad news.

"Of the remaining seventy thousand, only twenty-two thousand have been accounted for. Of those, six thousand are wounded, but should return to service. We believe others will report over the coming months but expect no more than a few hundred. The rest either died, remained in Melucia, or returned to their homes upon crossing back into the Kingdom."

"What about machinery? Siege equipment and transports?"

Marks's brow rose appreciatively. He hadn't expected his young queen to understand military matters, much less ask detailed questions during this audience.

"Carts and carriages accompanying the ten thousand at Huntcliff survived with only minor, weather-related damage. Roughly one third of our carts and other transports returned with the surviving troops. All our siege engines, heavy ladders, rams, and other machinery were lost."

"What about the navy?"

"Our fleet is intact. The Melucians never built anything stronger than merchant vessels, so we never encountered resistance. I have recalled our ships to their home ports."

"Well, that's a tiny rose amidst all the thorns," she sat back and pressed fingers into the bridge of her nose. "General, by my math, we now have a functioning navy with a dozen well-armed ships, and twenty-five thousand able-bodied men in our army, ten thousand of whom are green recruits stationed at the far end of the Kingdom. Our heavy equipment is gone, and only a small fraction of our transports used to feed and supply our troops remain. Does that about sum it up?"

"Yes, Majesty, give or take a thousand men."

She paused, then turned her gaze to the man standing to Marks's right. The golden badge of the High Sheriff's office glittered on his breast. Jess had only pinned it on the man an hour before this audience.

"High Sheriff, what of our constables? Surely, many joined the army and were lost. Are our cities secure? Is the capital?"

Bryan Cribbs, the new High Sheriff, bowed deeply. His unruly brown hair flopped as his head lowered, forcing him to flick it back into place as he rose. Curls flew in every direction. If the topic hadn't been so serious, Jess would've laughed at the spectacle. But despite the man's unkempt mane, his dozen years of service to the Crown had proved him an effective and loyal lawman. Of the immediate appointments pending Jess's attention, High Sheriff had been the easiest. Cribbs was a good man and an even better Sheriff, if a bit too enamored with his own visage.

"Majesty, our ranks are thin, but holding. Most of the losses to the army came from smaller towns and villages, so the capital and larger cities remain secure." Cribbs's eyes fell.

"What is it, Sheriff? What aren't you telling me?"

"Well, Your Majesty, it's just—"

"Spit it out. It's just the three of us." Marks turned and fixed Cribbs with a stern gaze.

Cribbs continued. "I've received reports of . . . disturbances in a couple of our port cities."

"Disturbances?" she leaned forward.

"Nothing violent, Majesty." He absently fidgeted with his badge of office. "Priests of a new faith are entering the towns. They're ministering to the poor, feeding the hungry, that sort of thing."

"I'm sorry, Sheriff, I'm not following. What's bad about any of that?"

"It's not their good works that bothers me. It's what they're preaching." He locked eyes with Jess for the first time. "They're openly prophesying the return of the One, an ancient legend only told to children to scare them. *The One* traditionally refers to Empress Irina, or some fictional version of her, but these clerics speak of the earthly return of some prophet or mystic god who will unite the continent's people under one faith—and *one banner*."

Marks's head snapped up to Jess. "*One banner*? Are they actually talking about their god replacing the Throne? Or the Queen being subservient to their faith's leader?"

"That's what we think, but they talk in circles. When pressed, they go back to their good works and encouraging the people to take care of their brothers and sisters, that sort of thing. I'm not even sure the people know what they mean by their veiled political references, but they're gaining followers through their ministry. Our agents fear they're building toward something; we just don't know what."

Jess thought a moment. "What are they calling themselves?"

"The men and women are called Priests, and their faith is referred to as the Order. The prophet or god they talk about is called "the One." It's strikingly similar to old tales of Irina's return and the insanity preached by the Children, but their Priests actually call Irina a "false prophet" and blame her—along with King Alfred and Queen Isabel—for the disaster in Melucia."

"They blame *my father*? He never wanted war."

He nodded and cast an uneasy glance to Marks. "It's all still new and reports are unclear, but I thought you should know everything as we're learning it."

"Thank you, Sheriff. Keep an eye on this group and update me regularly."

"Yes, Majesty," Cribbs said. He bowed again, took two steps backward, then wheeled and exited.

Marks relaxed his posture as soon as the doors closed. "I think he's a fine appointment. You did well."

Jess stood and stretched. "Thanks. We'll see how he does. What do you make of that Order talk? With all the wounded returning, the people need a little extra help these days. Sounds pretty harmless to me, save the part where they throw my parents under the cart."

"Theology was never my strong suit, though many soldiers turn to the Spirits in the heat of battle. I suppose any group offering food to our hungry in the dead of winter is welcome, but the whole part about 'the One' and putting their religious leader above monarchs and rulers could take us down a dangerous path. We need to learn more about their true purpose."

"And that's why I asked you to join these meetings today." She turned and strode to the Council table, then seated herself at its head in the High Chancellor's seat. Marks took the hint and followed, sitting in the chair closest to her.

"So, Uncle Ethan—"

"You know, *little Jess*, you only call me that when you want something." The corner of his mouth quirked into an uneasy grin.

"You think you know me," she said with mock offense and a nervous chuckle, then turned serious. "It seems I have several openings at this table."

Marks sat back. "I wondered when we'd have this conversation. With the loss of Bril, War makes sense. What else were you thinking?"

"There are others who can do a fine job at War. I need a *High Chancellor* I trust completely. Unless you know someone more qualified, someone who earned my family's trust over the years, I'd like you to fill this chair."

Marks's eyes popped wide, somewhere between surprised and nauseated. He looked away and stared at some distant, unlit point in the corner of the chamber. After several moments, he still hadn't spoken.

"Well?"

"Jess—*Your Majesty*—I have very little experience in diplomacy or dealing with nobles. You need someone polished in the art of kissing backsides. I'd be more likely to incite a revolt than quell one if I had to listen to those howling jackals all day."

Jess leaned forward and placed a hand on his arm. "Ethan, I can deal with the nobles. I need someone to watch my back, to question everything *and everyone*, to be my eyes and ears throughout the Kingdom. I need someone I can count on when everyone else turns away. You're the only man I trust completely." Her voice faltered. "With my father and brother gone—Spirits, with my *mother* gone, too—there's no one left. Please."

Marks opened his mouth to speak, then closed it. His hand reached up and tugged at his suddenly tight, itchy collar.

"If my Queen commands—"

"No," she interrupted sternly, then softened. "Uncle Ethan, this is *Jess* asking, not your Queen. You've given your life to this nation. I will not command you to serve more than you already have."

He stared into her eyes, then lowered his head and whispered. "I would do anything for you, Jess. Of course, I will protect you and your throne in whatever way you need me."

She schooled her expression, straightened her back, and extended her hand toward Marks. "Thank you, High Chancellor."

Ever the dutiful soldier, Marks dropped from his chair to one knee, bowed his head, and kissed the proffered signet.

"Thank *you*, Your Majesty."

A few days later, as Jess was setting her crown onto the velvet cushion beside her throne, ready to change out of her formal audience attire before dinner with Kendall, the page's head popped between the cracked double doors.

"Your Majesty, the High Sheriff is asking to speak with you."

Jess and Marks shared a look. Sheriff Cribbs hadn't returned to the palace since accepting his office.

"Send him in," Jess said, adjusting the crown on its pillow then turning to stand before her throne. Marks stepped to the bottom stair on her right and faced the doors.

One of the golden doors swung open and a harried-looking High Sheriff scurried across the long chamber and bowed before his Queen.

He eyed the crown resting by the throne. "Majesty, thank you for seeing me. I won't take long, as I'm sure you've had a long day."

Jess waved a hand as she'd seen her father do a thousand times. "Sheriff, our duty never rests. What brings you to the palace?"

Cribbs locked eyes with Marks for a moment, then looked to Jess. She raised a brow at the interaction but said nothing.

"Majesty, there was a murder in the eastern quarter last night. The victim was a shopkeeper who sells pottery near the Temple. No one of prominence."

When Cribbs didn't continue, Marks spoke. "And? Murders are rare, but they do happen, even in the capital."

"Yes, Chancellor, that's true, but two things concern me. First, the man was killed behind his shop, in a densely populated area of town where he could only have been alone for a few moments. His body was mutilated."

"What do you mean? How so?"

"It looks as though some wild animal attacked him. Massive rends across his chest and stomach appear to have been made by claws of some kind, and his face—it's barely recognizable."

Jess covered her mouth with her hand.

"The eastern quarter abuts the Spires. Is it unusual for wild beasts to wander down in winter, seeking food?" Marks asked.

"No, of course not. We see bears and wolves on occasion, but they are rarely bold enough to attack. There are so many people packed into the capital these days that most wildlife is too afraid to venture close."

"You said there were two things that bothered you. What is the second?" Jess asked, impatient to be done with her day.

Cribbs looked to Marks. "This is the third killing in three weeks that appeared to have been committed by wildlife. The other two occurred in Oliver and Featherstone."

"Oliver? I could understand Spoke. It sits on the eastern base of the Spires, but Oliver is a port town with nothing but fields at its back."

"It gets stranger," Cribbs nodded. "The victim in Spoke appeared to be mauled by a wolf or some other smaller predator. In Oliver—I hardly know how to believe the description. Constables there report the man appeared to have wounds consisted with a bear. There were wide gashes across his chest and arms. Worse, whatever attacked him didn't stop when he was down. It continued tearing at his flesh, his face in particular, until he was barely recognizable. In neither attack was the victim . . . well . . . eaten."

"Eaten? Right." The color drained from her face as images of the victims flashed in her mind. Jess stepped backward and sat on the throne, her mind reeling. "Three attacks, all completely different. Coincidence?"

"If there were two, I suppose they could be. But three? That's a pattern, even though there's no obvious connection between the attacks.

"What about the victims? Were there any similarities?" Marks asked.

Cribbs shook his head. "None that I've put together—a shopkeeper, a weaver, and an innkeeper—none were prominent or wealthy, ordinary in every way."

"Alright, thank you, Sheriff. Is there anything else?" Jess asked.

"No, Majesty. That's everything we have so far. I'll keep you informed as we piece the details together. This may be nothing more than morbid coincidence, but I thought you'd want to know about it before the papers piece things together."

"Thank you. Please keep us informed." Jess rose.

"Sheriff, wait a moment." Marks said. "Your Majesty, you have one of the most prominent investigators on the continent as a guest in the palace. Do you think he might like something to do with his time?"

Jess quirked a brow. "There's an interesting idea. I think he'd actually love a new challenge. He's been pretty bored of late."

"Majesty? I'm not following."

"Sorry, Sheriff. I would like a fresh set of eyes on this situation. Unless you object, I will ask Guard Lieutenant Rea to assist with your investigation."

The Sheriff thought a moment, then nodded. "I think that's a fine idea, Majesty. We can use all the help we can get."

"Excellent. I'll speak with him this evening. Thank you, Sheriff."

Cribbs bowed again then backed out of the room.

"What do you make of all that?" Jess asked as she strode toward the side door to the residence.

"Hopefully, it's nothing more than an overcautious lawman with three coincidental deaths. But we'll see." Marks bowed. "Rest well, Your Majesty."

"Good night, High Chancellor."

Chapter Twenty-Three

Danai

"Our Priests report great success in the towns and villages throughout the Kingdom, Excellency. Far better than we originally anticipated. Your approach offering basic necessities before attempting conversion is working brilliantly."

Danai steepled his fingers and stared down from his throne. His liaison to the capital was proving a most effective leader among the clerics, allowing him to spend more time on overall strategy.

"And the detractors? Were they able to chip away at our support before the Five handled things?"

"There will always be those wary of our faith, but the Priests haven't reported any more *vocal* opposition. Local constables are chalking their deaths up to animal attacks, just as you predicted. Each was handled well out of the view of anyone who might raise suspicion," Danym said.

"How many are we up to now?"

"Four have been eliminated so far, though that number may have increased since I received my last report. In some of the larger towns, that still leaves vocal detractors, but we followed your instructions to limit activities to one per town for the moment."

"Make sure our people stick to the plan. The constables are likely comparing notes, searching for a pattern. As long as we keep things limited, they won't find one."

"Yes, Excellency."

"Good." Danai rose. "What of the capital?"

Danym's brow furrowed. "Fontaine is . . . a challenge. The coronation was well received, and the new Queen rides a wave of popularity. This will change as her reign ages, but for the moment, the people flock to her whenever she leaves the palace. They hang on her every word and gesture."

"What else? I can tell you're holding something back."

"It's the Temple. Despite Irina literally going up in flames, adherents to the old religion remain strident in their beliefs. Our Priests have been welcomed with wary eyes, even when carrying blankets and food for the poorest in the city. It will take time for the people to accept our presence and good intentions."

"Press the Priests. I want Temples built in every city and town. Spring will be here in four or five weeks, and I want a toehold in each location by summer's end. If we had more golden collars, this would go much faster, but use what we have." He paused and thought a moment, then looked up at Danym.

"You've done well. Get some rest. I want you back in Fontaine as soon as possible. Our brothers in that city need your guidance, now more than ever—and I believe you have a date planned, do you not?"

Danym grinned as he nodded. "Oh, I do, Excellency. Your most generous offer should make for an interesting first audience with our new Queen."

Chapter Twenty-Four

Jess

Jess shifted, adjusting the cushion, wishing she had even more padding. When a new monarch was crowned, every vassal and village presented leaders and letters offering their service to the new ruler. It was as if the Crown had been reinvented and everyone was required to bend the knee all over again. Jess understood the significance of the tradition, as it forced even the most upturned of noble noses to lower themselves and pledge their fealty once more. They weren't exactly making a new promise, more renewing the lifelong one they'd made when accepting whatever appointment or office they held.

She sighed deeply. It was an important step, if a long and boring one.

"Guildmaster Devon Weaver, head of the Merchants' Guild of Featherstone," the Royal Page called out as the doors swung open once again. Jess straightened and tried to stretch the weariness from her eyes. She hoped the man entering the audience chamber hadn't seen her rolling her neck to ease the stiffness, but she really didn't care at this point.

The reed-thin man in his pale-blue doublet and brown breeches stopped when he reached the mark on the floor some twenty paces from the base of the dais. He bowed deeply, then continued forward to the final mark. He lowered his eyes and tried not to meet his new Queen's gaze.

"Guildmaster Weaver. It is a pleasure to see you again. It's been what, four years?"

The man's head snapped up. "Majesty? You remember?"

She smiled. "Of course, I remember. It was a wonderful visit, and I recall your kindness most fondly, though you might not say the same of my own . . . unfortunate behavior."

Weaver's eyes lowered once more, but Jess saw a grin poke out the corner of his mouth. "You were young, Majesty. A little precociousness is to be expected of a child, royal or common, wouldn't you say?"

"Precociousness? Yes, well, you are again generous with that description." She chuckled. "Nonetheless, it is good to see you again. For what purpose do you seek audience with us?"

The shift in formality of her words snapped him back to the present, and Weaver dropped to one knee. "I come to congratulate Her Majesty and give my Oath, such that this humble servant of the Crown may offer."

"Your humility is refreshing in this chamber so often filled with hot air." Another grin tugged at the man's mouth as she spoke. "Guildmaster Weaver, what is your pledge?"

"I, Devon Weaver, do swear that I will well and truly serve our Sovereign Lady Queen Jessia Vester and her heirs and successors. I will do right to all manner of people after the laws and usages of this Kingdom, without fear or favor, affection or ill will. By the Spirits and the Spires, I do swear."

Jess rose from the throne and placed a palm on Weaver's shoulder. This was the only ceremony in which tradition required the monarch to actually touch the person offering their pledge, but doing so carried significant symbolism to all involved. Jess also knew the magic of the Crown flowed through her and into her new vasal, binding their promises in a virtually unbreakable pact. As her hand contacted Weaver, the faint glow flared from her Crown, and the familiar tingle of magic trickled down until it vanished from her palm into Weaver. He looked up, and his eyes widened as she spoke.

"Guildmaster Devon Weaver, the Crown accepts your fealty. In return, we offer you and yours our hearth and home, protection and provision, justice and righteous vengeance, without fear or favor, affection or ill will. By the Spirits and the Spires, we do swear."

A tear fell from Weaver's eye as he watched her step back. "Thank you, Majesty. Thank you," he said, before standing, bowing, then backing out of the chamber.

"This might be the longest day ever, but that part never gets old," she whispered to High Chancellor Marks, who stood one step below the throne to her right.

Marks grinned. "You royals are all alike. Your father once said exactly the same thing after doing this all day."

"Really?"

Marks nodded, his eyes twinkling with mischief. "All alike, I say."

"Oh, hush. Just because you—"

"High Priest Danym Wilfred, Ambassador of the Order to the Crown, Bearer of the Keys to the Faith, and Voice of the One."

Marks cocked a brow at Jess. "*Voice of the One?* He sounds full of himself. This should be a good one."

"Ethan," she whispered urgently. "He said Danym *Wilfred*. Is that *my* Danym? The Sheriff's son? The one who betrayed me?"

Before he could answer, the doors swung open, and Danym strode into the room, his dirty-blond hair now draped against the shoulders of his silky brown robe. He also wore a bemused grin, as though he'd played some devilish prank that was now being revealed.

Jess stood before her throne, fists balled tightly at her sides, her chest heaving with labored breaths. Her guards noticed the change in their charge's posture and stepped forward to assume their not-so-ceremonial positions on either side of the dais.

Danym stopped exactly on the first mark and bowed exactly the minimum depth required to not be rude, then he marched purposefully to the second mark. His gaze never left Jess's eyes, and he did not bow or kneel again.

"It is customary to take a knee before the throne, Ambassador," Marks said.

"Forgive me, Your Majesty. The Faith *appreciates* the Crown for its, how should I say, worldly duties, but we do not recognize the monarch as sovereign over spiritual matters. I will show respect to you and your office, but the Order compels me not to kneel in submission or subservience."

Marks's other brow rose.

"Danym?" was all Jess could get out.

"Hello, Jess."

"You may not yet kneel, but you *will* address her as Your Majesty, *Priest*." Marks snapped.

Danym peered out the side of his eyes at Marks, as if viewing some bug on his shoulder. "And you may address me as *Holy Voice*."

The room began to spin, and her breath became shallow, so Jess sat back on her throne. Danym took a step forward, his hand outstretched, but the guards thrust their pikes threateningly toward him.

"No need for violence. I was merely offering *Her Majesty* a hand. She looks as if she's seen a ghost," Danym stepped back.

"I'm fine," Jess said, waving her guards back. "Let's get this over with. *Holy Voice*, why do you seek an audience before the throne?"

"Tsk, tsk. After all we went through, this is how you greet me. I was hoping for a happier reunion."

Jess gripped the arms of the throne and leaned forward. "You're lucky *my greeting* doesn't come with the sharp end of a pike. You deceived me, betrayed me, and nearly watched me murdered. Now you come into *my* house and expect a warm embrace?"

"I was talking about a welcome, but if you're offering an embrace—"

"Enough!" She shot off the throne and descended one step to stand eye level with him. The guards were at Danym's side before she'd settled. When she spoke, an angry, hissing whisper escaped her lips. "If you ever loved me, ever cared for me, you will get this farce over quickly and leave. If I never see your face again, it will be too soon."

Danym's smirk vanished, and she thought she saw a hint of the boy she'd known emerge. He whispered, "Jess, of course I loved you—*still* love you. It's not what it looked like. Give me a chance to explain."

Her throat seized.

She couldn't think.

The room spun again, and she had to brace herself against Marks's proffered arm to keep from falling.

Nothing made sense. Danym *had* betrayed her, given her over to the Children to be slaughtered on the altar of sacrifice. And for what? What was in it for him? He was a teenage boy who didn't want to live with his father anymore. He didn't care about power or religion. He barely cared about his place in Fontaine society. Jess had had to coach him through everything. Or was that all an act, too? Was the quiet, brooding boy who seemed to stumble over his own feet actually feigning all that? Did she ever really know the man she'd fled the safety of the palace with, only to travel halfway across the Kingdom to be kidnapped by murderous madmen? No, not kidnapped by, *delivered to*. Was that his plan all along?

And now he stood before her. He was so cocky, strutting down the aisle and barely showing respect due the Crown. How dare he? Who did he think he was? Who did he think *she* was? Some foolhardy, doe-eyed girl whom he could manipulate again—or worse? Well, he'd learn exactly who this Queen was, and just how mighty her commands could be, no matter what his fledgling faith might think.

She stepped back, straightened her spine, and spoke formally. "Voice Wilfred, the Crown will hear your words. Speak."

The boy in his eyes vanished, and the annoying smirk returned.

"I come with an offer of friendship. The Order wishes the Crown no ill. In fact, we offer to unite our strength with yours.

The One returns with a message of hope, and we believe the time is right for the Crown and the Order to stand as one."

"Unite? The Crown and the Order? What are you saying?" Marks spoke the words Jess couldn't voice.

Danym locked eyes with Jess. "The One offers a hand in marriage, to join through matrimony the spiritual guidance of our faith and the worldly governance of the throne."

Jess leaned forward, confusion replaced by a hawk's piercing gaze. "You said *a* hand in marriage, not *his* hand."

Danym actually laughed. "Oh, no, Your Majesty. The One could not marry, though I'm sure he would be honored by your offer. He seeks to give my hand to Her Majesty, in the furtherance of peace and prosperity for the land we share."

Jess fell into the back of the throne, stunned.

"You want me to marry *you*? Seriously?"

Danym finally offered a slight tilt of his foppish head. "I do." He grinned, then said, "Has quite the ring, doesn't it?"

Jess seethed as she glared at the man before her. "Get out. GET OUT!"

The guards rushed forward and took Danym by each arm, practically lifting him off the ground as they hauled him out of the hall.

As he vanished through the doors, she heard him call out, "So you'll think about it?"

The doors slammed shut.

Chapter Twenty-Five

Keelan

Keelan ran his fingers along the stem of his wine glass and stared into the pattern of interlocking gold and silver woven into the tablecloth. Servants stood stiffly along the walls behind each chair, ready to fulfill any wish or need. All he wanted was a few moments alone, a chance to talk and laugh as they had on that first stroll through the garden.

He'd only seen Jess a few times since her coronation, and there were always servants or messengers or the occasional soldier scurrying about. He understood. She was a monarch now, with more demands on her time and attention than virtually any other person alive, but he couldn't ignore the tugging at his heart.

Over the past month, he'd explored every inch of the palace, taking in both the extravagance of its interior and the natural beauty of the grounds surrounding the royal residence. Dittler hadn't seen any more of Jess than he had, and the stubborn stallion refused to let any of the stable hands near him. At their insistence, Keelan spent a few hours each day exercising, grooming, and tending his equine friend. For his part, Dittler had stopped nipping Keelan every time he approached—unless the Guardsman forgot his daily apple. Without the bribe, he earned a crisp snap of the horse's teeth in reprimand.

Keelan's other hours were filled more with boredom than anything. He wasn't a subject of the Crown, and therefore wasn't allowed to take part in anything meaningful. Jess included him in some Council meetings but was convinced it was inappropriate for a foreigner to become a regular attendee at meetings involving Kingdom security. He was grateful to be excused from those meetings. The Council Jess had assembled was made of fine men and women, but they still loved to hear themselves talk. Jess hadn't yet secured her Crown enough to stop the constant preening and strutting displayed by visiting nobles, and he wasn't sure he could endure her hours of platitudes without offending some pompous official with his fist, or at least his yawns.

He tried talking the Sheriff into letting him help with some of their case load. The man, still new in his role, had thanked him politely, but suggested internal matters were best handled by Kingdom officers.

If it weren't for his ever-present desire just to be with Jess, he would've already headed home. He wasn't sure what existed between him and Jess, that feeling of togetherness, that longing, but he felt it every time she was near. Then he felt it more strongly when she left. It pulled him, or pushed him, he wasn't sure. The logical constable's brain couldn't comprehend the utter illogic of him mooning over a woman he barely knew, but here he was, staring at her chair, willing to wait until the world stopped turning for her to arrive and smile.

Just as he was about to chide himself for being sappy, the doors flew open, and Jess stormed into the dining room. The servants, already stiff in their uniforms, snapped to absolute rigidity at the presence of their fuming sovereign.

A man in his mid-thirties with only a few strands of pulled-over hair scurried behind her, his eyes downcast and expression wan.

"Explain this to me, Lord Chamberlain. Did *no one* in this palace know the Sheriff's son had returned? The one who sold me to be slaughtered?" Her voice rose with each word, and the man somehow bowed lower in her wake.

"I don't know, Your Majesty. No one reported this to me."

She wheeled to face him. "Stand up straight and face me."

He did, reluctantly, though his eyes remained downcast toward her chin.

"Unless you want to be the *former* Lord Chamberlain, you will look me in the eye. Now." She waited as the man struggled to lift both of his chins. "I want you to find the High Chancellor and get me a report from our eyes and ears. I want to know our numbers, strengths, gaps, and how the best network on the continent could miss something so obvious. Then I want to hear the plan to never miss so much as a whisper on the wind again. Am I clear, *Lord Chamberlain*?"

The man bowed several times nervously. "Yes, Majesty. Perfectly clear. I'll find the High Chancellor at once."

"Now get out." Her voice had fallen to a low murmur, which was somehow more intimidating than the raised pitch from before.

As the man ran out of the room, the servants began their highly choreographed dance, pouring wine and water, removing chargers, and retrieving platters of rolled meats and cheeses from the kitchen.

Keelan sat back as Jess turned and noticed him for the first time. She sucked in a deep breath, then released it. She reached over her chair to grip her wine glass, drained half of its contents, then set it down.

"I'm sorry you had to see that. You're not going to believe who showed up in court today."

He raised one brow but didn't speak.

"*Danym*. Can you believe it?"

"You mean Ambassador Danym? The Priest?"

Her jaw dropped. "You *knew*?"

He threw his hands up to fend off her rising anger. "I knew a Priest named Danym was appointed Ambassador. He was at the coronation banquet, paid me a visit at my table. Are you saying he's *that* Danym?"

"Yes, *that* Danym." She spat. "The one who tricked me into falling in love and running away with him, then gave me away to be killed. The one who laughed at me as those robed monsters dragged me into their temple. *That* Danym!"

She grabbed her glass and finished the wine. A servant materialized and refilled it before she'd even set it on the table.

Keelan switched into investigator mode, insulating his newly found, highly confusing emotions from her wrath. He watched but didn't speak.

She sipped more wine.

"Well? No advice? Everyone else around here seems to have plenty. All day, every day. Nothing but 'You should do this, Your Majesty,' or 'Oh, no, don't do that, Majesty.' They never stop. Surely you have some counsel, too?"

Keelan didn't move.

She took another sip, eyeing him.

"I'm sorry, Jess. I didn't know."

She looked up from her glass and the icy glare thawed. He turned to the servant standing watch behind him and asked, "Would you ask the staff to give us a moment?"

The woman bobbed and actually looked relieved. Within seconds, Jess and Keelan sat alone. He stood and knelt beside her chair.

"Do you want to talk about it?"

A tear threatened to flee the corner of her eye, and he thought her lip quivered slightly. She didn't turn to look at him, but one hand reached down and gripped his tightly. He could feel her anger and pain through that simple touch. Warmth also flooded up his arm and into his chest at the feeling of her skin pressed against his own. He didn't know what to make of all the emotions competing for his attention at the same time. He'd never felt comfortable dealing with one feeling at a time. A swirling host of emotions was overwhelming—and confusing.

"I loved him." She said in a small voice he strained to hear. "I *really* loved him. I never thought I'd see him again after . . . everything happened. And today, I was so happy, and then he appeared. He just showed up."

Keelan had seen the glassy-eyed stare of survivors before, heard the monotone of their recollections, watched as they relived their terror again and again. Usually, their memories and emotions came in waves. Shock, pain, anger, grief, disbelief, belief, acceptance. Sometimes the waves respected the order, but mostly they came when their hearts allowed, disjointed and unpredictable. Keelan knew Jess's mind and soul were under assault by more than a few of those feelings, and he ached to help her cope, but he knew her own strength was required to survive such a journey.

He stood, lifted her from her chair, and held her in his strong arms for so long that the servants began returning before he released her to sit again. By then her tears were dry, though the redness of her eyes told of their passing. The servants spoke with a gentle kindness Keelan hadn't heard in the palace before. It was the sharing of a burden only found within a special bond, within a family. He realized in that moment how unique those who served the royal household must be, and how critical they would be to her future success. He made a mental note to learn more about each servant and guard, especially those who worked within the private residences.

As plates from the main course were cleared, Jess broke the silence that dominated the meal. "Are you tired of me yet?"

Keelan wasn't often surprised, but the look of utter shock that flooded his face actually made her smile for the first time that evening.

"*Never*. Jess, I—"

"Good. Me either." She reached across the table and gripped his hand again. "I need to ask you to do something for me."

Her tone had changed, and her back stiffened just enough for him to notice.

"Is this Jess or the Queen asking?"

Her eyes widened. "Am I that obvious? Sometimes I forget you're a trained investigator."

When he didn't reply, she continued. "There have been a series of deaths scattered in towns and villages across the country, seemingly at random. They appear to be the work of wild animals."

"But you don't believe that, do you?"

"No. It's *too* random, if that makes any sense."

He nodded thoughtfully. "Alright, what do you want me to do? Your Sheriff made it clear he didn't want me involved in Kingdom matters."

"Not to worry. I've already spoken with him, and he's agreed." She took a sip. "I'd like you to go to Oliver and see what you can learn. Our investigators have done their best but failed to uncover anything beyond the obvious."

"The obvious may actually be the truth."

"Right. I'd still like your eyes on this. Something feels wrong. I just can't figure out what it is."

"Of course, I'd do anything you asked, Your Majesty." He offered her a mocking bow of his head at the table.

She snorted again. "Not you, too! Stop that."

"As you wish, Majesty."

Another snort.

Keelan didn't say anything, just stared.

"What? Have I got something in my teeth?"

"No. It's just nice to see you smile again."

Her smile broadened, and a flush raced up her neck. "Ooh, it's warm in here. Would you mind accompanying me on a stroll through the gardens after dinner? We can walk off some of this meal."

"I thought you'd never ask."

They made it halfway across the gardens before either of them spoke. Jess raced fingertips across every plant and flower they passed while Keelan fiddled with his fingers and timidly avoided eye contact.

"Jess—"

"Keelan—"

They finally spoke—at the same time.

"You go first," she said.

He returned his gaze to his rapidly twiddling digits.

"It's nice out here," he said.

She snorted. "That's what you were nervous saying to me?"

"No." He didn't look up. "I guess I'm just nervous about the trip."

Jess looked up sharply. "What? You mean going to Oliver? Keelan, you're one of the most storied investigators alive. Why would taking on one more case make you nervous?"

"Because it's not just another case. It's a case *for you*."

"You've taken cases from the Triad. Why's one from the Queen of Spires so different?"

He finally met her eyes. "I don't care about 'the Queen.' I'm worried I'll disappoint *you*."

She missed a step and nearly stumbled. He caught her arm, and she gripped his hand and didn't let go. After a moment of silence, she looked from their clasped hands.

"Keelan, you're an amazing constable, one of the best, and you have magic that helps you serve people in need—but your skills and your Gift aren't why I fell in love with you."

His head snapped up, and his eyes widened.

She softened her voice and stroked his cheek. "Yeah, I said it. You'll owe me for that." She smirked. "You are a good, decent man, Keelan. You're smart and strong, and you would die before letting anything happen to someone you love. You act all tough, but I've seen the real boy inside the hardened shell. He's scared sometimes, but mostly he wants to be happy, to be accepted, and to help others. I love that boy, Keelan, with all my heart."

He stared down at her with wonder in his eyes. Never in a million years would he have dreamed she'd felt the same way he did. Part of the reason he'd taken the assignment in Oliver was to get away before he said something he'd regret, something she'd send him packing for. But she loved him. *Him*. He couldn't believe it.

His pulse started racing again, and beads of sweat formed on his forehead. He reached up and pulled at his itchy collar, and it suddenly became very warm in the gardens.

She grinned as only a woman who knows she's flummoxed a man can grin, and then she pulled his face toward her before he could gather himself.

She tasted his breath, and a magic all its own sent tingles down her spine. As their lips met, warmth exploded in her chest, and all thoughts of animal attacks or ex-boyfriends faded from her mind. He was startled at first, eyes wide in panic, and tried to pull back, but she held him in place until he kissed her back. Their eyes closed, and the world drifted away. She melted into him and knew she was at home in his embrace.

Chapter Twenty-Six

Keelan

By the time the outskirts of Oliver came into view, Keelan's backside and legs were achy and stiff. It had taken nearly four days. As much as he trusted Jess, his Gift told him she wasn't laying all the cards on the table. He'd worked for the Triad long enough to be used to knowing only what they deemed necessary, but it still bothered him that *Jess* didn't fully trust him.

It made him wonder why he stayed so long. Atikus and the Guard could certainly use his leadership and strong hands to rebuild. His *home* needed him. Yet here he was riding to some distant ocean town to investigate animal attacks that didn't smell right to a foreign ruler.

But she's a lot more than just some foreign ruler now, isn't she?
Dittler snorted.

Keelan reached down and patted the stallion's neck. "I know. It sounds ridiculous when I think it. Please don't make me say any more of it out loud."

Dittler looked back and whinnied.

Keelan slowed their trot as they entered town. Oliver was larger than he'd pictured in his mind. While scattered farmhouses dotted the landscape inland for leagues around, the town itself was composed of a variety of tightly packed wooden and stone structures. Well-maintained cobbled roads wove between them with little apparent pattern for traffic flow. Keelan knew from similar small towns in Melucia that village roads were often little more than the trails left by frequent visitors, merchants, and traders. Over time, and with years of wear, they became the arteries carrying the lifeblood of the place. This appeared to be the case with Oliver.

It was an hour or two past midday, and the sun was beginning his lazy descent over the ocean. Men and women in simple clothing moved about with purpose, most carrying goods or children in their heavily laden arms. As they passed each other, most smiled or nodded in greeting to their neighbors, and the sound of chatter and laughter echoed off the clustered building walls.

At first glance, Oliver was a bustling, thriving town with warm and friendly citizens, but as he watched life unfold before him, Keelan knew there was an undertone of something—a sense of loss and sadness—that seemed to drift on the ocean breeze as it wafted by. It was as clear to the Guardsman's keen senses as the salty tang on his tongue left by deep inhalations. Whether this undercurrent of grief was born from the mysterious death that had occurred two weeks earlier or from the war that had torn many families asunder, he couldn't be sure. It was probably some measure of each.

A man in a silky brown robe stopped as he strode past, looking up at the massive horse Keelan rode. "He's a beauty. Haven't seen a Cretian in years. I almost forgot how tall they are." The man whistled as his eyes traveled up Dittler's neck and met his eyes. The horse peered down, then snapped at the man's foolishly outstretched hand. Dittler whinnied and looked up at Keelan as the man snatched his hand back and clutched it against his chest.

Keelan smiled down. "He's a beauty, but not the friendliest beast you'll meet, especially not without a little bribe in your hand."

The man smiled weakly and nodded. "I hear you. If it's all the same, I'll leave the bribing to you."

Dittler snorted, drawing the man's now wide eyes.

"Yeah, he thinks he knows what we're saying, too. He's far too smart for his own good," Keelan joked.

Dittler turned and snorted at his impudent rider, who simply stroked his neck affectionately.

The robed man finally stopped gaping and cleared his throat. "I'm Seth. You look like you could use a break from riding. Been traveling long?"

"Keelan," he said with a head bob. "Just arrived from Fontaine."

When he didn't offer more, Seth asked, "I don't recall ever seeing a blue uniform like yours."

Keelan looked down at his dusty navy jacket. He'd forgotten he wore his uniform. "I'm a constable in the Saltstone Guard."

"Saltstone? Melucia's capital?"

"Yes. I came on behalf of our government to help repair the ties that were recently broken." The scripted and well-rehearsed line sailed off his tongue with barely a thought. Jess had insisted he offer only this explanation when asked why he was so far from home in what many still called *enemy territory*.

Seth was quiet a moment as he turned over Keelan's explanation. He finally smiled and looked up, apparently dismissing the oddity, at least for the moment. "Welcome. We're a friendly town, especially to those in need. I'm the local Priest. If this humble servant can help with anything, please ask."

This man was unlike most vicars he'd ever encountered. Keelan didn't sense anything false in his words but knew from painful experience not to trust men wearing silky brown robes. He decided to keep a wary eye on the man while in town.

"I *could* use some directions. The roads around here seem to follow their own whims. Can you point me to the local inn?"

Seth brightened. "There are two inns in town, but you'd probably prefer the Glory. The other inn is by the docks and tends to attract sailors and other less reputable sort of folks. I was actually headed there now. You're welcome to join me."

Keelan bobbed again. "Thank you, Priest Seth."

"Please, call me Seth."

Moments later, they stood before the entrance to the inn. Keelan eyed the two-story stone building with its stylized golden crown glittering above the door.

"Local story says the King stayed here and loved the place so much he allowed the owner to use the royal crest. People still talk about the court's visit, but nobody knows if the owner made up the last part or not. Either way, the Glory is nice and run by good people. You'll be comfortable here," Seth said as Keelan stared at the inn's signage.

A boy in his early teens startled the men, appearing from around the corner. "You checking in, mister? I'll stable your horse."

Dittler nipped at the boy's hand as his thin fingers reached for the bridle.

"If you'll lead the way, I'll take him back. He doesn't like most people. Some days, I'm not sure he likes me," Keelan said as he dismounted.

On cue, Dittler turned and snapped a Keelan's arm, earning a playful swat from his temporary master. "Enough of that. You behave."

Once Dittler was settled, Keelan and Seth entered the inn through the back to find an empty common room filled with the sounds and smells of an active kitchen a doorway away. Keelan's stomach made its presence known.

"Didn't eat much on the road?" Seth said with a smirk.

Keelan didn't want to like the Priest but couldn't help warming to his easy smile. "Just some dried meat in my pack. They told me this place serves good food, and I've been looking forward to it for days."

Before he could answer, a rotund older woman burst through the door, an empty pitcher in one hand and four beer mugs gripped by their handles in the other. Her head snapped up when she saw her guests.

"Oh, Seth. You're early today. I can't let our girl go for another few hours."

"It's alright, Ma. I'm just bringing you another guest: a constable from across the mountains who just arrived in town."

She set the pitcher down and gave Keelan her full attention, eyes widening at the mention of his homeland. She failed to hide her sudden unease. "Across the mountains, eh? What brings ya here?"

Keelan offered a shallow bow. "I'm here on a personal matter and need a room for a few nights."

Ma brightened at the sound of paying customer. "Of course. We can fix ya right up. You'll be wanting to wash the road off first thing. I'll have our boy bring you hot bath water. We just cleaned up the noon meal, but I can have some cuts and cheese brought up if you're hungry to tide ya over 'til dinner."

"You're right on both counts. I'm starving and"—he looked down at his dusty coat— "definitely need to wash the road off. Is there someone who could clean my uniform?"

Ma nodded. "Just leave it outside your door. Boy'll take it and bring it back clean before the day's out."

Keelan bowed again. "Thank you, ma'am."

"You hear that? He called me ma'am—and bowed *twice*!" Ma giggled and swatted at Seth. Through her laughter, she called over her shoulder as she left the room. "Wait one minute. I'll show you to your room."

Seth turned to Keelan. "I'll leave you to it, then. Hope your stay is peaceful and pleasant."

"Thank you." Keelan set his pack on the floor and nodded. "Before you leave, can I ask you about something?"

"Of course. How can I help?"

"How long have you lived here?"

"Oh, it's been a few months now. Feels like I've been here forever, though. The place really grows on you fast."

"Did you know a man named Hershel? Used to run this inn?"

Seth's face fell, and his eyes hardened. "Yes. I knew him."

Keelan held up a palm. "Forgive me. I know his passing was a tragedy. I'm here to learn what I can of how he died. The local constables' report was fairly vague, and the High Sheriff in Fontaine asked for another pair of eyes. He couldn't spare his own men, and I was about to climb the walls with boredom. So here I am."

Seth relaxed slightly, but his guard remained in place. "They say it was a bear attack. Awful thing. I didn't see his body afterwards, but folks who did said you wouldn't know it was Hershel unless you looked closely. His face—most of it had been ripped apart. If we didn't know an animal was to blame, I'd say someone who hated the man killed him with spite in their heart."

Keelan watched carefully. His Gift remained quiet, undisturbed. The Priest believed what he was saying and held nothing back.

"Thank you. I know it's hard to relive events such as this, but it's important we know what happened, to protect others from the same fate."

The stable boy appeared through the kitchen door and looked between Keelan and Seth, sensing a tension he hadn't felt before. Seth looked up slowly and nodded. "I'll leave you now, Guardsman. Good day."

A couple hours later, Keelan returned to the common room cleaned, fed, and somewhat rested. He'd exchanged his uniform for more comfortable civilian clothing, a muted-green tunic and dark tan trousers—something Jess had provided. The thought made him smile as he donned the shirt. He'd been away for only a few days and already he missed her. He hardly knew what to do with the foreign feeling.

He settled into a chair at a table near the hearth. The warmth of the newly stoked fire felt good against his back. A few other guests talked quietly at tables throughout the room, but most of the tables remained empty. That would change in a couple hours as the dinner rush began.

A girl of seventeen or eighteen winters with curly sandy-colored hair darted from one table to another. When she approached Keelan's table, she paused to catch her breath before speaking.

"Sorry for the wait. I'm Laurie. I'm the only one out here for now, so they've got me running. What can I get you to drink? Ale? Wine?"

"How about an ale and some water?"

She cocked her head when he spoke, nodded, and vanished to retrieve his order. A moment later, she reappeared with a mug in each hand, set them down with a heavy thud, and scurried to the table two rows away without even looking up.

Keelan sipped his ale. It was sweet with a touch of a citrus, unlike the tart beers he was used to back home—and there wasn't even a hint of the water he expected from most inns or alehouses. *This might be a good trip after all.*

The front doors clacked open, and he looked up to see a man with broad shoulders and a square jaw entering. The collar on his forest-green uniform cloak glittered, a common enough sight in Melucia, but a rarity in the Kingdom. The man stopped in the doorway and methodically surveyed the room, taking in each table's occupants before moving on to the next. When his eyes fell to Keelan, his scanning ceased, and he strode purposefully to stand before his table.

"Mind some company?"

Keelan's eyes found a piece of metal pinned to the man's inner coat, a crown over two small ships, their sails unfurled. He'd know a lawman's badge anywhere in the world. The symbols were different, but they *felt* the same. To Keelan, they felt like brotherhood.

He nodded and gestured with his mug. "Please, make yourself comfortable. Always happy to meet another constable."

The man smiled as he removed his cloak and sat. "That obvious? Guess it is to another lawman. It's the eyes, isn't it?"

Keelan shrugged and pointed. "I saw your badge."

The man's hand reached up and felt the pin. "Right. That'll do it, too." He chuckled. "I'm Chief Liam Kerr, head constable in town. It's a pleasure to meet the famous Keelan Rea."

Keelan's eyes widened. "Got all that from my eyes?"

"No, from a bird. Received word from Fontaine to expect you around this time. They told me to give you whatever assistance you needed, but to not ask too many questions."

Keelan relaxed and took another sip.

"So, what's this all about?"

Now it was Keelan's turn to laugh. "So much for no questions."

"Ever met a constable who could let a good mystery go? You're about the best mystery this sleepy little town's seen in a decade, and I've always been a curious lad."

The kinship Keelan felt when recognizing a fellow lawman deepened as the man spoke. His words were clear, his laugh deep, and everything he said rang true to Keelan's Gift. This truly was a brother in uniform.

"I'm honestly not sure what all the secrecy's about. I've been sent to see if there's more to the killing from a couple weeks ago than was in your report."

Liam's brows rose. "You mean the mauling? Why would they send someone to look into that? Poor man was torn to shreds just outside town. His whole body was covered in claw marks, at least what was left of it. I can't see anything other than a bear or some other wild animal causing that kind of damage."

"I was planning to come see you first thing in the morning, but since you're here, mind if I ask a few questions?"

"If I can have an ale while we do it, you can ask anything you want. Like I said, I'm under orders to help you however you need it," Liam said as he motioned Laurie over to the table. "The girl coming over here is Hershel's daughter. The round woman who'll bring out your meal is Ma, his wife. Best we not let either of them hear what we're talking about."

Keelan nodded and held his mug to his lips as Laurie chatted briefly with Liam, then hustled back to the bar.

Over the next few hours, Keelan and Liam reviewed every aspect of the investigation into Hershel's death. From the start, local constables had seen it as a clear-cut case of animal attack, though none could understand why a beast large enough to maul a big man like Hershel would be so far south and so far from any forested area. Liam couldn't recall a single bear sighting within fifty leagues of Oliver during his lifetime, and the next largest animals to wander nearby were wolves. They were dangerous enough in a pack, but wolves would eat what they killed, not tear it to shreds and vanish. That part didn't make sense, but the obvious nature of Hershel's death had quelled the constable's insatiable curiosity. The town would be on the lookout for a large beast, but everyone supposed such a wild creature would vanish as quickly as it had appeared.

Keelan sat quietly as Liam launched into his dinner of pot roast, a well-known winter special of the house that would soon be out of season. Virtually every table held the same hearty chunks of meat, dark sauce, and bowl of roasted potatoes. Keelan moved his own roast around his plate as he thought.

Hershel's murder, he thought as he sipped. *Nothing in the facts suggests a murder, merely a killing as the locals believe. It seems so obvious, yet my instincts are screaming there's something behind the mask.*

"I know that look. Had it often enough myself. What are you thinking?" Liam asked between bites.

Keelan sighed and set his mug down. "I don't know. Everything you said makes sense."

"But your gut's churning, and you don't know why?"

Keelan glanced up and nodded.

"Tell me about Hershel."

Liam set his fork down and looked around the room until he'd located Laurie and Ma. When he spoke, his voice was quiet.

"Hershel was a good man. Stubborn, strong-minded, loyal through and through. He and Ma bought this place twenty or so years ago. It wasn't anything until the royals blew into town. To hear Hershel tell it, the King kissed the floorboards and shat gold on the bar." He chuckled, but there was a sadness in his laughter.

"Was he well liked in town?"

"Liked? More loved than liked. He could be a surly bastard when something didn't go his way, but everyone knew to just let him cool down, and peace would be restored—usually at the business end of one of Ma's cooking spoons."

Liam sipped his wine and stared into the fire. To Keelan's eye, the man saw memories more than flames. Hershel was more than just another citizen to the Chief; he was a friend.

"Chief, I'm sorry. I know this is hard for everyone, especially those who were close with him."

Liam glanced up. "You don't have to do that, play the empathetic constable to get me to talk."

"I didn't mean—"

"Yes, you did. And you were right to, but it's unnecessary. I want the truth as much as anyone, but I'm afraid it's a simple one that won't give any of us satisfaction."

Laurie swung by and replaced their empty mugs with a pair filled to the brim. She seemed to sense the tenor of their conversation and slipped away without a word.

"Did Hershel have any enemies in town?"

Liam shook his head. "Not that I know of. He really was well liked. Oh, there's always one or two who don't like anybody, but they're that way with the lot of us, not just Hersh. I've been over this a thousand times in my head since he died, and I can't come up with one person who would've wished him harm, much less dead."

As the stable boy, who seemed to do far more than simply manage the stables, stoked the fire, a player took the stage. The room was now packed, every table filled, and two rows of standing patrons milled about the bar. With the first few notes of the gleeman's fiddle, the low murmur of the crowd swelled to a clamor in anticipation of the entertainment to come.

"Well, Chief, I thank you for your time—and company. Despite the topic, you've made a traveler feel at home tonight. If it's alright with you, I'll leave you here and start again in the morning." Keelan finished his ale with a long swallow and set his mug on the table.

Liam stood, gripped his arm, "The company was welcome. Get some rest. You look like you could use a good night's sleep."

Keelan started the next day with Chief Kerr, reviewing the written account made by officers who were first to arrive at the scene of Hershel's death. They were cursory and about what Keelan expected. Liam explained that unnatural deaths were rare, murders even more so. His constables might face one murder in a dozen years. With that lack of experience, Keelan thought it was a wonder the report contained more than "He was dead when we arrived."

The rest of the day was spent interviewing townsfolk. Each was friendly, respectful, and visibly despondent at the mention of Hershel's death. As Liam had told him, the man was well known and loved. No one could fathom a reason for foul play, and most expressed ongoing fear of the wild animal roaming free near their town. They spoke of early nights, shuttering their businesses before sunset for the first time in a generation, and few were willing to walk alone, even in broad daylight. The normally peaceful seaside town was now firmly in fear's grip.

But there was no talk of murder.

No one even gave that serious consideration. It was unthinkable, especially with a man like Hershel. It just couldn't have happened.

Something in their universal certitude made Keelan's neck itch. He knew it was an irrational reaction, but years of investigation had taught him to trust his instincts. He didn't know what it was, but he was missing something important.

He ran into Seth as he was making his way back to the inn around sunset. As the day before, the Priest offered a warm smile and gripped his arm firmly in greeting.

"It's good to see you again, Guardsman. Headed back to the inn?"

Keelan nodded. "It's been a long day and I hear tonight's dinner is roasted boar. I haven't had boar in years."

Seth grunted appreciatively. "And Ma knows her way around that kitchen. I was headed there myself, though the boar is welcome news."

Something tickled Keelan's senses and he eyed the Priest. "You visit the inn often?"

"Most days. It's a popular place around town, especially this time of year as Ma starts to run out of winter fare and move into the spring menu." His expression turned sheepish. "And Laurie is always there."

"Laurie?"

"She's . . . well . . . we've taken a few long walks together and . . . I don't know . . ."

"I didn't know holy men could have crushes on young women, much less court them." Seth's explanation rang true, and Keelan released the tension he hadn't realized he was holding in his shoulders.

"The Order doesn't teach celibacy like some faiths, thank the Spirits. I could even marry one day, should some woman be foolish enough to accept my offer."

Keelan mirrored Seth's smile as they reached the door to the inn. As promised, the common room was overflowing with townsfolk and the enticing aroma of well-seasoned meat. Festive music from a colorfully dressed pair on stage set the mood, and Laurie and two other serving girls raced from one table to the next.

"Join me for dinner?" Seth asked, noticing Keelan scanning the room for an open table. "Ma and Laurie have a table for me by the hearth, and I'd be glad for your company. I doubt I'll see Laurie much tonight."

They waded through the sea of tables to Seth's promised seats and settled in for the evening. As he took his first sip of the evening's spicy ale, Keelan was glad for the Priest's invitation and the fire's warmth.

Chapter Twenty-Seven

Jess

Jess strode into the throne room with High Chancellor Marks trailing a couple paces behind. He'd interrupted her breakfast with several urgent missives and news of one important, unexpected visitor seeking audience.

As she squirmed her way into a *somewhat* comfortable position on the throne, Marks unfurled a scroll the size of his thumb and began reading.

"Constables in Cooper are reporting a strange death that appears to be a wild animal attack. This time it was a dock foreman. I'll get this to the High Sheriff as soon as we finish this audience."

He rolled the scroll back up and shoved it in a pocket, then took the next scroll, then the next, and so on. Five messages later, he unfurled the final one and glanced up after reading it to himself. Jess was staring at the golden doors, lost in thought.

"Majesty, it appears Guardsman Rea left Oliver yesterday." The mention of Keelan caused her eyes to snap to his. "That puts him back in the capital tomorrow or the next day. The scroll doesn't say anything about his investigation."

"Did he say anything else?"

Marks couldn't hide the smile that curled the corners of his mouth. "No, Majesty. Just that he would be here soon. The scroll was actually written by the Chief Constable, not Guardsman Rea."

"Of course, it was," she huffed under her breath, just loud enough for Marks to hear. When he stifled a laugh, she shot daggers his direction.

"Sorry, Majesty. Very inconsiderate of him." His smirk widened to a grin.

"Don't you have somewhere to be? A message to deliver? A cliff to jump off?"

"I will find a cliff straightway, Majesty." The laugh finally escaped, and he offered an exaggerated bow. When he rose, his smile vanished, and his voice lowered. "Jess, please be wary of your next audience. The Order is growing in influence across the Kingdom, faster than I ever would've imagined. You've worked too hard building a solid reputation and good will to see a battle with the clergy do you harm. Most of their Priests are actually doing good work for people who need it. We may have ears in every corner, but they have wagging tongues and powerful voices."

She considered his words and nodded once. As Marks disappeared through the massive double doors, the royal page entered.

"Ambassador Wilfred, Majesty." The page bowed toward the throne and waited for her reply.

"Great," she muttered. "Send him in."

Danym strode slowly down the center of the room, his eyes locking onto Jess's and never wavering. She thought he looked a little too satisfied with himself and regretted holding this audience without Marks by her side to offer words of calming wisdom—or to just hold her back. She wanted nothing more than to strangle the life out of her guest.

He stopped a few paces from the dais and bowed. "Majesty, thank you for seeing me."

Marks's words echoed in her head, and she resisted the urge to spit curses at the man who'd betrayed her only a few months earlier. She stood and slowly stepped down from the dais to the Council table.

"Please, join me for some tea. It's been a long morning already, and my back can't take sitting on the throne one moment longer."

If he was surprised by her cordial offer, Danym didn't show it. He simply nodded once and stepped toward the table.

The same guards who *ushered* Danym out following his last audience stepped forward, taking up positions on either side of the seat Jess indicated Danym should occupy. Rather than sitting at the table's head where they would be close, she took a seat on the opposite side of the table.

A servant materialized from the darkness in the corner and filled two cups. Jess raised hers and quickly took a long sip. Danym's brow rose, but he remained silent.

"What does the Order seek of the Crown today?" she asked.

He lowered his gaze and spoke in softened tones. "I am only pleased to be in Her Majesty's presence once again. I've missed our chats, especially those in the forest at night."

The swirling ceased as her grip on the cup tightened. She had to set it down to keep from spilling her tea. When she looked up, the intensity of her gaze made him flinch.

"Just tell me why you're here so we can be done with this."

He actually had the good grace to look hurt. "Jess—"

"Don't *ever* use my name again. Address me as *Your Majesty* or not at all," she snapped, immediately regretting the venom in her tone. Marks was right. She had to control herself.

"I'm sorry. It's been a long day," she said.

His eyes fixed on a knot in the table's rich wood. "No, I'm sorry, Your Majesty. It won't happen again."

Silence loomed as they each stared pointedly at something, anything, that wasn't the other person. They might've been sitting across the whole country, not simply the table, in that moment. When one of the guards reached down to scratch an itch, the squeal of his armor scraping against itself turned Jess's gaze back to Danym.

"Where did you go? After—"

"The Temple."

"You mean you were there? When Justin—"

Danym's head snapped up. "No. I was in the Temple, but not the chamber. I didn't know your brother was there, or what they had planned."

"And when I was there? When they dragged me down that aisle?"

His head lowered again. "Yes."

"Yes, what?" Her voice was now hardened ice. "Yes, you were in the chamber when they were going to kill me? You were actually there?"

He didn't speak or look up for a long moment.

"Jess—I mean Your Majesty—I was under *her* Compulsion."

"When you wooed me? When you asked me to trust you? When you promised to start a life together? Or when you stood by and watched my own mother drug me and try to take my life?"

He looked up. His eyes pleaded in a way she hadn't seen since that first night they fled the capital. "I felt her Call after that night in the inn, the one with the old couple by the fire. Not before. *Never* before."

She thought his eyes glistened in the light of the table's candles. His lips quivered. Her mind raced almost as quickly as her heart. This was the man she'd loved more than any other, the one she'd pledged to abdicate her throne for. She'd been willing to give up the whole Kingdom for him.

Now, she was ready to have him executed the moment he stepped one foot wrong—yet he claimed his actions had not been his own.

It made sense. He'd loved her. She knew it. And she wanted desperately to believe him, to believe he'd never intentionally betrayed her. She *wanted* to believe.

He reached a hand across the table toward hers, but she pulled back as their fingers brushed. She clutched her hand to her chest and stared down at his empty embrace.

"No," she whispered. "We can't go back to what we had. Even if your actions weren't your own, I'll always be haunted by the betrayal in your eyes. I still dream about that mask you wore, that mask you looked through as you *laughed* at my terror. How could I ever see beyond that?"

The tear finally fell and trickled down his cheek. He reclaimed his hand and slowly nodded.

"I understand," was all his frail voice could muster.

She took another sip, desperate for strength and courage.

"Why do you still wear those robes? If her Compulsion died with her, why stay with those awful people?"

His eyes became distant, his voice again a whisper. "Where else could I go? At least in these robes I can try to help people, do some good with whatever life I have left. I lost the only thing that mattered. What do I have left?"

She couldn't listen anymore and stood suddenly. "I'm tired. Return to the palace tomorrow and we'll discuss whatever your Order seeks us to consider." She wheeled from the table, flanked by the two guards, and vanished out the side door, leaving Danym alone in the massive chamber.

Jess barely slept that night. Memories of Danym flooded her mind, and she couldn't find the magic to banish them. In her dreams, he smiled up at her as she rode Dittler through town, freshly splattered mud dripping from his hair. Then he lifted a pastry to her lips, eyes twinkling in the midnight moonlight. He gripped her hand from across a rough wooden table, adoration flowing beside sparks of flame through his skin into hers.

And then he wore a mask. *That* mask. His eyes held amused loathing, no longer twinkling with anything but cruelty and spite.

Unable to bear the dreams any longer, she rose and strode, bleary-eyed and grumpy, into the family dining room two hours earlier than her usual post-sunrise waking. Steaming platters of eggs and bacon awaited. The servants always knew *exactly* when she would appear and ensured she never waited for a meal. If she'd been more awake, it would've amazed her, made her smile.

She might even have said something to one of the invisible, uniformed purveyors of domestic magic.

One of her maids entered as she finished her meal. A short gasp was followed by cold hands gently gripping her shoulders.

"Majesty, please, come back to your chamber so I can do something with your hair before the Council arrives."

There was pleading in the maid's voice. *It must be bad*, Jess thought. She tried to run her fingers through and surrendered to the maid when they became stuck. She grunted with a last bite of bacon and nodded with a half-smile.

An hour later, she sat erect on her throne and greeted each member of Council as they entered the chamber. The domestic magicians had struck again, as her hair was as perfectly silky as her gown. All she could think about was her pillow.

By noon, the Council had beaten every dead horse from Fontaine to the mountains. They'd reviewed troop levels following the latest round of recruitment, discussed talks of renewed trade with partner nations, including Melucia, and even debated opening talks with the more primitive island nations to the south, hoping to increase the flow of goods.

Jess never spoke. Counselors looked to her for opinions or guidance, but she simply nodded and shifted her gaze to Chancellor Marks, a look he understood was his cue to make a decision and move the agenda forward.

Marks was about to call the session to a halt when the royal page rapped twice on the door, indicating the Queen had a high-ranking visitor outside. The page entered and called out, "Holy Voice Danym Wilfred of the Order."

Jess cringed. Every member of Council turned to her with astonished eyes. They'd heard rumor of the dead High Sheriff's son making a surprise appearance, but none had the temerity to believe its veracity. Yet here he was, begging audience with their Queen.

She looked to Marks and nodded once. He turned to the page. "Show him in, please."

No one stood as Danym entered. It violated protocol and custom, even simple good manners, but the Queen remained firmly seated, so her Council followed suit.

For his part, Danym looked as unkempt as Jess felt. His normally well-bushed hair tangled rather than hung to his shoulders. Its shine was somehow dull. His eyes carried bags she'd never noticed before, and his shoulders slumped in contrast to the proud posture he regularly displayed.

Good. At least I wasn't the only one to lose sleep, Jess thought. A twinge of something passed through her as she watched him enter. Despite everything, part of her wanted to comfort him, to rush forward, grip his arm, and help him into the room. She shook off that silliness and steeled her expression.

He stopped on the golden mark inlaid in the marble floor, bowed toward the Queen, and waited.

Marks spoke coldly. "Voice, to what purpose do you interrupt a session of Council with Her Majesty?"

Danym rose. The ice in Marks's voice somehow gave him strength, and his eyes hardened. He ignored Marks and looked directly at Jess.

"I came hoping you had considered the One's offer. It's been nearly a week, and he grows impatient for your reply. I fear, without this marriage, the Kingdom may experience . . . *difficulties* . . . that could otherwise be avoided."

Jess's brows rose, as did the heat coursing through her veins.

"Are you threatening the Queen?" Marks asked.

Danym shook his head slowly. "Only advising, as is my duty to the Crown."

Other Counselors began to speak, to ask questions, to raise voices. Jess silenced them with a raised palm. She stood and walked a pace from the table.

"What sort of *difficulties*? Please, advise us."

Danym tried to straighten, to stand taller, but was cowed by her imperious gaze. She was indeed her father's daughter.

"Your Majesty's people suffered great loss following the folly beyond the mountains. Husbands, sons, fathers—so many were lost. Our Priests minister to the needs of *our* people. They understand the value of faith in a time of sadness and grief. They seek shelter in our arms when the Crown's own embrace is lacking. The One fears *our* people's reaction should the Crown reject the faith's honest offer of alliance and friendship."

Jess balled her fists tightly and forced herself to breathe slowly and deeply. Not only had he threatened the Crown with possible unrest, but his continual use of *our people* also claimed *her* subjects were shared by his One. Everything he said was an affront to her, her family, her crown, and her Kingdom. She knew Marks had been right to advise caution and a level head, but she couldn't let this weasel spew such filth, not in *her* palace, before *her* Council.

"You think I actually considered marrying *you*? Or marrying your faith? Or whatever insanity you were proposing? Does your One think I've completely lost my mind?"

As she marched forward, unseen guards reacted, encircling Danym with pikes at the ready. Jess pointed with one accusing finger and spoke with the wrath of a royal.

"Tell your *master* the answer is still *no* and will *always* be no. I won't marry a dog on a leash, even if that leash is made of gold." She sucked in a breath and glanced apologetically toward Marks before returning her eyes to Danym. "And don't bother returning to the palace—*ever*. I, Jessia Vester, Queen of the

Spires, hereby sever all formal relations with the Order, and therefore expel the Order's representative to the Crown from the capital."

She waited a moment to gauge Danym's reaction. When shock appeared, she continued. "There will be no formal recognition of your Order. Your Priests may continue caring for those in need but will share *your* banishment if we receive one whiff of rebellious talk."

She turned and nodded to Marks.

"We're done here. Let's resume tomorrow. Guards, get *that man* out of my palace. Send two men to escort him to the city's border once he's gathered whatever belongings he might need. If he resists, send his head to the One as a token of our love and affection."

Then she marched out the door to the royal residence.

Part V

Chapter Twenty-Eight

Declan

Atikus braced himself against the rim of the Well as Declan pushed him up and out of its opening. The Mage sprawled across the floor and lay there as his adopted son bound up beside him.

"Atikus, are you alright?"

"Fine," his muffled voice bounced off the glassy surface of the cave's floor. "Can we not do that again—*ever*?"

A chuckle replaced concern as Declan gripped the man's arm to help him stand.

"We may need to make one more trip to get you back home, unless you'd prefer to take the Gate and walk all the way from the mountains to Saltstone."

Atikus wobbled and sat on the crystalline bench across from the Well. "I might prefer a few weeks of walking to riding that river of death again. How is your head not—?"

His last word trailed off as his eyes took in the cavern for the first time.

"What? You alright?" Declan asked.

Atikus spoke in awed tones. "For hundreds of years, I kept the secret of the Well. Velius and I spent hours privately guessing what the hallowed mountain might look like, how magic in the air might feel, at what wonders were hidden and would never be revealed to anyone beyond its Keeper." He sighed deeply at memories of his old friend. "When you returned from your first journey here, describing the cave with a boyish gleam in your eyes, I never dreamed *I* would gaze at the majesty of the Well. You've helped me live a dream, son."

He stood on shaky legs and braced himself against Declan's shoulder with one hand. His head turned slowly—very slowly—as he took in every crystal and crevice, every shade and shadow, with widened eyes.

Declan gripped the old man's hand in his own and watched as he surveyed the cavern. He spoke in hushed tones.

"I was pretty blown away the first time, too. Look down."

Atikus did and took a reflexive step back as azure mist curled upward toward its glassy ceiling, winding toward Atikus's feet. Once he realized it was harmless, he kneeled and placed a hand on the floor. The mist responded immediately, hungrily racing to mirror his bony fingers and palm.

Atikus erupted in a childlike laugh, and tears of pure joy began streaming down his cheeks.

"Oh, that's not it. Come over here," Declan said, hooking the Mage under his elbow to help him stand. He walked him to the opening that was the Well of Magic, where mist wafted upward, unabated by stone or crystal or glass. It seemed to sense Atikus's approach and warmly greeted him, enveloping his entire being in glowing, writhing fog.

Atikus's laughter echoed loudly throughout the chamber, and Declan's heart soared. He couldn't wipe the goofy grin from his face, so he swatted rebellious curls out of his eyes—an old childhood tick.

"Declan, I'm rarely speechless, but this—" He choked on a happy sob that wracked his chest.

Declan beamed as he witnessed the wonder in the old Mage's eyes. "I know. I get chills every time I come in here, especially when the currents greet me."

Atikus kneeled and extended a hand toward the opening, toward the gently rushing magic that flowed beneath.

"Oh, no. That's one thing you cannot do. Kelså says the currents will overwhelm and consume you."

"Then how did you Travel in them? How did you bring *me* here?"

"I honestly don't know. Heir of Magic thing, I guess." He shrugged. "The first time, I felt like I'd been dragged behind a horse for hours, though I never felt any pain. Órla said I would always be safe in the currents."

"Órla?" Atikus's head snapped up. "Didn't she—"

"Yes, she sacrificed herself, but her Spirit returned to the Well as it always does." He saw a confused look cross Atikus's face. "Atikus, she isn't just a manifestation of magic, as we thought. She *is* magic's essence and cannot die. She will be reborn one day in a new form."

"Sweet Spirits."

"For now, she speaks through the currents. You couldn't hear us talking?"

"I was more focused on staying in one piece than listening to you babbling into the void. Yours was the only voice I heard."

Declan leaned closer to the Mage. "Your eyes didn't change like mine did. That's weird."

"I may be the most knowledgeable Mage alive, but I feel like a new acolyte around you—and *all this*."

"Second most knowledgeable," a warm female echoed said from behind.

Atikus wheeled around. His eyes widened and smile broadened as Kelså strode toward them.

"Kelså?" the astonished Mage exclaimed as he struggled forward on unsteady legs. "It's been decades—no, centuries. You haven't aged a day!"

"And you still remember how to flatter a woman, you silver-tongued Mage." Kelså reached them and wrapped her arms around her old friend. She peered over his shoulder and winked at Declan, then gaped at his eyes.

"Declan, *your eyes*—"

"I know, but it's alright. Órla warned there would be changes when I entered the currents. She doesn't know if this is permanent or not, or if there will be other side effects later on. Nothing else changed—at least that I can tell—other than people's reaction back home."

She released Atikus and stepped past him toward her son, concern creasing her brow. "What do you mean, *people's reaction*? Last I heard you were being hailed as a hero pretty much everywhere you walked."

He shrugged and his eyes fell. "They act scared of me, like I'm going to attack them with my eyes or something. I don't know, Mom. Even the kids wouldn't come close. They either ran or hid behind their parents." His eyes strayed to meet hers, then shied away. He muttered, "Guess I'm alone again—"

Kelså closed the gap between them faster than he could've imagined her moving. Her palms cupped his cheeks and pulled his eyes to hers. "Declan Rea, you are *never* alone. You hear me? *Never*."

He stared into her loving eyes, lost himself in his mother's ideal of him reflected through her vision. She saw something he couldn't fathom, someone he didn't recognize. How could anyone believe in someone with such reckless abandon? He wished some small measure of her confidence in him would take root in his own heart and grow—but he knew it was likely too late for that, especially with magic literally seeping out of his eyes every time he opened them.

Now utterly self-conscious under her maternal gaze, he said, "For whatever reason, Atikus was unaffected by his trip along the currents."

Kelså gave him a look he couldn't interpret but said nothing, turning back as Atikus coughed.

"Unaffected? I can barely walk after bouncing from the continent to this island!"

Declan snorted, relieved the spotlight shone elsewhere. "I meant magically. We can't help that you're old and frail."

"Hey!" Atikus slapped Declan playfully on the arm. "I'm *distinguished*. And hungry, now that we're talking about our feelings."

"Of course, you are." Declan rolled his eyes.

"You boys come with me. I can take care of your stomachs while we talk about fixing Atikus's magic. As much as I would love to just catch up, Órla's warning has me worried we don't have time to waste."

Days passed, and nothing worked to restore Atikus's magical connection. They tried Healing, then Healing combined with Air, hoping Declan could somehow *breathe* life back into his Gift. It had seemed a silly idea at the time, but Kelså swore she remembered something akin to it working to Heal another Mage many years before. They were growing desperate, and Kelså's wild guess theory failed as all previous attempts had.

On their fifth morning together, Atikus, Declan, and Kelså sat around the table on the landing overlooking the standing stone circles. Each held a glass of restorative wine and a full belly. Atikus peppered Kelså and Declan with questions throughout their meal, eager to learn everything he could about the mountain and its mystical Well. Kelså took it in stride, joking the Mage asked more questions than a three-year-old but reveling in his enthusiasm and curiosity.

As they transitioned from lunch to wine on the ridge, the conversation turned to possible treatments to restore Atikus's connection to magic. Kelså was disappointed the trip within the currents had done nothing to aid him and was surprised when Atikus described feeling none of the tingling sensation that practically assaulted Declan as he Traveled. His lack of sensation, along with his inability to sense Órla's presence or hear her voice, underscored to her how complete his separation from magic truly was.

"I was afraid to let go of him while we Traveled," Declan explained. "Maybe he needs to be exposed to the currents without me protecting him with my touch."

Kelså shook her head firmly. "No, let's not try that. Putting him into the currents without you would likely kill him—or sear his consciousness so he'd lose all sense of identity or self. You are the only person in my thousand years of life who has touched the currents and lived. Let's save that for a last resort."

"What if I Called to his Spirit, like a Summoning, but inside?"

"Now that's just plain creepy, and I've lived long enough to see many things to make your skin crawl," Atikus said.

"You might be onto something, as *creepy* as it may sound." Kelså grinned at Atikus, then became serious. "But you'd have to be very careful. Interaction with a living being's Spirit is dangerous, and not just to them. The will of a Spirit is a fickle thing, and Atikus might not be able to control what it does."

"What are you talking about? It's *my* Spirit. Why wouldn't I be able to control it? Wouldn't its will and my own be the same?"

"Yes, it is *your* Spirit, as long as it's within you, but if Declan connected with it, there would be a path it could take through his consciousness to escape the bonds of your mortal body. In essence, Declan could be a conduit to allow your Spirit to become fully sentient in itself and then be loosed on the world to do who knows what. You know how dangerous freed Spirits are. That's why we're so cautions when constructing Summoning Circles. Think of it as a conscience-free Atikus in Spirit form roaming the land."

"Sounds like another Spirit I met recently, except *without* my sparkling personality." Atikus said sourly.

Kelså ignored his attempt at humor. "Exactly. Irina's Spirit maintains her personality and some of her will, but now lusts for vengeance on its own. The woman I knew would never kill innocents indiscriminately."

"The woman you knew was entombed for a very long time. I expect that dark prison changed her, even in Spirit form," Atikus said.

Declan cleared his throat. "We're wandering. Back to helping Atikus. I don't like the Spirit interaction idea anymore. Let's shelve that for now. What else?"

And so the evening went, each idea more audacious than the last, and each being added to a very large and growing shelf of unpopular suggestions. When night's darkness fell and the stars' light guided their vision, they were nowhere closer to an actionable plan than before.

Kelså stood and downed the last of the wine in her glass. "Let's get some sleep and start fresh in the morning. I don't think my mind can take any more tonight."

The next day, the trio sat eating a hearty breakfast and chatting about recent events on the continent. Kelså soaked in every bit of news about Keelan and the goings-on in her homeland. As Atikus reached across to fill his plate for the third time, a voice, clear and commanding, boomed throughout the mountain. It sounded—no, *felt*—like the mountain itself was speaking.

Órla's voice was filled with urgency. "KELSÅ! Someone has made it past the hut, past the wards. Hatred and anger burn in her wake. She is almost at the Well!"

"What in the void—" Declan started, but cut off as his tunic flared with brilliance, the Phoenix practically leaping from his chest.

Kelså shot to her feet and squinted. "Declan, come with me. If someone is powerful enough the pass the wards, I may need your strength to protect the Well."

Declan rose, and Atikus moved to follow, but Kelså looked to the Mage. "Atikus, stay here. If we get into trouble, you're the only one left who can go for help."

The old Mage started to protest but relented with a nod as they raced out of the room.

Declan charged after his mother through the winding corridors of the mountain. The crystals embedded in the walls, normally glowing with gentle light, now pulsed brightly, as if angered by the intruder. As he skidded to a stop in the entrance to the Well's chamber, Declan was stunned to see its crystalline walls and ceiling pulsing even more brightly than the hallways had. The lazy river beneath its glassy surface roiled and raged, white caps pluming atop its cerulean waves. He thought it felt almost like the currents begged for escape, for the opportunity to join in whatever fight was to come.

Kelså darted toward the platform containing the Well's opening and panted as she stood a few paces from the billowing mist that gushed forth. Declan raced to join his mother. The hairs on his arms and neck snapped to attention, and his skin pimpled at magic's touch. His tunic's glow became urgent, insistent, almost painful to look upon.

And that's when Kelså saw the intruder in the entrance opposite.

"Larinda?" Kelså asked, dumbfounded. "How did you get in here . . . or even know of this place?"

The old woman strode forward without a hint of the ailing joints Declan knew plagued her. Her chin was high, eyes bright, but it was her smile Declan noticed above all else.

"It's not Larinda," he whispered to Kelså.

The woman waved a hand in the air while continuing her trek forward. "Listen to the boy, Kelså; he's brighter than he appears." She cackled at her own double entendre.

Kelså instinctively called to her Light, and the mist surrounding the Well poured into her mouth and nose, drawing itself into her. Her skin began to glow, and her eyes blazed with the light of the sun. With a thought, she erected a shell of swirling air around the Well to guard against whatever evil the inhabiting Spirit might attempt. Declan gaped, having never seen the strength of his mother's magic.

Larinda cackled again, more amused than concerned by the Keeper's display of power. She waved her hand once more and shattered Kelså's shield without so much as a grimace. Sparks of spent magical energy exploded throughout the room, forcing Declan and Kelså to throw up shields of air to protect their faces from the blast. When they lowered their arms, the woman who was no longer Larinda stood only a few paces away, raging fire blazing in each palm.

"Boy, I was using magic long before you were born. Don't waste my time. I've waited a very long time to *deal* with your mother, and your pathetic magic isn't going to stop me."

Without warning, she flung both palms forward, and the fire flew forth, one blaze aimed at each of them. Declan threw out his arms and pulled moisture from the air in the cavern. Discs of water the size of his head appeared before his outstretched hands, flew forward, and doused the balls of flame.

Then Kelså threw her head back and cried out, "Eveth erna fertu!" A dozen glowing crystals broke free from the wall to Larinda's left and hurtled toward her. The ancient woman ducked and threw up a bony hand in one motion. A shock wave of air and energy pulsed from her raised fist, blasting Kelså's missiles away to shatter against the walls of the cavern.

Again, Kelså didn't hesitate. With Larinda distracted by deflecting the crystals, she drew more mist into her chest and formed balls of pure azure magic in each palm, similar to the fire Larinda had thrown before. She hurled one ball, arcing it high in the air toward Larinda, while sending the second in a blazing streak directly toward the woman's chest.

Larinda managed a quick shield, absorbing the missile headed for her torso, but the second attack landed a half-pace from where she stood. The soundless eruption lit up the cavern with a kaleidoscope of colors and brilliance, forcing Declan to shield his eyes with his arm. Sparks of shimmering magic flew in every direction, and Larinda screamed as the force battered her body and mind. The attack bore no heat, but its strength weakened the connection to her own magical core.

Sensing an opening, Declan reformed his shield, this time drawing both air and water. He stepped forward, shield wall extended two paces before him. Another step, then another. Larinda's eyes widened, and she took an instinctive step backward. Declan threw his arms forward again, hurling his shield into her. The impact of hardened water and air slammed into the aged, frail body she now inhabited, sending Larinda's form flying backward and into the crystalline wall. Blood streamed from a gash on her forehead, and more flowed from another on wound on the back of her skull. The inhabiting Spirit didn't feel disorientation as Larinda would have felt from such a blow, but the body of her servant was slow to rise on unsteady legs.

With moisture and heat nearly exhausted within cavern, the temperature plummeted, and thick clouds billowed each time they breathed. Kelså began to shiver as she screamed a warning to her son.

Declan lunged forward and drove a fist into Larinda's sternum, doubling the old woman over. He gripped her by her hair and pulled her head upward, readying another blow, but Larinda was faster. Her bony fingers bent, and hardened knuckles thrust upward into his neck. He gagged and gripped his throat, straining for air as he staggered backward.

"Irina?" Realization dawned on Kelså as her teeth began to chatter. Her eyes widened in recognition.

The woman's head snapped unnaturally toward her, then cocked to one side. "Took you long enough, *witch*. It's only been a millennium since you stripped me of my power and cast me aside—you and your *family of Mages*." She spat the last words as if they tasted bitter on her tongue.

"Irina, I wasn't even there when the last battle occurred—or when your parents—"

"Enough!" Irina screamed. "I will reclaim my power and send you where you belong: into the void."

A wave of Compulsion slammed into Kelså, nearly knocking her backward. Declan's tunic resisted the spell, but Kelså's eyes glazed, and her body relaxed.

"Cast him into the Well." Irina commanded.

Without hesitation, Kelså stepped forward and gripped Declan by both shoulders. Startled, he began turning, but she pulled with all her strength. His feet had been well set, shoulder width apart, in anticipation of Irina's next attack, but he hadn't expected the assault to come from behind—*from his mother*—and he staggered into her embrace.

"Mother!"

Kelså couldn't hear him through the incessant muttering of Irina's magic in her mind. She yanked backwards and dragged her son toward the Well's opening. He threw an arm behind but couldn't dislodge her grip.

Irina, seizing the moment, flew onto the platform and punched Declan's chest with her Enhanced Strength. His tunic blazed at her touch, and her hands came away scorched. She screamed in agony and staggered back, gaping at her angry red palms.

But her unexpected shove had been enough.

Kelså tripped over her own feet and, still gripping Declan's shoulders as Irina had commanded, tumbled backwards. Declan cried out but was helpless to stop their momentum. Kelså's grip vanished as she reached the current. He threw his arms out, reaching for the edge of the Well, but its glassy surface slipped from his fingers.

A thunderous clap rang through the chamber as the Keeper and Heir vanished beneath the raging river of magic.

Irina looked around her to find the mist moving faster, glowing brighter. She took a step toward the Well then froze, head cocked to the side.

The chamber fell silent as the world paused.

Then the mountain began to tremble.

The pulsing of light inside the crystalline cavern raced faster and faster as pieces of lattice began falling from the ceiling onto the gleaming floor. A scraping sound roared from somewhere deep beneath the well, and tremors grew as the mountain woke.

Irina stood before the Well and stared into its angry waters, oblivious to the chaos erupting around her. She muttered rapidly in the guttural language of Mages, a whisper that grew into a cacophonous shout, her head bent backward so she screamed the final words of her wicked incantation.

With her spell's final words, the scraping sound grew to a roar that echoed through the chamber. It sounded as if the whole world were being broken apart. Irina looked down in wonder and fear as a fracture appeared in the floor, and mist began seeping through the rend. It started at the base of the Well and clawed its way across to the far entrance of the cavern, dividing the room in two and allowing the river of power to swell and spill onto its unmarred surface. Everywhere the currents touched, mist sizzled and snapped. In its wake, plumes of dark vapor clawed against the pure blue fog, infecting it with its malice, turning it from glowing life into something dark and foul.

Near panic gripped Irina as she watched the brilliant cavern descend into darkness, yet she managed to calm herself enough to picture *home* in her mind, her small house in the Kingdom where her father and mother had raised her, had loved her—*and where they had died*.

With that thought, she vanished.

Atikus reached the entrance to the cavern as Larinda vanished, and the Well was cast fully into night.

Chapter Twenty-Nine

Danym

Danym's knees ached. His back ached. He knew his legs would ache if Thorn ever let him stand again. He'd been kneeling before his master for over an hour, only allowed to look up when answering a question. He'd never seen Thorn so angry.

"Do you honestly believe you had *any* other use to me? Or had you deluded yourself into thinking your brilliant wit could actually serve some purpose to my cause?" Thorn's words dripped with contempt as he stared down from his ivory throne.

"Master—"

"Shut up, Danym. That wasn't a question. Even *you* should understand sarcasm when you hear it." Thorn stood. "You had only *one* mission, and you failed. What more could possibly be said?"

"Excellency, forgive me. Jess—I mean the Queen—wouldn't be moved. I managed to get a private audience with her, to get her thinking about our time together before—"

"I don't care!" Thorn shouted, emphasizing each word. "You *failed* me, and now you—and any other representative I might wish to install—are banished from the capital. I can't begin to calculate the harm you've caused. I should get my staff and Turn you here and now. At least then you *might* be of some use."

"Master, no—"

"Stop it, Danym. Just stop groveling. You've destroyed months of work. I can't allow your incompetence to threaten our mission any longer."

"But Excellency—"

Danym's words cut off as Thorn absently waved a hand and bright flame enveloped the younger man. He writhed and screamed until the fire's hunger had stilled his voice; all that remained was the charred ruins of a Priest and his robe.

Moments later, a lanky Priest entered. His loose-fitting robes flowed behind him as he strode the length of the chamber. He wriggled his nose and covered it with a sleeve as he snaked around the charred corpse that lay before the dais. Then he knelt and remained cowed until Thorn bade him rise.

"Efrem, our plans for the Queen have failed. *Danym* failed. If I can't have her join us, I need her out of the way. Unless I miss my mark, that child brother of hers should be much easier to handle. He's simple and gullible and has no ill memories of the man I was at court, unlike our current monarch."

Efrem's expression never wavered, his eyes never blinked. He simply stared and listened. *The perfect Priest*, Thorn thought.

"Do you have a preference as to method, Excellency?"

Thorn steepled his fingers and thought a moment. "No, do what you must—but whatever you do *must not* be traced back to the Order. Understood?

"Yes, Excellency. Your will be done."

As Efrem vanished through the towering golden doors, Thorn removed the crown and cradled it in his hands. He traced a finger along its interwoven gold and silver, landing on one of the diamonds inlaid in its base. The bloodred pulse echoed through every facet of the stone, drawing him into its fearsome beauty. He wondered what the imprisoned Spirit must think. Could he or she see or hear what went on before them? Could they even still think? Their power pulsed through the relic and into him when he called, yet he knew nothing of the individuals trapped within.

And he really didn't care to. It was more curiosity than anything. Like his Priests, they were tools, weapons to be wielded for his greater cause. And like Danym, when they failed or served no further purpose, they were dead to him.

He sat staring into the stones for long moments, lost in thoughts and plans for a world beneath his banner. For the briefest moment, as Jess's face passed through his mental vision, a twinge of regret pricked his soul. He shrugged it off as quickly as it had arisen and chuckled at his own foolish sentimentality.

Chapter Thirty

Atikus

Atikus gaped into the darkness of the Well's chamber. What had been the most beautiful, vibrant sight the old man had ever seen was now utterly devoid of light or life. Even the residual glow of the crystals along the hallway through which he'd raced as the mountain shook had begun to dim. His head swiveled, searching for any speck of light or trace of Kelså or Declan.

"Declan? Kelså?" he cried over and over, stumbling into the darkened cavern. The only answer was his own voice echoing through the mountain's heart.

As he nudged his way forward, his foot caught on something jagged that shouldn't exist where he knew smooth, transparent flooring should have rested. He knelt and felt carefully with his fingers. Sharp edges scored a line across one bony digit, and unseen blood trickled into the chamber's gaping wound.

"Damned darkness," he muttered, wishing for light to see how deeply he'd cut his finger.

A ball of swirling, pulsing light bloomed before him, lighting the chamber in a dim, flickering glow similar to that of a dwindling torch.

"Sweet Spirits, how—"

He looked down at the massive crack in the floor, and horror entered his eyes. The currents of magic he recalled drifting lazily beneath, with their gentle mist warmly reaching upward, now oozed like sludge, bubbling and hissing as they passed beneath the crack. It was as if water had been turned to syrup or oil—or some wretched combination of the two. A foul scent of *wrongness* prickled his nose, and he smothered a cough in the crook of his elbow.

The glowing orb waited patiently a few paces before him. When he moved to inspect the Well's platform, it knew his intent and led the way, casting its eerie light some twenty paces in every direction. He wished for brighter light, and the ball blazed brilliantly.

"How—"

The rational scholar seized control and began testing the insane theory that flooded his mind. First, he held out his palm and thought of ice. An instant later, the air around him *warmed*, and a ball of pure, frozen water formed in his palm. He'd pulled the heat from the surrounding air, combined it with moisture, and frozen it, all with a simple thought.

That's not possible.

He tossed the ice aside and held out his palm again, this time thinking of fire. The surrounding air cooled, and sapphire flame erupted and hovered above his hand.

His stomach offered an involuntary grumble, and he pictured the platter of bacon still sitting on the kitchen table. Less than a blink later, the blaze was replaced by the platter of fried pork. Atikus gasped and stumbled backward, dropping the platter to shatter and scatter across the floor.

"I wish Pel could see this," he said without thinking, closing his eyes and pinching the bridge of his nose with gnarled fingertips.

"Atikus?"

The Mage's eyes flew open, and he found himself standing above Mage Pel's bed, the bleary-eyed man staring up at him, confused by his mentor's arrival and the blazing ball of light hovering far too brightly above his head.

Kelså opened her mouth to scream as bolts of terror traveled up her spine, but the mist, now thick with a dark residue permeating its natural blue brilliance, raced into her lungs. The mist had never inhibited her breathing. In fact, throughout her centuries tending the Well, it had only ever given her strength and confidence. She was connected to the currents on a spiritual level—at least, she had been before the infernal infection flooded magic's arteries. Now, she felt her chest heave painfully with each breath.

She spun her head, searching for Declan's face. Their hands remained tightly clasped. The currents churned, tossing them feet over head again and again, threatening to break them loose. She felt Declan squeeze tighter.

Waves of heat and angry power battered her body and mind; her Light, normally her peaceful core, felt like a dagger's tip digging deeper and deeper.

"Don't let go of my hand, no matter what!" Declan cried in her mind. *"We just have to hang on until we reach the opening at the Guild. Hold on!"*

Their bodies spun as if tossed by angry waves. The light in the flow was dimming as darkness began winning its battle over Light. Declan's tunic still beamed, a beacon in the growing darkness, an anchor in Kelså's mind that held her to her son as firmly as his grip. A few times, as they bounded over each other, she saw his face. Her boy, the one so unsure of himself or his place in the world, looked *confident*, even amid such frightening tumult. If she hadn't been so frightened, she would've glowed with pride.

"We're almost there. I can feel the Silver Mountains."

The currents twisted and turned, bouncing them off unseen walls of the river's course. Kelså's body was battered, and she felt his grip loosening. She squeezed even harder. A finger came loose, and she began to panic.

Another finger slipped.

"Mother! Hold on! Grab me with your other hand! We're almost there!"

She could hear him, feel the panic in his voice, but couldn't see him through the blackness. His tunic was nearly invisible in the inky blackness, and she felt her connection to magic failing as the strength in her fingers slipped away.

Then Declan was thrust upward, expelled from the river, and spat onto the shores of the Silver Mountains. He gasped at the coolness of the cavern's air against his skin. With his free hand, he threw himself down and reached for his mother's arm. It was impossible to see, but he managed to feel her shoulder. He pulled her up by two fingers and tried to grip her blouse, but a wave of power slammed into her body as her face neared the surface. His hand fell away from her shirt as her final finger slipped from his grasp. Through a film of murky magic, Declan watched in horror as his mother's form dissolved into specks of dim light, then faded and dispersed within the blackened flow.

"NO!" he cried, and he dug into the current with both hands, desperate to feel his mother touch once again.

But Kelså Rea, the Keeper of the Well and Protector of Magic, was gone.

Chapter Thirty-One

Jess

"Majesty, we're now investigating *nine* mysterious deaths across the Kingdom; all appear to have been vicious attacks by wild beasts that occurred in different locations and against random members of their community. We've still found no commonality regarding sex of the victim, station, occupation, or any other measure we use. In some cases, the victims appear torn apart by massive claws, like those of a large bear. In others, the attacker was clearly a raptor or other bird of prey." The High Sheriff folded his hands and stared awkwardly across the table. His eyes were lined with dark circles, and his normally well-kept uniform was as disheveled as his stringy hair.

Jess strummed her fingers against the wood of the Council table as she mulled over his written report. She glanced up. "Chancellor Marks, any word from your ravens? Or our network of ears?"

"Actually, Majesty, something interesting arrived by raven just before Council assembled. I haven't had time to relay it to my people for further review, but it may provide us another avenue of inquiry." He reached into the leather folio containing sheaves of parchment and removed a tiny scroll. He unfurled the finger-thin strip of parchment and read,

"The dead innkeeper in Oliver was angry at the Order's Priest and his speeches about the Crown. Rumor has it, he was stirring up a small group to chase the Priest out of town before he was killed, though none of that group will speak of him or their plans. This was overheard in the dockside tavern by the barman." - V

Treasurer Dask scoffed a laugh. "Are you suggesting a wild bear was angered by the man's hatred for a Priest? That may be the most ridiculous thing ever spoken at this table."

Sheriff Cribbs chuckled, but his smile didn't reach his weary eyes. "It does sound far-fetched, Ethan. Is that all we have?"

Marks held the Queen's eyes, despite the others' reactions. "On the surface, Treasurer Dask is right. This sounds ridiculous, but we have little else to go on, so I suggest the High Sheriff have his men in each town revisit interviews, ask about the Priests and their speeches. Local constables may already know of royalist passions but failed to link them to the killings."

Sheriff Cribbs leaned forward. "Majesty, I can have my men ask quietly in their respective towns, but this whole thing sounds like a child's fever dream."

Jess looked from Cribbs to Marks, then raised a brow. "It sounds like dreams *I* had as a child, thanks to stories our dear High Chancellor told me before I was sent to bed. But he's right—we have little else to go on, and asking a few questions seems simple enough."

Cribbs nodded once. "Yes, Majesty. I'll send birds when we finish here."

"Good," Jess said, squinting at the upside-down writing on the parchment before Marks that detailed the lengthy agenda to be discussed. "What's next, Chancellor?"

"Trade with Melucia and Vint. Our representatives—"

The audience chamber doors flew open and slammed against the stone of the walls as Mage Ernest raced into the hall with the royal page a step behind. "Majesty! Mage Dane Ernest," the flustered page called belatedly.

Everyone at the Council table jumped at the startling interruption.

"Majesty! They're gone! They're just *gone*!" Ernest cried out.

His eyes were wild, and his arms flailed as he ran. Halfway down the aisle, he remembered where he was and slowed to a not-so-stately brisk walk until he stood, huffing in heavy breaths, before his Queen.

"Mage Ernest? Are you alright?" Jess stood, her own eyes rising at the man's unusual agitation.

"No, Majesty. *None* of us are." The Mage finally remembered to bow, then rose and met her eyes. "The Gifts are gone."

"What are you babbling about? Whose Gifts?" Marks asked in annoyance.

"Majesty," Ernest sucked in a few breaths. "All our Gifts have vanished. I can no longer sense the currents, and none of our Mages can cast even the simplest spell."

Jess shot a look at Marks, then turned to Dask. "I can't tell if my Gift works without an animal nearby. Treasurer Dask, please try yours?"

Dask shot the Queen a hard glare.

"Barnabus, just do it. You're the only one present who still thinks your Gift is a secret."

Amused eyes turned to Dask as he looked from Marks to Cribbs. Then his eyes were gripped with panic.

"Majesty, I can't—"

"Dear, Spirits," she muttered.

"Majesty, people all over the city are coming to the Guild Hall, seeking remedy for what they believe to be an ailment. This isn't limited to Mages. Our Gifts, *all of them*, are gone."

Panic erupted as every Counselor stood and began talking at once. It was impossible to hear what any one person was saying as they shouted over each other. Mage Ernest dropped to the floor and pulled his knees to his chest. Jess gaped at the self-assured Mage who was now reduced to a helpless, muttering child.

She drew a deep, calming breath, then another, as her father taught her. He'd warned of many things, but his lessons on crises were his most frequent—and most forceful.

"Jess." He'd pointed his forefinger for emphasis. *"Every crisis will be different, but two things will always remain beneath the noise. First, everyone will look to you for leadership, even if you have no knowledge, background, or training in the matter at hand. You will be Queen, the only one wearing the crown. As such, people will expect—no, they'll demand—you to make the impossible choices.*

"Second, you will want to run out of the room. Your heart will race, and sweat will pour from places you never knew could sweat. And those same people demanding leadership will see it all. They'll watch your every movement, hang on every word. They'll seek meaning where you offered none, all in a desperate attempt to feel secure in a time of uncertainty. You must gird yourself, especially in those times. Find strength within yourself. Widen your stance, breathe slowly and deeply. Speak slowly and with purpose, if for no other reason than to buy yourself time to think."

In that moment, with the Mage Ernest in a near panic, her Counselors chattering like Temple gossips, and word beginning to spread through the city like summer flames, she knew the wisdom of his words.

And she breathed deeply again.

"Everyone sit." Her clear voice pierced through the cacophony, and every head turned. "Don't stand there staring at me. I said sit!" She punctuated the last phrase, practically spitting with each word.

Slowly, the leaders of the Kingdom gathered themselves and took their seats. Marks helped Mage Ernest to his feet and ushered him to his chair at the foot of the table, then took his own. All eyes turned to Jess, who was still standing before her own chair.

"I want each of you to listen to me right now. I need you. The people need you. *This Kingdom* needs each of you." She looked around the table with a stern gaze. "The people look to us for strength, and *they will see strength* when they look at each of you. Do you hear me?"

Mutters of "Yes, Majesty" scattered around the table.

"Good." She took her seat, back straight, head high. "Sheriff, send your birds. Find me answers regarding the killings. Chancellor Marks, I want other birds sent to every Guild in every nation, starting with Melucia. Find out if their Gifts are also affected."

General Sento, her new Minister of War, began to protest. She silenced her with a raised palm and defiant glare.

"I understand we're tipping our hand by asking the question. They will know we are wounded without our Gifts. Your objection is noted. Chancellor, send the birds. Everyone else, assess how to move forward with your respective areas assuming there are no Gifts to assist with your work. I want outlines of your worst-case plans by tomorrow. Mage Ernest, stay with me a moment. Everyone else, get to work."

The Counselors rose and quickly made their way out of the chamber. None had ever seen Jess command the room as she just had, leaving more than a few remembering her mother's famous wrath. When the last of them vanished and the doors closed, she walked the length of the table and sat in the chair closest to her Mage. His head was bowed, and he didn't look up.

"Mage, look at me," she said. His eyes slowly rose to meet hers. "Do you know of any time in our history when the Gifts failed?"

He shook his head. "No, Majesty. I've had our historians scouring the Royal Library since the first report. Since the time of Irina, the Gifts have flowed through the bloodlines without interruption."

She thought a moment. "Is there a spell . . . or some artifact . . . that could block someone's Gift? Mute it?"

"I know of one man who could Silence those within a certain radius, but he died many years ago. If such existed, even in the other nations, the Mages would've shared that information. It would have frightened every serious magician to their core. To have someone able to steal—"

"Stay with me, alright," she rested a hand on his arm to try to calm him, but the Queen's touch made him jump nearly out of his robe.

"Majesty, forgive me. I was startled. You *touched* me."

She let out a sigh. "My touch isn't poison."

"No, but you are Queen."

"Fine," she sat back. "Just focus. I know your people are working on this already, but the Mages are our best hope of finding a solution. Do whatever you must. Ask for whatever you need. There is no price too high for the return of our magic. Understand?"

"Yes, Majesty," he stammered.

"And, Mage, please *remain calm.*"

He nodded frantically, "Yes, ma'am—I mean Majesty."

Chapter Thirty-Two

Keelan

It had taken nearly four days of steady riding for Keelan to make it back to the capital. He was tired, hungry, and covered in sweat and dirt. The last thing he wanted was to deal with the mass of people clogging the streets. He didn't think it was a festival or market day, but who knew what days were special in the Kingdom? So, he reined in Dittler and picked his way carefully through the crowd.

As he passed the first handful of people, he thought an odd fear painted their eyes. This definitely wasn't a festival crowd. An old woman and her daughter scooted out of his way following an angry snort from Dittler. When the woman looked up, Keelan nodded his head respectfully and asked, "What's going on? Is there a market day today?"

The woman's daughter tugged her arm, urging her to ignore the large man in his dusty blue uniform—his *foreign* uniform—but the old woman stepped closer and stroked Dittler's neck. The stallion allowed her touch without so much as a whiney.

"Everybody's gathering at the Temple. The Gifted are asking the Priests for help."

"Help? Why do the Gifted need help? Especially from the Priests?"

The woman shushed him, looking over her shoulder nervously. "Who else are they going to turn to when their Gifts are gone? The Queen can't do anything about magic. They need the Spirits now," she whispered loudly so Keelan could hear atop his horse. Her daughter gave Keelan a dark look and pulled the woman away.

Keelan sat up straight and scanned the crowd. He had paid little attention before, but every sense he had screamed to be on alert.

He passed another small group who were clumped together around a small child who wore the Gifted gold. The girl was crying hysterically. Keelan stopped and dismounted, then carefully made his way to the group. When they spotted his own golden collar, they parted to allow him to kneel before the girl.

"Are you alright? Don't be afraid. I want to help if I can," he said in as gentle a tone as he could muster.

She eyed him through wary, reddened eyes and wiped her tears with her balled fists.

"I can't hear Gretta anymore," she managed before her sobs returned.

Keelan waited, then gave a questioning look to the woman who held the girl.

"Gretta's her cat. Her Gift lets her hear animal thoughts, or see their images, however it works. She's the only one with a Gift in our family, so we don't really understand it all," she said. Then she noticed Keelan's collar. "How are you being so strong without yours? All the others wearing gold we've seen are a wreck."

Keelan fingered his collar. He hadn't even thought to test his own Gift.

"I'm a constable from far away, and my Gift is telling whether or not someone is being honest with me. Unlike your girl, I can't make my Gift work; someone has to lie to me for it to trigger." Then an idea struck. "Can you tell me something about yourself that's true, but throw in some false things?"

The woman scrunched her nose as if smelling something rotten, then nodded. "My name is Macey Brie, and I work as a weaver around the corner." She paused, thinking. "Um . . . my girl here, Bess, takes that darn cat with her everywhere. At least she did before all this."

Keelan waited, but the woman stayed silent.

"Well, anything?"

Keelan cocked his head. "Are you done? I was waiting for you to tell me something false."

She patted his arm with her weathered hand. "Son, this is my granddaughter. Her name is Jemma, and she hates that raggedy cat, even if its thoughts keep her company sometimes. Just about everything I told you was a lie, except for my name and where I work. Looks like your gold is just as tarnished as the rest of the Gifted."

Keelan stared blankly at Macey. He felt his pulse quicken and his breathing become shallow, but still couldn't believe what she'd told him. His Gift had been his constant companion since its first manifestation. It wasn't just some talent or learned skill—it was part of him. How could something woven into the fabric of his being simply vanish? His legs became numb from squatting so long, and he nearly toppled backward into Dittler. Macey gripped his arm and held him up.

"You might want to join those folks heading to the Temple. Maybe the Priests can help you, too."

He shook his dazed head. "No, I need to get to the palace." Without another word, he stood, mounted Dittler and continued threading his way through the crowd.

Jess watched the Mage vanish through the doors and slumped back into the chair. First mysterious killings—by animals, no less—and now magic had failed. *What's next?* she thought. *Is this really what being Queen will be? Chasing one disaster after another?*

A moment later, she rose and turned to head to her chambers. She needed a long soak in a hot bath.

"Your Majesty," the page's voice called from the entrance.

Jess tilted her head back and breathed. *What now?*

"Yes? What is it?" she asked, turning toward the voice. The liveried boy scooted out of the way and a tall, broad-shouldered man in a dusty blue uniform entered. Their eyes met, and her exhaustion vanished.

"Keelan!"

He dropped his pack and stood just inside the doors. When they slammed closed, he barely blinked.

Jess took a few steps forward, her brow now creased with concern. "Keelan, what is it? What's wrong?"

"Jess, I—" his voice broke.

She raced to him, and despite his road-worn state, wrapped her arms around him and held him tightly. She felt the warmth of his breath on her neck, then the pressure of his hands against her back and his strong arms encircling her—and then she felt his chest heave.

"Oh, Keelan. What's happened?" She couldn't imagine what could reduce such a strong, steady, stoic man to tears.

She'd lost track of how long they'd held each other in the doorway when he spoke in a hushed voice. "I can't feel my Gift anymore. Jess, I tried over and over. I can't feel the nagging sensation when something isn't right. I can't protect you or Atikus or Declan—or anybody anymore."

She pulled back and gripped his face with her hands. "Keelan, look at me." She waited until he gathered himself enough to hold her eyes. "*Everyone's* Gift is gone. Everyone's. It's not just yours. Something has happened to magic that we don't understand, but we're working on it."

He tried to look away, but she turned his face back to her.

"We're going to fix this somehow, make it right, but your Gift isn't what makes you special. It isn't how you protect people. It's just a tool. Yes, it's powerful, and yes, it's part of you, but it doesn't define who you are, and it certainly doesn't take away your ability to help those you care about."

He nodded, but she wasn't convinced he believed her.

When Jess entered the family dining room, Keelan was already standing politely behind his chair. He'd shed his dusty uniform, showered, shaved, and donned a sharp, tightly fitting charcoal-gray coat piped with golden thread. His eyes were so brilliant against the darkness of his coat she nearly missed a step, wobbling on one foot before righting herself. Keelan was there in a flash, offering a hand to steady her, and never looking amused at her predicament.

That simple act made her heart flutter even more.

Dinner was served exactly one half hour from the time Jess asked her maids to alert the kitchens. Being Queen might carry unfathomable weight and responsibility, but the food and service were to die for. The staff brought platters of roasted turkey and vegetables lathered in garlic and butter.

Keelan hadn't eaten that day and was starving. He dove into the turkey with ravenous abandon and savored the rich sauces that drenched the vegetables. Midway through, a frightening thought struck - would the stink of the herbs frighten her lips from a repeat performance of their kiss in the gardens?

Thankfully, her little tumble had given him a chance to recover his wits and do what he did best: rescue her from a fall. That was a task he knew well. That gave him confidence.

And then she'd cupped his cheek as he lifted her, and all his defenses had melted away once more.

What was she doing to him? Was this what it was supposed to feel like? The Guard never trained him for this. He didn't even know what *this* was.

Conversation was awkward at first, until Jess caught one of the older serving women grinning, her eyes glittering knowingly. The Queen emerged and sent that woman to the kitchen for more . . . *whatever*. The woman giggled as she scurried out of the room to bring her moonstruck Queen a giant platter of *something*. From that point, they had pulled it together enough to start a proper conversation. He asked how things were going with her Council appointments, knowing that particular duty still nagged at her daily. She asked about Keelan's journey, avoiding the gruesome parts of his investigation, and he obliged with small talk of the people and village of Oliver. She asked how

Dittler was treating him, grinning as she remembered how the stallion nipped at the giant man every time he came near.

He looked up at the mention of her beloved horse. "Jess, I'm so sorry. I completely forgot. You haven't seen Dittler in over week. I'm sure he'd love a visit. Care for a walk by the stables, then through the gardens?"

She beamed excitedly. "I can't believe I hadn't thought to visit him either. Yes, I'd love that."

He set his fork down, having licked it clean of the blueberry dessert they'd just devoured, then rose and extended a hand. "May a humble constable take the Queen for an evening stroll?"

She giggled and stood. Taking his hand, she held her chin high and said in her most formal voice, "We are pleased with your offer. Lead on, good sir."

Jess stood outside the stables, still wearing her garnet gown and pearl necklace. The plan was to pay Dittler a quick visit, then stroll through the gardens. She'd come back tomorrow in her riding leathers and give her stallion a bit of proper exercise—not that he'd missed out during his journey with Keelan. The ride would be more for her than her horse.

Keelan appeared in the opening to the stables, reins in hand, with Dittler playfully nipping at his shoulder and whinnying every time Keelan tried to shoo his bites away. Jess grinned at the pair.

"Looks like you two learned to get along."

"If you count me getting nipped every five seconds as getting along, then sure." He chuckled and pushed the horse's toothy snout away again.

At the sound of Jess's voice, Dittler's ears shot forward, and his head snapped up. He began prancing on his front legs and surprised Keelan by yanking the lead out of his hand with a quick tug. Within seconds, the massive stallion had knelt on his front knees before Jess, his snout nuzzling nip-free against her chest. She laughed heartily and stroked the horse's ears in exactly the spot she knew could make him weak. He let out a gruff snort—something akin to what a thousand-pound cat might do when given a good scratch.

"That's my baby boy," she said, pressing her cheek against his forelock. The powerful-beast-turned-helpless-puppy dared not move; he simply breathed and snorted happily as his mistress praised and stroked him. After a few peaceful moments, he pulled back and eyed her.

"What is it boy?"

He snorted and stamped once, then resumed staring at her.

"I don't know what you're saying, Dit. My Gift isn't working, and I can't see your thoughts in my mind."

He snorted and stomped again.

Keelan stepped up beside her, careful not to startle the stallion. "I think he senses something's off but doesn't know what it is or why you're not understanding him."

Dittler leaned toward Keelan and nudged his arm with his muzzle, then nickered and bobbed his head.

"Did he just agree with you?" Jess asked in amazement.

Keelan laughed. "Jealous? I'm pretty sure we bonded on this trip."

On cue, Dittler lunged forward and nipped Keelan's coat.

"I see how you boys bonded." Now Jess laughed. "And I think you're right. He's always been more perceptive than people think. Part of it's being a Cretian—everybody knows they're the smartest of horse breeds—but there's magic at work here, too.

It might not be a Gift exactly, but he's shown me many times over how much he understands."

That earned her another nuzzle.

"I see how you are, traitor. Nip me but nuzzle her."

He turned and nipped Keelan again.

Both of them broke into a fit of laughter, and Keelan thought he heard Dittler snorting a little too merrily himself.

Then Dittler let out a deep throated roar of surprise.

All at once, the peaceful night turned into a blur of motion. The sound of another horse's hooves on the cobbles clanked through the yard, and a mottled gray broke through the darkness from around the stables, headed straight for Jess. Keelan pulled her to the side just as the horse reared and missed striking her head with its front hooves.

"Get back inside!" Keelan yelled as he ducked the horse's angry teeth.

Jess turned to run, but her gown and shoes were made for dinners, not sprints, and she sprawled face first across the cobbles a few paces away. At the sound of her cry, the gray horse turned from Keelan and charged for her prone body. Dittler, enraged, snapped at the horse's neck, gripping a mouthful of its mane in his mighty teeth. He yanked backwards, twisting the smaller animal's neck and head around. The gray pulled himself free and in the same motion turned his hindquarters toward Dittler, landing a painful blow with both his rear hooves straight into Dittler's side. The Cretian roared in pain, stumbling back a pace, then he charged forward again, teeth bared. The two reared on hind quarters and exchanged vicious blows on the other's neck and head.

In battles for dominance, such fights were common. To an outsider, it would appear the challengers were trying to kill one another, but this wasn't usually the case. Horses generally fought until one submitted, then the order of supremacy in the herd was restored or remade.

But the gray horse wasn't trying to dominate. He wanted to *kill*, and while he fought Dittler, his eyes kept returning to Jess.

Keelan darted out of the way of the dueling beasts and helped Jess to her feet. She threw off her heels and turned to run for help. The gray broke free of Dittler and charged again, this time slamming his shoulder into Keelan, knocking him several paces away and onto his back. Her protector out of the way, the gray locked eyes with Jess and reared. His wild roar tore through the night, and sharp hooves glared down at their helpless target.

As its hooves were just hands from crashing into Jess's face, Dittler charged and slammed his entire weight into her attacker's side. The gray, still on just his hind legs, was knocked off balance and flew into the side wall of the stone stables. His head slammed into the hard surface, and blood oozed from a massive gash the impact had created. The horse's eyes lost focus and he struggled to rise on wobbly legs, but Dittler was there before he could stand, battering him with fore hooves and biting unmercifully into his throat and withers.

Keelan finally shook off the last blow he'd taken. He ran to the stables' entrance and searched for any tool he could use as a weapon, finding only a manure fork hanging on the wall. It wasn't perfect, but it would have to do. He ran back to where Dittler continued to pummel the wounded gray. It might've been disoriented and pinned beneath the blows of a far heavier beast, but the gray continued to bite and struggle. In one lucky thrust, it managed to rake Dittler with a hoof, scoring a bloody line across the stallion's chest. Dittler roared in pain and staggered back a few paces, leaving an opening for the gray to try to rise.

Keelan was there before he could stand, driving the fork into the gray's head and side again and again until the horse lay motionless on the bloody stones. Keelan's chest heaved from the effort, and Dittler snorted wildly. His eyes were frenzied as he struggled to comprehend the end of the threat, so Keelan staggered away slowly, giving him space to calm.

Jess ran to Keelan and wrapped her arms around him. He winced as she gripped his bruised and likely broken ribs but still pulled her tightly into him. A moment later, silver-plated guards began pouring out of the palace toward their Queen.

"The Queen! To the Queen!" they yelled.

Before Keelan could think, they were safely surrounded by a protective ring of men sworn to guard Jess at any cost.

"I'm alright," she said in a small voice as she pulled away from Keelan's embrace.

A man with a bright-green plume on his shiny helmet was let into the circle. He bowed, then locked eyes with Jess. "Your Majesty, are you hurt? What happened?"

Jess sucked in a few breaths then looked up at the man. "I'm fine. Keelan may need a Healer, and Dittler definitely will, but I'm unharmed beyond a few scratches. That horse came out of nowhere and, I don't know, attacked me. It all sounds insane now, but that's what happened."

The man's brows knitted in confusion as he looked from Jess to where the gray horse lay then back to her. "A horse attacked you, Majesty?"

She nodded, "That's right. He's right over—"

Her words caught in her throat as she turned and pointed to where the horse had lain only moments before.

There was no horse.

There, lying in a pool of his own blood that still poured from his head and chest, was the body of a man in long brown robes.

Pieces of a shattered mask depicting a snarling gray horse with stubby antlers lay a pace away.

Chapter Thirty-Three

Declan

Tears flowed freely as Declan searched the inky flow with both hands. With a thought, he cast a swirling ball of light and thrust his hands beneath the river's surface once more. Each time they rose from the current, they held nothing, simply dripped with oozing blackness.

His mother really was gone.

He sat back against a stone and stared blankly. He looked down and scrubbed his hands against his trousers, angry at the poisoned substance that had made him an orphan, desperate to remove its stain from his skin. How long he sat in that grotto, revisiting every moment he'd had with his mother on the isle, he would never know. Minutes? Hours? It felt like a lifetime—but a lifetime wasn't enough.

He hadn't had enough time with her.

There could never be enough time.

He wept again.

When weariness of heart and body finally seized him, he rose and made his way to the cavern's entrance. Darkness had fallen on the early spring night, and stars shone brightly in the cloudless sky. He could make out the lights of the Guild and trudged slowly toward them.

Why were so many burdens laid on his shoulders?

"Declan, can you hear me?" a familiar voice called in his mind, startling him out of his pondering.

"Atikus?" he asked. "How—"

Declan *felt* the Mage's rumbling laughter in his mind. *"I have no idea, but you're not going to believe what else I can do now."*

"Atikus, where are you? I need to tell you something and I'd rather—"

"Wait! You can respond Telepathically! Does this mean your Gifts still work?"

"Yes, my magic works . . . just differently. It's hard to believe, and even harder to explain. Where are you? We need to talk."

"I've returned to the Guild. I just thought about home, and the next moment I was here. It's incredible!" Excitement flooded through their mental channel.

"Alright, I'm almost there. I need a bath and a meal, but we should talk first. This is really important."

Atikus's voice sobered. *"Son, are you alright? What's wrong? I can feel it through this bond, whatever this is."*

"I'm fine. Meet me in the dining hall in fifteen minutes. I should be there by then."

"Okay. I'll head down and ask cook to whip up something to eat. See you then."

Declan sat across the table from his adopted father. They'd eaten their fill of cold cuts and dried fruits, and Atikus had recounted the events in the mountain as he'd experienced them, letting Declan finish his meal before having to deliver his news. He tried to tamp down his excitement, but Atikus beamed as he talked about his newfound abilities.

"I didn't just get my Gifts back, I got *all* of magic!"

Declan looked up from his plate, said, "Me too," then took another bite as if he hadn't spoken anything of import.

Atikus gaped. For once, the man was speechless.

"Maybe I should tell you what happened while you were still in the kitchen," Declan said as he washed the last bite of his dinner down with ale. For the next fifteen minutes, Declan wove his way through the events in the Well's cavern, the battle with Irina, and his harrowing journey with Kelså in the currents. When he got to the last part, his somber demeanor cracked, and he wept. Atikus stood, stepped around the table, and gripped him tightly until the tears ebbed, never uttering a word.

"I couldn't save her, Atikus. I tried, but the currents were raging, and the poison was killing magic all around us. I could barely see, much less hold on." He looked up with reddened eyes. "She vanished while I watched. I saw her break apart in the current."

When Atikus remained quiet, Declan pulled back, anger blazing in his eyes. "Irina did this. We need to banish her once and for all, Atikus. I don't care if I die fighting; that witch is going to the void where she belongs."

Atikus let out a heavy breath, then nodded. "You're right. We can't let her Spirit continue wreaking havoc, but I don't even know where to begin looking for her, much less how to actually banish her." Then he sat back and gripped Declan's arm with his bony fingers. "You look like you could use a bath and night's sleep. I know I need the rest. We'll both think better in the morning, and I can get some of the Mages I trust to help us plan."

Declan nodded weakly, then locked eyes with the Mage. "I never said *thank you*."

Atikus cocked his head. "For what, son?"

"For being the only family Keelan and I ever had. For taking us in and always believing in us, even when we—or I—didn't believe in myself."

Atikus's face softened, and his eyes moistened. "Declan, son, you two have given me so much more than I ever gave you. You filled my life with laughter and my heart with joy in ways I never knew were possible. I should be thanking you."

The two men embraced once more, then left the dining hall to find rest.

The next morning, Declan found a note that someone had scooted under his door instructing him to meet Atikus and several other Mages in the study for a private breakfast. He grinned broadly as he entered the paneled room and saw the rotund, ever-jovial Pel piling his plate with eggs and bacon. The Mage fumbled for a place to set his breakfast down, then waddled quickly to the entrance to greet him.

When all the reunions were complete, Declan fixed his plate and took his seat around in one of the large leather chairs, which normally faced the hearth but had been turned to form a circle with the room's other seating.

Atikus set his steaming tea down and cleared his throat. "Keep eating, everyone, but let's get started. What we have to discuss is too important to wait. I'll ask you to forgive my caution in advance. What Declan and I are about to reveal must never leave this room, and I will bind each of your minds with magic to ensure no one could ever pry these memories from you, something I wish had been done for me before Irina could rummage through my head." He looked each Mage in the eyes, waited for their nod of assent, then cast the binding spell that would wipe any trace of their conversation from their minds within a few days. He hated taking the step but knew the secret of the Well was too important to expand the circle of knowledge.

He then summarized the events that had occurred over the past days, which translated into weeks in non-island time. Declan interjected at points, but Atikus's perfect memory had clearly returned, and his details were impeccable.

Hours later, Declan marveled at Atikus's perfect recall as the Mage recapped the plans they'd devised.

"First, we have to locate Irina," Atikus began, as if reading from a list. "She's powerful; we assume she's regained *all* Gifts, just as we have. We need one Mage to Scry for her. I'll power his efforts with my magic. With her new powers, she should light up like a star in any scrying bowl.

"Second, we have to banish her. Unfortunately, we have far more questions than answers on this one. Is banishment even possible with a Mage of her power? Is her Spirit separate from Larinda's body, or do we need to kill the woman formerly known as Larinda and *then* banish Irina's Spirit? If so, will a Summoning Circle be needed to contain her Spirit until it can be banished?"

As happened all too often when a group of Mages sat in the study, the conversation meandered on and off topic, and Declan found his mind wandering. He snapped back to the present when they moved on to the final challenge.

"Finally, we have to cleanse the currents and restore Gifts to the world." Atikus said.

A tiny voice inside Declan wondered if he would lose many of his newly acquired powers if Gifts were restored. He was just getting to know his new powers, and here they were talking about stripping him of them, returning him to only what he, as Heir, possessed. He would be reduced to what, six or seven Gifts? Then he chided himself for such selfish thoughts. His charge was to protect the people and magic itself, not hoard it like a dragon with a pile of gold. He realized in that moment how bitterly Irina was likely to resist having her powers taken from her once again, especially after a thousand years of imprisonment. This was going to be a lot harder than any of them thought.

Atikus turned to the historian in the group. "We need you to dig through the stacks of historical scrolls maintained in the Guild's vault for any reference to the spell used to splinter magic and create Gifts. It *has* to be there. Mages were the original pack rats. We never destroy anything, especially if it was written on parchment."

The Mages chuckled knowingly at their own penchant for hoarding.

The group disbanded shortly after lunch, each Mage hurrying off to research his or her assigned task. They would reconvene for dinner and review each other's progress.

Declan and Atikus headed to the Guild Hall with the Scrying Mage, hoping the circle embedded in that building would be powerful enough to find their quarry. It would've been a simple matter from atop the Mages' Tower, but that option crumbled when its stones fell.

Declan had never seen the gold and silver inlaid circle in the casting chamber of the Guild Hall—he'd had no reason to since he grew up believing magic had shunned him. Now, upon entering the well-lit room, his eyes widened appreciatively as he took in the craftsmanship of the perfectly laid circle. One golden circle in the center surrounded by a silver square wrapped in a final golden circle. The whole thing flared brightly when Declan and Atikus entered.

"Well, that's new," the Scrying Mage said.

Atikus shook his head. "We're seeing all sorts of new things these days. It appears anything invested with magic responds to our presence."

"Interesting. That might be helpful when we get to the fighting stage of the plan," Declan said.

A white marble pillar stood waist high in the center of the circle. The Scrying Mage poured water from a pitcher into a shiny brass bowl and placed it on the pedestal, careful not to spill anything inside the circle.

"It's too much to hope you have something personal to Irina, isn't it?" he asked.

Declan barked a laugh. "I don't know that anything matters to her anymore. She's the purest kind of evil."

"Declan's right that we don't have an item of hers, but he's wrong in painting her with one solid color. While I agree she's turned dark, no one is completely evil—or good, for that matter. We are all shades of various colors."

"Maybe shades of *black*," Declan mused. "But let's stick to finding her. What do we need to do?"

The Mage stepped up to the bowl. "It's a simple process. Whichever of you is performing the Scrying, place both hands on the outside of the bowl, but don't touch the water. Then, call your Light. When your magic responds, focus your thoughts on Irina, what she looks like, every detail you can remember. If she wore a certain scent, try to recreate that memory. Everything helps. We wouldn't normally need to be this detailed, but without an artifact, your mind will have to be the bridge. If you do everything correctly and maintain steady focus, the water will ripple and show images of where Irina is currently."

Atikus looked at Declan and raised a brow. "Would you like to do the honors?"

"I'm not sure this counts as *honors*, but sure," Declan said, stepping up and gripping the sides of the bowl. He closed his eyes, and his Light flared brightly at his touch. He heard a gasp and opened his eyes, disrupting the process.

"What happened? Is everything okay?"

Atikus chuckled and looked to the Mage whose eyes couldn't grow any wider.

"I don't think he's seen your tunic light up before. Excuse the pun," Atikus said with a flourish of bushy brows and a chuckle.

"Sorry," the Mage said. "It's . . . incredible. I'll stay quiet this time."

Declan allowed himself a grin, then closed his eyes to focus again. As before, his Light responded quickly. He then replayed the scene from the Well in his mind, first with him and Kelså running into the chamber in response to Órla's alarm. Then Irina had appeared wearing the mask of Larinda. He focused on the details as the Mage had instructed, recreating every wrinkle and weathered spot on the old woman's face and bare arms, her stringy snow-white hair, and her colorful island dress. He could hear Larinda's voice, the warmth and depth in her laugh, taste the salt in the air as he breathed deeply. He held that image, those sensations, for five minutes, then ten. Finally, he felt a hand pat his shoulder and the image fell away. He opened his eyes to find the other two men staring at the bowl in frustration.

"Were you able to remember details?" the Scrying Mage asked.

"Of course. I spent a lot of time with Larinda. That wasn't hard."

"Well, the water didn't so much as bubble once, much less ripple and show us anything," Atikus said. "I could feel waves of power wafting off as you focused. Having strong enough magic is definitely *not* our problem here."

"Wait," the Mage said excitedly. "You said *Larinda*."

Declan nodded, confused. "That's right. That's the face Irina wore when I saw her."

"True, but we're not looking for Larinda, we're looking for *Irina*. Her Spirit could've left Larinda's body to inhabit another. Regardless of what body she wore, it's *Irina's Spirit* we're trying to locate. You'll need to try again, this time focused on Irina."

"This just got a lot harder. I've never seen Irina. No one has, at least not in a thousand years."

Atikus raised a hand like a schoolboy.

"You've got to be kidding," Declan said.

"Perfect memory, remember? I've studied the Kingdom War, read much of what still exists detailing Irina's rise. There aren't any remaining busts or sketches of her, but her appearance is described in vivid detail in Matias's Histories."

"And he even remembers the name of the boring book he read," Declan grunted.

"Yes, my boy, I do. Stand aside and watch your Arch Mage work."

Declan rolled his eyes, more for the Scrying Mage's amusement than for Atikus's sake, but he backed away from the bowl and watched as Atikus took over the process. Within a minute, he'd closed his eyes, called his Light, and caused the water to ripple violently, then settle into images of a building none of them recognized.

"It looked like an old warehouse. There were candles hanging everywhere; there must've been a hundred of them hanging from lines stretched across ceiling. I've never seen so many in one place. Does that mean anything to either of you?" Atikus asked.

The Mage shrugged, but Declan looked pensive.

"When I was on border patrol, there were a few traders who would come through from the Kingdom with carts sagging heavily with candles. We're normally the producer in the trading relationship with the Spires, but there are a few items where they do most of the production and selling. Candles happens to be one of those items."

"Do you know where they're made? Where the merchant sells them?"

"No, but Keelan's over there, right? Why don't we pay him a visit with our shiny new powers? He may know someone who can help—*like the Queen.*"

"My boy, you may become the smartest of us all," Atikus grinned. "I've been to the palace several times, so Traveling there won't be a problem. Let's go see your brother."

Chapter Thirty-Four

Jess

The next day's duty started early for the Queen. By the time she walked into the audience chamber shortly before sunrise, the entire Council was already seated and heartily devouring the proffered pastries and spiced tea. As she approached her seat with Keelan following closely behind, everyone stood. The portly Trade Minister, Destin Carver, was startled by the sudden appearance of the monarch and fumbled his pasty, exploding confectioner's sugar all over himself. A cloud of white powder lingered above the table near his seat a moment after he recovered the rogue pastry. Jess stifled a laugh.

"Good morning, everyone. Please sit," she said with a voice that brooked no discussion. "I assume each of you has been briefed on the attack that took place last night. Were it not for the heroic efforts of our guest from Melucia, Guardsman Rea, you might have been having a succession crisis this morning."

Heads bobbed.

"This was clearly planned and orchestrated by the Order. Their Priests have been infiltrating our towns and cities, winning over the hearts of *my* people, and preaching against the Crown. They pose a clear threat that must be dealt with. Does anyone here disagree?"

She looked from one Counselor to the next. Some wore bewildered looks, clearly having missed the aforementioned briefing. Others masked their expression, either unsure how to respond or afraid to challenge their Queen when her mind appeared set.

Marks waded into the deep waters. "Majesty, while I agree we must deal with those behind the assassin swiftly and without mercy, the Order and its Priests have established themselves across the nation as peaceful caretakers of the poor and destitute. Whether true or not, the crisis with Gifts has cemented their role as intercessors for the Spirits."

"You've got to be joking. *They're the Children* without the masks. They're the people who kidnapped and tried to kill me—*twice* now."

Marks held up his hands in surrender. "I know that, and you know that, but the people have bought their story. What we initially thought were a handful of Priests scattered through the countryside turned out to be one or more Priests in *every* town, village, and hamlet in the Kingdom. There isn't a place with more than three families without a Priest ministering to their needs, preaching goodwill and the call to care for a neighbor."

"And the need to supplant the Crown!" Jess shouted. "I get it. They've taken a huge lead in the propaganda war, but we didn't even know we were in a war, much less put up a fight. That changes today."

The men and woman at the table we speechless. They worked shoulder to shoulder with the people—well, with the *rich* people of the nation—and the nobles had bought the Priest's message just as the commoners had, likely more so since they wore most of the golden collars and were desperate to recover their magic. The idea the Queen would go to war with the Priests who were embedded in their communities was beyond belief.

"No one? Not *one* of you will speak up?" Jess glared at her new members of Council. "When I see you again, I want options to take down the Order. If we need to leave the Priests in place with a narrow mission of good will, fine—but I want their leaders dealt with so they can never threaten the Crown again. Am I clear?"

A muffled chorus of "Yes, Your Majesty" made its disorderly way around the table. Jess turned and stalked out of the room. Keelan, unsure whether he belonged with the angry Queen or her befuddled Counselors, nodded to Marks, then turned and followed Jess.

Chapter Thirty-Five

Laurie

Laurie was exhausted. Her day had begun, as it always did, long before the sun bothered to show its lazy face. She helped her mother prep, cook, and serve breakfast to their guests, then rushed through a cursory cleaning so she could make it to the market before other merchants gobbled up all the fresh produce.

The air was blessedly cool with a light breeze blowing in from the ocean, but she still arrived sweaty and stinking from her day's effort. Ma sent her upstairs with orders to make her bath quick so she could help cut vegetables and roll dough for pie crusts.

That night, the common room was overflowing. Every major city in the Kingdom was holding qualifying rounds of the annual Tournament of Spires, the chief sporting event of the year where stupid men tried to poke other stupid men with pointy things. At least, that's how Laurie thought of the games. There was sword fighting, jousting, marksmanship . . . yeah, she was right—stupid men and pointy things. Whatever one thought of the games, they drew crowds from all over, and that was good for business.

She raced from table to table taking orders, delivering food, and slinging more mugs of ale than she thought they owned. Three separate times, she was called to the kitchen for an emergency cleaning of piled up tankards only to immediately fill them for delivery to new patrons. The seasonal nature of the inn's business could be maddening in slow times, but when it was good, it was *very* good.

The musicians finally started their slower songs, the part of their set designed to calm the rambunctious, highly intoxicated guests before the staff shuffled them off to bed or on to other adventures around town. Laurie shared an appreciative smile with the fiddle player as his bow caressed the strings with a sad, harmonious rapture. His magic worked as the guests quieted and settled into the emotional ballad, moistening a few eyes by the time the players struck their last chord. With that final note, the players began packing up their instruments and passing their very deep hat one last time to squeeze every drop of juice they could. Laurie began clearing and wiping tables as most of the patrons took the hint.

One pair of men remained at a table in the corner. Something in their posture, the way they leaned a little too far and whispered too low, made her uneasy. She knew both men. They were among the more successful business owners in town.

What are they scheming about? she wondered.

Unable to overhear any of their conversation, she continued about her work. When the last of her tables was cleaned and the dishes in the kitchen put away, she gave the common room one last scan. The two men were still there, still whispering, with eyes darting around the room every few minutes. They were *definitely* up to something. She couldn't resist and walked over to their table.

"Can I get you gentlemen anything else tonight? We're about to close up."

"Oh, no, Laurie. We're just finishing up. We'll be out of your hair in a few minutes," one of the men said. The other simply stared at his hands and avoided looking up at her.

"In that case, mind if I wipe down your table real quick? I can leave you to your conversation once the table's clean. You can stay as long as you like."

The talkative man smiled. "Go right ahead, and thank you."

As she walked away, taking as much time as she could without looking obvious, she caught a tiny snippet of their conversation.

"This has to end. Tomorrow's our best chance to take care of him. Are you with me?"

The other man, the hand starer, finally spoke. "Aye. Tomorrow."

And with that, the pair stood, bade her goodnight, and left.

Laurie let out a long breath. Nothing in what she heard made any sense, but it caused her stomach to do flips all the same. She didn't like it one bit.

"Laurie," Ma's voice called from the kitchen, snapping her out of her thoughts.

"Yes, Ma. I'm wiping down the last table. Be there in a minute."

The kitchen door swung wide, and Ma appeared in the door, her lips pursed to one side. Laurie knew instantly she was about to run another errand when all she wanted was a warm bed.

"Dear, I completely forgot Mrs. B. We were supposed to drop dinner off at her place an hour ago. She's been laid up with a terrible cold all week, and I told her we'd handle her cooking tonight. If she's not miserable, she'll be madder than . . . well, that doesn't matter. Would you mind running this over to her place? I'll finish up out here and in the kitchen."

Laurie knew both the common room and kitchen were finished but smiled at her mother as if she'd saved her days' worth of cleaning. "Yes, ma'am. 'Course I will."

She walked to Ma and exchanged her apron for the wrapped box in her hands, then gave her a peck on the cheek.

Mrs. Betner, known as Mrs. B to anyone who'd passed through Oliver, lived in a small wooden home on the outskirts of town proper. At her leisurely pace, it took Laurie forty minutes to make the trek. The widow had been asleep and hadn't even realized dinnertime had come and gone. She was normally one of Ma's more talkative friends, but Laurie got off easy. She called out for Laurie to leave the box on her porch, so the dear girl didn't risk catching a fever. *If one could catch a fever*, Laurie thought.

She was more relieved to have avoided what surely would've been an hour-long chat than any cold. She could cope with the sniffles, but diarrhea of the mouth was incurable.

The night was chilly as Winter still battled Spring for supremacy. Clouds blanketed the sky. She folded her arms and rubbed for warmth.

Only a minute from Mrs. B's house, she heard a muffled cry off to her left. She thought she recognized the voice but couldn't quite place where she knew it from. She slowed her pace and crept toward the sound, stopping cold as she rounded the apothecary's dull brick facade. Her mind struggled to process what she was seeing.

A man lay bleeding on the ground, his arms raised as if to ward off an attack and blood pooling beneath his head and chest. Towering above him with mighty paws poised to strike was a massive brown bear. She'd never seen a bear in person, but she was sure the sketches she'd seen didn't mark bears at seventeen hands tall with claws as long as this one had. They looked more like daggers protruding from his digits than an animal's claws. As she watched in horror, the bear flung its full weight down on the man, ramming its razor-sharp claws into the man's head and chest until only the meat of its paws was visible. The mad didn't twitch or moan. He didn't spasm. He just died.

But the bear wasn't finished. As if he held some personal grudge against the poor guy, he lunged again and again, digging and clawing until there was little recognizable left on the bloody street. Laurie covered her mouth with her palm to keep from screaming and told herself to breathe quietly. The bear's back had been to her, but she didn't want to give him any reason to turn.

And then, as strange as the mauling had been, something she could never fathom happened. The bear dropped to all fours and lumbered a few paces away. It then reached down and picked up something off the ground and held it up to its muzzle. The gigantic bear shrank to average human proportions. Its fur vanished, and a silky brown robe flowed with the breeze in its place. She ducked behind the building as the man turned toward where she stood.

If she'd been afraid before, she was now terrified.

She waited a long moment, until she heard the sounds of footfalls fading, then peered carefully around the corner. The masked man was gone. She took a few tentative steps out from her hiding place and strained to see the dead man in the darkness. She didn't recognize his face through all the blood and gore, but a piece of his shredded shirt caught her eye, and she finally realized where she'd known his voice.

He was the quiet one at the table in the corner. The one who wouldn't stop staring at his hands.

Chapter Thirty-Six

Declan

Cooks raced between boiling pots and sizzling pans as they prepared the royal household's noon meal. Heavenly aromas of herbs and fresh-baked bread hung in the air. The Royal Chef, leader of the brigade, kept a watchful eye each time a cook added ingredients or seasoning. He wore a perpetual scowl as he dipped one of the dozen clean tasting spoons from the pocket on his sleeve, then thrust a taste into his mouth. Most of the time, his scowl turned into a relieved grin, and he would nod appreciatively to the cook.

When Atikus and Declan suddenly appeared where one of his white-coated cooks had stood only seconds before, the Chef nearly jumped out of his puffy hat. The smallest cook, who looked to be no more than fourteen years old, raced out of the room screaming, "Guards!" at the top of her lungs.

"You *would* have to land in the kitchen of all places," Declan turned to Atikus with a smirk and an eye roll.

Atikus wiggled brows above twinkling eyes. "It's lunchtime. If I remember correctly—and you *know* I do—the palace has the best chefs on the continent. Just smell that bread! *Of course*, I landed us in here."

The Royal Chef ventured a nervous step forward, baffled by their banter as much as their sudden appearance. "Uh... hello?"

Atikus smiled broadly and offered a shallow bow in greeting. "Please forgive our rude arrival. We didn't mean to startle you. I am Arch Mage Atikus Dani and this is Declan Rea. I'm not quite sure what title he has now. We're here to see your Queen and her guest, Guardsman Keelan Rea, but... would you mind if we tasted a bite of that hot bread before we see them?"

Silver-plated guards arrived as Atikus finished his roll. He was still licking the butter off his fingers when swords appeared at his collar. The pair was ushered into a small room that looked strikingly similar to the study back at the Saltstone Guild, and Atikus promptly flopped into a leather chair, kicked off his shoes, and poured a glass of liquor from a nearby decanter.

Declan shook his head. "Really? Just make yourself at home. Think I should ask one of the guards outside to bring us a pillow for your feet?"

"That would be nice," Atikus said, wiggling his toes through stockings that showed more of his big toe than fabric. He held up the decanter. "They wouldn't put this here if they didn't want us to enjoy, now would they?"

Declan chuckled, then tossed himself in the chair across from his insufferable traveling companion.

A moment later, the door flew open and Keelan barged in. When he saw Atikus, his entire face lit up—and then he saw Declan. He nearly stumbled, eyes wide.

Declan saw his big brother's discomfort and flinched back. "I know. They're weird and everybody's scared of me now." His head drooped.

Keelan closed the gap between them in two strides and wrapped his brother in a tight hug, lifting him playfully off the ground.

"You'll have to do better than swirling eyes of death to scare me away, Dec. You should know better."

Declan didn't fight the embrace the way he had when they were children. He wrapped his arms around Keelan and buried his head in his shoulder.

"It's good to see you, Kee. You've got no idea how much." The beginning of a sob shuttered through his chest, and Keelan started to release him and step back, but Declan clung to him as a desperate man clings to life raft. That's what Keelan had always been for him: the beacon in the storm he knew would be there no matter what. Keelan's arms were the safest place in the world for him. Even now, as a twenty-year-old with immensely powerful magic, Declan found comfort in his brother's presence.

Keelan finally pulled back to find Declan's face streaked. "Declan, what's wrong? What happened?"

Atikus finally stepped forward and placed a hand on Declan's shoulder.

"Our mother is dead," Declan blurted out. "I mean . . . I lost her. Keelan, I tried so hard, but her fingers . . . I couldn't hold on." He began sobbing uncontrollably. Atikus guided him to one of the chairs, he took the other, and Keelan kneeled beside his brother.

For what felt like an eternity, no one spoke. Keelan watched Declan carefully as he mourned. Atikus, racked with his own sudden grief, stared with pooled eyes into the dwindling fire in the hearth.

Finally, Declan spoke, sounding very much like the small boy Atikus had first met seventeen years ago. "I know you never got to know her, Kee, but she was so strong, and she was beautiful, inside and out. There were so many times I thought about just staying on the island with her and never coming back, but she knew what was at stake. She gave me strength and taught me to believe in myself for the first time. Imagine that. The mother we never knew did the most motherly thing possible just before—" He couldn't finish as another wave of sobs overcame him.

Atikus finally pulled himself out of his own thoughts and leaned forward. "Declan, I know she was proud of you—of both of you. I can't imagine a greater gift a son could give his mother than the time you spent with her. On the island, it was what, a year? More?"

Declan took a deep breath. "More like a year and a half, the way we counted it. It wasn't enough."

"If it had been a hundred years, it wouldn't have been enough. Take that from someone who's lived a *very* long time."

Keelan's leaned back against Atikus's chair and asked, "What happened? Are you okay talking about it?"

Declan let out a humorless laugh. "Guess we'll see. But yeah, you need to know."

Over the next thirty minutes, Declan walked them through everything, starting with Órla's first warning about Atikus being attacked through his own arrival in the cavern at the base of the Silver mountains earlier that day. Somehow, he managed to get through the whole thing without breaking down again.

He sucked in several breaths when he finished, as if to ensure he really was okay after reliving those events.

"I still don't understand." Keelan turned to Atikus. "Don't get me wrong, I'm happy to see you, but *how* did you get here? Everyone else's Gifts fell silent weeks ago."

"The Gifts are part of the reason we're here, but first we need to find Irina's Spirit and send her where she belongs—to the void. If she's allowed to continue roaming free, there's no telling what kind of havoc she'll cause. From what we can tell, she may also have the same unrestricted use of magic Declan and I now share."

"Unlimited magic? What are you talking about?" Keelan looked between them with wide eyes.

Declan gave him a weak grin, the best he could do in the moment. "Let's just say we don't have Gifts, we have magic. Remember the old stories of the original Mages and how they could do most anything? Back before Irina?"

Keelan nodded. "Yeah, I remember tales about that. Never believed any of it."

"Well, it was all true. Turns out, several of those Mages sacrificed themselves to cast a spell that stripped the others of their unrestricted magic and gave it as a Gift to normal people around the world. The spell had to be performed at the Well, the same Well our mother was the Keeper of."

"Holy Spirits," Keelan whispered.

"Literally," Atikus chuckled despite the somber mood in the room.

"Anyway"—Declan shot the old man a mock-annoyed scowl—"when Irina took over Larinda's body and did whatever she did to the Well, that spell was shattered. Gifts don't exist anymore. We've talked about it and believe we received our magical abilities because we happened to be the only people in the room. If we hadn't fallen in the Well, Kelså might've had the same powers, too."

"But that still doesn't explain why you popped up out of nowhere to scare the schnitzel out of my kitchen staff."

The three men's heads whirled to find the voice, stunned to see the Queen standing in the doorway. None of them had heard her enter. Declan scrambled to his feet, and Atikus followed suit as quickly as his old knees allowed. Unsure how to greet a monarch, Declan fumbled an awkward bow, then extended a hand as if to shake hers. Keelan reached up and gently lowered his brother's hand with his own.

"A bow is fine." He exchanged an amused, knowing look with Jess. "Gentlemen, may I preset Her Royal Majesty, Jessia Vester, Queen of the Spires."

"Oh, stop that." She stepped forward and waved a hand like she was swatting a fly. "It's just us here. There's no need for bowing and scraping, though I do rather enjoy it when Keelan shows deference to me, *as he should*."

Keelan reddened, causing Jess to chuckle.

Atikus looked from Keelan to Jess, then back to Keelan. His eyes widened, and he turned and poured another glass of amber liquid. This time, he handed it to Declan. "Here, you're going to need this."

A befuddled Declan took the glass, shrugged at Keelan, and downed the liquor.

Jess cleared her throat. "Declan, it is nice to finally meet you. Keelan can be tough to pry conversation out of, but when he opens up, it's usually with some story about you."

"Really?" Declan looked genuinely surprised.

Jess nodded. "Declan the Terrible, I believe was one of your first nicknames?"

"Jess . . ." Keelan tried to cut in.

"Great, thanks a lot," Declan jabbed him with his elbow.

Atikus stepped forward. "Your Majesty, it's good to see you again, too. You look much better than the road-worn girl I recall."

She smiled, and her eyes drifted as she remembered their flight from Irina's Seat. "That was . . . a very different time. I'll never be able to thank you for rescuing me and helping me."

No one quite knew what to say after that, so everyone stood and stared awkwardly at the floor or their hands.

"So," Jess said to fill the void. "We're all glad you here, but you still haven't answered why you nearly scared the life out of my cooks."

Declan barked a laugh. "Because Atikus's first thought would be of food if the continent were sinking into the sea."

"Well, now that you mention it, I am a tad hungry," the Mage said seriously.

"I think we're curious what drove you to visit." Keelan chuckled and saved Jess from pressing her question a third time, something he knew the young Queen hated doing.

"Ah, right. I suppose lunch can wait a few moments longer," Atikus said. "We did a scrying in search of Irina's Spirit. We know from the vision that she is here in your capital, but neither Declan nor any of our Mages recognized the building. We thought one of the Queen's constables or staff might be able to help. Declan and I have a plan to banish her, but we have to locate her first."

Jess nodded pensively. "Of course, my people will help. I'll summon the High Sheriff to join us for lunch. He knows this city as well as anyone and will be able to coordinate assistance from his force, should you need it."

Atikus offered a shallow bow. "Lunch would be most welcome—oh, and the assistance, too."

As they were finishing the last of their meal, Sheriff Cribbs and Chancellor Marks entered and paid respects with deep bows.

"Ethan, Bryan, come join us. We need your help on a critical matter," Jess said. "Are either of you hungry? We were just finishing, but the staff can bring you whatever you like."

They thanked her but declined more than water and tea as they took their seats. Marks studied Declan intently, his eyes returning several times to the golden tunic poking up from beneath his cloak.

"There is a *person of interest* hiding in a building here in the capital," Jess threw pleasantries aside and aimed straight for the point. "Mage Dani and Ranger Rea need your help to identify the location they saw in a scrying. Once determined, I need you to provide them whatever assistance they may need to deal with the culprit."

"My constables will help any way we can, Majesty, but may we know more about this person? What they've done? Who they are?" Cribbs asked.

Jess looked to Atikus and Declan and cocked a questioning brow.

Atikus thought a moment, then nodded. "Of course. We are looking for Irina's Spirit. She is currently inhabiting an elderly woman from the island of Rea Utu, a mystic of great value to their people. We saw her walking around a darkened shop or warehouse filled with candles. That is all the information we have."

Cribbs whistled as Marks sat back, eyes wide.

"Irina's Spirit? Really?" Marks asked Jess. She nodded once.

"And you're sure she's here?"

"We are certain she was here roughly two hours before we arrived. Whether she is still in that building, or even in the capital, we don't know," Atikus said.

Marks leaned forward again. "Speaking of your arrival, I've heard some fantastic rumors today. Care to share how you made it from Saltstone to Fontaine so quickly?"

"Later, Chancellor," Jess said, wanting to keep on topic.

"There's only a couple places that could be. We supply most of the candles for both the Kingdom, Melucia, and some of your neighbors to the east, too. There's a large factory on the southern edge of town that handles most of the manufacturing, but there's also a fairly large shop that makes and sells sticks only a few blocks away from the palace. Do you have any idea why she would want to go to a candle factory?"

Atikus shrugged. "No clue."

"Alright, it will take a little time to gather the men and get them there. I can have teams in both locations in an hour, maybe a little after. Would that work?"

Atikus looked to Declan, deferring to his service in the Rangers for the operational component of their mission.

"I think so. But Sheriff, tell your men not to enter either building. We believe she has an overwhelming arsenal of magic at her disposal. If we're right, she could kill your men with barely a thought," Declan said.

Cribbs nodded. "Why don't you meet me at the constabulary in thirty minutes? We can go over the plan and ride to the buildings together."

"Good. I have other meetings this afternoon. Declan, Atikus, please let Chancellor Marks know if you need anything else. The Kingdom is at your disposal," Jess said.

Marks and Cribbs caught her tone of dismissal, rose, bowed, and left.

Jess stood, gave Keelan a peck on the cheek, and left to begin her afternoon audiences from the throne.

Declan and Atikus stared openmouthed at Keelan.

"The Queen just *kissed* you!" Declan exclaimed.

Keelan chuckled. "She does that a lot these days. You'll get used to it." Then he winked at Atikus.

"This just gets stranger by the moment," Declan said.

Atikus grunted.

After a moment of consultation, Atikus and Declan decided to split up so one of them could accompany each team. If Irina really was at either site, they were the only ones who could do anything about it. They also decided not to enter the building if Irina was present at either location but wait and call for the other magician to Travel to that location so they could fight her together. Uncertainty around just how powerful she really was, as well as fear they'd only get one shot at banishing her, drove them to extra caution.

Atikus and his team approached the southern warehouse, a huge building that spanned the length of three or four moderately-sized homes. It was far enough from the center of town that there was no traffic—foot or carriage—seen nearby. A dozen constables fanned out and quietly surrounded the building.

The sounds of a working factory drifted out of open windows but weren't nearly as strong as the overpowering mixture of melting wax and the dozen aromatic oils used to create the candles' scents.

A few quiet moments passed before one of the constables appeared from the back of the building and walked unhurriedly toward Atikus and Sheriff Cribbs.

"Sir, we looked through several windows. It's only workers inside going about their routine. Nobody matching the description."

Cribbs thought a moment. "Alright, sergeant. Have one of your men go inside and interview the foreman, see if anything seems amiss."

The man snapped a nod and turned to carry out the Sheriff's orders.

"These are some of my best men. If there was anything out of place, they would've noticed it. My guess is that Declan is at the right place," Cribbs said.

"I need to warn him. Give me a moment."

Atikus closed his eyes. It wasn't necessary, but it helped him concentrate, and he'd learned over his centuries of life the little stagecraft helped those without magic understand it better, regardless of its utility to the casting.

"Declan, she's not here. I'll be right there."

"Understood. We're outside the shop, but there are civilians everywhere. This is a busy market district and a terrible place for a magical showdown. I'm not sure we can do more than observe."

"Keep watching. I'm coming."

Atikus opened his eyes.

"Sheriff, I need to get over there. Declan said there's a lot of people around, so we might not be able to go in to confront her."

Cribbs nodded. "It would be a lot better to do that at night. We can reassess after you learn whatever is there."

Atikus nodded, then vanished. Cribbs shook his head and stared at now the empty space before him.

Declan stood by a fruit vendor's stall across the road from the candle shop. Its wooden facade was painted blue, and a bright yellow sign swung above the door. An artistic rendition of several candles of various colors marked what waited inside. Dozens of well-dressed men and women strolled by, some carrying shopping bags or boxes, others wrestling children. The road lived in a state of perpetual motion. On any other day, Declan might've enjoyed sitting and watching the people pass by, but not today.

Atikus appeared directly behind Declan.

"Anything?" the Mage asked.

"Freakin' Sprits!" Declan exclaimed a little too loudly.

Atikus chuckled, then whispered. "Sorry, thought you heard me pop up behind you. I guess Traveling doesn't make noise."

"Guess not," Declan snorted, then looked back toward the building. "We have constables all over the place, but there's too much foot traffic here to do anything. They can't even get close enough to look inside."

"Why not? It's a shop, isn't it. Just go inside like you're looking for some candles."

Declan turned and stared at the Mage. "Well, I feel stupid."

Atikus grinned and shrugged his bushy brows.

"I would send you in there. Who'd suspect a frail old man?" Declan said, poking back. "My riding leathers aren't as highbrow as most of these shoppers, but they're better than a constable's uniform or your robe. You practically scream Mage walking around in that thing."

Atikus grunted. "You're right about the robe. Just be careful. Try not to use any magic while you're in there. She might be able to sense it. I know it makes the hairs on my arms stand up whenever you do anything powerful."

Declan nodded, then turned, wove his way through the passing throng, and approached the shop. The tinkling of tiny bells rang merrily as he entered, and the door closed behind him.

Chapter Thirty-Seven

Irina

***T**wo hours earlier (island time)*

In a moment of sheer terror, as the Well began to blacken, its cavern darkened, and the mountain shaking with anger, Irina had closed her eyes and focused on the safety of home. The magic coursing through her responded, understanding her need, and she Traveled instantly. She was utterly bewildered when she appeared in the storeroom of the candle shop, and several sticks dangling from lines strung across the ceiling clattered and smacked her in the head.

How was this possible? Her Gifts were strong, but *she couldn't Travel*, could she?

Then a different line of questions flowed through her mind. She had been thinking of home when she Traveled, but that home, where she was born and raised by loving parents, and where those parents were murdered, couldn't still stand. That was a thousand years ago. So where had magic delivered her?

The room spun and nausea threatened from the depths of her stomach. She forced herself to calm. There wasn't a mountain about to crash down on her, so this was an improvement. She just needed time to think and would figure everything out.

She started by surveying the musty room. Only a sliver of light trickled in from the partially covered window. She ran a hand across the candles that had assaulted her when she'd first arrived. The ancient, weathered look of the back of her hand gave her a moment's pause. She used to be so young and beautiful. She longed for that day again, a day when men would turn as she entered a room, would stumble over themselves if she glanced their way, a day she was wanted and desired. She pictured her smooth skin and lustrous black hair, her brilliant green eyes. Then she sighed.

She'd lost so much from her imprisonment.

When her attention returned to the candles above, and her hand continued its journey, she was astonished for the second time in an hour. Smooth, supple skin that smiled back at her. The hand flew to her face and felt the absence of age, the same smoothness of youth she'd seen on her hands. Had her magic answered her call again? How?

On a whim, she held her palm before her and called moisture from the air, forming a swirling, wobbling ball of water. She gasped and the ball fell apart, spilling on the dusty wooden floor.

That's not one of my Gifts either. I've never been able to call or manipulate water.

Her head spun at the implications. Something had happened to her at the Well, far beyond simply taking her revenge and breaking that wretched place apart. Somehow, *her true magic*, the magic of her youth, had returned. She was powerful again, invincible so long as that blasted Phoenix stayed dead. The boy who'd fought her, the one with Kelså—he was powerful, too, but she'd seen him fall into the Well, dragged under the sickened waves by that witch. Now, she was the last living Mage, the only *true Mage* left.

A wave of euphoria washed away the prior moment's nausea as she realized she could do anything, *be* anything. She could rule the Kingdom. Spirits, she could rule them all. That had been her goal all those years ago, and now she could actually accomplish it. The only question was, did she want it? Destroying her enemies was so much more satisfying than ruling. As Empress, she had to pretend to listen, pretend to care what her people thought. How tedious could life be? She'd have to think on that.

She shook herself out of her thoughts and returned to her present situation. This was definitely a storeroom. By the combative wax sticks dangling above, she guessed it belonged to a candle maker's shop. On the wall with the window, several barrels stood stacked on one another, ingredients for the maker's craft. On the opposite wall sat a small writing desk littered with parchment. She crossed the room and scanned a few pages, mostly invoices or inventory tallies, even a few personal letters. She set the last of the letters down, careful to place it exactly as she found it.

Satisfied there was nothing of interest in the room, she quietly crept to the door and peered out onto the large sales floor. The shop was still. She thought it odd for the owner to leave in the middle of the day, but customs of this time might differ from her day. Or maybe the maker had simply gone out for lunch or to run errands. She really didn't care.

She stepped into the sea of tables and candles and surveyed the room. Nothing jumped out until she started to leave through the front door. Pinned to the wall by the door, where exiting patrons would see it, was a flyer. She reached up and plucked it off the wall. Local Priests were holding a meeting to support their efforts in the city later that week. The image of a man in long robes was pictured to the side of the lettering. The flyer proclaimed, "The day is coming soon. The One shall return and the faithful shall take their rightful place by his side."

She stopped reading as realization slammed into her.

The room was suddenly small and sweltering. Anger boiled inside her.

Thorn, that bastard! He's stolen my *prophecy. That conniving, thieving snake.*

In that moment, she knew her goal wasn't to rule. She didn't need a crown—and she had more than enough power to do whatever she pleased.

No, she wanted one thing, and only one thing.

She wanted *vengeance*.

The door closed behind him and Declan looked up. A tall woman with waist-length silky black hair was glaring at a parchment in her hand. Despite the tinkling of the bells, she hadn't seemed to notice him.

And then she looked up and their eyes met.

Somehow, she *knew* him. The answer came to him immediately; he'd forgotten about his eyes and their swirling magic.

Before he knew what had happened, a wall of air slammed him into the back of the heavy wooden door. He lost his footing and landed on his rear. Dazed, he looked up at the woman. He could feel the venom and hatred glaring back. And then she vanished, and the crinkled parchment she had been holding drifted to the floor.

Chapter Thirty-Eight

Declan

Declan climbed to his feet and stared at where the woman had stood a moment before. He threw up a shield of air in case she returned, then took a couple tentative steps forward, scanning the area. His head swam a moment before settling.

The door squealed as it flew open, and two uniformed constables entered with swords drawn. "Are you aright, sir? We heard the crash and thought you might be in trouble."

Declan released his shield and turned to the men. "I'm fine. The shop is empty now. The woman got away."

"How?" The men glanced at each other. "We have the place surrounded. There's nowhere for her to go."

"Officers, would you get the High Sheriff, please. We'll explain everything to him," Atikus said as he entered.

Declan was already kneeling to pick up the parchment Irina dropped as she vanished. He turned and started to say something, but Atikus silenced him. *"Not until we're alone."*

As soon as the constables closed the door, Declan stepped forward and handed the flyer to Atikus. "I'm not sure if this is relevant to finding her, but she was reading this when I walked in. I caught her crumpling it up, and she looked angry."

Atikus skimmed the flyer and grunted. "Hmm. The Order again. Seems like they're in the middle of everything these days. When we see the Sheriff, I'll ask him to assign some men to sniff around about this. Now, tell me what happened."

Declan recounted the two-minute encounter with the woman he presumed was Irina. When he described her hair and eyes, Atikus nodded. "That's her. She's used her magic to change her appearance back to how she looked before. If I understand the magic correctly, that's akin to Illusion, and not a true transformation. She should still be inhabiting Larinda's body, which means the physical limitations of an old woman still work to our advantage."

"Maybe. She's a *magically enhanced* old woman. She tossed me back like I was nothing."

"Her magic is strong, but she caught you by surprise. In a fight you knew was coming, I doubt she could do that without you having time to shield yourself." He smoothed his beard as he thought. "Using magic takes a physical and mental toll. That's its price. Larinda's constitution is strong, but she's still old."

"You're already planning our confrontation, aren't you?"

Atikus nodded slowly. "We'll need to get this right when the time comes. If we can keep her contained and throwing her magic around long enough, her body will wear itself out. It should be like watching a flame flicker and go out. Then we can banish her without her power resisting us."

"We just have to survive her attacks long enough while keeping her contained somehow. Sounds easy enough."

"This was never going to be easy, but that's the best idea I have at the moment. You're welcome to come up with a better plan."

"Oh, no. I'm a Ranger, not a tactician. I'll be the hammer; you be the brains."

Atikus laughed. "Finally, you recognize my mental prowess and your . . . well . . . *other* abilities."

"Thanks a lot, I think." Declan smirked. "We should get to the Sheriff."

They'd made it a dozen paces out of the candle shop when another uniformed officer approached with a message from Sheriff Cribbs asking them to join him at the palace. There had been other developments, and the Queen wanted them to be part of his briefing. After a short walk, they passed through the golden doors to the audience chamber and were greeted by Jess, Keelan, Cribbs, and Marks, all seated around the Council table.

Heavily armed guards were everywhere. One stood quietly along the wall, ten paces from the next. Four additional guards stood near the Council table, two on either side of Jess's chair, and the other pair on either side of the throne.

Keelan noticed Declan's eyes widen as he scanned the room.

"There was an incident here at the palace. Security has increased," he said simply.

Jess stood and greeted them, then asked them to the meeting already in progress.

"Sheriff, why don't we hear from Declan and Atikus? Then you can brief everyone on Oliver," Jess said.

Declan and Atikus brought everyone up to speed on their action at the two candle shops, each interjecting when the other needed help to fill in details. As they concluded, Atikus withdrew the flyer from his robe and handed it to Cribbs.

"This is all we have to go on at the moment. We're not even sure it's connected to anything," Atikus said.

Cribbs glanced at it and handed it to Jess.

"These are all over town, Majesty. Nothing unusual there," Marks said leaning over the table, then settling back into his seat.

Jess set the flyer down and turned to Cribbs. "If there's nothing else there, Sheriff, it's your turn."

"We received a bird from the constabulary in Oliver. Unfortunately, the scrolls are tiny, so our information is limited. I'll just read it to you."

Another murder. Witness came forward, saw large brown bear maul victim. Witness saw bear don mask and change into man following killing. Man wore brown robes. – FL

Cribbs handed the scroll to Jess. "Majesty, without speaking with my officer or the witness, I have no way of affirming the veracity of the claim. This could be a drunk who saw nothing, or something far more troublesome."

"He's right. The message doesn't give us enough to go on," Keelan said, once more in his element discussing a criminal investigation.

"We have—" Declan started.

Keelan cut him off. "What we *do* have is a pattern. First, the Order shows up trying to strong arm the Queen into submission to their faith. Then, murders begin, but only one in a particular city, all committed by animal attack. Has anyone here ever heard of such a wave of murderous beasts within such a short window?"

He watched as everyone considered his words.

"Then the Queen is attacked by a horse who Shifts into a man after he's killed—a man wearing brown robes," he continued.

"And now, another animal attack, but this time with a witness who saw the live assailant Shift back into his human form and walk away from the scene—again, wearing brown robes."

"Your Majesty," he said, turning to Jess. "We cannot act on supposition, but it should guide the next steps in our investigation."

She stared at him for a long moment. "Go on. What are you proposing?"

He looked toward Cribbs. "I need to go to Oliver again, interview this witness and the officers, confirm whether or not the story is credible. While I'm there, Atikus and the Sheriff continue working toward locating Irina."

Jess leaned back and crossed her arms.

"It's a three-or-four-day ride. By the time you get there, do the interviews, and get back, who knows where Irina will be or what she'll have been up to." Cribbs mirrored his Queen, crossing his arms.

Declan leaned forward and cleared his throat. "I can help with that. Using my magic, I'll take Keelan to Oliver, then bring him back. Your four days will be a blink if we Travel, and Atikus and I can coordinate using Telepathy. Now that we both have that ability, we can actually conduct a two-way conversation."

"I like it," Atikus said. "Jess—I mean, Your Majesty, do you think your Mages would be willing to help? I could use some extra minds thinking this through."

"I'll have Mage Ernest summoned to the palace. He's sharp, and a good man. You'll like him. He can get whoever you need involved." Jess leaned forward again and placed her palms on the table as if to rise. "Are we agreed? Anything else?"

Everyone looked around at each other, but no one spoke.

"Fine." She stood and turned, then looked back at Declan. "Ranger Rea, please be careful and keep Keelan out of trouble."

Declan shot Keelan a startled glance.
Keelan returned a lopsided, boyish grin.
Jess rolled her eyes and walked out.

Declan gripped Keelan's arm. "You may be a little dizzy when we get there. It'll pass in ten or fifteen minutes. Now, picture the area just outside the inn's front door in your mind—as detailed as you can."

Keelan nodded and closed his eyes. When he opened them, the inn was dancing in front of him—but not just the inn, the whole square where it sat swirled in and out of focus. Even Declan, who still gripped his arm, was doing a weird wiggling thing.

And then he threw up all over Declan's trousers.

"Aw, really? You couldn't hold on for just a minute?" Declan groaned. "Are those chunks of apple? Ugh."

"Sorry, but if you'd just stand still—" and he threw up again.

Declan walked his woefully pale brother to the front of the inn and sat him on the ground.

"As big as you are, I thought you might be able to handle that better. Just sit there until the nausea passes. I'm going to find somewhere to clean up."

Keelan didn't look up for fear of his brother doing the wiggly thing again. He just raised a hand in acknowledgement and let his head loll forward. Declan disappeared into the inn, returning several minutes later with somewhat cleaner trousers and Laurie in tow.

"Lieutenant?" Laurie said from behind Declan. "Didn't you just leave us?" She kneeled down and helped him drink some water from the mug she'd brought out.

"It's a long story," Declan said. "We need to see your Sheriff, or whatever you call the head constable in the town."

"That would be Chief Kerr. He's a few streets over. When the Lieutenant is back on his feet, I'll take you there. It's right on my way to the market."

Keelan finally looked up, focus slowly returning to his eyes. "Thank you. I should be alright in a minute."

It took another twenty minutes for Keelan to stand without wobbling, then another ten to reach the constabulary, but they made it. The brothers thanked Laurie and entered the building as she turned to perform her daily market ritual.

"Ah, Keelan, come in." Chief Kerr rose from behind a heavy wooden desk in the back of the one-room space to greet them. Four other desks faced the door from various points in the room, and two were occupied by green-uniformed officers.

They settled into a pair of simple wooden chairs opposite the chief's desk and were promptly handed mugs of steaming tea.

"Chief, this is my brother, Declan. When we get into what we have to tell you, you'll understand why he's here. Would it be possible for us to have some privacy as we talk?"

Kerr quirked a brow, but before he could ask his officers to leave, Declan held up a hand. "No need to send your men out, Chief. I'll silence the room so only the three of us can hear our conversation. There, done."

Kerr's eyes widened. "How—" He looked up at one of his men working at a desk across the room. "Edward. Hey, Edward!" The man didn't flinch, just kept scribbling on a parchment.

"No one's Gifts are working, haven't been for a bit. How did you do that?"

Keelan leaned forward and whispered, despite his brother's magic. "There's a lot going on, and we're neck deep in it. We can't talk about parts of the investigation, but what brought us here may be the key to securing the new Queen's throne from danger."

The lawman leaned back and whistled. "The Queen? Really?"

Keelan nodded, then launched into his prepared explanation detailing what they knew about the attacks in the other cities and the one on the Queen. He left out the whole Irina-has-returned side of the investigation.

"And now you want to know more about the bird we sent, about that last killing?"

Keelan nodded again. "That's right. As crazy as it sounds, your witness's story fills in a lot of holes for us."

"Crazy is right, but explain something to me. Why would the Order and their Priests do something like this? Most of the people have come to love the Priests. Those who don't at least respect the work they're doing. Why go after the Queen—or any of these people, for that matter?"

"We're hoping your witness, or someone in town who knew the victim, can help us with that. We might also want to talk with anyone who knew your first victim, Hershel?"

"That's right. Town was torn up over his death, now one of his best friends gets killed. It's just too much."

Keelan's eyes narrowed. "One of his best friends? The victims knew each other?"

"That's right." Kerr nodded. "You think there's a connection?"

"I don't know, but it's another piece, and there's been too many pieces showing up for them not to paint a picture at some point."

"Alright, where do you want to start?"

"Right here. I'd like to talk with your officers who dealt with the latest killing first. Then we can move on to witnesses and acquaintances."

Kerr gave a smile that didn't reach his eyes. "Solid plan. I'm starting to see why you're Melucia's famous top cop now."

Keelan shrugged. "Not sure I deserve all that. I'm just trying to protect people best I can. Who should we start with?"

The constables were friendly and helpful, offering detailed accounts of their investigations and interviews, all of which resulted in more questions than answers. Keelan thanked them, and the brothers moved on to a witness list the Chief provided them, complete with locations and directions.

"Wait," Keelan said as he read through the list. "Laurie? Is that the same Laurie who works at the inn?"

"And the same Laurie who's Hershel's daughter. That's right." Kerr confirmed.

"Huh," was all Keelan said, drawing a curious gaze from Declan.

Kerr offered to accompany them as they left the constabulary, but Keelan waved him off, and they made their way to the first name on the list.

Four hours later, Declan and Keelan were down to the last name, Laurie. As they walked toward the inn, Keelan turned to his brother.

"Did you sense anything from those people we just talked to?"

Declan raised a brow. "Sense anything? What do you mean?"

"You know, feel anything strange? Get a tingling sensation, say, between your shoulder blades?"

"Are you feeling woozy again? That's the strangest thing I've heard all day—and we're dealing with some pretty strange stuff."

Keelan grunted in agreement. "I'm talking about sensing Truth, like I could do before the Gifts vanished. You remember my bees? How they'd sting just below my neck? You teased me *for years* about calling it that. That only happened when somebody was hiding something or lying."

"Oh! That?" He paused and thought through the conversations they'd just completed. "No, nothing jumps out. That one guy, the butcher, wasn't very talkative, but I didn't get any tingly magic alarm or anything. I'm pretty sure I would've noticed a hive attacking me."

"Nice. Keep rubbing it in." Keelan smirked. "I thought the same about that guy. Maybe we should pay him another visit before we leave. For now, just pay attention when we talk to Laurie. I've got a feeling—"

"Alright, I'll keep an eye—or a neck—out for the bees." Declan quipped, earning a brotherly punch in the arm.

A short time later, they sat at one of the round wooden tables in the common room of the inn. Laurie stared across, fingers fidgeting.

"I know it sounds crazy, but I swear that's what I saw. The bear reached down to the ground, grabbed a mask, put it on, and turned into a man, then walked away into the night. I was hiding behind the apothecary not twenty paces away."

Keelan looked to Declan, then nudged him with his foot.

"Uh, ok. It does sound crazy, but I believe you're telling us what you think you saw."

"I *saw* it. It's not what I think. Don't you call me nuts, too. I deal with that enough around here already. The whole thing was supposed to be kept secret, but it's all anybody's talking about." She put her head in her hands as if to cry.

"I know this is hard, but what you're telling us is important." Keelan tried to reassure her. "The bear put on a mask and turned into a man. What did that man look like?"

She looked up slowly, her lips pursed as she tried to remember. "It was dark, but I could see he wore robes. The moonlight reflected or shimmered off them as he walked away. I never saw his face, but he had short hair. I think it was brown or black."

"Was he tall or short? What was his build like?"

"It was hard to tell. He was so big as the bear, then he shrunk down. I guess he was average height, maybe a little taller. His robes were flowy, so I couldn't really tell anything about his body."

Keelan watched her fidget.

"Laurie, what aren't you telling us? I can see you're holding something back."

She looked up. "I've told you everything I know, everything I saw."

"But not something you suspect?" he guessed.

"How—? Her eyes widened, then she looked back to her hands.

Keelan decided to go in a different direction. "How well do you know the local Priest?"

Laurie's head snapped up. "Seth? Pretty well, I guess."

Declan leaned forward and gave Keelan a meaningful look over his shoulder.

"What's he like?"

She sat up straight and crossed her arms. "He's a good man who helps people. What more do you want to know?"

"Easy," Keelan raised a palm. "We're not accusing him of anything, just trying to get to know the people in town. I've been an investigator for years, and you never know what tiny clue might help crack a case."

Her arms unfurled and her hands dropped back to her lap, clutched tightly. A far-away look came over her eyes as she remembered and spoke. "Seth and I started seeing each other a few months after he came to town. He visits in the morning as we're getting ready for the breakfast crowd. We have dinner a few times each week and take long walks around town. He's even helped me with my market runs a few times. Like I said, he's a wonderful man."

"What can you tell us about his work with his faith?"

She beamed at this. "He helps more people that anyone I've ever known. He says it's why the Spirits called him to the Order, to help those who can't help themselves. Poor, lame, sick, old, it doesn't matter to him. He does whatever they need, whatever he can,"

"How does he spread the word about his faith? Does he hold meetings in a temple, or speak somewhere?" Keelan asked.

"Oh, yes, he holds meetings a couple times each week in the town square. There isn't a temple here, so he stands on the steps of the courtyard and folks gather around. Most folks make at least one of his meetings each week."

"I assume you attend these meetings?"

She nodded. "I don't miss many. I like seeing him talk, watching how the people react to his message of kindness and generosity."

Keelan sat back in his chair and tapped his forefinger on the table as he thought.

Declan leaned in, surprising Keelan. "Laurie, I'm not a constable, just a Ranger. We take care of animals and trees mostly. Keelan and I haven't seen each other in a while, and I thought traveling together might give us time to reconnect."

She smiled tentatively, unsure where he was headed. "That sounds . . . nice."

"It has been, except for him throwing up on me, of course." He smiled innocently. "But I've listened to most of his conversations today and something you said tickled my neck. Can you go back to before you left on your walk that night, the one where you saw the bear? You said you saw the man who was killed lingering at a table, chatting with some other man. Could you hear anything? See anything?"

She scrunched her mouth in concentration. "I tried to listen in. They seemed so secretive. It made me curious, but they were whispering most of the time. It didn't make any sense, but I think they said something like, 'This has to end,' like they were planning something. I'm sorry, I really couldn't hear them."

Silence lingered before Keelan finally leaned forward.

"I only have a couple more questions."

She nodded.

"What does Seth wear? Does he have a uniform or some symbol of office? As a Priest, I mean."

"He wears his robe," she said.

"Long, brown, shimmers in the light?"

She sucked in a breath and nodded, then looked up.

Keelan waited.

"I . . . It can't . . . He wouldn't hurt *anyone*. I know Seth."

Keelan tapped his finger on the table. Even Declan shifted in his seat before the silence was broken.

Laurie whispered without raising her head. "I don't know. I can't believe Seth would do anything—would *be* that."

"It might not be him, but we need to find out. No one in town will be safe until we do." Keelan rose. "Thank you, Laurie. I know this was difficult, but you've been very helpful."

She shot to her feet. "What are you going to do? Please don't hurt him."

Keelan put up his palms again. "We're just investigating. Hopefully the facts rule him out, but we have to follow them, not decide what we want them to be."

Her head drooped again. "I know you're right. This is all so terrible."

Declan stepped forward. "It is, but we're here to help."

She nodded in thanks and gave Declan a weak smile.

"We need you to keep this conversation between us for now, OK. Whoever killed that man—*and your father*—wouldn't take well to a witness walking around."

She nodded and walked them to the door.

"We'll check on you later tonight, alright?" Keelan said as they exited.

The brothers walked outside, and Keelan asked Declan to shield their conversation like he'd done in the constabulary.

Declan nodded, then Keelan asked, "What do you think of her story?"

"Something was nagging at me about the victim's conversation that night, but everything else lines up with what we already knew. I couldn't feel anything false from her. She's dating the Priest, but she didn't rule out him being the bear-shifter-thing, whatever you call it."

"Let's go with *bear* for now. If we're overheard somewhere, it'll raise less suspicion in the community," Keelan said. "I agree with you on her being honest. She didn't want to make her suspicions real by talking about them, but opened up when pressed. I believe her. Now we need a way to rule Seth out."

"We could just ask him," Declan said.

Keelan laughed, then looked up. "You're not joking, are you?"

Declan shook his head. "No joke. Remember, I have your Truthreading Gift now. If we ask him and he lies, I'll know. Bam! Bear trap."

Keelan groaned. "Now he jokes."

Declan laughed and gave his brother a playful punch in the arm. "You missed me. Go ahead and admit it.

Keelan chuckled and shook his head. "Let's go *bear hunting*, little brother."

They found Seth playing with a group of children at the edge of the market square. Keelan had a hard time picturing the man as a menacing bear as he ran in circles with three-year-olds dangling from his legs and laughing hysterically.

After a moment, the Priests noticed the men watching and forced the children to set him free so he could greet the newcomers.

"Hello, gentlemen. Were you hoping to be the hunter or the pray today?" Seth asked with a broad smile.

Keelan stiffened, but Declan laughed.

"He means with the children, dummy." Declan whispered in Keelan's mind.

Keelan shook off the odd sensation of having his brother in his head and nodded toward the Priest. "Forgive us for interrupting, Seth. Looks like you had a real fight on your hands. This is my brother, Declan. Mind if we ask you a few questions?"

"Of course not. How can I help?"

Keelan motioned for the trio to step out of earshot of the children and the woman tending them. Declan nodded to his brother, indicating the Silencing shield had been erected once more. Seth looked at Keelan expectantly.

"Have you ever heard of a man who could turn into an animal?" Keelan asked without preamble.

Seth rocked back and barked a laugh. When the brothers continued glaring, he sobered. "You're serious?"

Keelan waited, his eyes never leaving Seth's.

"Only in children's takes."

"What about within your Order? Are there *tales* of men with this ability?"

Seth's brow furrowed. "I've never heard of such. Where is this coming from, Keelan? Why are you asking *me* these questions? And what would the Order have to do with something so horrific?"

Keelan watched him a moment, then sighed. "I'm sorry, Seth. We're following leads found at the scene of the mauling. Some are disturbing and don't make much sense, but they're all we have."

Declan finally spoke. "I think we have everything we need. Thank you for your time."

Keelan gave him a questioning look, but Declan simply motioned for them to leave.

"We may have more questions later, if that's alright." Keelan said.

"Of course," Seth said. "You don't think the people here are in any danger, do you?"

"We think the bear fled after the attack and hope that's the last we see of him," Keelan said.

The brothers had made it around the block when Declan turned to Keelan. "He's telling the truth. He had no idea what you were talking about when you mentioned a man turning into an animal. The shock on his face was real."

"I could tell that *without* magic. He would've been the best liar I'd ever met otherwise."

"What now? That really was the best lead we had."

Keelan rubbed his chin. "I guess we let Laurie know her man is innocent, then head back to Fontaine."

Chapter Thirty-Nine

Keelan

Keelan staggered forward as the pair appeared back in the palace. He took two steadying steps then threw up all over the audience chamber floor.

"Well, that's a first during my reign," Jess said with a raised brow from her seat at the Council table.

Chancellor Marks, Sheriff Cribbs, and Atikus turned.

Declan grinned back at their audience and bowed. "My carriage rides are a tad bumpy for the uninitiated."

Keelan retched again.

Jess turned to a servant standing in the shadows near the door and nodded sharply. The woman curtsied and vanished, returning a moment later with two others, a bucket, and a mop.

Keelan stumbled to the bottom step leading to the throne and sat with his head in his hands. Declan walked over and placed a palm above his brother's shoulder. Light exploded from his hand, then winked out.

Keelan looked up with wide eyes. "The nausea's gone!" he exclaimed. Then he scrunched up his face his brother. "You could've done that all along, couldn't you?"

Declan grinned and shrugged. "Honestly, I didn't think of it until now. That's the first time I've used Healing since gaining all these new powers, but I did owe you for ruining my breeches."

Keelan gave Declan one last annoyed glance and stood, surprised how solid the ground now felt under his feet. The pair then joined the Queen's meeting.

"Atikus was just about to tell us about a scrying he did with our Mages, but I think we should hear from you two first." Jess turned to Keelan and gave him a hint of a smile.

His return smile was more than a hint, and the others shifted in their seats, watching the reunited couple.

"Your Majesty," Keelan began formally. "Most of the interviews were fruitless. However, we spent a good amount of time with the witness to the latest killing and believe the killer wore the robes of a Priest once he resumed his human form. We also questioned the resident Priest, but found no evidence he knew anything of the killer or anyone else in the Order with the ability to Shift. Declan can now Truthread and found no lies, nor did he sense either of them hiding any information. We found them both to be forthright and highly credible."

Cribbs leaned forward and shook his head. "Incredible. I was certain this was a talk of a drunk woman."

"I was too, until we met her and the Priest," Declan said.

"Did you find anything else, a motive, anything else connecting the Order to the killings?" Marks asked.

Keelan shook his head. "No, nothing solid. The witness recalled seeing the victim talking in hushed tones with another man hours before he was killed, but she only overheard a couple random phrases, nothing that made any sense."

"What did she hear?" Cribbs asked, quill in hand.

"Something like, 'this has to end,'" she thought. She wasn't completely sure and had no idea of the context."

Cribbs made a note. "What would they be plotting about that could cause one of them to be killed? Oliver is decent-sized town with healthy trade from both the ocean and roads. There hasn't been a serious crime like murder or kidnapping there in years. What's changed recently?"

Declan started to speak, then stopped.

"What? Don't hold back at this table," Jess said.

"It's just . . . the Priest. I know we're already wary of them, and I don't want to jump to conclusions because of that, but he showed up what, five or six months ago?" Declan asked.

"Right, but you heard Laurie. He's basically the town saint." Keelan said.

"If they can Shift into murderous animals, they can fool us into thinking they're good people."

"What about preaching against the Crown? Did you hear any more about that?" Marks asked.

Keelan shook his head. "Not really. A few of the people we interviewed said they'd heard the Priest talk about unifying under the One, but they thought he meant as an addition or support to the Crown, not anything like rebellion."

Silence lingered a moment as the brothers' report sank in, then Jess spoke. "Thank you both for going down there so quickly. Atikus, would you tell us what you and the Mages found?"

The old Mage leaned forward. "Mage Ernest suggested we scry for Irina using the crumpled flyer she was holding before she vanished. It had only been a couple hours since she possessed it, so he thought we might still get a reading. If we had waited another few hours, it wouldn't have worked at all." He paused and took a sip of water. "We are now certain she Traveled to Irina's Seat. The image in the scrying bowl was clearly the stone Temple in that village."

Keelan sat back and ran a hand over his head. "Irina's Seat? I really hoped to never see that place again."

Jess muttered. "That makes two of us."

Declan cocked his head. "Atikus, what aren't you telling us? I can sense you're holding something back." "Bees get ya?" Keelan said with a smirk.

"Shut it," Declan said with a grin of his own.

Atikus looked between them and shook his head. "I thought of something while you were talking about your trip to Oliver, but it may be too crazy, even for this situation."

"I doubt this could get any crazier. Let's hear it," Declan prodded.

"Well, the flyer referenced an upcoming meeting the local Priest was holding, and it highlighted a message about the Return of the One. That's an ancient prophecy we all assumed referenced Irina's return. What if this One is using her prophecy for their own gain? How do you think she would react when she learned of it?"

"That insane, murderous witch? She'd want to rip their eyes out," Jess spat.

Atikus nodded. "She just Traveled to Irina's Seat, and Declan, the last person to see her before she went there, said she looked angry as she read the flyer."

"Holy Spirits. That actually makes sense." Keelan exclaimed. "Dec, Atikus, we need to go there right now. We may not get a better shot at her."

"Woah. Hold on there, Big Brother. Remind me what magic you have to fight an all-powerful, wildly angry sorceress."

Keelan glared a moment, then shrugged. "Fair point, I guess."

"Atikus and I are the only ones who stand any chance of banishing her once and for all. I just hope she really is the only other person with magic. If she were to team up with this One and they had power, it might be more than we could handle."

Atikus grunted. "That's all true, but we have to try. Keelan might not be able to join us, but he was right about not missing this chance. We need to go quickly."

No one at the table objected, and Jess reluctantly agreed, though she hated the idea of anyone returning to that awful place. Within ten minutes, everyone had wished them well, and the pair had vanished.

"I hope we did the right thing sending them," Jess said, as she and Keelan stood alone—save for her guards—in the throne room. Keelan wrapped his arms around her and held her close.

"Me too," he whispered. "They're the only family I have left now."

Chapter Forty

Irina

Thorn sat on his throne, crown glittering on his head as its bloody diamonds pulsed their eerie, magical heartbeat. Two Priests knelt before him. Irina's sudden appearance in a darkened corner of the massive hall went unnoticed, and she crept forward to peer around a large column.

"Excellency, there was no way to know the girl was watching. I checked the area before killing the man, and it was clear." The kneeling Priest sounded terrified, even from where Irina listened.

Thorn leaned forward and sneered. "And yet she was there, watching you. She reported everything to the Crown, you idiot!"

The second figure spoke, a woman with a high-pitched voice made shriller by Thorn's wrath.

"Excellency, if the four of us remaining approached the palace at the same time—"

"You want me to send you back to the palace? After the Horse's failure with the Queen and your inexcusable negligence in Oliver? The Queen's guards will be on high alert now. You won't get anywhere near her. It's more likely you'd all be killed—and, as *displeased* as I am at the moment, you are far too useful to die—*yet*."

Irina's blood boiled watching Thorn act as though he ruled the world and everyone in it owed him their allegiance.

Then she realized he was wearing *her* crown.

She held her palms before her and called a swirling ball of flame into one; water mixed with air in the other. With a thought, she froze the water solid, creating a spiked ball she recalled seeing many times on the end of mace's chain. She threw her palms forward and urged her missiles into the air. Then she drew more air and shoved it behind them, propelling them faster and faster. The ball of ice struck first, slamming into the back of the man's head with a sickening crunch that echoed throughout the chamber and splattered blood, skull fragments, and brain matter all over the woman and the floor. His body lurched forward, immediately still. The fire didn't strike the woman as much as it engulfed her the moment it touched her skin, crawling hungrily until her entire form was covered in writhing flame. Her robe blazed brightly, and she screamed in agony. She managed to stand and run several paces before the flames overcame her and she toppled to the cold marble, a burning, billowing pile of unrecognizable flesh. The stench nearly made Irina want to flee—*nearly*.

Thorn shot to his feet, eyes wide, but he paused only a second. His gaze followed the line traveled by Irina's missiles, and he locked onto her stare with a hate-filled scowl of his own. One of the bloody diamonds on the crown flared brightly as he called its Enhanced Strength and hurled a heavy silver pitcher across the hall. Irina easily avoided the blow by ducking behind the column, but that split second gave Thorn time to prepare a real attack.

He gripped the silver staff that leaned against the throne as another diamond flared. A column of flame as tall as Thorn erupted a few feet from where Irina stood. It inched toward her, expanding with every second, curving at its ends as if to embrace her whole being.

In all her centuries, she'd never seen a wall of flame called before. Her heart raced and she began to panic as the heat swelled around her. The flames pressed her into the corner of the chamber and began to lick at the edges of her dress. She called as much moisture from the air as she could hold and threw it outward. The wall sizzled angrily and dimmed but would not be stopped by mere water. It pressed forward.

Then she remembered she had far more that her simple Gifts. She Traveled the length of the room, away from the flame, and immediately in front of Thorn. He leapt back, startled by her sudden appearance, and tripped over the bottom step of the dais. Irina shot forward and drove her own Enhanced punch into his gut. He crumpled and clutched his stomach, gasping for breath. She called Fire once again and hurled it into the fetal form before her, engulfing him immediately. Thorn writhed, but a third diamond flared, and he Healed himself as quickly as he burned. Shimmering light flared from the length of the silver staff in his hand, and the flames surrounding his body turned from hues of auburn, golden, and scarlet to a translucent azure.

He stood, a man still consumed in flames, yet unburned.

Irina staggered back, horror and shock streaked across her face.

Thorn gripped her arm, and angry flames clawed at her dress and skin, crawled up her shoulder, and began searing away the fabric on her back. She screamed in pain and rage, cast her own Healing, then hurled a gust of wind at Thorn's head.

He laughed as the spear of air sailed over his head.

She'd missed.

Standing not two paces away, the fool woman had missed.

Then he heard the clanking of metal on marble, and his heart seized.

"Looking for something?" she asked from behind, as she bent and retrieved the crown.

He whirled around to find her leaning casually against the throne. He howled and tried to step forward, but the flames still raging across his body, again the colors of the sun, were now free to burn and destroy. The staff dropped from his hand and clanged loudly against the marble as it fell down the steps of the dais.

Irina holding his crown was the last thing he saw before darkness took him.

Declan and Atikus appeared on the balcony above the ceremonial chamber, just as Keelan had described it. They were both relieved they hadn't ended up Traveling themselves into one of the pillars or walls since neither had ever seen the place.

They could hear a man speaking below. He sounded arrogant and angry, but they couldn't make out what he was saying. Declan sneaked a peek over the railing.

"There are three people down there. One on a throne wearing a crown and two kneeling in front of him. The two on the floor are wearing robes and masks." Declan whispered in Atikus's mind.

Before Atikus could respond, a bright flare lit up the far end of the hall. They watched as the echo of its light streaked the length of the aisle, then struck something. They heard the sickening sound like a large melon splattering against a wall, then a blood chilling scream that lingered for many seconds before dwindling to nothing.

Atikus braved a glance over the railing and was transfixed. Blood and gore littered the polished marble before the dais. Smoke curled from what had to have been a body moments earlier. Thorn held a crown, his eyes fixed on a point at the far end of the chamber. Atikus followed his gaze and his throat caught.

"Irina's down there. She just ducked behind a column," he said without turning.

"What the—" Declan started, as he peered over the railing next to Atikus.

His thought cut off as a battle erupted below. He was sickened and fascinated at the same time.

"Should we attack now, while he's distracting her?" Declan asked.

"No, let him wear her down. Whoever survives will be weaker when they face us."

When Thorn finally fell and Irina stood with the crown in her hand, Atikus slumped back behind the banister. *"Now it's time. You go to the right side; I'll take the left. Hit her with everything you've got."*\

Irina watched Thorn's body burn, then turned her gaze to the crown, *her* crown. The diamonds pulsed their steady rhythm, as if welcoming their mistress home. She grinned and placed the golden band carefully on her head, reveling in the wave of white-hot power that rippled through her body.

She turned to exit the chamber, eager to walk the halls of her former capital once more, when the sound of leather slapping marble caused her head to snap up. The man from the candle shop stood twenty paces to the side of the dais, the *same* man who'd attacked her at the Well—but it wasn't the man or his strangely swirling eyes that drew her attention most; it was the solid-gold tunic emblazoned with the Phoenix on his chest that arrested her breath. It glowed brighter than the fire she'd thrown at Thorn.

The man took a step forward and threw out a hand.

She reacted on instinct, erecting a shield of air before her. The man's attack pressed her backward but couldn't penetrate her defenses.

Then she heard something behind her. She chanced a glance over her shoulder as Atikus raised his arms, and the massive throne rose from the dais and hurtled toward her. It cast a mighty shadow just as she Traveled to avoid its crushing blow. The entire chamber echoed with the roar of a mountain's rage as thousands of pounds of marble slammed into the ancient stone of the dais. Shrapnel of jagged stone burst in every direction, but none caught Irina as she reappeared midway down the aisle. Declan had to lunge behind a column to avoid being sliced by dozens of razor-sharp fragments that pinged against the nearby wall.

Atikus wasn't so lucky.

The old Mage, so focused on his herculean lifting of the throne, failed to shield himself when it fell, and pieces of rock battered into his chest, arms, and face. He tumbled to the ground and didn't move.

"Atikus!" Declan screamed in his mind. *"Atikus!"*

There was no reply.

A woman's voice cut through the clamor.

"Everyone around you dies, don't they?" Irina needled. "First your mother falls into the Well, now your old Mage. Who's next? Who's left for you to lose?"

Her voice came closer with every word. Declan's heart thudded against his chest, and anger burned through his mind. He wanted to squeeze the life out of this woman with his bare hands, watch her struggle for air and then fall limp as Atikus just had. He'd never felt rage so intense, so powerful—it consumed him in that moment.

The column behind which he'd hid suddenly shuddered, and he heard stone rending against stone. *She's going to bring the temple down!*

In a blink, he was behind her, casting his own wave of fire and air, using magic as a bellows to nurture his ire. Without turning, Irina raised a palm, and a massive wave of water fell from above, extinguishing Declan's flame. She then yanked the column she'd cracked and hurled marble into the insolent boy. Two of them, over a thousand stones each, blasted where he stood. A deep crater opened in the floor where they struck, and a plume of dust and debris rose into the air.

She waited a long moment, but no attack came. There was no sound, no movement.

She finally breathed deeply and willed her heart to calm.

And then the point of Declan's dagger appeared out the front of her chest. She looked down, confused, then saw blood beginning to flower on her dress around the blade. He withdrew it, then dragged it across her throat. She gasped for air. Her hand flew to her throat and was immediately slick with blood that poured out of her weakening body. She felt the crown lift from her head as she fell to her knees.

She tried to Heal herself, but her magic only trickled into her wounds. The hole in her chest began to knit, but far too slowly. She shifted her focus to her gaping throat, and the bloody flow lessened but didn't cease.

Declan appeared before her, crown in hand. She looked up, and a mix of pain and fury flooded her eyes. He closed his eyes, then opened them, but she couldn't see that anything had changed—until she looked down at the gold and silver lines newly emblazoned in the marble. Terror added its thrill to her roiling emotions.

Then Declan did the unthinkable.

He placed the crown just inside the outer circle. Using his Enhanced Strength, he shattered one of the bloody diamonds. Her eyes widened as the form of a man rose like mist from the shattered gem. He lunged at Declan, but the circle flared, and the man's hands slammed against in invisible barrier. Declan stepped into the circle and snatched the crown. He crushed a second stone, releasing a woman in tanned leathers. Her form flitted about the circle, confused, pressing her hands to the invisible wall, keeping her from the world of life.

Again, he smashed.

Again, another Spirit appeared.

Five, then six, finally the seventh.

Prince Justin's innocent face glowed with ethereal light as he drifted to stare down at Irina's bleeding form. The other Spirits joined him, forming a circle around the fallen, bleeding woman.

Finally, the man, the first to emerge from his stone, turned a wretched gaze toward Declan. "What do you want from us? Set us free!" His voice was the grinding of metal against stone, a whisper of pain and loathing. In that moment, Declan knew this man was no longer a man, but a fiend bent on hatred and vengeance.

"I will give each of you rest," Declan said, his voice that of steel, unflinching, resolute. "But only if you help me banish this abomination. Until she is vanquished, none of us will be free."

The Spirit laughed. "Why would I care if you're free, boy?"

Declan's tunic flared to life once more, and the Phoenix leapt from his chest, an apparition of the mighty bird soaring until it filled the chamber. It turned its beak toward the Spirits and roared so loudly that Declan fell to his knees and covered his ears.

"BECAUSE I COMMAND IT!" Órla's voice bellowed throughout the hall.

Declan felt the waves of Compulsion as they drew from his own core and were magnified a thousand-fold by the Phoenix. All seven Spirits flew toward him and slammed against the barrier of the circle. They clawed and scratched and released otherworldly cries that filled the hall.

A light burst from Declan's chest and cloaked the Spirits, transforming each into a beacon of white. Their eyes flew wide, and rage fell from their faces. A moment later, their heads lowered and stilled.

Declan drew his will into his Light and cast it into each of the seven, commanding them, Compelling them into action.

As one, they turned to encircle Irina once more. Each Spirit placed an ethereal hand on her body, and their energy flooded into her. Declan watched in awe as the seven's images dimmed and Irina's grew brighter and brighter. It was as if they poured their very essence into her.

When the Spirits were barely visible, and Irina glowed so brightly it hurt to look upon her, each released their touch and began to shatter before his eyes. Irina released one final scream, and her Spirit was expelled from its mortal shell. The body that fell to the floor transformed, its hair turned from black to silver, its skin wrinkling, until Larinda's kind eyes looked up at Declan. She smiled fondly as the Light faded and her own soul drifted into night.

Irina's Spirit, now in ethereal form, raged against its confinement, but the circle would not yield, its lines blazing as the sun each time she tried to penetrate its borders.

Declan braced himself for the jolt of magic he knew would come, then began the incantation his mother had made him learn before he'd lost her in the Well. The words were foreign and meant nothing to him, but their invocation stirred ancient magic to life. Irina's Spirit began to writhe as she resisted his commands. She darted around the circle, raged against its shield, and screamed every curse a thousand years of life had taught her. Yet nothing would stop the unshakable force of Declan's will.

As he uttered the final words, Irina's Spirit howled one last time and burst into brilliant points of light. When Declan looked back after shielding his eyes, nothing remained of the great Empress Irina.

He slumped to his knees, exhausted.

One Spirit, barely visible in her faded blue smock, floated to Declan. He looked up and they locked eyes. As the wind whispers across a winter field, her voice drifted across his consciousness.

"Tell Keelan thank you for trying to save me."

Tiana's form scattered, sparkled like shimmering snowflakes, then winked out.

Declan grabbed Irina's ruined crown and ran to the end of the chamber where Atikus lay unmoving. Blood no longer leaked from the cut on his forehead, but there was a drying pool beneath his neck and more cuts on his hands and face. A trickle of blood dribbled from the corner of his mouth.

Jagged chunks of stone lay strewn about. Declan nearly panicked when he saw one the size of his head a hand's width away. No doubt the Mage had taken several blows.

"Atikus, look at me! Please, if you can hear me, open your eyes."

The Mage lay unmoving.

Declan steadied himself, then placed both palms above the Mage's chest, and brilliant light flared from his hands and flowed gently into Atikus. Declan explored and found more bruises and cuts, then a few broken ribs, one sharp bone now piercing the Mage's lungs. The cuts began to close at magic's touch, but the internal wounds would take more time—and far more effort—to mend. But Declan now knew the Mage would be whole again.

A stone fell from the broken pillar across the room, sending an echo throughout the chamber. Declan's head snapped up at the sound, and his heart pounded as other noises, leather soles slapping marble and men shouting, drifted toward him from outside. He couldn't afford another battle with Atikus bleeding internally on the ground. They had to get somewhere safe quickly.

As he turned, the glint of a brazier's light flickered off the staff that had fallen when Thorn had burned. Without thinking,

Declan released his Healing light, ran, and grabbed the staff, hooking his arm through the crown to carry them both. Then he returned to grip the Mage's arm and Travel to the refuge of the Queen's palace.

Chapter Forty-One

Atikus

Weeks had passed since Thorn had fallen and Irina was banished. The palace Healers declared Atikus fully recovered, though he still used his brush with the void to skip heavy lifting or gain special treatment at every turn, mostly in the form of extra meals.

"I feel like I could eat for days," Atikus said as he stuffed another buttered roll into his mouth.

Declan laughed. "And that's different from any other day how?"

"Son, you know better than anyone how grave my wounds were. It was a close thing, you saving me. Any Healer worth their blues tells a patient they need solid food to recover their strength. I'm only doing what's prudent. Call it *taking my medicine*. Now, pass me that bacon again, and maybe those eggs."

Declan shook his head and laughed again but passed the bacon.

Keelan and Jess strode into the room, their fingers interlocked. Jess winked conspiratorially before releasing Keelan's hand and taking her seat at the dining table.

"You two seem to be in a good mood these days. I can't remember the last time I saw Keelan smile this much—or show *any* emotion, for that matter." Declan teased.

"Yeah, yeah. You're just jealous."

Jess had barely lowered herself into her chair before the team of lurking servants leapt into action. Her charger vanished, teacup filled, and fresh plates of every breakfast food imaginable appeared on the table near her. Keelan still gaped every time the palace staff cast their spell, but Jess hardly noticed as she reached across to grab a piece of still-sizzling bacon.

In the weeks that had passed, the absence of Gifts had made itself keenly felt. For a thousand years, magic had been engrained in daily life. Simple tasks, such as moving heavy equipment, that previously only needed one Gifted person with Enhanced Strength, might now require an engineer's mind and the muscle of twenty stout men. Spring had yet to bloom in its fullness, but farmers dreaded the planting without Gifts of horticulture to speed up and enhance growth and ward away pests. Royal advisors were sent to every corner of the Kingdom to gather information on the impact and assist with what everyone hoped were temporary solutions.

Midway through breakfast, Declan suddenly set his fork down and looked at Atikus. A furry gray brow rose in questioning reply.

Declan spoke in his mind to guard their shared secrets. *"I don't know why I didn't think of this before. Mother talked about the spell used to create the Gifts. I think she referred to it as the Sundering Spell or Spell of Sundering, something like that."*

"Spell of Sundering. That's right." Atikus looked back to his plate and kept eating, not wanting to alert anyone to their conversation. *"I've had the Mages here in Fontaine looking through the library and vault, but they've come up empty. Our own Mages in Saltstone should also be looking for reference to the spell, but they don't have a Telepath to report progress, so I don't know if they've found anything or not."*

"I think Mother said there's a copy of the spell in her library in . . . that cave."

The fork slipped from Atikus's hand, clanked against his plate, and fell to the floor. Jess and Keelan looked up from their engrossing conversation.

"You alright?" Keelan asked.

"Fine, fine. My fork slipped. I must've had too many of those buttered rolls." He grinned innocently.

Keelan shook his head and turned back to Jess.

"You mean there's a copy of the spell in the cavern where Kelså lived? A whole copy?" Atikus said, taking a replacement fork from one of the ever-diligent servants.

"Yeah, that's what she said, though I never saw it. There really wasn't a need, and I was still so new to magic it wouldn't have meant anything to me. But there's a problem."

"What?" Atikus asked, turning to look at Declan.

"She said it took five of the original Mages, using their combined power, to cast the spell—and it consumed all of them—except her. By design, she wasn't part of the casting—she was an object of it. That's how she became Keeper."

Atikus nodded slowly. *"I knew about her becoming Keeper through the spell but hadn't realized the other Mages were consumed by it. I'd assumed a couple had died, but the others were simply lost to history after leaving the island. The bigger problem here is how much power was needed for the casting—and they were casting into a purified Well, not the muck we're dealing with today."*

"We need to go back to the island. The answers are there. I can feel it."

Atikus held his eyes a moment, then nodded. *"After I finish breakfast."*

Declan actually laughed out loud, turning Jess and Keelan's heads once more.

"Care to share what's funny?" Jess asked.

"No," Declan said through chuckles. "Just Grampy and his appetite."

Two hours after Atikus finally tossed his napkin on his plate, he and Declan hugged Jess and Keelan goodbye. With the temporal difference between the mainland and the island, Keelan knew it might be months, or longer, before the pair were seen again.

Atikus told Jess they were headed to Saltstone to review scrolls his Mages had unearthed, a lie that deeply bothered Keelan. He might not have his Gift of Truthreading, and he certainly understood the need for secrecy, but the idea of being untruthful still burned him. And yet, given the Compulsion cast on his mind when Declan told him of his mother and the Well, magic's binding wouldn't allow him to correct the misinformation, even if he wanted to.

With a last wave and pair of tight smiles, Declan and Atikus vanished.

On their third day, by island time, Declan's magic-enhanced voice bounced through every corridor of the cavern. "Atikus! Come quickly. I found it!"

A moment later, the old Mage shuffled into the library, wheezing from his brisk walk from the kitchen, where he'd been making their lunch. He passed the rectangular worktable that was now buried beneath dozens of unfurled scrolls to find Declan pacing between two stacks near the back of the grotto. A ball of undulating magical light bobbed as he walked, somehow keeping up with his frantic movement. His eyes never left the scroll he held.

Atikus gripped his arm to stop his pacing, then peered around his shoulder to peek at the parchment.

"What language is this? I don't recognize it." Atikus said.

Declan grinned. "Keep looking."

Atikus furrowed his brow at the strange symbols, then something astonishing happened. They began shifting. Symbols splintered apart and formed letters in Melucia's lilting dialect. Whole words vanished as others appeared. The inky dance was mesmerizing.

"Sweet Spirits. I've never seen magic do that." Atikus murmured.

When the spell settled and Atikus could read each line, he let out a long breath and allowed himself to relax. "My boy, you've done it. You've found it!"

The two grinned giddily, then Atikus sobered. "There's just one problem."

"What now?"

"The Well is still poisoned, and I don't know how to cure it."

Declan looked back to the scroll. "Could casting this also purify the currents?"

"Hmm." Atikus fiddled his beard as he thought. "Maybe — or it won't, and we could waste an immense amount of magical energy and blow our only shot at fixing things."

"Immense amount of magical energy. I've heard you use that exact phrase before." Declan dove into his memories. "What about using the crown? The one we recovered from Thorn and Irina?"

Atikus shook his head. "That won't work. The crown lost its magic when the diamonds were shattered. It magnified whatever Gifts the wearer possessed, but also granted the Gifts of the Spirits trapped within each diamond. All that was lost when the Spirits were freed."

"Wait! I think—you weren't talking about the crown when you said that phrase, you were talking about *Irina's staff*, how it magnified her power." Declan paced excitedly. "What if we used the staff to magnify our power as we cast the spell?"

"Thanks to your quick thinking, we have her staff." Both bushy brows raised. "I've never studied it, but in theory, I suppose it could work."

"We've got to try. If there's even a tiny chance we can restore the Gifts, we have to try."

Atikus sighed. "It's never this easy, Declan, but I suppose you're right. We do owe it to everyone back home to exhaust every avenue. It's why we came here, after all."

Declan retrieved the staff from his chamber, where he'd leaned it in a corner and forgotten about it. The broken crown stared back at him from the writing desk. On a whim, he grabbed it, too, then headed to the Well's chamber to meet Atikus.

A few moments later, adopted son and father stood on the glassy dais of the Well of Magic staring down at the blackened ooze that was once magic's untainted lifeblood.

"When you brought me here, and I saw the current for the first time . . ." Atikus swallowed hard. "Declan, when you think about the past, do you have one or two moments in time that seem frozen in your mind? If you close your eyes, you can see every detail, hear and feel and taste *everything*. In all my long life, I remember three or four *perfect moments* like that. Standing here with you, seeing the Well and its majestic flow that first time, was one." Atikus gripped Declan's arm. "I don't know how to explain. It felt like I was an excited, innocent child again, thrilled at magic's first touch, though I had no idea what it even meant. It filled me with wonder and a sense of possibility, with dreams so distant a moment earlier, but suddenly within reach."

He let his hand fall, then turned, sat on the stair, and stared down into the murk. It absorbed much of the light normally present in the cavern, and Atikus had to cast several globes above them just to see a few paces around the Well.

"Now, all I see is darkness. This poison is the absence of hope. Son, we have to succeed, because my heart tells me the whole world will dim if we fail."

Declan sat and put an arm around the Mage.

"You are the smartest, strongest, *kindest* man I've ever known. And I'm Keelan's brother, which means I have to protect everyone and be grumpy doing it."

Atikus spit a laugh despite his mood.

"We'll make this work. One way or another, we'll find a way."

Atikus looked up at Declan, and his lip quivered slightly as he spoke in a strained whisper. "I'm so proud of you, Declan. You've grown into quite the man."

Declan's eyes dropped, and his face reddened. Then a grin quirked the corner of his mouth as he ran a hand dramatically through his curly mess of hair.

"I know. It's a burden being so awesome sometimes."

Atikus barked another laugh as the mood lightened.

"Enough of you! Let's cast a spell."

Atikus stood and gripped the staff in both hands. His heartbeat quickened at the touch, and he could feel the thrum of power—*his own magic*—reverberating through the cold metal. Declan rose, and they approached the opening of the Well shoulder-to-shoulder, father and son. Declan uncoiled the scroll and held it so they could both see its contents. They called their Light and poured it into the scroll.

Triggered by the touch of their magic, the scroll's lettering glittered to life, transforming from faded black to brilliant gold. With each spoken word, the symbols and letters brightened, and their strokes *flowed* on the page.

Declan's tunic flared to life, quickly outshining the dim globes hovering overhead.

With a mutual nod, they began reading aloud as one, and the incantation began.

Biotáille solais, glaoimid ort. Éist linn.

Pinpricks of iridescent cerulean light appeared amidst the charred current.

De réir cumhachta táimid faoi cheangal. D'fhéadfaimis réimeas.

Light bloomed amidst darkness, and a translucent mist rose from the mire and engulfed both casters. Their voices rose, and unnatural wind began to swirl and howl about the cavern.

De réir cumhachta theipeann orainn. D'fhéadfaimis titim.

The air in the chamber grew thick with power, and Declan's eyes blazed with intensity. Atikus strained to stay on his feet.

Ceangal ár n-uacht. Ceangal ár gcumhacht. Briseadh ár slabhraí agus sever dúinn. Briseadh sinn.

Light now balanced darkness in the flow as the power of pure magic fought against the insidious poison leeching its warmth from the world of life, but the infection would not be banished easily. It strained against the invocation now damning its existence. Pain seared in Atikus's chest, and the staff scored livid burns across his palms, yet he held firm. He continued to chant, now more wail than prayer, as magic warred within his soul.

Declan fell to his knees as lances of agony pierced his eyes. The Phoenix on his chest burst forth, now freed from the golden fabric of his tunic, an ephemeral beast bent on serving its fallen master. The mighty bird grew to consume the space before them, then dove headfirst, with wings dripping power, into the embattled river below. The blackness convulsed, coalescing around the Phoenix, enveloping it, clinging to wing and beak and claw. Yet when the mighty bird vanished, far more blue than black flowed in the ancient brook.

One line remained.

Sunder cad a tugadh agus Tabhair cad a bhí sundered.

They shouted louder.

Sunder cad a tugadh agus Tabhair cad a bhí sundered.

And a third time.

Sunder cad a tugadh agus Tabhair cad a bhí sundered!

Power flooded up from the current and out from their chests. Declan screamed as magic was ripped from his core, his soul torn asunder, and he was thrown to the floor.

Atikus, weakened and spent, was lifted from the glassy stair as raw magic tore from his Spirit. Higher and higher, the light raised his body, until he hovered ten hands above the Well. Unable to speak or move or scream, he gaped in terror at the raging rush below.

The staff slipped from his weakened grasp and fell into the opening of the Well.

The river writhed at its touch, and a wave billowed forth. There was nowhere to hide. There was no spell or power to protect from the current's ire. Atikus fell from its grasp and plunged beneath its foaming waves.

Declan cried out and dove toward the Well. He would give his life to save the Mage, and there would be no regrets.

He leapt above the opening in the glassy surface and threw out his hands to push the Mage to safety, but magic would not be robbed of its price, and Declan watched in horror as Atikus fell past him and vanished beneath the surface below.

Chapter Forty-Two

Declan

Declan sat staring at the mountains across the island, his feet dangling off the edge of the cliff. He'd been out there for hours. The sun had begun his graceful descent, and the sky was painted with more hues than he thought were possible. A gentle, salty breeze tickled his nose, and he relished the taste of the island air, inhaling deeply.

A week had passed since the spell was cast. A week in island time.

Declan wore his tunic and still enjoyed the Gifts he'd studied with his mother, but his limitless grasp of magic no longer availed itself. Fire wouldn't bloom in his palm. He couldn't speak in another's mind at will. Healing's restrictive rules had returned, as he learned the first time he tried to Heal himself and was punished with bouts of nausea that lasted hours.

Worst of all, he could no longer Travel.

That had become his favorite power.

He released a wistful sigh remembering how it felt to blink and instantly appear anywhere in the world. There was far more than power in that ability; there was *freedom*. He longed for that freedom again, yet it refused him.

At least the pitcher of magical wine was still bottomless. He chuckled as he drew another sip from his glass.

"You've been out here for hours. Aren't you hungry yet?"

The deep warmth of the familiar voice soothed his angst. The perpetual hunger made him laugh.

"Atikus, you old goat, will you ever stop eating?"

Bony hands dug into his shoulders, but in a playful, fatherly way—the way that actually hurt just a little more than intended.

"Never! Besides, after all that Healing you did on me, I could eat for days. Come on now, let's fix some supper."

Declan reluctantly peeled himself from nature's canvas and followed the Mage into the mountain.

Over a meal of roasted turkey, seasoned vegetables, and mango pie, the two joked and laughed as if they hadn't just saved the world of magic from a bitter end. That all seemed too big for either of them to face aloud. They needed the comfort and safety of little things just now.

And yet . . .

"Atikus, I still don't understand how you survived the currents. Magic had been Sundered when you fell. You should've dissolved, and your Light returned to the flow."

Atikus set his fork down, and Declan knew it was about to get serious.

"Son . . ." he struggled. "Magic always demands her due. There is a price to every Gift and every spell. When the staff fell into the waters, its power completed the cleansing we began, but no price had yet been paid for the Sundering. It wouldn't be complete without one."

"But it didn't take you. Magic gave you back."

Atikus struggled to meet Declan's eyes. "Not *exactly*."

Declan thought his heart would stop in that moment.

"Declan, there's no easy way for me to say this, so I'm just going to say it. Magic didn't give me back. It kept me. Well, technically, I'm keeping *it* now. I will live, but only so long as I remain on this island."

Declan's puzzled expression turned to excitement. "Wait! Does that mean—"

"Yes, I'm now the Keeper."

After a moment's pause, Declan exploded from his chair, wrapping his arms around the old Mage. "Atikus, that's amazing!"

Atikus returned his smile, but his shoulders slumped.

"What? This is a good thing, right?"

Atikus stared into his plate, unable to meet Declan's eyes. "One day, you or Keelan, or both of you, will find someone to love. You'll marry and raise a family. You'll see the world and conquer it. And I'll miss it all. I know being Keeper should be a gracious, selfless act, but I can't help thinking about all the things *I* will sacrifice for magic."

Declan braced him with strong hand on either arm.

"Atikus, I know you'll miss Saltstone and the Guild, but there couldn't be anyone better suited to protecting Magic and the Gift. Keelan and I can come visit you. I love this place. Spirits, I'm a little jealous." He smiled broadly. "We'll find a way. Between the two of us, we've held more power in our hands than anyone alive. We understand magic and casting in ways most could never dream about. You will always be at the center of our family, no matter how small or big it might get. We'll make this work. I promise."

Atikus had prepared himself for anger, bitterness, rage, even childish fury, but he hadn't prepared his heart for this. He peered up at the boy he loved more than life itself and tears brimmed in his eyes. Declan fell into another embrace, and the tears finally fell.

Chapter Forty-Three

Jess & Keelan

By the time Declan returned to Fontaine, six months had passed on the continent. Spring had turned to summer, and summer surrendered to fall. The Spires were ablaze with leaves of red, orange, and yellow, and a brisk wind blew, heralding the coming of colder months. It was a beautiful time to visit the Kingdom.

He strode down the cobbles of the main thoroughfare with a crisp new suit Jess had had made for him. She would've had it delivered to his chamber at the palace, but he'd waited so long for his fitting that she'd made him fetch it himself—and he knew she'd skin him alive if he was late on *this* day, so he walked quickly.

People were already lining the streets, most wearing their brightest green and gold to honor the royal house. Vendors selling everything from trinkets to funnel cakes barked out their pitch, luring festive citizens to their cart or door. Everywhere he looked, people smiled and laughed. He couldn't remember the last time a city felt so good.

Guards in polished silver plate, now wearing equally shiny helmets plumed with towering feathers in the Queen's colors, greeted him at the gate as he passed. He expected a flurry of activity in the palace but hadn't planned to walk into a full-scale battle in the throne room.

"Jess, please." Chancellor Marks said. "I'm not asking you to do anything other than consider all perspectives, to think through all the consequences of every decision you make. It's what your father pressed me to do for him, and what my oath to you demands."

She paced a few strides away, then returned to glare at him. Her voice was low, restrained—but only barely. "I appreciate your advice, Ethan. I really do, but I'm pretty sure we passed the point of this lecture months ago."

He crossed his arms. "If you'd allowed it, we would've had this *conversation* months ago. You shut it down every time I brought the topic up."

"Maybe you should've taken the hint."

"Jess—"

"Ethan, there are three reasons today will move forward, and my High Chancellor *will* respect them."

She led up one finger.

"One, being Queen is lonely and hard and . . . *impossible*. It's particularly impossible when I'm doing it all by myself. I need someone who loves and supports me, someone I can trust."

She held up two fingers.

"Two, the Kingdom has yet to heal the wounds *we* inflicted. I know we're doing a lot of good work on this front, but it's not enough. The people—all people—need more than sacks of grain and carts of wood. They need hope. Today will give them that hope."

She held up three fingers.

"And three. I am Queen, and I will marry *whoever I want*, and I'm marrying Keelan Rea. Today. Do I make myself clear, High Chancellor?"

Marks eyed her for a moment, then something softened in his eyes, and he smiled.

"What? Why are you smiling?"

"Because you are your father's daughter, and I am so proud to stand in his stead and give you away."

She cocked her head, sucked in a breath, then pushed him back with both hands.

"If you make me cry and I ruin this face paint, I will exile you to the smallest island on the farthest corner—"

Marks's arms pulling her close silenced whatever decree she was about to issue. A small girl's voice whispered as her chin settled on his shoulder, "Thank you, Uncle Ethan."

Chapter Forty-Four

Declan

Declan's feet dangled over the edge again.

He'd returned to Rea Utu and Atikus as the last of the wedding festivals had ended. Keelan and Jess made a striking couple, and he'd even seen his big brother smile and wave at the cheering crowds. Magic was definitely still alive in the world.

He knew he should go inside, see what the old Mage was destroying in the kitchen, but something in the night air drew him to remain. As much as he always said he craved freedom, he was coming to realize that the *peace* he felt in this place was far more important than the power to roam freely.

Here, he was alive.

Here, he was free.

A faint scraping noise caused his head to turn. He squinted in the dimness of the waning sun but couldn't make out what had caused the sound. His eyes turned back to the last rays of the dying day.

Then the scraping came again.

Slowly, he peered out the side of his eyes, careful not to make any sudden movement.

There, on the ledge, not ten paces away, skittered a tiny red ball of fur with a fluffy tail and giant eyes. Ever so slowly, he turned his head to face the intruder.

The eyes blinked and it shuffled back a pace.

He froze.

Curiosity got the best of the little beast and it shuffled within a few paces. Now within the light from the lantern sitting on the table, Declan could clearly see his guest. A baby fox, whose tail was larger and fluffier than its entire body, stared up at him.

"Shy little fella, aren't ya? How'd you get up here, anyway? You know we're on a cliff, right?" The fox cocked its head as if listening or trying to figure out what the crazy man was doing talking to a baby fox.

Declan carefully reached to his other side, found a couple of whole macadamia nuts, and set them on the fox's side of his body. He wished he had some of the dried meat he carried when traveling but figured the nuts would at least show good faith.

The fox cocked its head to the other side, scooted forward a couple of paces, then back to see if Declan would remain still. After another few seconds, it repeated the dance until its prize was within reach.

He avoided the animal's gaze, not wanting eye contact to scare it away. He was surprised when the fox ignored the nuts and began tickling the back of his hand that was palm down on the ledge's stone. He chanced a glance just as the fox made it onto his left leg. It sat and stared. When he didn't respond, the fuzzy creature let out a tiny yawn, scratched at Declan's breeches a few times, then curled up in his lap.

Declan glanced down to find his new friend fast asleep. He'd always had a way with animals, but this was beyond strange—and cute. He gave it another minute before reaching a finger down to stroke the fox's head. At his touch, it emitted a high-pitched whirr that sounded oddly familiar.

Declan's heart nearly leapt out of his chest.

He stared down and barely whispered, "Órla?"

The fox's eyes flew wide, and she nuzzled his outstretched hand, cooing and purring the entire time. Then she curled back into the safety of his lap and drifted off to sleep.

Also by JD Ruffin

J.D. Ruffin is the author of multiple bestselling novels, including the epic fantasy Kingdom War series.

Ironically, he never really enjoyed reading until a friend loaned him a dog-eared copy of J.R.R. Tolkien's Fellowship of the Ring. From that day, he was hooked, discovering fantasy authors Robert Jordan, Brandon Sanderson, R.A. Salvatore, Terry Goodkind and many, many others.

Becoming an author was never part of the master plan, but...

As a fourteen-year-old bespeckled and befreckled boy, J.D. and his friends would gather around the D&D dice for hours on end, trading reality for fantasy, if only in their minds. In his quest to "stump his friends" with an impossible campaign, he dreamed up a storyline that captured his imagination.
Then... well... nothing happened. He grew up and went to work

in a completely different world.

Too many years later, that story pulled at the corner of his mind, demanding to be heard... to be written.

Hence, an author was born.

J.D. lives in Florida with his three Australian shepherds. In his spare time, he enjoys playing amateur chef, hitting the tennis courts, traveling, and watching Survivor.

About the Author

J.D. Ruffin is the author of multiple bestselling novels, including the epic fantasy Kingdom War series.

Ironically, he never really enjoyed reading until a friend loaned him a dog-eared copy of J.R.R. Tolkien's Fellowship of the Ring. From that day, he was hooked, discovering fantasy authors Robert Jordan, Brandon Sanderson, R.A. Salvatore, Terry Goodkind and many, many others.

Becoming an author was never part of the master plan, but...

As a fourteen-year-old bespeckled and befreckled boy, J.D. and his friends would gather around the D&D dice for hours on end, trading reality for fantasy, if only in their minds. In his quest to "stump his friends" with an impossible campaign, he dreamed up a storyline that captured his imagination.
Then... well... nothing happened. He grew up and went to work

in a completely different world.

Too many years later, that story pulled at the corner of his mind, demanding to be heard... to be written.

Hence, an author was born.

J.D. lives in Florida with his three Australian shepherds. In his spare time, he enjoys playing amateur chef, hitting the tennis courts, traveling, and watching Survivor.

Ingram Content Group UK Ltd.
Milton Keynes UK
UKHW021815240723
425688UK00017B/164